NO EXAGGERATION

By Cee Cee Evans

Pharos Books

ISBN: 978-93-91384-22-7
eISBN: 978-93-55468-20-8

©Author

Publisher: Pharos Books (P) Ltd.
Plot No.-55, Main Mother Dairy Road
Pandav Nagar, East Delhi-110092
Phone: 011-40395855, +4049916623
WhatsApp: +91 8368220032
E-mail: sales@pharosbooks.in
Website: www.pharosbooks.in
First Edition: 2022

NO EXAGGERATION
By Cee Cee Evans

CONTENTS

DEDICATION

I dedicate this book to the two big D's in my life, for their immense forces are gravity to my soul. For my lovely mother who nurtured me and for my Cuckoo, the beautiful Jennifer Daisy, who has taught me that a mother's love is absolute and unconditional. Finally, a nod to the sadly late, yet forever irrepressible Mr. R., who helped to shape my former self, for which I thank him. As without my then, I would not have my now.

Chapter One

Meeting the Big Man

I t is early in the evening, mid-October 2014, as I sit on the balcony of our holiday apartment. The doors are open; and a light breeze is fanning through the flimsy curtains. The accommodation has a typically Spanish interior, with pale, painted walls and tiled floors, that are intended to try and cool the rooms from the heat outside. The Sun has climbed high in the sky during the day. This morning, I had watched it rise determinedly from the West, catapulting itself with the force of a meteor, until it hung, glistening and shimmering in the cobalt, blue sky. If clouds had dared to show their crystal faces, they would have been quickly banished by the many sizzling ripples of solar power. Now, as I continue to gaze, the Sun glides slowly East, disappearing beyond the horizon of the ocean and the sudden cooler air of dusk is soothing on my skin.

I raise my face to the heavens, to welcome the Moon to its celestial center stage. As it creates a magical bridge through the darkening sky, with silvery rivers of light, the hypnotic lull of the tide becomes mesmerizing, lapping against the beach with reassuring swishes, moving against the magnetic pull of the Earth. Stars are slowly revealing their own special diamante twinkles, as I watch with my usual wonder, searching for the brightest. Thinking as always of my father, wishing that he knew that he was in my thoughts. There it was, sparkling majestically, as if it had a special force of its own.

Another perfect day in this holiday paradise is ending, beckoning another perfect night with sultry fingers and I walk back into the apartment, humming the tune of 'Moon River', the song that always reminded me of my father.

'You ok babe?' 'The Big Man' asks me, with a worried expression on his face.

'Yeah, bit sad, I wish I could talk to him, say I'm sorry.'

'Your father?'

'Yes baby, but it's an impossibly stupid idea, ignore me.'

Gentle background music is playing; and a few scented candles have been lit, adding to the exquisite ambience of the evening My body and soul are warmed by the day's fierce heat and the potent red wine that I am drinking. My eyes are half-closed, I am not thinking of anything now, just relishing the fact that all my senses have been heightened by this special moment in time. I am acutely aware of the smoke from an expertly rolled joint as it wafts past me; and I am also blissfully aware of my husband's presence in the room. The Big Man smells of sun oil and sex, and he has literally changed my life in so many ways, that it has been a mystical experience.

My name is Catrin Thomas, and I am fifty-four years old, five-feet six-inches tall, really five and a half inches, but the acceptable ratio of height to weight deemed the addition of that extra half an inch into my personal equation to be essential, my battle with calories having been a lifetime war. Large-breasted and slim-hipped, I carry the inevitable wine belt of the fifty-plus woman on my midriff. My facial features are defined by a nose that is slightly too long and a determined chin, both of which reinforce the fact that I am no shrinking violet. I have full lips, which express my serious or even sullen side if I am not smiling or laughing, which is seldom and my mouth frequently transforms itself on those occasions, when I regularly emit an explosion of cackles, giggles and hoots of mirth.

I have 'good skin' as the expression goes, having as a teenager, never been plagued by spots or acne, but a few telltale wrinkles give my age away, mostly in the crease between my eyebrows, telling of many frowns, whilst puppet lines, from my nose to my mouth, reveal more evidence of a lived-in face. I had never considered Botox however, this would have been unthinkable, as I have seen enough faces ravaged with Botulinum to dismiss the procedure out of hand. I think, that unadorned with make-up I could be considered plain, but I am a blank canvas, on which my features when painted, transform me into the sultry beauty who he had met that night. This is apparently how the Big Man had described me, trying to track me down afterwards.

The memories of the rest of that night, eight years previously; even now, burn vividly in my mind and recalling the images of the deep, frantic fucking which had followed our chance meeting, can still harden my nipples and send spasms through my clit. The definition of my name is 'Pure', which certainly applies to my soul. For despite all the shit I have faced, my soul has remained intact from the blows that have been inflicted on it, by the 'monsters' that wanted to own it, but this is where the analogy stops. 'Dirty', would be a better description of me, dirty-minded, with a dirty laugh, far better sums me up.

It was by total chance that we had even met, but once the connection had been made, it was destined never to be broken and despite any normal concerns about inviting a stranger home, that incredible evening, November 5th. 2006; I felt I had no choice. We talked into the early hours, the wine flowing, until suddenly I found myself straddling his body, my arms wrapped around his torso as I pumped up and down on his extremely large, erect cock.

'Fucking Hell! Fucking Heaven!!' Were my initial thoughts, until lost in the experience, there was no thinking. Instead, I succumbed to pleasure, just total fucking pleasure. He took control of the situation easily and led the pace with consummate skill, penetrating me with deep rapid strokes, then slowly withdrawing and teasing me with delicate butterfly touches, constantly watching my face. His eyes travelled to the liquid core in the middle of my spread-eagled legs, the fleshy folds engorged and dripping. He scooped up the juice with his hand and wiped it around my open mouth, finger fucking my equally swollen lips, that were panting out my guttural appreciation. He rammed his cock back into me, gasping at my reaction as I came again. His thumbs parted the wet, matted pelt covering my pubis, one day he would regularly shave me, but for now, he continued to fondle the sticky, coarse hair before plunging his tongue through it. Sucking up the squirting, he replaced his tongue with his throbbing cock and fucked me again. Starved of such amazing sex for far too long, I took the ride of a lifetime, as orgasm after orgasm ripped through me.

Clinging onto him, I breathed in his smell, tobacco and alcohol, a faint hint of subtle aftershave, sweat and fresh sex, all making for a heady combination. He smelt of pure male, he smelt like chocolate, he smelt like my father. He was built like a powerhouse, about fifteen stone in weight and five-feet ten-inches tall. His chest was barrel like, covered in short, curly body hair that mirrored the colour of the cropped, grey hair on his head. His eyes were piercing blue and still fixed on me, as I reverently stroked the thirty-year old army tattoos that adorned his body. Dragons and mythical sea creatures, all inked in red, blues and greens, the glorious designs may once have been brighter, but were still simply stunning, in all their aged glory.

'I always wanted a tattoo.' I nuzzled the words into his neck.

'Well, we'll have to see what we can do about that then, won't we babe!'

I fingered the silver rings piercing his right nipple and left ear lobe, as they shone in the darkened room. I wanted more of him, lots more, I wanted to drown in the deluge of sexual pleasure that was washing over me.

'Again!' I demanded.

'Greedy girl!' He laughed in reply, but our actions were soon to be cut short, as the living room door suddenly opened; and the carnal coupling was rudely interrupted by the eyes of my twelve-year-old daughter, shock shining from her prim, little pupils. The frenzy did an emergency stop and the Big Man was banished into the night, leaving me, his new lover, squirming with desire and mortification. Despite this rather unfortunate end to the proceedings, whether it had been by chance, or an intervention of fate, that night was to be the start of the rest of my life.

I, Catrin Thomas am of humble Welsh birth; with no royal lineage to boast of and the rich colour of my casually styled, shoulder-length brunette hair, is deceptive. Once natural, it now has the odd helping hand and I have lost count of the number of times that I have been asked about to my origins.

'Have you got Spanish blood in you, or Greek?' I always laughed, as I answered this question and invariably my reply was always the same. It is Celtic blood that roars through my veins. Strong Welsh men and women; have been my forefathers and mothers and I am proud of this history. My father had told me many times of the poverty in which he had been raised, with old newspaper lining holes in shoes and piss poured into ears, to ward off infection. All reflecting a family history of mining, hardship and sheer willpower.

My eyes are large, pansy-centered, dark brown with hazel green flecks. My eyebrows are carefully plucked, but not too much; and there is not a hint of any fashionably thick penciling of them. My fingernails are cut short with an application of clear varnish, which is the extent of my idea of a manicure, as I have never been tempted to try gels or falsies. In fact, there is nothing false about me at all, apart from several crowns amongst my teeth and two perfect porcelain caps, replacing my originally slightly crossed front ones. All testament to previous years of fast drug abuse, notorious for its ability to leach enamel and destroy perfectly good teeth. There is no high maintenance for me at all, but I'm not in bad shape considering everything, which was extraordinary, since the 'everything' has taken my mind and body to edges, that had I toppled over them, there would have been no rescue for me.

We are halfway through a blissful fortnight in October 2014. We have travelled to a tiny island in the Atlantic, a jewel of a place, just a drop in the ocean. The resort is jolly and laidback, the sort of place that teenagers on an annual break with their friends, without parents, would reject as a holiday destination. This is a place for young families and middle-aged couples; and of course, the seventy plus oldies who desire peace and quiet. One solitary nightclub starts banging out its nightly tunes, at about the same time that most holiday makers are turning in for the night. For us it is a perfect place to create a do-as-you please holiday, where the only decision we need to make is what to do next from the pleasurable tick list of choices available to us. Eat, drink, swim, sleep, or fuck, all of which we embrace with gusto, but it is hard, dirty fucking, which is our essential mutually shared goal, the benchmark having been set the night we had first met. Both of us being highly sexed beings, who had met our ultimate matches in the fornication stakes; and we have continued to revel in our ability to fuck each other senseless, on a regular basis.

Then there is the final choice on the tick list, an acute pleasure during such a holiday, far removed from the timescales and deadlines of busy, everyday working life, which was just to be with each other. This was one of those 'just being' moments, relaxing idly in the evening after another day in the sun, when the idea sprang into my psyche, formed from the numerous paperbacks that I have mentally devoured. Eyes suddenly wide, my pupils enlarged with the rush brought by the thought, that had crystallized so clearly as to become vocal. My mantra of never looking back imploded into the blackest of holes in my mind, in the form of a psychedelic kaleidoscope of memories. A myriad of past

NO EXAGGERATION

places, people, tastes, colours, sights and sounds, all fused madly into this one poignant idea. The power of this mental cocktail, hallucinogenic almost, raced through my head as I would imagine magma would have erupted, should the slumbering volcano on the nearby sister island, have awoken. I heard whispers from the 'monsters' that I had firmly banished into purgatory and the black clouds of my past started to roll towards me again, until suddenly jolted back to the present, I proclaimed aloud.

'I could write a book! No exaggeration, baby!' And so, it began.

'I guess you could babe.' He had smiled at my outburst, knowing me as he did, not one iota surprised by the statement.

The last week had been spent drinking in the sights and sounds of the island. I had discovered a large supermarket, a mere stone's throw from the apartment and I sang along softly to the melody of 'Bright Eyes' being piped over the tannoy, as I meandered along the aisles, unaware of the other shoppers who were casting admiring sideward glances at my tanned legs in denim shorts. Little did I know that in less than two months, one of those legs would be gouged deeply in a bizarre accident and would consequently forever bear the thickest of scars. Nor could I have possibly known that the bright light in the eyes of the pet rabbit at home, safely boarding at a local pet ship, would be distinguished and I would cry over a little, hand-dug grave.

I used my limited knowledge of the Spanish language, to decipher the contents of strange packets and jars and fingered fruit, some familiar, some unknown. The warm, ripe avocados; and Sharon fruit, were so reminiscent of how the chubby bodies of toddlers on the beach would feel, if squeezed. I had watched them squeal with joy at their first experiences of sun, sea and sandcastles, as their carefree, laughing parents supervised them carefully and I was reminded poignantly of the holidays when I had played on foreign beaches with my own daughter, when she too was a podgy, waddling baby, in times long past.

We gulped down pints of ice-cold beer, found different back street restaurants where we ate hot, garlicy meals washed down with warm house red; and spent lazy hours reading novels whilst settled on sun loungers by the pool, working on the obligatory tans to show off proudly at home. The beach was our favourite place of all, swimming in the warm sea water with snorkels fixed firmly on faces, we explored the depths for glimpses of silvery blue and green fish and other aquatic treasures. We jumped waves and threw ourselves down on towels afterwards, to dry off in the sun, loving the feeling of sea salt crystallizing on our hot skin.

I looked over at him a few days later, he was lying on his back, his eyes seemed closed behind dark glasses, but I knew he was aware of me as I spoke.

'I could do this baby; I could write a book.' And now it began.

That evening I texted home. 'Hi, it's me, how's the boy? x'

'Fine and dandy! x' The reply came straight back.

'Going to write a book! x' I typed my exciting news.

'Well baby girl, if anyone can, you can! x'

'Yeah, think I've got a few yarns to tell! You're 'in it obvs! An interesting character with a twist! x'

'Start spinning baby girl! x'

'Why are you being so nice.' My mood had changed abruptly.

'Wasn't aware I was being nice.'

The connection was cut off as I slammed the phone down, very conscious that this was an extremely rude way to text the guy who was looking after our dog back at home, even if he happened to be my ex-husband. I opened another bottle of mind-pleasing wine and accepted the spliff offered to me. Toking deeply, I returned my thoughts to the concept that was now becoming exciting, a bloody book!

NO EXAGGERATION

'Yes, you were nice and yes I am horribly hungover x' I sent what I hoped would be construed as an apology, the next morning.

'Get on with your holiday doll x' Came the reply an hour later; and so, we duly did. Shaking off the cobwebs swirling around my head, I gathered up our beach stuff and a cool box filled with a picnic lunch and four cans of iced lager, before we ambled to our usual spot, to nest on the sand for another idyllic day. We had found it by trial and error, rejecting the main beaches with their sterile rows of plastic sun loungers and parasols available to rent for a few hours. Our special place was at the edge of a cove, where the tide lapped musically; and some degree of privacy was ensured. The rocks around us were volcanic, densely black and Jurassic. They had been there for millions of years, robust against the gentle elements that swept across the island.

'You cold babe?' He asked the question as he pointed to my bikini top.

'Cold? It's boiling baby!'

'Big babe!' The Big Man rolled onto his side and ran a finger around one of my erect nipples, as I proceeded to stroke what was clearly a massive erection underneath his swim shorts.

'I wanna join your party!!' A random guy making sandcastles with his children, shouted over to us, smiling as he did so. Whether it was the visible sexual tension between us or the beers we were gulping that had made him make the comment, was unclear.

'This party's only for two!' I laughed back, watching wistfully as he dug a deep moat, filling it with sea water for the delight of his offspring. We lay on our backs, watching planes as they took off every fifteen minutes. As they banked around and shot up into the blue before disappearing completely, I suddenly remembered another island from my past, nearly thirty years ago. There had been no planes to watch then, only ocean liners had been able to access that jewel of a place, deeply hidden in the heart of the Aegean

Sea. I had been standing at the Port of Piraeus in Athens in May 1986, waiting to board such a ship, wondering if the monsters that I was desperately trying to run away from would have the strength to follow the five-hour sea crossing to the Cyclades Greek Islands. Hoping against hope that I would leave them dockside and that they would leave me in peace, albeit temporarily.

'You ok babe? You look sad, what're you thinking about!'

'I'm fine baby!!'

'If you write about it, it could upset you.' I had told him everything about my life before we had met; and explained that I was going to try and turn it into a story.

'You'll make me happy then! You've always made me happy and kept me safe baby!'

'Sad!! You idiot! This is paradise' I murmured, drifting off to sleep, as my idea of writing a book mixed with the heat on my skin and the drowsy, intoxicating effect of the cans of beer, in an irresistible combination, luring me into its literary spell. Unaware that just like Icarus flying too close to the Sun, my written words were going to soar far too close to long-gone memories, for them not to hurt me again and that the frozen demons from my past would temporarily come alive in its pages. But for now, on this most idyllic of days, the only thing to invade my dreams as I dozed on the beach, was the 'Something', as the story began to unfold.

Chapter Two

Such a Something

I was dreaming about my mother and how she would tell anyone within earshot, that I had written beautiful poetry as a little girl, which was true, but when said Mother went on to elaborate further, my dutiful daughter's smile was automatically switched on and subjects got changed swiftly. My 'lovely mother' was alone now, after losing her husband, my father, after what seemed like a lifetime ago. She would sigh sadly, recalling life before his death at sixty-six, having lost him to a cancer that was diagnosed too late for there to be any hope. They had been scary, fearful times; watching him being reduced to a pathetic ghost, fading to grey, calling out pitifully for breakfast in the evening. Having to witness my mother begin the grieving process that would change her forever, as we tried to hold it together as a family, during our last Christmas with him in 1996.

There were three children present, my own daughter and my sister's offspring, joint ages a mere thirteen years, who were all overly excited about the Yuletide magic that was their absolute right. It mixed sourly for the adults present, with the fear of what was to come, as come it had to. His death on 2nd April 1997 was followed a week later by his funeral, that took place in an austere, chilly service chapel on a cold, overcast morning, accompanied by some bizarre, tuneless Methodist hymns, that had been selected especially for the occasion.

'I'm not sure you would have appreciated that choice, Dad.' Was my only thought, as I stood in the receiving line, thanking the mourners as they exited the building, my smile fixed and glazed.

'You mustn't blub.' Mother, stony-faced, had suddenly whispered the order in my ear, but how was I supposed not to, having just witnessed the coffin containing the body of that once great and powerful man, disappear behind the curtains in the grim crematorium.

A few years later, the urn containing his ashes was taken to the Welsh hills where he had played as a boy.

'Not sure if you would have liked this choice either.' Again, my thoughts were unspoken as I played along with the charade that had been planned, Mother not saying a word, pretending she didn't know what was about to happen. With a sign from an uncle, I left my then six-year-old daughter, secretly and affectionately known to me as 'Cuckoo', with her silent grandmother. We took the urn away, to do the scattering in a place that I would never be able to find again, even if I tried, which I never would. The contents were granular, pale; and dry.

'Christ. Is that all that remains of a person, lumpy ashes.' Another sobering thought had crossed my mind as the two of us stood in silence. With a final glance back, we walked away; and black comedy reared its head, as a lone mountain goat snuffled around in the sad, little heap of matter.

'Bloody hell, Uncle Merlin, it's trying to eat Dad!' It was a standing joke for my family, that as a child I was one of a few to have a wizard as an uncle, it was a common enough old Welsh name, but magical still, to a little girl.

As I continued to sleep in the Spanish sunshine, my reveries accompanied by the soothing swish of the tide, my dreams turned to August 2013, when, aged eighty-one, Mother had decided to have a breast scan, which was unusual for a lady of her years. Once the cancer had been discovered, it brought the fear straight back into the mix. Eventually it was all ok, apart from a few very messy moments. I had travelled with my nineteen-year-old Cuckoo to the West Country, where my parents had retired to, several years before my father died. We had planned to stay for a few nights, to fuss over Grandma after her operation. She'd seemed quite perky when we arrived, considering her age and the trauma of general surgery and overall, it seemed that everything was going to plan. Cuckoo was put on a London bound train the day before I too, was due to return home. All had seemed well until the early hours of the morning, when lovely mother had collapsed with a loud thud, falling out of bed at three a.m., waking me with a jolt. The events that followed became a hideously surreal experience as I dialed 999 in a shaky-voiced, dry-mouthed, panic.

'Mum!! Wake up!!' I'd helped her back onto the bed as she came to, but her eyes looked strange, unseeing almost.

'I think she's had a stroke.' My voice was trembling as I spoke to the emergency operator, remembering the television advert. 'Face, Act, Speech, Time.'

We were blue lighted to A&E, and I gave a garbled account of the incident to a succession of doctors. Brain scans and examinations followed, during which the patient kept falling asleep. They were interspersed by me pacing the corridors and sneaking out for cigarette after cigarette. It all turned out okay and I ferried her home in a taxi, much later that afternoon. That evening I sat on the balcony of my mother's flat, lighting up yet another cigarette and looked up to the stars, thinking of my father.

'I'm so sorry Dad, but maybe I'm a little bit vindicated now.' I heard myself whisper the words softly into the dark, wishing that he could hear me, as my mind meandered between the past and the present.

I saw myself sitting with him during a sad lost afternoon in early 1997, as he faded, neither of us aware of the time.

'Do you want to talk?' I gently asked him.

'Not particularly.' Was his answer from the bed, but I spoke anyway, wanting to make him a pledge, a promise to look after my mother afterwards, which was sadly the very least I could do. I owed him that much, as apart from this terminal cancer that was taking him over, I had been the only other thing he had never been able to control. Furthermore, the head-first spiral in my twenties, into the life of an addict, had nearly broken both of my parents. Not that I had given a shit at the time, whilst yet again, poetry was falteringly written.

'I underestimated you, my nearest, dearest friend.

The danger in your bad white lines, no promised pot of gold.

The tears you cry are crocodile, how many souls you sold?'

'I followed the night round in circles, that shadow boxed under my eyes.

You hold me at such a cold distance, no wonder I'm high as the sky.'

Those scribbled lines of verse, never finished, were reaching out for the perfect rhymes that never came and the collection of tatty pieces of paper, having survived so many upheavals in my life, was stored in a box of paperwork in the corner of the bedroom that I now share with the Big Man; and as my sub conscious continued to play tricks as I slept on the beach in October 2014, much more recent events took centre stage, in a crazy random order, as only dreams can make happen.

Before this much-needed holiday, we had undertaken the solemn task of protecting each other by writing our wills, should an unthinkable 'Something', happen. We then vowed never to refer to them again, apart from letting my ex know that he was the executor and would find the legal documents in my knicker drawer.

'So, no unnecessary rummaging!' I'd ordered, when we dropped the 'Beloved Pooch' off with him, which had tickled all three of us immensely. We then began the pre-holiday countdown with a succession of precision-made plans, the first of which had been orchestrated by entrusting the dog to the man who probably loved him as much as we did. Next on the list was taking bunny to the pet shop. A bizarre conversation followed as to what should happen in the event of sudden death, whilst the animal was boarding.

'We can keep her in the freezer for you.' The shop assistant suggested, looking suitably serious as she explained that an eight-year-old rabbit was a very venerable being. I wasn't sure how old that was in human years; it didn't work like dogs, multiplying by seven, but as bunny was probably in her eighties in rabbit years, the matter indeed had to be discussed.

'Well yes. If you think that's for the best.' I tried not to giggle, as I gravely agreed that the freezer was indeed an excellent idea.

The bunny had been a present for my daughter, when the two of us had moved from our family home, into a neat mid-terrace just down the road, in early October 2006, after I'd finally called time on my marriage to Cuckoo's father. It was a heart-breaking, gut-wrenching time for me, but for the girl, aged twelve, it was a time of mammoth experiences, both the move and the bunny. It had been a surprise present, an apology of sorts, for the night that I had met the Big Man. The cross, little girl, who had been most displeased about the uninvited house guest and even more shocked, by having to witness me bouncing up and down on his cock, had fled to her father's new home for a few days. This had given me some thinking time and breathing space, as well as an opportunity to get to know my new lover, whose personality and stature matched his fucking skills. He'd helped me choose the bunny and created an indoor area for a pen, under the stairs. When the child returned, he was discreetly nowhere to be seen and the sight of the tiny, soft white Angora rabbit immediately wiped the scowl from her face. She called it Daisy, in the spring the bunny would be moved, to a double-story hutch at the bottom of the garden. My lover had created a large run that was attached to her new home; and there, Daisy bun made her world, where she would often be found happily humping a stuffed toy, much to the amusement of all.

Years later, aged twenty, living in London, Cuckoo's memory of the small furry mammal, had sadly receded considerably and became just as unimportant as her memory of the move, with all the angst and upheaval that had accompanied it. The Beloved Pooch had been another present for Cuckoo, long after the troublesome business of witnessing her parents lash themselves apart both verbally and physically, whilst also trying to deal with the equally troublesome business of morphing into a teenager. None of this helped by the fact that she had to witness me unexpectedly falling in love again, within a few weeks of us marching down the hill to our new house. In her then childish eyes, this should have been a sanctuary for her and me alone. 2009, aged fifteen, she had picked him from a litter, an adorable, fat, wriggling, Jack Russell Terrier puppy, with the distinctive brown and white markings of his breed. He was given as another attempt to salve her mojo when she was battling some different demons. The Beloved Pooch was a bundle of joy, capturing the hearts of anyone who met him. There was a definite love affair between this fur baby and Cuckoo's father, 'Daddy Two', which was very handy for holidays and short trips away.

Cuckoo's father, 'Mr. R'., was sixty-two, a good-looking man with dark hair peppered with grey, a Roman nose ala Pacino and thin lips, shielding an acid tongue that I had been the victim of for many years, until he'd called me names for the last time. That was a pivotal moment, as decisions were made which, at the very least I hoped would eventually prove calming for me and which at the very best, as I was to find out, would become wonderfully life changing. We had no choice other than to cohabit during the long months as we waited for our house to sell. It was a truly horrific summer, and I broke down constantly, begging and berating in turn, as he continued to shout insults at me.

'Cunt! Control freak!' He would scream, up and in my face. I knew I was no such thing, I just wanted to be finally able to control my life. The strength came from somewhere, the shielding of my daughter was paramount in my eyes, but there were too many occasions when I failed to do so. The whole episode had been unbelievably stressful, mental; and physical carnage, but I survived it and the old saying proved to be so true.

'If it doesn't beat you, it makes you stronger.'

'Time's a good healer.' Another proverb, that was also bang on.

Mr. R., Daddy Two, had mellowed over the years and I wrote to him eight years later, with a poem about the irony of life, after the true love of his life had died from the dreaded cancer.

'I'll be your friend, if you'll let me be, to see you back together.

Another of life's ironies, there's no such thing as never.

I'm feeling your despair my dear, I know how much you've lost, and if the tables turned on me, I couldn't take the cost.

Now there's a new star in the sky, and it's ok to look and cry.

So, I can be your friend it seems, just know you're on my mind.

I'm waiting in the wings for you, until the day you find,

Your pieces back together.'

The awful disease had reared its head again in Mr. R's life, having been diagnosed with it himself, fourteen years earlier. I had nearly prayed on the day of his surgery in January 2000. I had passed a church whilst I was walking aimlessly around the streets near the Royal Brompton Hospital in London, killing time, waiting for the five-hour operation to be over. The removal of half a lung saved his life, leaving him with a shark bite of a scar ripping through his back. Had I but known it, also with a fresh desire to follow his own desires, that absolutely did not now include a wife. A good few years later, after the fall out of our separation had settled and I had met the Big Man, poor Daddy Two had finally found his soul mate in a man who had also battled cancer, but whose war with it was about to be lost.

'Are you ok?' I had asked him during a routine telephone call about our daughter.

'I am bereft.' The tone of his voice was subdued, not the brittle one I was used to.

'Oh no!!'

'I know.'

'You can tell her.' My next words, after I had quickly realized the enormity of the tragedy, by the broken spirit in his voice over the phone.

'You can talk to her, she will understand.'

He duly did so and the once confused child, who had grown up and matured so beautifully, was able to reverse their roles, offering her father the support he now needed. I drove Cuckoo to his house, having explained the situation. Of course, she had worked it out already, her father's friend had been visiting one day and their body language was enough for a streetwise girl to be able to read between the lines. I stayed for a while, genuinely hurting for him. They had met in a bar in Brighton, Mr. R. haltingly told me.

'Hi, I've been watching you.' Had been the chaps opening line apparently.

'Oh, that's what he said to me.' I replied, recalling the very first words uttered to me by my Big Man. We continued to talk, Cuckoo taking it all in, so grown-up in her ability to absorb and understand, the gentle conversation that was taking place between her parents.

'Why didn't you tell me at the beginning?' I had to ask the question that had puzzled me for a long time, meaning his sexuality.

'I couldn't.' This, I understood. Homosexuality in the 1980's was so much more frowned on than these days. He had a reputation to maintain and had tried so hard to live the lie.

'I would have been happy to just be your friend, if I'd known you felt like that.' I said quietly.

'Well, you wouldn't have had me, if he had!' Cuckoo piped up. We both looked at her, then back at each other.

'You are quite right, darling!' He told her, as I nodded my head vigorously in agreement. Mr. R. went on to confess that he had loved me very much, in his own strange way.

'You never told me.'

'I couldn't.' I half smiled on hearing him admit to having felt any degree of the emotion that I had once longed to instill in him. There had been a time when I would have done anything to hear him speak to me in this way, but now it was just mildly irritating.

'Anyway, forget it. At the end of the day, we were toxic together.' Was my only possible answer to his disclosure. He went on to add, that I had broken his heart several times, when I'd had to up sticks and leave him, after events that had equally shattered my own.

'You never told me that before either.' My reply was gentle, but non-committal. It might have made a difference back in the day, but it didn't matter now. Neither did the crazy way we had lived our lives together, but my sudden memories of that life caused the monsters to bare their teeth at me, from their crypt where they lay buried.

In March 2014, we drove Mr. R. to London. It was the day his lover was predicted to die. Daddy Two had been a dark secret in his life, therefore it was impossible for him to be able to say goodbye in person and he didn't want to be alone, waiting for the final call from the only mutual friend who was privy to their relationship.

Cuckoo had mannequins displayed in several branches of a well-known men's clothing retailer, part of her university coursework and we decided to go and see them. The four of us traipsed the city, tolerating the smog and noise of the relentless traffic, fighting our way through the crowds of Londoners and tourists. We walked for miles in search of the shop windows, finally, proudly viewing the life-sized puppets, that had chimney brushes for top hats and designer clothes draped perfectly around them.

'The Artful Charmer.' Each one had been labeled with the quirky title and all had Cuckoo's own name, on a label below it. We took many pictures, as Japanese tourists craned their necks to see what had caught our attention, shop assistants too, curious as to our actions.

'That's my daughter's work!' I proclaimed loudly, with a huge grin on my face.

'Ma, you're so embarrassing!'

Mr. R. was subdued, we three others had popped out for a smoke during a stop off at a restaurant for lunch and we all peeked in at him, through the window His face was grimly set, and his mind was clearly elsewhere. That night, we left the Beloved Pooch with him. It would be too terrible to be alone with all that raw grief. I pictured poor Daddy Two sobbing into the furry warmth of his companion and despite every reason from the past, which should have made me not give a damn, I still felt his pain. Several times during the following weeks, when I took the dog out for his evening constitutional around the block, I looked up to the stars and cried for the messed-up man with whom I had spent twenty-five years, on and off. Why on earth I was able to be that emotionally generous, had everything to do with the awesome Big Man, who had changed everything for me one Bonfire Night, when sexual attraction and fireworks had combined with a potent magic.

Yes, I had nearly prayed the day of Mr. R.'s surgery, but religion is not part of my personal belief list. Not religion, not God, but 'Something'. The morning of my father's funeral, I had been smoking on the terrace at the back of my parents' house and, as I had always been instructed, chucked the still lit butt into a flower bed below. As it landed, something else started glowing, an old cigar end which must have lain in the soil for months over the winter. My father hadn't been able to smoke a cigar since the previous autumn and had also thrown the discarded ends, still lit, into the same flower bed. The elements should have mulched them down to nothing and it would have been impossible for any of them to catch light, so there was definitely a Something in that. Years later I was sitting in a pub garden, when a drinking buddy started doing her party trick, psychic reading. Intrigued, I gave her a ring that I wore constantly.

'There's someone looking out for you in the spirit world, successful businessman, not always well liked, but he adored his family and he's got a full head of hair.'

'Really!'

'Sounds like your father to me.' My mother was quizzical when I told her. She had been with him when he passed away. His last word had been 'Iridescent.' He had opened his eyes and gazing beyond the woman stroking his face, had uttered that one word, then simply stopped being.

'Mum, it sounds like he saw angels!' Such a Something, indeed.

'Babe, wake up, you're burning! It's bad to fall asleep in the sun!'

'I was dreaming!'

'What about?'

'I'm not sure baby, something.'

Chapter Three

Introducing Cuckoo

The journey to our holiday destination in October 2014, had been uneventful. Whilst the flight was on time, during the enforced wait at the airport we had longed for a cigarette, reminiscing about the good old days, when there had been a smoking bar at the airport and looking back in time even further, to the days of being able to smoke on a plane. Gatwick was its usual hectic self, as hundreds of excited outward-bound travelers yielding heavy suitcases were flocking towards their designated gates, ready to embark on journeys that would take them to places all over the world, in search of their own personal eutopia. Immaculate airport staff were overseeing the huge operation, each dressed in the corporate uniform of the airline they worked for. Despite the professional smiles slicked onto glossed lips I knew what they were really thinking, as I watched them survey the inexperienced hordes, fumbling for their passports and boarding passes.

'Reminds me of Spain in 1988 baby!'

'When you were a holiday rep?'

'We thought we were so special!'

'Bet you looked hot in the uniform!' I giggled at that.

'When were you in the Greek islands babe?'

'Oh, that was 1986, been around the world baby!!' I started dancing around him, singing the words to Liza Stanfield's iconic pop hit, as the smiles on the faces of the airport workers turned to ones of genuine delight.

Both the Big Man and I had been seasoned travelers before we had met; and we took our time during the delay in being allocated a gate for our flight. We boarded smoothly and without incident, settling into the four-hour long journey easily, with a regular bar service providing plenty of alcoholic distraction.

'Fancy the mile-high club babe?' He smiled as he posed the ridiculous question.

'We wouldn't fit in there!' I chuckled, pointing towards the cramped airline toilet cubicle. We settled for cuddling up together, my hand stroking his cock, which was responding admirably. Arriving at the apartment, however, the key wouldn't work properly; and the Big Man had gotten extremely cross, ranting like the proverbial bull, especially when the promised English TV channels didn't work either. Quietly I unpacked for us both and poured large duty-free vodkas.

Later we sat outside on the balcony breathing in the sweet, warm air, watching the tropical palms as the night turned them into strange, silhouetted creatures with Rastafarian dreadlocks, wildly waving hands; and noses that would have done Pinocchio credit, making us laugh helplessly. The Moon and the stars accompanied us into the early hours as we stared into the night sky, humbled and overawed by the celestial display, that was so much brighter and larger than that of home. The proximity of this jewel of an island to its African neighbor ensured the magnification of everything magically stellar, as thoughts of my father lapped through my mind again from the river of moonlight, that was flowing through the dark void above; and the special star that I would always be drawn to, seemed to take a bow.

'Done it!' The Big Man announced with glee the next morning. I had known straight away exactly what he'd meant; we had this way with each other, of knowing what was intended, without explanation.

'You got the telly to work!' I'd shouted back with delighted relief. It was time to declare this amazing feat on Facebook, to a work friend who was always outraged that a television had any part to play in a holiday.

'That's just wrong.' Her message pinged back instantly.

Later in the week, after our day on the beach when I had fallen asleep in the sun dreaming of my past, the idea of getting ready to go out, dressing up and making up had lost its appeal. We decided that mooching around in the apartment for the evening was a much more blissful idea instead. There was plenty of alcohol of course and we counted the number of bottles that we had bought so far.

'Now that's really wrong!' I laughed to myself as I meandered again to the supermarket and bought everything that I would need to prepare Spaghetti Bolognese. The pasta dish had been easy to cook on the hob in the dinky kitchen, though ensuring that I had really bought minced beef had been slightly more complicated.

'Vache?' I hesitantly hoped that I was asking if I had picked up the right ingredients.

'Si. Senora. Beef!'

Later, replete, we lolloped on the settees, comparing degrees of suntan; and reveling in the chilled togetherness of the moment.

'Wanna watch a film babe? "Cape Fears on later." He asked me.

'I love De Niro! Yes, please!'

I proceeded to tell him that it had been twenty years since I had watched that epic classic in a maternity ward, whilst recovering from the serious business of birthing a massive, ten-pound-plus baby girl, admitting wryly that it probably hadn't been the best choice of film to try and watch after my ordeal of the previous twenty-four hours. He listened intently as I went into more detail, as interested as always to hear more of my past stories, as I was his. The labor had gone on relentlessly, every medical trick having been applied by the increasingly concerned consultant and eventually I'd been rushed to theatre, where to the strains of 'Who wants to live forever?' my daughter was presented to the world. The doctor had been drop-dead gorgeous, with floppy, blonde hair and blue eyes, that suddenly looked very relieved. It had been such a shame that his main memory of this patient would have been a view of my gaping nether regions. As he was busily stitching up the neat incision created by the caesarean delivery, he'd commented that should I have more babies; an elective C-section would be needed, as my pelvis was naturally narrow.

There would be no more babies for me though. This hadn't been my first pregnancy and it was to be my 'third time lucky.' So instead of sadly dwelling on the past, once I had stopped shaking from the epidural anesthetic and I was handed my amazing bundle of creation, I'd just counted my blessings, knowing that she had been so worth the wait. I held my baby tightly that night, analyzing every inch of my new-born daughter. She was a sumo infant compared to the other average sized, bald occupants of the cots in the maternity ward, with a shock of black hair and features that were so ugly, squashed from her exertions of trying to eject face first into the world. She was a veritable cuckoo in the nest and as I gazed at my Cuckoo in wonder, I fell head over heels in love.

Tomorrow, that baby, now a beautiful, young lady at a fashion university in London, that fact so sweet as there had been some terrible times in her teens, was flying out to join us for the last four days of the holiday.

'Our own little 'Love Actually' moment.' I smiled up at the Big Man as we waited impatiently in the cool of the air-conditioned Spanish airport, anxiously checking the arrivals board and peering between the automatic doors that were opening and closing, to let the travelers through.

'Bet she's wearing leggings!' He had commented in the taxi on the short drive to the airport, en route to collect her. Finally, there she was, Cuckoo had landed safely, grinning from ear to ear as she burst through the doors, suitcase in hand. She was wearing the predicted leggings and her long, richly brown hair was tousled and newly styled. I spent a few stolen seconds admiring my daughter. She was such an amazingly physically perfect combination of myself and her biological father, all our good bits had been rolled into this one scrummy creature. She was exquisitely made up and casually dressed in designer labels of course. Such a mini-me, in her facial appearance.

'God babe she is such a ringer for you!' The Big Man, her proud stepfather, whispered in my ear before kissing me full on the lips.

'Are you sore babe?' He patted my sun burnt shoulders.

'Everywhere!' I was referring to the previous evening, after our day on the beach when I had indeed burned badly; and our evening chilling in the apartment, the torrid heat of the night had combined with the lack of inhibitions that too much alcohol could cause. He had fucked me fast and furiously on the floor of the living room, covering my naked body with his own, as I responded to every thrust from his pulsating cock with the rhythm of the erotic, horizontal dance that we had perfected.

'You two are so embarrassing!!'Okay, let's go!' She had chirruped, leading us out of the arrivals lounge into the blazing early evening heat.

'Phew it's boiling, wish I hadn't put these leggings on!!'

'Here we go baby, Hurricane Cuckoo's made land!!' He grinned in agreement at my words.

'Hola 'guapa senorita'!' The taxi driver wolf whistled at Cuckoo, his eyes full of excitement as she returned the Spanish compliment for sexy beauty, with a Mona Lisa smile and a demure twinkle from her dark, almond shaped eyes. I shuddered, glimpsing the tiny silver scar in her left pupil as it shone in the fierce sunlight, remembering the day that the monsters had struck out at her. This frisson of fear was swiftly replaced by amusement as I watched the driver catch sight of the Big Man's face, his expression clearly giving a silent warning about the dangers of eyeing up his stepdaughter.

'Hola senor, Hola senora. Donde vamos? Where we go?'

'Bloody hell, I'm never guapa these days.' I sighed inside, remembering when I too had been feted as a 'guapa senorita', attracting the same sort of lascivious interest from hot blooded Spanish men.

'Oh Ma, this is lovely!!' Cuckoo squeaked her appreciation as we opened the door to the apartment and she raced to the balcony, flinging the doors open to be able to admire the swimming pool below, as the Big Man poured drinks for us all.

'Oh yeah, what were you going to tell me yesterday?!' I had found my daughter very mysterious over the phone.

'What!!' Her grin deepened as she answered my question.

'You've met someone!' The penny dropped in my mind.

'Might have!' She said coyly and then Cuckoo consented to give us the rundown. Her stepfather's face was now an even grimmer picture. He is naturally a very possessive man, alpha male incarnate, which personally I adore. Ex-army and all mine, every sexy, little bit of him. I was more than happy to listen to her chatter, when my waking mind suddenly drifted back to the night that I had met the Big Man.

A few weeks after the war in my marital home was over and I had successfully moved with a young Cuckoo, to the much longed-for house of our own, I had decided to take the girl to a Bonfire Night party at a local pub. She deserved this treat and I had tried to give her many after the previous horribly crappy six months, having to watch with innocent, childish eyes, as her parents' relationship deteriorated with the fallout of a nuclear explosion. This was supposed to have been a fresh start for the two of us, a little house for me and her alone, with a front door that we could close against the world and only invite in those who we wanted to. Our old life had been full of random drunks invited back to party-on after nights in local pubs and I was bitterly ashamed of the scenes she had had to tolerate. There had been many other past debacles that I had survived, but this one had had a totally negative effect on my girl, so no, I was not proud at all. This twist in my chain of thoughts was horribly unwelcome, I hadn't wanted to remember any of that shit and my face must have given this away.

'Ma! What's wrong!!'

'Babe, what's the matter!!'

'It's ok guys, just too much to drink, we need to get some food!' I reassured them, dragging my thoughts back to the present. They both seemed satisfied with my answer as we walked slowly down towards the sea front and Cuckoo shooed us into a funky restaurant, stopping to eagerly study the menu that was advertised on a billboard outside.

'Tell us then, does he like football?' The strange question came from the Big Man, who was sitting opposite us at the table. She and I smiled privately between our-selves, at his attempt to try and be civil about another of her potential boyfriends. As they playfully argued about what to order, I concentrated my thoughts purely on my first encounter with him.

Cuckoo and I had arrived at the Guy Fawkes party early in the evening of November 5th. 2006. We were both wrapped up warmly against the cold night air, which had become soured with the smells of damp foliage and burning wood. Eager for a drink, I left her safely with her friends in the crowd of locals, her eyes gazing widely at the splendid roaring fire and made my way into the busy bar.

'I've been watching you.' The words were spoken by the silver-haired vision standing next to me, he was no one I recognized and there was no lust in his smile, like most of the drunken advances I was used to. But whilst there had been no lust then, there would be plenty of time for that in the future and I would later see it change the color of his eyes. His pupils always enlarged massively as he approached orgasm, I would always love watching his eyes during sex and loved the words that he always whispered urgently.

'I like that, babe, God, your wet!' He would groan as he fucked me.

For now, his eyes were intent with interest, totally fixed on my face. Staring back in surprise, with a jolt I dived into the serious blue gaze of the extremely sexy man standing before me. Later I would realize that the detour to that pub, in search of fireworks, had been a stroke of genius and indeed a walk towards my future destiny.

'I'm going to write a book!' I suddenly announced, changing the subject, we had grilled Cuckoo far too much about this new development in her love life.

'Really, what about Ma?'

'Oh, something, you know, this and that!' I replied nonchalantly, going on to explain the meaning of this and that, as she nodded appreciatively until I recited the line about ripe avocados and baby flesh.

'You can't use that Ma!' She gasped. Apparently, it was too close to the bone. Well, I would use it anyway; only a mother would understand the reference to stroking and squeezing baby skin, without seeing it as immoral. Much later that evening we stumbled back to the apartment, laughing; and puffing as we climbed the steep incline back to base.

'Blimey Ma!!'

'They don't call this cardiac hill for nothing!' I gasped back.

'Keep up you two!' The Big Man was yomping determinedly ahead of us both, racing to be the first to the top of the hilly street that wound down to the beach road. Later, I slept like a log, unaware that there were going to be more ghosts from my past who were going to disturb my dreams that night and on a regular basis in the future. 'Grunty' monsters who would pad around the perimeter of my imagination, impotent now but still there, trying to huff and puff, longing to blow my house down again, angrily mindful of the Big Man's powers to keep them at bay.

This time I dreamt of past holidays, adventures and my childhood. My first jaunt abroad, aged fourteen, was with my family, probably enjoying one of the first package holidays of its kind, when such trips were an ultimate and novel, luxury. Crème caramel was always for pudding and waiters had regularly eyed me up and down. Years later I still reveled in the thrill of descending from a plane, having landed on exotic foreign soil and sniffing the air that was warm and sticky, permeated with the unforgettable smell of sewage, mixed with garlic and hot, sweaty bodies.

'Hola guapa senorita!' I had always replied silently to the age-old compliment with the same smile and hint of flirtation in my eyes, that my daughter would adopt many years later. Watching my father glower at them, much as the Big Man had done when she had silently flirted with the Spanish taxi driver. I had adored the attention, but years later, 'Hola senora.' told me all I'd needed to know about the passing of time on my face and body, relegating me to a much less desirable item. I was loving the knowledge that those horny Spanish men had wanted to bed the teenaged me, then not knowing that there were going to be others in the future, who would want to fuck me over in a much more sinister fashion. Cunty, grunty apparitions, devils, who weren't interested in me, yet.

I dreamt about the very beginning when I was 'Daughter Number One', of two little girls, a product of the union between a boy and a girl, both from poor working-class backgrounds, living in towns with little to offer them. I saw this couple of hopefuls, my parents, forging their way, untwining themselves from the roots of their respective childhoods, but never forgetting the debt they owed to their families who had played their own parts in making this escape possible, by giving them love and support in abundance. I watched as university life had opened unique doors for them and how they'd met whilst studying, when the stars had aligned for them also. My father had made advances, my mother recounted to me many years later, during one of our confidential chats. She had broken down, as his inexpert fumbling had upset her and as she sobbed her own sad story into his chest, he had cried too.

He had listened hard and wrapped his arms around her, forging the beginning of their own magic, which would last forever, they'd believed. Indeed, the words of the marriage vows they were to make would prove solid and true, as their separation would only be with his death. There had been no money to give them as a head start in life, but my father had been ambitious. His career soared, with my mother right by his side, birthing and raising two little female cherubs, 'Daughters Numbers One; and Two'. We were eighteen months different in age and poles apart in anything else. This would inevitably lead to estrangement between us sisters as we grew into adults. I became indifferent to this eventually, but our mother suffered from the situation and for her, I felt nothing but sympathy.

I saw my childhood, Punch and Judy shows and fish and chips in newspaper, on family holidays; and daytrips to piers at the seaside, where I was scared by the gaps between the wooden planks, fearing that I would fall into the murky water that was splashing below. There were no mod cons in the 1960s, when we visited a large static caravan in a Welsh field every year, yet for me, it was the most perfect place to be. My reveries took me back to the early 1970s, when I was thirteen or fourteen. We'd toured Europe, with a compact mobile caravan hitched proudly to the back of my father's car, intent on finding the next camp sites, where my mother insisted on checking out the toilets before we could park up for a few days.

'Fair le plein! Fill it up!' I could hear my father's voice, as he merrily shouted out to the bemused attendants at French petrol stations. I could smell the tinned corn beef dinners, with sizzling, salty chips that we collected in a saucepan from the camp site kitchens, and I could taste the sweet crêpe suzettes cooked on the same grills. I saw us all playing Monopoly in the pokey caravan, where my sister always lost badly, in a temper and as I dreamt, I felt the most special echo from those halcyon days, as it lightly stroked my unconscious mind with a gentle kiss. We had parked overnight on a cliff top in France, when my father first introduced me to the delights of red wine. He and I had sat quietly on deckchairs outside, watching the Moon as it shone a translucent, silver path over the sea. 'Moon River' would forever be an anthem to my father, and I requested the tune at many a piano bar.

'Para mi Padre, pour favor.'

I heard his voice again, listening as he introduced me to 'The Chariots of the Gods' theories. They mixed the celestial with mankind, explaining a version of the origin of Stonehenge and other impossible ancient creations. I watched as we stared for hours at the twinkling, milky white constellations in the richly dark velvet skies and I felt once again, the irresistible urge that had been born in me on that special evening. An impulse to look up to the stars at night, no matter when or where I was to find myself, another legacy, from this legendary man. Off we went, continuing our European adventures, Mother perched firmly in the front with her map, tracing the coming route. We two well behaved children, snug in the back, falling asleep watching raindrops trickle down the car windows, lulled by the murmuring from our parents as they negotiated the highways together.

In my dream I could feel the sense of safety that was eternally evoked by that memory and I cried in my sleep, subliminally so sadly aware, that years later I would have to experience the fears that come with adult life. I heard a drugs councilor ask my earlier, fucked-up, grown-up self, if I blamed my upbringing for the demons I was battling and heard myself reject this idea out of hand. I saw us, as we moved around the North of England as a family, my father rising meteorically in his chosen industry. I watched myself develop, as my bolshie, teenage juices started rising and with my sex itching, my interests in the wrong subjects started to grow. Daughter Number Two was trailing behind me, in the wake of what would become my near self-destruction. Number Two, always the good girl, never causing any problems, explaining to a degree, her fermenting resentment towards me later in life.

I revisited the summer of 1974, when I had a school exchange visit with a family near Paris, where I was given an improvised bedroom, created in a very dark, dingy dining room. I saw myself hiding under the covers, trying to ignore the strange, shapeshifting nature of the scary pictures that the old pieces of furniture were conjuring up in my head and to avoid the annoying mosquitos that were buzzing angrily around, intent on sucking my blood. I laughed inside as I slept on, remembering secret drinking on the ferry on the way over to France, when I was cornered by a disgustingly garlic-smelling French sailor and running away from him and his determination to shag the drunken, young English traveler who he was lusting after.

As I slowly woke the next morning, that last vestige of my previous night's reveries was at the forefront of my waking mind, reminding me that it was my teenage adventure in Paris which had given me a pretty good smattering of their language, a lingual skill to help me in the future, if I had but known it then.

'Morning Ma, did you sleep well!' Cuckoo chirruped in the doorway.

'Wow, I had some vivid dreams darling!' I answered her, as the shadowy specters from my past slowly retreated, to whence they came.

'You were laughing Ma and crying!'

'Was I darling, how weird I can't remember a thing!' I dismissed her concerns, whilst mentally hugging every piece of my nocturnal visions.

'You were talking about 'Grandpa Poorly' Ma!' My bombastic daughter wasn't going to let the subject drop that easily.

'Oh, that's so cute darling, I'd forgotten you called him that!' I deftly avoided her suggestion that I had been sleep talking to my father, who she had had always referred to as Grandpa Poorly, as tragically that was how she remembered him.

We decided to spend the next day on 'our' beach. The holiday was flying by for me and the Big Man; and now that Cuckoo had joined us, we wanted to make the last three days extra special. Cuckoo had insisted that we buy her a lilo and armed with the brightly colored blow up and a cool bag rammed with more ice-cold cans of lager, we settled on the sand for the last time, wiggling it between our toes. The following day, our penultimate, we took an obligatory boat trip, the price of the tickets had included fried chicken and chips and as much beer or sangria as we could drink.

'Fancy a fishing trip, girls!' The Big Man had asked us.

'I've never been fishing!!' This from Cuckoo.

'Not on my watch!' I laughed in return, vehemently wagging a finger at him.

'Why Ma!!'

'What's up babe!' He knew exactly why I loathed the idea and he bought three tickets for a much more agreeable alternative.

'Ma! why were you crying last night?!'

'Were you crying, babe!!'

'Ffs, leave me alone you two!! I had a bad dream is all!!' My eyes met his and although he knew well enough to leave the subject alone, he couldn't resist one last comment.

'I warned you babe, it's this idea of a writing a book, it's making you unhappy.'

'I'm fine!'

'Sure?'

'Can we drop it please.' I snuck my head towards Cuckoo, I didn't want her to know that my dreams had been invaded by monstrous nightmares.

'Mmmmmm.' He wasn't convinced, but she was, and that would do.

The boat trip was superb, standing at the prow of the sizeable craft that was easily holding fifty other passengers with room to spare, we watched as it cleared the harbor walls, pointing directly out to sea.

'You ok babe!' The Big Man asked the obvious question, concerned after seeing me suffer during past nautical experiences with him.

'It's brilliant!' I shouted back, easily adapting my sea legs to the roll of the deck. We sailed for about an hour, before approaching calmer waters that surrounded a practically deserted beach.

'Playa nudista, nudist beach!!' The captain announced proudly over the microphone.

'Ma!!!' Cuckoo gasped, casting a shy peek at the very evident crown jewels contained within the Big Mans shorts. Sadly, or gladly, it turned out that the waters were too choppy to be able to launch the on-board tender to transport any hopefuls to the naturist beach; and when he next announced that a banana boat was still available for rides, Cuckoo was much more amenable.

'Come on Ma!!!' She shouted, but I was more than happy just to watch as the other two clambered up onto the yellow, torpedo shaped inflatable, life jackets securely tied around them, waiting to be towed out to sea. Laughing at their faces, that were pictures as they clung on, fighting to stay on board as they were pulled around in crazy circles.

Too soon it was our last day and tattoo time. I sat down as the artist inked my idea on my forearm, a daisy for Cuckoo and a poppy for the Big Man, their initials adorning the two little flowers, like leaves.

'Have you been drinking a lot of alcohol?' The tattooist had asked in his thick Dutch accent.

'It thins the blood you know.' He fretted out-loud, trying to stop the excessive, bright red flow, as his needle stabbed its work into my skin.

'I've been here for two weeks, what do you think!' I laughed in reply, deciding not to elaborate too much. I already had other tattoos, as the Big Man had once promised I would. Cuckoo's name was inked on my lower back, and I had an image of a guardian angel standing on a crescent Moon, on my left shoulder blade, represented by a sketch of my daughter.

'Wow babe!' He'd exclaimed, when he'd seen it. I had wanted to surprise him, so I had kept this appointment alone. I was very proud of my first two symbols, but I couldn't see them. Today's result, the bloodied and sore, little flowers, their stems reaching out to each other, was right in my eyesight. Cuckoo had a third inking, a depiction of the Sun to add to her own collection and we walked slowly away, with my new tribute to my cherished family permanently etched on my arm.

The flight home was crap. Night flights always seemed like a good idea at the time of booking, to make the most of the final day of the holiday. It wasn't funny however, when at one a.m. there were still two hours of flying time to endure, and the plane seemed to be full of scratchy-eyed zombies and unhappy, vocal babies. We'd parted ways back at Gatwick, Cuckoo returning to London life and us, finally arriving back home at five a.m. on a cold, dark English morning. We hadn't wanted to be intimate whilst Cuckoo was staying with us and now, we were able to enjoy another slow fuck, with room to spread my legs and take it all, sleeping soundly afterwards, as the dreaming continued.

Chapter Four

No Looking Back

I could see my childhood, where I was a perfect little girl, until accordingly to my father, when I reached my teens.

'Sex reared its ugly head!'

I swapped horse riding lessons for pocket money to buy lurid eye shadow. Parties were discovered, drinking cheap cider and cherry brandy necked during games of 'Spin the bottle' were followed by acts of forbidden, inexperienced groping with randy boys in darkened rooms. I wore hot pants and flared jeans with 'God is an Alien!' scribbled on them in permanent marker pen. My father had wholeheartedly disapproved of this, which I saw myself laugh at scornfully.

'Dad, you introduced me to the idea!!' I recoiled in my sleep as I watched his head droop on hearing the unwelcome and new, harsh tone of defiance in my voice from the past.

'I didn't mean it like that!!' I cried out as I slept on in October in 2014, shouting back down the years, desperately and futilely wanting him to hear me.

It was the mid-seventies and hair was tortured into place with curling tongs and gallons of hair spray. Cheese cloth and clumpy heeled shoes were part of the fashion of the day. Pretending to smoke pot in the toilets at school and poopooing the teachers behind their backs, were all part of the pleasures as I grew up. I played my part in the act of teenage rebellion passionately, starting to smoke secretly, swapping my dinner money for a packet of ten Players No6 cigarettes and dating a succession of boys. Oh yes, how sex had raised its ugly head indeed! My virginity was finally properly lost at one of the house parties, as the inevitable start of my rebellion against my parents began. How horrified they must have been to see their sunny Daughter Number One, who had hung on to every word they'd uttered, turn into a sullen and insecure little goblin, defying them at every step of the way. Sadly, they had no benchmark to fall back on to help them understand, as such emotional tribulations had not been theirs to experience, life had not afforded them such luxuries at that age. I would be determined to try and remember this when Cuckoo hit puberty and would always try to understand, however hard if not impossible this would prove to be.

I was given a record player one Christmas or Birthday, so old-fashioned these days. Forty-five rpm vinyl was all the rage and as the mechanical arm of the machine moved down onto the grooves of my cherished, black discs, as I continued to dream, I watched in horror, the teenaged me bopping along to the tunes of the day, with 'Puppy Love' on constant repeat, my face horrendously made-up, shaking my head with regret in my sleep, witnessing my father's face as it dropped even more. He preferred the sounds of military band music and was obviously totally perplexed as to what was happening to his beautiful Daughter Number One, whilst trying feebly to protest about the war paint that I was slapping on again. I remembered the summer of 1976 and with my O levels completed, I could feel myself just starting to understand my transition through my middle teens, when suddenly my father's work took us as a family to what might as well have been another planet, the South of England! It was a total culture shock where everyone talked posh and where I, at the age of sixteen, was an alien creature, with my flat, northern dialect, my huge, over-made-up eyes and my defiantly 'don't fuck with me' attitude.

I was such a square peg in this southern, round hole, with my dark hair, strong facial features and a curvy body that for years I could never appreciate. It was therefore no wonder bulimia crept into my life, which became a way of controlling the binge-eating that I had fallen prey to. I saw myself buying packets of laxative at a string of different chemists, lest my guilty secret was discovered. I could feel the pain of the sleepless nights, when I writhed in agony, shitting bricks through the eye of many a needle, following hours of literally stuffing myself, until my stomach was so distended and swollen with the quantity of food it had been forced to contain. This was the start of many erratic forms of behavior by the younger me and they were certainly strange at their best. Harbingers of the monsters, as I was going to refer to the demons who were going to blight my life. 'Cunty grunts', born of my own stupidity and released from behind the doors that I was going to open into dark places. It would be many years later after I had managed to banish them, that I would understand that such monsters were everywhere and that they weren't exclusive to me. This lesson would one day be taught to me by my father.

I saw an old photo that I had found years later. It had been taken at a beach bar when I was twenty-four. The girl staring back at me from the picture was laughing, her face suntanned, hair thrown back, wearing an off-the-shoulder top, with a figure to die for. It was not the way I had remembered that day at all and the memory of the feelings of uncomfortable self-consciousness that I had experienced that afternoon, made me whimper as I dreamt. No wonder discovering amphetamines was like a gift from God the Alien, the drug was appetite-curbing, confidence-boosting and of course, price-paying. More poetry was written during those nights of wide-eyed restlessness, when the high had subsided and only alcohol and dope would settle the jumpy, jangly residue of forty-eight hours on speed. I heard myself shouting at my father, in my mid-twenties, trying to blame my drug use, which was by then in full swing, on the family's earlier cross-country move and drooped my own head, listening, thirty years later, thirty years too late, as he crossly rejected my theory.

'Drugs would have found you wherever you were, young lady, THAT was the problem.'

It was only now in my dream, that I had the only answer that he had deserved to hear and once again I muttered down the years, hoping that by some miracle he could hear me.

'Oh Dad, you were so right; and I was so wrong. It wasn't the drugs that were a problem, it was me and the way they seemed to help me deal with the pain of the reality of who I had become and how I had failed. THAT was the problem.'

We woke up at lunch time after the long night flight back from our late autumn holiday in October 2014. It felt strange to be home, feeling the holiday reality recede and ready to deal with imminently important issues, such as picking up the bunny and the Beloved Pooch.

'She's not in the freezer then!' I laughed, as I pushed open the door of the pet shop to see Daisy, alive and kicking, nose twitching and ears pricked, ready to be brought home. Mr. R. had looked after our dog for two solid weeks, and we gave him a bottle of expensive brandy, as a present for being a good Daddy Two, plus a bottle of cheap Spanish plonk to wash it down with, a love of all thing's alcoholic being a common denominator between the three of us.

Soon it was Bonfire Night, I had been with the Big Man for eight years and for the first time in my life I had been completely monogamous, without an iota of any desire to charm another man. I took the Beloved Pooch for his walk around the familiar block. There was to be no stargazing that night, as the first rockets lit the skyline his little legs went bonkers trying to get home, terrified of the noise as always. This was indeed a home, our home, I had lived in probably more than twenty-five places in my life, having stopped counting when I had tried and failed to remember them all. Knowing that none of that mattered now, only that my final dwelling was a real home, with a real man.

'Happy anniversary babe x' The Big Man had texted me that morning. We had two anniversaries, 5th November, when our eyes had met for the first time and the stars had realigned for us and 13th February, when we had taken the plunge into marital bliss in 2010, the second time for both of us. I smiled to myself, having got the Beloved Pooch indoors safely where he was able to hide under the bed, remembering that the old romantic had wanted Valentine's Day as the date for our wedding, but the registry office wanted four hundred and fifty pounds for that privilege, whereas the day before was a tenth of the price. There were only four of us, with my lovely mother and Cuckoo both acting as witnesses. I had looked up at the Big Man and for the umpteenth time he locked his eyes with mine, as we both repeated the short heartfelt vows, saying 'I do' with every atom of our bodies and souls.

Another equation I had once tried to work out was how many men I had bedded, again I quit after about twenty-five, supposing that it had been a desire to be wanted that had driven all that promiscuity. Having said that, the night that we had met and fucked so urgently before Cuckoo had caught us in flagrante, had not been the best of starts to a meaningful relationship. The next morning, I had woken up with the old, familiar feeling of abandoned misery swirling around my head.

'Oh no, what have I done.' I was thinking of the sight I had exposed my daughter to, as well as letting her down already; and for what? That evening he rang me.

'How did you get my number?!' I asked with delight.

Apparently, he had done some rather good detective work at the pub. He'd told the landlady he had met a sultry, dark-haired woman and needed her phone number.

'Hello babe.' He'd said, and my misery was replaced with delighted anticipation. This time things would be so different for me. We were meant to be together, two parts of a whole, unlike my first marriage. My father used to compare it to a broken pair of scissors, cutting each other up and completely useless. It had indeed been so terribly toxic, but it had produced that fine bouncing baby Cuckoo and both my-self and Mr. R., if pressed, would surely both have admitted some blame for the failure of our relationship, in one form or another, whilst thanking our lucky stars for our daughter.

In November 2006, the terrace house with its dinky garden was a blank canvas, Cuckoo and I had only been there for four weeks, before my first encounter with the Big Man. He was superbly sensitive to the objections of the girl and he would only visit when she had gone to stay with her father. Gradually he became a fixture in our lives and together he and I created our own little bit of Heaven, buying stuff and acquiring even more.

'Oh baby, you are such a gatherer!!' I had laughed in delight at what he brought home; and proudly presented to me. My Big Man, as an army veteran was HGV-trained and now delivered and collected, huge metal skips. His ability to rummage through other people's trash and find treasure was completely awesome, beggaring all belief. A few months later I introduced him to my lovely mother, who took to him immediately.

'Such a pipe and slippers man!' Mother had commented with pride. I didn't have the heart to tell her that a spliff and dressing gown man was much more appropriate. Shortly after that meeting, he had proposed to me, it was so unexpected and so typical of his thinking process. He did a lot of that, whilst driving his chunky lorry.

'I think we should get married babe.' It was the most beautiful of beautiful thoughts that he had ever shared with me.

'I need to get divorced first!' Laughing and crying at the same time I accepted his proposal, but to my surprise, lovely mother was initially skeptical.

'Stay loose.' She had advised me in her infinite wisdom. Her reservations about a man who seemed to have no tangible past, were understandable. He had no friends or family at our wedding, nobody to prove who he was, but time eroded mother's reservations and her trust in her new son-in-law grew. As for me, I believed every word of the sad stories he had told me, which of course, down the line turned out to be completely true; and the military medals that he had kept safe over the years and wore proudly on his chest every Remembrance Sunday, bore testament to that truth.

That night, when the fireworks had stopped screeching and banging, I dreamt about the day that the eighteen-year-old me walked out of the family home. I had no such mementos to pin to a jacket as I left, without looking back. We had limped on as a family for a few short years after our geographical relocation. I had tried to fit in at the sixth form college I was enrolled at and my parents had made every effort to reconcile their own hopes for me, with my own silly dreams, but the generation gap was too vast. I packed my belongings into cardboard boxes and gleefully stepped out on my own, leaving them astounded, confused and bitterly upset, perhaps even blaming themselves for my departure. If I had looked back, I would have seen tears in my father's eyes; but there were tears in mine now, as I relived that moment.

'I'm sorry Dad, I'm so sorry' The same unspoken apology, words that I wished so much that he could hear.

My blinkered sights had been firmly set on a new-found freedom, away from what I saw as their stupid, archaic parental rules. They never did understand how Daughter Number One with a future at university ended up preferring to live her life away from them, in a shabby bedsit. With good old hindsight being such a powerful medium, it would be many years before I finally did look back at myself with wiser eyes and totally understood their point of view.

Miss Incredibly Selfish 1978 got a job at a high street bank, earning one hundred and twenty pounds per month in wages, which was a fortune when fags were just fifty pence a packet. Now dating a boy that my parents considered most unsuitable and sporting a solitaire engagement ring, I plunged head-first into the delightful world of bedsit land. In the first one I would swear, I could have jumped off the bed and landed on the tiny grill/kettle area provided. It didn't matter, with a sturdy lock on my door and a loo just down the landing, I had everything I needed. The late Seventies were the era of big hair, jump suits and nightclubs. We had no mobile phones, but we did have the youth and excited determination to prove that we were the new generation, disdaining anyone or anything who was not hip or trendy enough to be accepted.

Contempt was easy to garb ourselves with, along with the fashions of the time and the beats of the day. Top of the Pops ruled weekly, and the music of the decade heralded the end of the power of the 1960's, as the original golden age. I also had the kudos that my fiancé was a part-time guitarist with a crappy club band, which in my immature mind gave me so much more exclusivity in the brave, new world that I was embracing. Wearing brightly coloured, many zipped jumpsuits with great pride, I strutted around in stiletto heeled shoes that made me look and feel six feet tall. I spent my nineteenth Birthday drinking Brandy and Babycham, at yet another rubbish gig, but my twenty-first was spent at a joint family party to celebrate the momentous milestone and my father's fiftieth.

A photo of us was taken that night and it sits next to my bed, kept safe over all the years, stored lovingly with those tatty pieces of paper containing my unfinished rhymes. There we were, the two of us, so similar in looks. He had a pipe clenched between his teeth and a bottle of champagne in his hand, whilst my head was on his shoulder, laughing out-loud. It was a moment of reconciliation, a good moment, but the picture was so bittersweet, as the innocence in our faces belied the future tragedies that lay ahead for the both of us and how the unravelling of my life was going to hurt him so badly. As a grown woman many years later, I would never study the yellowing photo without feeling sorrow and pure regret, always talking to it, always with the same sad acknowledgment.

'Dad, I'm so sorry.'

I fell pregnant of course, living in a rented flat with my betrothed. There was no double glazing, and it was so cold in the winter that the toilet and bath both froze over. My parents were about to move back up North. Daughter Number Two was at university there, so they had no choice than to begrudgingly leave me in the hands of the wannabe Rockstar, whose twitching guitar fingers impressed nobody but himself and a few diehard groupies who followed his band around at various weekly gigs in dingy, smoke-filled dives. Yeah, the girl at a high street bank with a great IQ was pregnant at the tender age of just twenty-one. I didn't have a maternal bone in my body at the time, in fact, I never actually did until I came face-to-face with my Cuckoo fourteen years later, when the awesome experiences of feeling a mother's love and the realization of the mother lion's instinct, both hit me like a ton of bricks.

I dealt with the pregnancy situation coldly and calmly, without a word to my own mother. I would have been appalled if one day Cuckoo had behaved in this way, without confiding in me. I brought my daughter up to tell me everything and anything, no matter how dire the subject matter could be. It wasn't until I'd had my first glimpse of Cuckoo, that I picked up the phone to speak the words that later I would have given the world to have done so, much, much earlier.

'I'm sorry, I'm so sorry.' I sobbed.

'What for?' My parents had laughed gently.

'Everything!' I wailed, as finally I had come to realize just how much they must have suffered, having to watch me self-combust during the crazy years.

I remembered the journey on the underground to a clinic on the other side of London, where the pregnancy was terminated. Waking up there the morning after the procedure, with a huge belly pain and a tiny sense of loss. Crawling back to the draughty, rented flat, with decisions made and a horribly sordid job done.

'Never look back.' As I repeated the mantra, I was trying to convince myself not to do so, creating a tool for my near destruction, as not looking back meant not really learning from mistakes. I was going to catapult through life, swinging from one ridiculous disaster to another Relying only on my sheer grit and determination to get out of my rolls in the shit and dusting myself down with rose petals, enabling me to career on. I would one day admit that the rose petal tinted olive branches used to drag myself out of the mire, were always proffered by my father.

'You never cut the umbilical cord.' Was a saying that he regularly used about me in my twenties and thirties. I expect he was trying to believe in a Something too, having to take my behaviour on the chin, time after time. Mr. R. was always a bit confused by the statement. It wouldn't be for many years later, as Cuckoo's father, that he would truly understand my own father's, intended meaning of his words.

Once the little matter of the lonely stigma of my experience in the abortion clinic was over, I arranged to meet my parents, half-way up the country.

'Got something to tell you'. I muttered.

'Oh my God, what?' From my mother.

'I'm leaving him, I'm bored.' Mother sat down suddenly, weak with relief.

'Oh my God, I thought you were going to say you are pregnant.'

Onwards, I lurched to my next adventure and was offered a room in the flat above the bank branch I worked in, it was going to be single girls party time, unfortunately.

A few days after Bonfire Night the Big Man drove us to the West Country, on the Saturday of the Remembrance Sunday weekend in 2014. The journey was quite tedious as usual; almost all the way following a straight line along the Roman road of old. Milestones along the route included the mammoth rocks of Stonehenge, with its potential evidence of visitors from the stars, the slaughter stone suggesting dark murders and diabolical rituals. I looked right sadly, as we drove past the historical site.

'It always reminds me of him, baby.' I was talking about my father.

'I know babe.' He understood, his eyes firmly on the road as he drove, his left hand squeezing my right knee. Finally, we pulled into the all-too-familiar parking bay allocated to my mother's airy second floor flat. She had eventually moved from the fabulous house that she had lived in with my father, ten years after his death, swopping flower beds and lost dreams for something more manageable. The town hadn't altered over the twenty-odd years that I had been visiting it. Once upon a time it had been to stay with my parents, but for a long time it had been to see lovely mother only. We strolled to the seafront that afternoon and as the fresh, salty air and spray from the choppy waves lashed the prom, it blew away our travel tiredness.

'Funny to think it's the same ocean we were swimming in a few weeks ago.' I remarked to the Big Man. This side of the Atlantic was bleakly dangerous in October and November, so different from the warm, calm sea lapping the magical island that we had been sad to leave. The sky was full of angry, grey, scudding rain clouds and squawking sea gulls riding the gusts of cold wind, but the weather was kind to us for the rest of the weekend, cold but sunny. We had walked hand in hand towards the memorial service on Sunday 9th November, my dashing Big Man was wearing a black jacket decorated with his war medals and I felt so proud, that my heart was beating out of my chest.

The view that night over the balcony of mother's flat, was of the Moon and bare trees that were moving spookily in the breeze. Laughing and a little bit drunk, having also shared a surreptitious spliff together, the Big Man and I created more surreal images in the swaying tree branches. No mystical, tropical creatures here, only spikey oak and elm trees, bared of leaves they splintered the dark with slashes of woody fingers. Later, as we talked and reminisced, Mother told me that she had been afraid of the Moon as a child, another of the little secrets that she had confided to me over the years.

'I'm going to write a book!' I dropped this into the conversation.

'Well, you always could write poetry!'

Have you kept in contact with anyone?' She asked next, changing the subject and told us about friendships that she still had, which was quite a feat, as some of these spanned sixty plus years.

'No, not really.' We had looked at each other before I answered for both of us; and falling asleep that Sunday evening, I reflected on earlier days, after deciding to go solo when she had been my age, making friends for life, not waves, as was going to be the case for me, her Daughter Number One.

My new job with a bank back in the day had pleased my parents, who obviously thought a career could be salvaged from the mess I had made of things so far. This was not quite how things were going to turn out, however. That night whilst the Big Man slept soundly, I tossed and turned, remembering everything about that time and as I eventually fell into a troubled sleep, my dreams were of the events that had followed, after my decision to go my own merry, single way, when the first six months were full of hot, sticky partying in nightclubs, before inviting random strangers back to the flat, for sticky, hot, drunken sex.

'No parties.' Had been the only stipulation of the bank manager to whom I paid a pittance for the privilege of sharing his precious flat. My hair was even bigger, hugely permed and blow-dried, my stiletto heels were even higher; and I now sported shoulder pads in jackets that had become part of the crucial 'look' of the times. I danced around my handbag to the current sounds, as flashing lights and plumes from dry ice machines added to the fun of a night out. I drank sweet, gag-making cocktails whilst selecting my chosen target for the night, with seductive glances from my overly made-up eyes. My new home, the bank flat, was very austere, with high ceilings and plain white walls, more of an office than a cosy dwelling. I shared it with a colleague from the bank, she was a like-minded soul and another heavy drinking party animal.

The work in the bank was okay, nine to five, if I was lucky and all the books had balanced. I learnt how to use what were probably the first computers, they were beasts of machinery, with clumpy keyboards and clumsy components, which future generations of bank workers would doubtless stare at with incredulous incomprehension. I moved up the ranks to become a cashier, sitting primly inside my glass window. Counting notes and coins, hours and minutes, until I could leave the day job and walk out of the heavy door of the bank, up a flight of metal steps and into the welcoming solitude of the flat, where I would plot my next move in the search of my idea of a good time.

The pill was the contraception of choice at the time. Condoms were shunned as being for amateurs; but considering that this was the era before Aids was discovered, the most deadly of all the sexually transmitted diseases that were already rife; and bearing in mind the sexual exploits that occurred weekly, that were the most dangerous of games. Friday night was the highlight I craved for, although no drugs had been dabbled with yet, this was swiftly to come and they were waiting impatiently in the wings of my life, soon to be discovered. Given the small-town nature of the clientele of this nightclub circuit, it was inevitable that eventually I would get to meet every 'groover and mover' within it and it was a sure bet that one night I would bump into the one who would become Cuckoo's father. A much younger Mr. R., as hip and as cool as the star of 'Saturday Night Fever', surveying his disco kingdom with pleasure and disdain. Every chat up line was well versed and slickly used on the females who were lapping up his attention and hanging onto his every quip, oblivious that deep inside, he was hiding his true yearnings.

Our meeting was an introduction of fire to oil, two brilliant minds, rampant bodies and darkly attractive faces. Unfortunately, there was also an inherent inability to understand and appreciate the soul of each other. If only we had known the personal suffering that we were going to cause each other, we would both have avoided that chance meeting like the plague.

'Chanson Papillon.' The lyrics to that song and so many others would add bitter- sweet music to the times we were going to live. His style was amusing and direct, his was the art of one-liners which had been well practiced and honed, to be delivered with a touch of silky venom. Despite his interest in this new girl in his sights, he laughed at my mane of dark, permed hair and ridiculously heavily made-up eyes. He gave me a nickname and called me Panda. losing my identity of twenty-two years, I would spend the next twenty-four, on and off as this character. I loathed the tag, but like many things, was powerless to prevent it becoming the norm. When I rose from the ashes of the furry Frankenstein, aged forty-six, finally freeing myself, many acquaintances had no idea of my real identity and I took great pleasure in telling them who I really was. Now however it would be the time for dabbling and the sirens were finally released.

'Try this.' The young Mr. R. casually introduced me to 'Billy' one night.

'What is it? Ok!!!'

To be fair, he couldn't have known what a fatal blow he was delivering, as he suggested I mix a little bit of speed in my drink. The damage, however, was done and I had found my perfect high, not realizing that the desperate low which accompanied it, was never going to be worth the cost. We partied madly, not together but in a crowd, any crowd, finishing up at the end of the night or the beginning of the morning, with each other. But I would feel so alone, as my inability to sleep and his way of holding me mentally and physically at arm's length, was frustrating my mind and body. How could I possibly have known either that this punishment was not because of my behaviour, but a consequence of his own suppressed desires?

A group of cronies evolved, including another colleague who I had befriended in the bank and her husband. Both were fucked-up characters, even before they latched on to the new-found pleasures that fast drugs had to offer. Both were shagging behind each other's backs and both were exceptionally greedy to share the sulfate high. They lived locally and were keen to have me as a lodger, after my shameful banishment from the bank flat.

'No parties!' Yeah right.

Chapter Five

Waking the Monsters

It was only one party, then two and then a few more. At the beginning I managed to contain things within the sturdy, thick walls of the flat. There was only one other occupied building at night on the street. A seedy Indian restaurant that was responsible for the rats and huge flies which plagued the open doors and windows of the flat in the summer. No concern there, about complaints arising from noise. The size of the partying grew, as did my drug use. I never did learn to roll the perfect spliff, but I sure could 'toke' on them. I would be wide-eyed, wild-eyed, talking absolute bullshit and swigging on anything to hand, until the ultimate party, where the place was packed to the rafter with random people as high as kites. I suppose it was today's equivalent of advertising a party on Facebook and in the event, it was just as catastrophic.

The flat had two floors and was quite isolated. A solid metal door with intercom was the first hurdle to negotiate, when entering from the pavement. The next obstacle to overcome in accessing the front door of the flat, was a flight of nasty metal stairs leading to a patio area overlooking the said Indian. Then finally there was yet another door, with another intercom. Clearly this had once been much more than a flat, it had probably once contained bullion, now it was going to store trouble. The door in, from the street was adjacent to several local shops, including several newsagents-cum-general stores, the owners happily selling me overpriced fags and out-of-hours booze on many occasions. They were also valued customers of the bank manager, paying in rolls of cash and cheques and bags of coins, daily. The everyday use of debit and credit cards was going to be a thing of the future.

My parents visited regularly, my father was soaring very high in the world of business and whenever he had the need to travel South, he would book my mother and himself into one of several rather posh and expensive local hotels, always arranging to treat me to dinner. I was still masquerading as a potential financial genius and the three of us would spend the evening enjoying the rather good food presented; and quaffing the wine that my father had carefully ordered. Now, I watched as they returned to the comfort of their hotel room, excited and happy and I listened as they chattered away merrily about how well I was progressing in life, despite the wobbly beginning, when I had chucked away my university potential. Only now, in my dream, could I tell him the truth.

'I'm so sorry Dad, I'm so sorry for the bullshit that I fed you.'

I introduced the young Mr. R. to them, as the new man in my life, wanting as much as they did to believe the charade I was acting out. He blotted his copy book with a throw-away sarcastic comment about my front teeth, which at the time were naturally slightly crooked and my father never forgot this. I would lovingly kiss them goodbye and continue to weave between the strands of the life that I was living, trying to avoid the muddle I was making of it, trying and failing badly. My nemesis owned his own house and I stayed there now and again. The womanly part of me was desperate to be nurtured and I would try to please him by cooking dinner, but that wasn't what he wanted. He wanted the she-devil, who to a degree he was responsible for unleashing. I was just twenty-three, learning to live without roots, a chameleon creature, still binging, drinking and taking speed, a recipe for disaster, for which there was bound to be a catalyst.

The morning after what was to be the final party, the remaining stragglers had piled out of my flat as usual. Unfortunately, a bag of powdered tar had been left next to the front door of the inner sanctum and regrettably it had just started raining, hard. The bag was knocked over, mixed with the rainwater into a sticky, black sludge and walked through by the departing rabble, who left tarry footprints as they went. Across the patio the gooey marks travelled, down the metal steps, onto the pavement and into the premises of the early-bird shop keepers. A few angry words were exchanged with the now extremely pissed-off bank manager, who really had had only one rule that he had expected me to obey.

'I said, NO PARTIES!!' He had shouted at me in an apoplectic rage, as he evicted me the following Monday morning, chucking me out by my perfectly pierced ears and sacking me to boot. My flat mate managed to retain her position as luckily for her she had been away the night the black gunk had done its damage. I found out many years later that she had died of cervical cancer and it was eventually proven that sexual promiscuity had contributed to many a female falling foul to this fate, I was to escape that destiny at least. With my tail between my legs, I moved in with the fair-weather, friendly married couple. At twenty-two, I was jobless and moneyless, with a drug habit to feed. Moving on again without looking back, I found a few random positions, bar work and the like and became relatively happy in my lodger bubble.

1983 came along and it was to be the summer of magic mushrooms. Again, this was the responsibility of my significant other. The young Mr. R. was eight years older than me, well-travelled and well-versed in his ability to work the room, with an even bigger need than my own, to get as high as possible. Many years later I would learn that potentially gay men are aggressive sexually with women, which explained the bites he would leave on my breasts and the emptiness I was filled with after the event. I was initially grateful for the warm welcome I'd received from my married landlords. There was nothing sexual there between us, partly because neither of them was my type, both resembling overcooked, overweight, anemic, pink pigs. Not to mention the fact that they were both far too busy fucking around with anyone else who showed an interest, to have thought about a threesome with me, an idea that I would have found repulsive even if it had been suggested. They learned to eagerly troughed-up the magic white speedy powder and were led quite happily to the mushroom tea being wickedly brewed for them.

The young Mr. R. showed us how to graze and pick at twilight, near cowpats in the local fields where the shiny, tiny, pale mushroom heads shimmered malevolently in the gloom. We picked them by the hundred and took our crop back to the house, to be chewed, brewed and simmered. The best thing was to stay indoors, not to answer the phone and trust no one, as we tripped off our faces. He had created the ultimate hallucinogenic medium for us. Trying to get back to my lodgings, after a session at his house, I was so fuddled and muddled, that putting one foot in front of another proved to be a mountainous step, and I watched, as a cat lurking in the dark grew into a six-foot-tall monster. Staggering back, I lay in a bath for hours unaware of the time or the rapidly cooling temperature of the water, as I stayed there, suspended in a mental blancmange. It was an extremely messy episode, aided and abetted by frequent top-ups of anything else at hand that could be snorted or imbibed.

We must have functioned on a day-to-day basis, me, the young Mr. R., my landlords and several other individuals, all bonded in our mission to take as many drugs as possible. One of our motley crew worked as a bank manager, who later emigrated abroad with his then girlfriend who vehemently disapproved of his extra-curricular activities and who despised the antics of his friends, one of whom was an extremely upper-class dude indeed. He had had a rather exclusive upbringing, having attended a local private boarding school, home to politicians' sons and foreign princes, he also happened to be screwing the landlady and not very discreetly either. We were all aware of their liaison, as their hands would be stroking each other's bodies whenever possible and openly flaunting the affair. The landlord was seemingly oblivious to the behaviour of his wife, it turned out that he was far too busy 'getting jiggy' with his secretary, to notice or care.

During the night of the cold bath and monster feline, the landlady and her posh bit on the side had joined in with the drinking of the disgusting fungal concoction. The three of us had been invited back to his own house by the young Mr. R., who had brewed up a mushroom storm. It was disgustingly rank, like consuming warm, stagnant pond water. What occurred next was the stuff of an embarrassing nightmare. Landlady took too much, the effect of the shitty soup, like hash cake, led to a delay before the drug kicked into the brain and there was always a thin line between overdoing it; and doing it just right. Impatient and greedy as always, she had slurped too much. Eyes rolling, she fell backwards onto a settee.

'Reality, real tea, reality, real tea.' She slurred, over and over. Mr. R. had passed out and I left, leaving the posh boy to sort his woman out. We never found out the true details of what had happened next, but the little we did manage to glean sounded gruesome, especially whilst being under the influence of the psychoactive delirium, which was pounding through their bloodstreams.

The next morning, I returned cautiously to the house that I had fled the night before. Landlady was sitting quietly on her own, the young Mr. R. was nowhere to be seen. She wasn't her usual brash, overconfident self as she explained what had taken place and that her upper-class totty had left, after abruptly terminated their relationship.

'I think the magic has gone.' She later lamented.

Summer turned to autumn in 1983 and December was just around the corner. I was bored with the saturated seasons of drugs and slightly sickened by the clique who I had been spending so much time with. I had no money to speak of, I had turned twenty-four that year and felt that the page I was currently on also needed turning. The parties and the frenzied nights spent in night clubs, that were followed by dawn joyrides to the coast. The baking of dope cookies and the brewing of fungi cocktails; had all merged into one big, pointless high. I needed to make some changes, my part in this remake of the 'Lord of the Flies' was most definitely over. Idly flicking through a local paper, I saw a job advertised.

'Private book shop requires an assistant.'

'Mmmm, bookshop eh?' I had always loved reading, not that much literature had grabbed my interest in the last year, but this was intriguing and so picking up the phone, I arranged an interview.

'What should I wear?' I asked the unseen guy on the other end.

'Stockings and suspenders.' The throaty answer rattled. Undeterred, I arrived outside the blackened-out windows of the bookshop a few days later, wearing jeans and an off-the-shoulder sweat top. He laughed when he saw me, my interviewer; and led me into the musty interior of a sex shop. He talked me through the merchandise. Dildos, vibrators, magazines on transsexuals, poppers, bondage equipment, videos, masks, the list was endless; and he watched my face intently during the interview, clocking that I seemed unfazed by the situation. He explained the ins and outs of the day-to-day management of the shop.

'When can you start?'

'Tomorrow!!' Suddenly it seemed that I had a new job, just before Christmas 1983.

As I slowly woke up, on Monday 10th November 2014, I was beginning to think that the Big Man had been spot on about how my mad idea of writing a book and opening doors to the past, could also open a very unpleasant Pandora's box. Doors that should have remained firmly locked and bolted in my mind. I decided that looking back was indeed proving to be a huge mistake and concentrated on looking forward to the Christmas of 2014, that was approaching fast. The Big Man adored Christmas, festooning our house with colour and twinkling lights, positioning every ornament and bauble, just so. He took so much care and attention that it was heartbreaking to watch, knowing that his own childhood had robbed him of this magic. My contribution in return was total appreciation and wonderment, both of which came without prompting.

I was working for a well- known retailer, a very different sort of shop from the bizarre store that I had found myself running, over thirty years previously. Retail work always meant little time off over the festivities, which was always a pain in the back side, but fate was about to conspire to cancel my obligation to do so this Christmas, after I had a strange random accident involving falling over a broken clothes dryer that was kept in our small third bedroom. I had been intending to hide Cuckoo's Christmas presents in there, as she had suddenly announced a few days previously, that she was coming home for the first weekend in December.

'It's nice being home for a few days, Ma.' She had said when she arrived.

'What's wrong then?!' I could see by her face that something was amiss.

The boy she had glowingly talked about on holiday, had turned out to be a total dick and she needed to lick her wounds, returning to do so in the bedroom that we had always kept the same for her. Old perfume bottles and childhood stuffed toys were still there, waiting for her in her bolt hole, as were the presents, I had suddenly remembered, before we all decided to turn in for the night. Hastily I moved them into the single bedroom, tripping over the dryer, I took it down as I fell and somehow an exposed metal sliced deeply through my leg. Shocked, I looked down at the injury to see bright red blood pumping from what looked more like a knife wound. The wide open, bloody flesh wound looked like a manic grin smeared with lipstick, revealing layers of yellow muscle.

'Help me!!' I screamed, as Cuckoo and the Big Man both rushed into the room.

'Ma, what have you done!!'

'Oh babe, that looks really bad.'

A trip to A&E was inevitable, with Cuckoo accompanying me in the ambulance. The female paramedics had insisted on seeing the scene of the accident, as it was clear that they too thought I might have been attacked. The presence of these uniformed women, plus the unknown but doubtlessly delicious scent of his mistress's fresh blood, sent the Beloved Pooch into a frenzy of fear and desire, so the Big Man stayed at home to clean up the blood-soaked carpet and calm the shivering animal. By five o'clock in the morning we had managed to crawl home in a taxi from the hospital. The medics had been unable to stitch the deep wound. The thin flesh on my shin had split like a peach, which necessitated being referred to a plastic surgery unit nearby, to be told that I was going to be out of action for weeks.

A few days later, Daisy bunny decided to check out. I found her one morning, she was still and flat, lying like roadkill in the bottom of her hutch. There would be no more pert ears and inquisitive, twitching whiskers. I had known this day would be imminent, as for pities sake the bunny was truly old, but at that moment my world was suspended in shock. I limped to the phone to call the Big Man, explaining with faltering words the scene that I had witnessed.

'Don't touch it.' He'd barked and rushed home. There was a makeshift funeral, he buried bunny in a pillowcase, accompanied by her stuffed, shaggy friend, the tatty toy that she had merrily humped away on. He dug a deep hole and covered the cold ground over when he had finished, after I had made him show me her bunny face, that was peacefully still, at the end.

'Oh, bless you, bunny bright eyes.' I cried, as salty tears poured into my pillow that night. Oh, bunny, bunny bright eyes had cost us a fortune over the years. She had been carefully tended to and fussed over. This care had included annual jabs and several expensive visits to the vets in her last months, when old age was creeping up on her; and she had survived an appalling case of flystrike in 2010, which had cost a small fortune to be treated successfully. I had been expecting the eventual demise of what was indeed a venerable rabbit, but her death still hurt me horribly. I had had such loveable fur balls as pets, as a child and had helped Cuckoo tend for several in her own childhood, but there would be no more little creatures for me to look after once Daisy passed away. I just hoped that there was a menagerie, somewhere in the heavens, for all the animals that I had loved. Hamsters, guinea pigs and rabbits, all whooping for joy, in their very grassy, ever sunny, fly free and fox safe, place in the stars.

I was now legitimately signed off work for the long haul and with ample time on my hands I spent one morning poring through old photographs. I found one marked 'Panda's Den 1984.' It was a picture of a blacked-out shop window, with a sign above it, proclaiming that it was a 'Private Shop.' Suddenly exhausted, I hauled my bandaged leg up onto our bed and as I sleepily studied it, against all my better judgement I reluctantly took another step back in time, hoping that in looking back I could have more chances to tell my father how sorry I was, knowing in my heart of hearts that he couldn't hear me. I found myself walking back through the door of the sex shop in December 1983. It had to have been one of the strangest and most bizarre periods of my life up to then, interspersed with moments of dark, satanical comedy as I manned the shop alone, waiting like a greedy spider for the blackened door to open into my web, when the jingle of a tiny bell above it signaled the entrance of the next brave visitor.

They came in all manner of guises, giggly hen parties looking for something to shock in the way of crutch-less and nipple-less lingerie. Awkward, young men bashfully in search of poppers, 'Rush' and 'Liquid Gold', would also be tempted by the promise of hardcore porn. Of course, I had to try the amyl nitrate for myself, which resulted in a catapulting rush of blood to my head, from the fumes sniffed in from the tiny bottles. It led to a moment of delirium, followed by the worst headache ever and was not to be recommended. Pathetic, old men enrolled for the video library that was advertised; and they eagerly handed over the membership fee of sixty pounds. It was easy money, as the tapes they scuttled out with in damp shaking hands, were nothing but blanks with handmade covers that falsely depicted hard cocks and cum shots inside the cases. Should they have dared to return to challenge the con, they were reminded that on joining they had stupidly and willingly supplied addresses and telephone numbers. It was a devious and unspoken threat that the loss of sixty pounds was a small price to pay to ensure their dirty, little secret was kept just that ... a secret.

I had frequent requests for sex, as it was always assumed that a girl who ran a sex shop was on the game. The scary weirdos were the worst, asking for male vibrators, fake fannies and then returning, to ask to be shown how to use them, creeping closer to the counter which divided me from the rest of the shop. The loan of my area manager's Dobermann came in handy on several occasions, he lay unseen next to me and knew by the tone in my voice when to make his presence known, with a low, prolonged growl. A few months after I had moved on from this madness, I heard on the news that the assistant in a sister shop elsewhere in the country had been found behind an identical counter with her throat slashed, proving that it was a really risky business to be involved in.

I was invited to consider escort work. It was explained I could make an incredible amount of money and that a minder would be provided, I was told that I could be very good in the role, as I had the looks and curves that would be very appealing to the clientele in question. I did consider the proposition, but despite agreeing in principle, the silky tones of my new prospective madam on the phone, explaining my first assignment, gave me a moment of lucidity and I politely declined. Drugs however had no part in my morality; and I was soon buying by the ounce, selling gram after gram of speed and gobbling as much as I dealt. So much cash changed hands during the winter of 1983 and the spring of 1984, as Wham's 'Last Christmas.' warbled on a cassette player and Sade's 'Your Love is King.' crooned through my lonely hours at work, whilst I chain-smoked and maintained the dangerous, false high.

I continued to rent a room with the two pigs then abruptly it was all to change again; and it was to be my last Christmas in my career in the sex shop industry. The young Mr. R. was still on the scene, clearly, secretly impressed with my choice of employment, but our relationship had hit a stalemate, as both of our unfulfilled needs were winning the fight against my sad, futile hopes for us. A new boy had joined the ranks of our weird group and one night my desires found a new haven as we looked at each other with different eyes, instantly strongly attracted to each other. He was an outsider, but his well-built body, dirty blonde surfer's hair, intelligence and good looks, had made him appealing to our screwed-up gang. He too had a penchant for drug use; and he was attracted to the inner girl in me, having seen beyond my fast talking, brittle persona.

We moved to London, hoping for a new beginning; and with a whoosh of the tyres of his much-envied black sports car, we left everything behind, apart from our drug habits and far too much personal baggage. The relationship barely lasted six months, as our inevitable need for uppers and downers led the fresh start to fail miserably. I had heard that my departure had left the young Mr. R. heartbroken, and I returned to his arms, that were held as wide open as he could, until like an unsuspecting insect in a Venus flytrap, once I was securely inside, as his heart hardened, the trap closed, allowing me no escape. Catrin vanished and the growly black and white doppelganger reappeared in her place. It was beyond belief that he could treated me like shit, cry bitter tears when I managed to escape his mental clutches and be able to do it all again once I returned to his fold. This was to be the start of a pattern between us that would repeat itself many times, again and again, until the last time, way into our future, over twenty years hence.

It was the hard-core mid 1980s now and my look had become slightly gothic, with my hair dyed raven black, tumbling in carelessly permed snakes over a tight black leather jacket. My make-up, always overdone, was accentuating the huge eyes in my pointy face, my regular consumption of fast drugs keeping me skinnier than ever. I had packed so much into such a comparatively little time and yet, despite all those experiences, I had learnt nothing and had even less to show for it. Flying by the seat of my impeccably fitting ski pants, I continued on my merry way to proceed to mess up every opportunity that life presented to me. My parents desperately wanted to keep in contact with me, but the physical distance between us enabled me to keep them at bay, choosing when to let them into my life. On those rare occasions I would be able to hold my head up and look them in the eyes, convincing them I was fine, but they were beginning to realize that I had a problem. The extent of that problem was not yet understood, yet they sensed that things were not adding up. The last thing they could have expected was that Daughter Number One had become addicted to a nasty, cheap, teeth-rotting chemical substance called amphetamine sulfate and that it was leading me down a path, to the monster's lair.

I still had to fund my habit, but there would be no venturing into more sordid realms to make my money, my soul had managed to remain intact to a tiny degree. My father bought me a shiny, red moped and I meandered from job to job, my diesel driven chariot popping me around. I worked in a petrol station and found other odd jobs, all of which lasted less and less time, as I became more and more unstable and all the while, bags and bags of the dirty, white powder were being procured, sniffed, swallowed and sold. I would forever recognize its disgusting smell, that at the time was the scent of Heaven. A true addict now, up for days and nights, I would then crash into a comatose sleep which would last for as long as the high did. A few days of feeling a vestige of normality always followed, but then, just as before, I would go up, up and away on the deadly roller coaster.

Impossibly during the mayhem of this chaos, I managed to open yet more doors into the nether world of a true drug-fueled life. I was still living with the young Mr. R., the guy who had proclaimed to love me but then beat me with verbal sticks of chastisement. The poor sod had no clue as to how to control me and would despair when I disappeared for days on end, returning bedraggled and dirty, sometimes with bruises, some on my neck. It must have turned the knife in him, seeing these signs of obvious betrayal. With nowhere else to go I would limp back to his house to sleep, having spent my time with random people who I met in my travels. Not on my magnificent moped, as there was always someone with wheels and I would pile into stranger's cars, not giving a shit about lack of insurance, MOT and car tax. These were alien matters to me and of no consequence in my fuddled mind. I frequented local nightclubs, one particularly notorious for shady nights, there was no dancing around a handbag here, cocktail in hand. This was a place of shadowy beings with dangerously sparkly eyes, dancing to the tribal beats of underground rhythms and I was feeling right at home.

I met the 'Barbarian', a tall, imposing, strange character who was to slip in and out of my life for the next decade. He too used my given name, whilst deliberately playing with my head, as he introduced me to places that would only have credence in the pages of a horror story. The monsters had finally come out to play, hiding behind a tortured side of humanity that was horribly vivid and real. He showed me benders out in the woods, man-made dwellings with sticks and sheeting used to make the domed, shallow tents. There were caravans on travelling sites, where slouched in piles of dirty blankets around campfires, I took acid tabs that created jagged images and crazed thoughts in my head, watching as heroin was injected and offered, but with another rare moment of lucidity I just shook my head in refusal. I accompanied him silently as we visited ramshackle houses inhabited by dry-mouthed, grey-skinned creatures, who now considered me one of them.

I never fucked the Barbarian, yet we would lie close together as the hold of the drugs loosened; and the dawn forced our fatigued eyes closed. There was an attempt between us but there was no magic in the making and I often wondered afterwards what his personal turn-on could have been. One morning his finale had been to wheel spin me around a field after a particularly crazy night, when he had supervised me swallowing as many tabs of acid as he deemed safe for me to take. The night had involved witches and warlocks, a nucleus of pariah people, wrapped in any rags they could find, huddled around the ever-present fire, staring unblinkingly, wide-eyed, minds elsewhere. Dreadlocked and pierced, they were silent, apart from the odd chant. I had taken my place amongst them, unaware of the monsters who were circling the camp, but they knew I was there, they could sense my presence, they could smell my soul and they wanted its purity.

The Barbarian kept one eye permanently on me, protecting me from the baying creatures looming in the shadows, who were ready to pounce at any minute, to drag me screaming into the dark abyss that I had revealed by turning the handle of this door into Hell. They hid in the trees, grunting and grumbling, prowling the perimeters of the campfire as the first slices of morning sunshine struck and like their fictional counterparts in the best zombie films, they lost their powers, but not the memory of the prize they had lusted after. The soul of the girl who had dared to peek into the darkness. They would sleep for a long time, but one day at some point in the future, they would wake up and try to find me again.

He took me to a friend's house, where a solemn, little girl was watching me warily.

'Are you his girlfriend! Do you love him!?' She asked me. I was unable to answer as my eyes met hers, knowing only that he had been my passport into an underground Hades, and my ticket out.

Chapter Six

Running Away

I must have slept for a long time that afternoon in December 2014, the Big Man was at work and Cuckoo was in London, tying up ends before her two-week break from university. It was Thursday 18th., a week until Christmas Day and the house was quiet. The Beloved Pooch had curled up around my undamaged leg under the duvet, like a warm, furry, breathing hot water bottle. I stirred a few times, only to fall back into a deeper sleep, as my dreams flew me back to the late spring of 1985. I was in Southern Spain with my parents, they had booked a holiday in a luxury hotel when they realized that their innermost fears about my physical and mental stability had been realised. The early warmth of the Spanish Sun did wonders for my damaged body and soul, as I had glimpses of how life could be with the natural highs of a few drinks, laughter and normal sleep patterns. These were good days for us all and they saw for the first time in a long time, the girl they wanted to believe was their true Daughter Number One, relaxed and happy with no falsehoods in her eyes.

My father decided to offer me yet another olive branch, in the form of a fresh start and a new life, away from that in which I had been drowning. He had bought a factory, an hour or so from where I was living; it was to make him his millions eventually, but for now he ran it with a steel grip, a cigar always clenched firmly between his teeth. He commuted regularly from the North of England and

NO EXAGGERATION

his dream now was to train me to be able to take over the reins, believing that I had the ability to do so, somewhere deep inside. He found a flatlet for me, within walking distance of the factory and settled me into the offices. The staff were naturally suspicious of the boss's daughter, but I was down to earth, had no airs or graces, smoked like a trooper, necked pints with them and liked a dirty joke. I fitted in instantly and they quickly decided that there was nothing not to like about me. I had no choice but to take the opportunity offered, hoping my alter ego would slink away. My long-suffering, part-time partner, poor young Mr. R. must have been relieved to see me go, who would blame him, as the disruption I had caused to his life had been colossal, but part of him probably grieved again for the loss of the girl who had gotten so far under his skin.

I was so bored, trying to show an interest in learning the ropes of the business during the days, whilst at night I was stuck in my two rooms, isolated from everything that had become my normal, no matter how bad that normal was. I struggled badly, trying to adapt to this new regime, but there were no mobile phones or laptops in 1985 and I had no friends in the town who could be invited round for a bottle of wine and a chat. I started taking a train back to my old stomping grounds at the weekends, where inevitably my old habits resurfaced, with itches that would need scratching until satisfied. I became increasingly unreliable at work and more and more reliant on waiting for Friday night, when I could catch the train back to where my dealers were happy to supply my needs.

This new circle of life stopped abruptly one night a few months later. I had woken up in the pokey bedroom of my flat, with the most incredible stomach pains and heavy bleeding. Bright red blood was soaking the sheets between my legs and there was nothing I could do but lie there terrified, while my stomach cramped more often and more violently. This continued for hours, until suddenly with pure panic I realized that something was trying to push itself out of me and in terror I decided that I must be having a miscarriage.

My periods had become very irregular, a known symptom of heavy drug use and I had no idea that I might have become pregnant again; but was now vividly certain that I had. The next few hours became a living nightmare of agony, as the pathetic entity which would have been a baby, was being squeezed out of my body.

Somehow, I caught the train again and as its clickety-clack motion on the rails was mirroring the contractions that were ripping through me. Somehow, I got myself to the local hospital where the experts calmly took over and the dead foetus which my body had been trying to expel was finally removed. I was wheeled to theatre, pumped full of painkillers and antibiotics and a day later I was discharged. It totally beggared belief that my first decision, regardless of the trauma I had endured, was, with shaky legs, to set out to score once more. My parents were away, abroad on business, so it was easy to pull the wool over their eyes and gloss over the sad episode, trying not to look back at it as the year rolled on and the seasons changed.

Suddenly it was December, with its promise of magic and tinsel. I had physically recovered from the damage that the miscarriage and the ensuing surgery had done to my body, but mentally I was still crippled. I was planning to travel North to see my family, the factory had closed down for the festive holidays and although my father was aware my performance at work was erratic, his staff had not been willing to incur his wrath, by telling him quite how rubbish I was. He was blissfully un-ware of my descent back into the pit that he had been so desperate to drag me from; and I was invited back into the fold for a family Christmas. I spent a few days with the young Mr. R. beforehand. He had been aware of my miscarriage, not knowing what to do or say, but he asked me to spend some time with him, the Christmas spirit allowing him to stretch out a hand of friendship.

We went to his local pub for drinks with his weird work mates, irritating men with smelly breath, who probably had equally irritating wives, but who didn't let that stop them making innuendos and brushing up too close to me in the crowded bar. Seriously sloshed at this point, we stumbled into a local shop for last-minute present buying. He furtively purchased something in a large box, quickly asking the assistant to bag it so I couldn't see what it was. I giggled, pints of beer and vodka chasers had done wonders for me and I felt no need to take the emotional anesthetic that the balls of white powder wrapped in cigarette paper provided.

'It's not for you!' The shop girl had laughed but the fun of the moment had released my inner child and of course, I knew that the contents of that box just had to be a present for me. Total shame on him then, for handing me the secret gift, a baby doll, a chubby, plastic, unseeing, baby doll. The pain it caused me was crushing, it wasn't the reminder of an unborn child, but the realization that he could be so callous and cruel. I collected my thoughts and a few things for my trip North and boarded another train, this time only my quiet sobs accompanied the clickety-clack of the Christmas Eve Express to Manchester. Time passed and time tried to heal my spirits as I battled on into the New Year, losing my fight against the serious business of learning to be the heiress of a manufacturing dynasty.

I kept the young Mr. R. at a distance for a while, which of course brought him a-wooing, but when in the spring of 1986 he landed me with another betrayal, I had no choice but to get as far away as possible. He had diffidently suggested that we might get engaged. Daring to believe this amazing turn of events, I picked out a pretty ruby and gold ring in an antique shop. Everything I had really wanted was eclipsed in that moment, until he had the brass neck to request that I wear it on the other hand and that the arrangement be our secret. I had done some terrible things to him, as consequences of my actions, but none deliberate and as his casual, thoughtless and mean-hearted proposal floored me once again, I felt as unloved and unwanted as a dog turd that he might have had to wipe off his shoe.

When the idea of completely disappearing raised its head, I had no choice other than to follow it. A plan was hatched, I was going travelling and as it slowly became a reality my parents were astonished and horrified when I broke the news to them.

'Thanks for the incredible opportunity, but actually, no thanks.' Or flippant words to that effect, explaining that I would rather swap my future seat on the board for a backpack, what a selfish, spoiled and horribly damaged bitch I had become.

As I tossed and turned on that Thursday afternoon in December 2014, I saw my father sitting alone in the board room at his prized factory, his head between his hands.

'You don't understand Dad, I had to go, it wasn't your fault!!' For one split second I thought he could hear me, as he raised his head sharply.

'Good night Boss' It wasn't me who he was listening to, just one of his management team clocking off for the night.

I packed a few possessions and prepared to hit the road with a one-time friend, packing rucksacks, sleeping bags, passports and as much money as we could squirrel away, until finally we were off, taking a train to Folkestone where we boarded a cross channel ferry to France. This was certainly a point of not looking back, it was May 1986 and my latest adventure had begun. We had bought roaming tickets that would take us anywhere in Europe and back again. We boarded the first train to leave Paris and it shunted slowly into the French countryside, it's next stop Venice. I was twenty-six, without a clue as to where I was going, moving as fast as I could to get away from the events of the last few years. Running away had seemed the only option, running and running, moving towards the light, trying to erase the horrors that I had experienced, the blame for most of which could be laid firmly at my own feet.

We had changed trains in the Italian city without a clue as to where the next one was going to take us. We didn't know where we were going, the train journey itself was enough, the most splendid and exciting of experiences. They were invincible ironwork giants spouting roaring plumes of angry smoke, as they careered their way across through Europe. Ensconced in a sleeper carriage we woke up to the magnificent sight of the Alps, snowy and majestic, looming above the railway tracks which had been hewn through the mountains. On and on we sped, day and night, the countryside changing constantly. The train rushed through the interior of what was then Yugoslavia. At the time, the country was open to travel, before borders were closed and its name changed. Years later a ferry crossing at Brindisi would be the only allowed route, but now we were awed and privileged to be able to stare at the incredible sight of mammoth green forests, spectacular waterfalls and completely uninhabited lands.

Among our belongings which were crammed into two rucksacks, was a quarter of cannabis, the size of an Oxo cube. When we eventually stopped at some unearthly time of night at a bleak railway station in the middle of nowhere, that little package was going to become a huge problem. Unbeknown to us foolhardy travelers, we were about to change trains for one that was headed to Greece. The carriages on this train were old-fashioned and each private compartment had windows, which were flanked by a corridor running from end to end. There was a Russian sector, where the occupants were not allowed to leave their designated carriage, although other European passengers could pass through it. I couldn't help but stare through the glass, furtively peeking at the families resplendent in traditional costumes, pouring tea from enameled silver and gold samovars. I had heard of their lifestyle of course, but to see this for myself was extraordinary. Neither could I help but stare at the new presence of several Greek police officers armed with live guns and nasty attitudes. They had started doing routine searches of luggage. Suddenly I was in a

'Midnight Express' scenario and dealing with the horrific knowledge that if our stash was discovered, we were dead meat.

'Bag!' Growled the mustached officer. I met his eyes and reached for my companion's rucksack; the contraband was in my own, so this was a moment of pure Russian roulette. He made a cursory search, as the British passports that we hastily opened for him were enough to protect us to some extent. And from the glint in his eyes, beneath his hostile exterior he probably fancied the 'arses' off us, literally. I would find out later there was a foreign penchant for a rosy bottom. I went to reach for my own bag.

'No.' He snapped and moved on. I felt as I had been holding my breath underwater for too long.

'That was a close shave.' I muttered wearily as the train moved slowly out of the station, onwards and onto Athens, which was the next stop and the end of the line. As we walked out of the station the heat hit us, as did the noise and the smell of the car fumes pumping through the air in the city centre. We passed high, austere stone buildings, trying to avoid crowds of bustling people. Normal tourists would have lapped up the history and stayed in a nice hotel whilst doing so. There would be no culture fix required by us two vagabonds however, as one night in a crappy hotel, with a bottle of wine and a tin of corned beef, was enough for us. Early the next morning we hailed a taxi to the port, where we bought tickets for the first passenger ferry of the day, bound for the Greek islands. We didn't care where it was headed, any of the islands would have suited us, all we cared about was that the adventure would continue.

Crammed with fellow travelers, Greek families and holiday makers about to start the first leg of island hopping, the enormous ship gracefully headed out of the harbor and into the open South Aegean Sea. The temperature was heating up already. I raised my face to the welcoming glare of the Sun, feeling it reflected off the water as the prow of the vessel launched up and down in the choppy waves of the fathomless ocean. There were many shades of deep and murky dark colours; and the almost oil slick like swirls of moving water were menacing in contrast to the bright neon blue of the sky above. Were the monsters swimming silently alongside us? I wondered, were they following in the wake of the ship, diving through the bottomless sea water with the speed and dexterity of giant serpents, hell bent to hunt down the soul of the girl that they had yearned to own that night?

We were firmly on course to the island of Naxos. We had been at sea for nearly six hours, fortified by bread rolls and bottles of warm beer, as we watched the horizon from the deck, jostled by crowds of like-minded people. Babylon was resurrected with the sounds of excited chatter in Greek, French, Scandinavian and English, all nationalities waiting eagerly for the first glimpse of land. Suddenly there it was, a tiny speck in the distance, just a drop in the ocean, growing larger and taking shape as the ship neared its destination.

The trip had been sweaty and uncomfortable. Heavy bags that had been tossed onto the deck on embarking, were now wearily hoisted onto aching backs, as hot and bothered we waited for the liner to slowly negotiate the harbor walls of the island. Throngs of locals were waiting to greet us; and produce was unloaded and reloaded on for the return trip. A few cars and motorbikes were revved up and driven out of the bowels of the ship. It was noisy, smelly and searingly hot. I was dripping with sweat and squinting against the glare of the fierce sunlight that was bouncing off the bleached, whitewashed walls of the buildings. Being at sea had at least tempered the heat with a breeze, but the temperature on land was almost at a boiling point, a dry heat that was sucking the oxygen out of the air, a sensation that I had never known, and it was only May. The real summer heat of these islands had yet to be experienced.

Naxos was a beautiful 'Shirley Valentine' place, with its cobbled streets, a multitude of bars and restaurants galore, plus exquisitely pretty beaches where the crystal-clear sea lapped tiny coves. It was an absolute gem of an island, this drop in the ocean and once we had discovered it, we were eager to explore the delights it had to offer. Finding lodgings was the main priority and a fat, merry landlady waiting patiently by the dock for potential guests, soon rounded us up.

'Pssst, Ella! Room?' She escorted us to her house, where a twin-bedded room awaited me and my equally knackered companion. Cool, white sheets welcomed us in. It had been about five days since we'd left home, a very long and tiring five days. We needed to recoup our strength and sleep in the irresistibly inviting beds, until we were ready to plan our next move. Our stay on Naxos lasted a couple of months, eight weeks, as we proceeded to live the dream, until the bubble burst. We dined on salads and kebab meats, washed down with whatever took our fancy. We were introduced to metaxa, a potent brandy, ouzo and retsina, which was a fortified paint stripper masquerading as wine, with the kick of an angry donkey and having the capacity to get me so drunk, that legless didn't describe it. We became used to lazy days in the sun on the beach and hanging out with the locals in the several bars and clubs, where the sharing of dope which we had heroically smuggled onto the island made us the belles of the ball. Then to top it all, there were the erotic liaisons with random strangers, leading to hours of steamy, sexual pleasure. We were living as if there was no tomorrow.

Tomorrow did have to dawn eventually though; bringing with it the realization that we only had a few drachmas left between us. Our passports were hidden carefully in the bottom of our backpacks in the rented room, along with our tickets back to Blighty, all intact and safe until needed again. We would meet folk so desperate for money that they had sold both these lifelines, but somehow; we managed to keep ours protected through the craziness of that summer. I had heard that the neighboring island of Paros was good for work and so, boarding another ferry, we waved goodbye to the melting frying pan of one island, heading straight for the fire of another. Swapping the relative luxury of a room with clean sheets, a lock on the door and a civilized bathroom, for a pitch on a campsite. With our travel documents stored in a locked cupboard in the campsite office, the next stage of the adventure had begun!

There had been other reasons to leave Naxos. We had not been popular with everyone we had encountered, as several girls before us had made the same journey and settled down with local men. The advent of us two sexy madams, one blonde and me darkly brunette, both tanned and toned, was too much of a threat. As we eyed up their men, looks that they reciprocated, we were warned off by the women who had already staked their claims. It was time to beat a hasty retreat and discover the art of slumming in the process. The 'facilities' offered by a Greek camp site, mirrored the well-documented design of many a continental loo. The toilet block had a series of holes in the ground, with a central water pipe connecting them; and squatting over them was the only choice. But when the renowned dodgy water pressure changed the direction of the flow of water, the result was gruesome. Oozing pats of human excrement were pushed back up into plain sight, making this an indescribably nauseous and disgusting way to have to use a toilet, but compulsory, nevertheless. There was also the small matter that we hadn't thought to pack a tent, not having a spare bean to buy or rent one, only our sleeping bags, a cardboard box and a piece of string tied between two trees marked our latest accommodation.

Personal hygiene also proved to be a major challenge, but I soon got used to washing my body without any qualms in the cold outdoor showers that were provided. I was, I supposed, quite a luscious sight, with an all-over suntan, amazing breasts and a toned, flat stomach, with smooth buttocks. At my peak now, the effects of the chemicals that I had been poisoning myself with over the years were completely out of my system. As for laundry, we simply wore our clothes hard and often, the few we needed, as night-time temperatures were starting to reach over thirty degrees, with forty maxing out in the middle of the day. The lure of trying to score was the last thing on my mind, as there was no gear to be easily bought or bartered for and having had my close encounter with the hair-bristling officer on the train from Hell, I had no intention of facing a second.

I avoided the island police, who loathed the camp site dwellers with a passion. People like me brought nothing to the island, unlike paying tourists whom they fawned and lusted over. We penniless travelers were vermin in their eyes and any excuse would have been enough to throw any one of us into a cell for a night or two. Many of the bar owners felt the same, I met a blonde English girl, dripping with blood from her face, dazed and in pain, calling out for help piteously, like a frightened kitten. Apparently, she had approached the owner of a restaurant, asking for work.

'Scum.' Or a Greek equivalent insult had been spat at her before he smashed her over the head with a metal coffee pot. I never found out what happened to her, doubtless she, like me, hadn't taken out any form of insurance before setting out. Even if it had crossed my mind to do so, I wouldn't have acted upon the thought, I was as young and foolish as that injured girl, in believing that that sort of thing happened to other people, not me. I later met two Dutch guys, travelling on heavy, shiny motorbikes. The sight of these blond gods tanned and laughing astride their metal steeds, was enough to have the glowering, jealous officer who spied them, fabricate a reason for a night in the cells, so to have tried to score would have been my crossover into insanity, not just madness.

Bikini tops, bras, knickers and shorts were my chosen garb as the Sun climbed higher into the sky and lasered the pavements into slabs of furnace-like heat, that no one could walk on with bare feet. Despite the horror stories I had heard concerning the attitude of the locals to those seeking work, I took the risk and was soon rewarded with several opportunities to earn money. Perhaps it was my dark hair and swarthy complexion which made me blend in with the natives, but whatever the reason I had no trouble with the islanders as I washed hire cars in the afternoons and worked in a kitchen from five p.m. until one a.m. As I scrubbed massive industrial pots with a metal scourer the palms of my hands turned pallid and spongy, but still my nightly reward of the equivalent of five pounds and a free pizza was worth it, whilst I also learned a bit of the Greek language.

'Pssst! Ella, Ella!' Were words regularly spoken to me by the proprietor of the restaurant I was slaving in. I kind of got the drift of this, it was their way of catching my attention.

'Yamas, Yazoo!' Hello and cheers!'

'Malaka!' An essential insult, not to be used lightly though, you didn't call the Greeks wankers, without incurring the power of their wrath.

Straight from the kitchen and into the night, drinking my wages I danced like a dervish, fueled with liquor and animated by party drums and beach bonfires. Dropping like a stone at dawn, as the fires were extinguished and the music ceased, exhausted, I would try to sleep after the excesses of the night before.

There was a multiple choice of randy, gorgeous, single young men on the island, Dutch, American, Irish, Norwegian, English and even the odd young local Adonis. It was a human smorgasbord of delicious male choices and I sampled the whole buffet. It was amazing what you could get up to without a tent, but in the middle of the night the guttural sounds of drunken sex were the norm, as all inhibitions were freed in this insane environment. Finally, there was the Statue Bar where I worked for a while, with its amazing sunsets and dangerous, winding stone stairway that I ran up and down, serving drinks to the sounds of Simply Red's 'Money's Too Tight to Mention' blaring from the speakers. How totally ridiculously true those lyrics were during that summer of 1986, on that mad party island so far from home, but I had achieved my wish to forget about all the shit I had left behind me. It seemed that the past was too far away, with too much water having been crossed, to allow the grumbling, crumbling, cunty, grunty monsters that had been preying on my mind and body, to find me.

The weeks rolled by with all the craziness imaginable, concentrated on a small island, with its hedonistic population and with me, happily bang in the middle of the blood-boiling heat and glorious carnage, until one evening, when I was given an envelope that had arrived at the camp site office. The young Mr. R. had managed to track me down.

'Bastard! Malaka!!' The young, good looking male receptionist looked up and scowled at me as I spat the words out.

'Not you!! Someone back at home in England!'

'What's it like there?' He asked in his broken English.

'Nothing like this!!'

'I would like to go there one day, meet the Queen.'

I laughed kindly, still concentrating on the fact that the knowledge of my presence in Paros must have somehow made its way back to my on and off boyfriend. My manic desire to live for the moment was quashed; and tears trickled down my sunburnt cheeks as I read the letter. He had enclosed a Greek bank note and a mere hint of the fact that he missed me. I wrote another poem that day, knowing that the party was nearly over. It was time to go back, to discover whether my absence had finally made his heart grow fonder.

'I sat on the edge of an island, a magical place, just a drop in the ocean.

I followed the swell from the passenger liners, the holiday trade, and sometimes reminders, that home was beyond the horizon.

I sat on the edge of this magical island, with the sound of the waves, such crashing heart breakers and the sense of the shape shifters, changing their makers.

I sat all alone with my thoughts on my island, with you out of sight and we out of touch.

Desperately wanting so little so much, knowing home was beyond the horizon.'

Our last day dawned, we had planned to catch the midnight ferry and partied harder than ever for the final few hours. We finally boarded the ferry and as the ship slowly left the harbour walls, we watched as the lights and sounds on shore receded. Our fellow camp mates were grouped on the dockside and we waved goodbye furiously, until there was nothing more to see but the sea and the stars in the midnight blue sky.

The journey back to England was tedious and long. I was 'skint', filthy and exhausted, we had been away for five months and proper sleep had always managed to elude us. After docking back in Athens, we managed to find a direct train to Paris, changing for Calais. We boarded another ferry, one bound for Folkestone and found a few English coins in the bottom of our rucksacks, enough for a cold pint of lager and a bag of crisps. At customs in England my bag was thoroughly searched, which I found hysterically funny, and more tears ran down my face, as I howled with laughter.

'Look at my stuff, its rags!' I spluttered in protest. Indeed, it was, all that I had was a collection of holey, dirty rags, hardly contraband. On to Waterloo, and there he was, the young Mr. R. waiting for me. He had grown his hair and had it streaked with blond highlights, so typical of a mid-eighties man. Whilst away, my own long dark hair had turned into a matted mop and it had been cut short. We stared silently at each other, taking in the changes in our appearances during the months that we had spent apart and for a moment, things nearly fell into place. I had lived on a diet of very little, with only enough food to sustain my body, but enough alcohol to compete with the volume of the ocean that I had crossed a few days ago. No fast drugs had been taken that summer; and I had found in the process, a passage to my own self-worth without the false crutch that they had provided. There was to be no happy ending of course and my true, pure soul slipped back into the shadows, drawn into the dark by the beckoning fingers of old. I found myself relying again on the false esteem provided by the contents of the familiar, tiny, custom-made envelopes. Inevitably we sank back into the discord that had and would always haunt us, until way into the future, when one day we could become friends.

Chapter Seven

Viva Espana!

I woke up with a jolt, my latest dream had been so vivid, but it had been like watching someone else's life, not my own. I was becoming aware that wanting to look back was turning into an obsession and that the Big Man's warning that it wasn't doing me any good, was right, but I couldn't help myself. I wanted so badly for my deceased father to know how sorry I was for the way that I had treated him. I also knew that this was as pointless as the rest of my stupid idea about exploring the past and writing a book about it.

'You need to get a grip woman!!' Shaking myself up, I tried once again to concentrate on the present and all my plans for the best family Christmas ever. A huge pile of carefully wrapped presents was hidden away, in preparation for the big day. A jewel of a gift, a gem-encrusted, rose-gold, designer watch was amongst them, de rigueur for a young lady of style and street cred. Cuckoo was currently living her own dream at university, living in a rented flat on the outskirts of London and commuting without a fear, into and out of the city. Her hair could be straightened into a glossy curtain; or left to retain its naturally gypsy-like curls and she had my eyes, dark and soulful. One marred by the scar that crossed the pupil of her left eye. Her rosebud lips were constantly seen to pout in the selfies that she reveled in. Her figure was to die for; and she had a stubborn chin, the shape of which was inherited from her father, along with his determination and downright selfishness.

These traits I did not begrudge her one jot, as they would stand my daughter in good stead, even though I found them annoying at the least, and at times downright upsetting. She was a popular soul among her circle of friends at home and those she had made the acquaintance of in the Big Smoke. Individually they were all as lovely as she was, but as a one, they considered that 'having a good time' was a major priority in their lives, drinking and taking recreational drugs being essential to that quest. This constantly worried me, but I couldn't judge them. That would have been far too hypocritical given my own behavior at their age, but I did feel it would have been a blessing to have been less au fait about such subjects, as most parents, who were blissfully unaware of the habits of their offspring. To me, this knowledge was a curse. Cuckoo and her friends had holidayed in the usual haunts for their age group, Zante, Malia, Magaluf and Ibiza. It didn't take much imagination for me to picture the antics they would have been up to, when the memories of the frenetic mania of my Greek summer were obviously still so clear in my mind.

Cuckoo came home for Christmas the next day, Friday 19th. December 2014, but she was unusually bolshie and up tight, not seeming to enjoy the chilled bottle of rosé wine that I had carefully selected for her and turned her nose up at the takeaway menus that we presented to her. Her Mona Lisa smile from our three days on holiday as a family, two months earlier, was nowhere to be seen.

'You choose honey, it's our treat.' The Big Man told her.

'Not very hungry.'

I looked at him and pulled a face.

'How's it's feeling, Ma?' She pointed to my bandaged left leg.

'What's up with mini-you?' He asked me when we were on our own.

She was spending the first night of her three-week break with us and was clearly very unhappy.

I'm going to bed now.' She sighed at ten o'clock.

'Ok darling, sleep tight, love you.'

'Love you too Ma.'

'Night sweetheart.' The Big Man hugged her tightly.

'I'm sorry about last night Ma.' She apologized to me the next morning, confessing that her use of fast drugs was becoming too regular and that the boy she had fretted about on the night of my accident, was history. Lovesick and revolted by chemicals summed up her state of mind. I understood of course; and after listening, gave her the benefit of my opinion on her woes.

'You've got to stop that nonsense!'

'I know Ma!'

'You don't need it, it's a one-way street, I should know.' Cuckoo knew that I had once travelled a drug lined path.

'I'm not you though!'

'And you're so gorgeous, darling, clever too.'

'Thanks Ma!'

'You'll find a boy who deserves you, but you've got to rein it in!'

'Ma!!! I know what I'm doing, I'm not a child!!'

'God help you!!' I didn't bother having the last word, just settled for thinking it, as our conversation turned to her latest idea, going to work in Ibiza after university had finished.

'It's not a bad idea, I suppose.'

'Oh, Ma, you always know what to say!' With that, Cuckoo flew out of the house to meet up with her friends. I was happy with the advice that I had given to my beautiful, intelligent, avocado squeezable daughter, who was not so little in the ridiculously high heels that she insisted on wearing. They were potential ankle breakers and made the girl six feet tall, reminding me of my own footwear at her age. For now, though, all was well.

That couldn't be said for my injured leg. It had been two weeks since my accident and we had driven to the hospital earlier that day, only to be told the wound wasn't healing and given instructions to dress it every three days, plus a certificate signing me off for at least another four weeks.

'They'll go ballistic at work!' I shrugged that concern off immediately and concentrated on simply enjoying the festive winter wonderland that my Big Man had turned our cozy house into. For the first time in twenty years, I could have a prolonged Christmas and New Year with him.

'Don't start drinking too early!' The previous year I had demolished a bottle of sherry pre-lunch, which had ruined the rest of the day. I made the vow whilst staring thoughtfully out of our bedroom window, reflecting on the grave for Daisy that the Big Man had created a week before, as 'When a child is born.' played quietly in the background. At that moment nothing could have summed up my mood more than those lyrics. Suddenly very tired, I decided to take an afternoon nap and continued to dream about my checkered history.

1986 had turned into 1987 and I was going to be twenty-seven that year. My crippled relationship with the young Mr. R. was dragging on and on, sexless, pointless and futile. In the spring I was invited to go to Amsterdam without him, for a long weekend with a group of cronies, travelling by coach and a cross channel ferry. It was a much shorter hop compared to the long-distance land and sea journeys that I had taken the previous year. We found digs on a barge called 'The Dutch Cockney.' The cabins were cramped and uncomfortable, but it wasn't far from the centre of the city, where we proceeded to get as stoned as possible, visiting the notorious coffee shops and Bulldog bars. The normal delights of the place had no interest for me, the canals with their colorful boats bobbing about on the water and the novelty of the tram system, the stunning flower markets where all one's senses would be assailed with the heady smell of tulips and daffodils that permeated nostrils with their delicious scents. All of this passed me by as I hunted for the fast stuff again.

I was offered a job on the boat, with my school-girl French proving to come in as handy as it had promised to, during my enforced stay with the non-English-speaking family, back in my teens. The owner of the boat, having heard me translate for several other guests, suggested summer work. My bilingual skills coupled with my eye-candy looks, made me very appealing as a potential crew member. But the draw of home was too much, longing to have the young Mr. R. love me, I refused this offer and made the most of the debauched weekend, sleeping during most of the return leg to England. Finding my dream impossible to fulfil, a few months later I packed my stuff and left him again, moving into another shared, rented flat.

I partied, drank, smoked and continued to rely on my faithful, deadly crutch. 'Relax.' By Frankie Goes to Hollywood, was the anthem of the summer of 1987. I slept through the great storm that year, when a hurricane, poo-pooed by a well-known weather forecaster, hit the South of England with devastating results. The sound of breaking glass in the middle of the night was all that briefly disturbed me; and I was oblivious to the carnage that the storm was wreaking. The problem was that the other storm, which was buffeting my own life, was not abating either as I started to convince myself that if only the young Mr. R. could be persuaded to marry me, it would make things better.

What a sad, mad, druggy soul mine had become, a blackened, withered soul with a false light at the end of my rainbow. How I had survived the events of the last few years was beyond comprehension, the zombies around campfires, the summer of magic mushrooms, the sex shop escapade and the Greek experience. There was that old saying again, if it doesn't kill you, it makes you stronger. I didn't realize how strong I could be, or how strong I would become. I was too close to the problem that was slowly destroying me and too close to understand that the solution to that problem was probably myself. There was no looking back, what would be the point, it was all rotten anyway, but the idea of being his wife became an obsession, an all-consuming passion, in my increasingly illogical mind.

My sister, Daughter Number Two, was about to take the plunge into married bliss in the autumn of 1987 and this act was to become the catalyst for my next adventure, had I but known it. As chief bridesmaid I stood in a church, dressed in a peach taffeta gown, feeling very stupid and later took my place in the receiving line at the wedding reception. The relatives attending this fussy event made the appropriate cooing noises to me, seeing my singledom as the eldest sister, as a situation to be sympathized with. My mother had doubtless confided in them of the chap who I was involved with, and as he was conspicuous by his absence, several bank notes were pressed into my hands.

'You'll be next!' Were the words of condolence uttered by the suited and frocked guests before they moved on to gasp over the wedding couple. I gracefully accepted the sentiments and the money. I counted it later, to discover I had been given over a hundred pounds.

'Wow, they did feel sorry for me.' I spoke into the mirror of the lady's cloakroom.

'Give a shit!' My inner self laughed back at me. Of course, I absolutely did give a lot of shit, an awful lot of emotionally painful shit and after several failed attempts over the next few weeks, trying to discuss any sort of a future with the young Mr. R., I spotted a newspaper advert for holiday reps and promptly applied for a position.

The interview process in February 1988 had been extremely daunting. The head office was on the other side of London and several years after taking the underground to the austere abortion clinic, head down and frightened, I took the same tube, head up and determined. It was one of the most nerve-racking afternoons that I had ever experienced, but bit by bit I passed each stage and the final test nailed it for me. I had to prove my command of my spoken French, having given it as my known foreign language on the application form. I bumbled through the questions and was offered a job at the end of the day, forgetting that I had also ticked 'yes' to having a full driving license.

The next few months were spent in preparation for leaving for Salou, on the Costa Dorada in mainland Spain, the resort I had been allocated to. I had made my peace with my parents for the factory debacle and for running off to Europe without any contact for months. I think they secretly knew that I was still heart-broken about the young Mr. R. and I had behaved extremely well at my sister's wedding, in their opinion. Many years later when I was a Mother myself, I had asked my own lovely mother how my disappearance had made them feel, because I would have gone off my head with despair if Cuckoo had done the same to me.

'Quite frankly my dear, we were glad to see the back of you!' Her answer was instant.

Shortly after I had shocked them by announcing my intention to up sticks to go travelling in 1986, they had retired to Devon, the factory having been sold and millions made. They had bought a huge property with its own grounds and there was lots of potential for little projects. No one could have possibly known that just over ten years later, my father would be dead; and nothing more than a smoldering cigar butt would bear witness to the fact he had designed and created the perfect flowerbed that it lay in. Now they were tickled -pink that their errant Daughter Number One was going to be a holiday rep for a leading company and happy too that she was again trying to sever the tie, to what they believed was a doomed and destructive relationship.

I visited them often, before the day I was due to fly to Spain in late April of 1988.

'I told them I could drive Dad!' I'd wailed. Rolling his eye, he decided to give me lots of driving practice in my mother's car. His own vehicle, a magnificent bottle green Jaguar, his pride and joy, would have been far too powerful for a learner driver. He made me repeat countless times, the maneuvers essential to pass the dreaded driving test. My head was spinning with trying to master reverse parking and three-point turns.

'I don't want to do it anymore!' I shouted at him, after over two hours of practicing the exercises in a local carpark.

'Again! Do it again!'

'You enjoyed that, didn't you Dad!' Speaking to him in my sleep, as I remembered the delighted expression on his face as he bossed me around, relishing the fact that he had regained a temporary control over the daughter who had become the bane of his life. It did the trick though and I eventually passed the test.

I went on a week-long residential training course, at the end of which I strode proudly back through Waterloo station, dressed in the distinctive red and blue uniform of the company that I would soon be working for. I had a new briefcase under my arm and a cap cutely perched on my upheld head. There was an official badge declaring my name decorating my left breast; and a trademark scarf tied around my neck, just so. There was a group of us fledgling holiday reps., all going our separate ways home for now. As we passed through the crowd; we were gleefully aware of the appreciative glances made towards us by the rest of the mere public. Wearing a waist-nipping jacket and stylish pencil skirt, I had no desire for a false, druggy high that day. The pleasure of the intoxicating sense of success had made me feel ten-feet tall; and I needed no chemical crutch to sustain the natural high I was enjoying.

I was busy over the next few weeks as I packed up my belongings from the dingy rented flat and moved them, along with the faithful red moped, into the young Mr. R.'s garage, but despite all the bravado I could muster, until the last day before I was due to fly, I was praying that he would change his mind about my leaving and ask me to stay. He shook his head every time I brought the subject up.

'You have to go; I can't give you what you want.' How ironic I now found his answer, as I slept on during the peaceful December afternoon over fifteen years later, knowing that he would never have been able to give me what I needed.

At Gatwick, he literally had to push me, blubbering and shaking, through the departures entrance. As I continued to protest it wasn't just tears, that were pouring down my face but rivers of snot-infused, bellowing grief, as I turned back for one last time to watch him slowly walk away. I continued to cry silently during the two-hour flight, aware that several of my fellow passengers were eyeing me sympathetically, but also aware that some of them were travelling with identical briefcases to mine and that I needed to calm down. As the plane started its descent, I began composing myself in time to walk down the metal steps of the aircraft onto the concrete concourse of a mainland Spanish airport, re-emerging like the proverbial phoenix from its ashes, to rediscover myself yet again and face this new adventure.

'Welcome to Reus Airport.' The sign proclaimed.

The coming two weeks were to be crammed full of meetings and activities. It was pre-holiday season and time for us rooky reps. to learn the ropes. Firstly, we were allocated the accommodation we would be responsible for, but there was to be nothing five-star for me to be based in. No swanky hotel for me to hold court in and intermingle with the shiny sun burnt guests No chilled cava to pour for them and lap up their adulation, as I impressed them with my local knowledge. There was no gleaming reception desk for me to sit behind whilst selling expensive excursions to eager tourists, I ended up with the shabbiest block of flats in the entire resort.

Part of the job was greeting planes, being an elite airport rep. was seriously good fun as we waited with aloof smirks, pencils at the ready to strike names off the list on our clipboards, smiles that turned to ones of disdainful pity, when we asked the newly arrived clients where they were staying.

'Spain?' was often the questioning answer.

'Clearly.' We stayed professional, as with poker faces and clip boards at the ready we queried which specific resort and hotel they had booked.

'Sir, I meant which accommodation would that be?' We switched on even brighter holiday rep. smiles like light bulbs, as we herded them into the waiting coaches and dumped them at their respective hotels. Then, no matter what time of the day or night it was, it was straight to a bar to toast another successful job well done.

I spent most of my remaining working days troubleshooting the same issues within the apartment block that I looked after. Cockroaches were a big ongoing problem, especially inside the ground floor flats of the old, decrepit complex. Several fridges and cookers didn't work and were never going to be properly fixed, plus the swimming pool was closed for repairs for the first six weeks of the season. Finally, there were no lifts in this four-storey dinosaur of a building, which for a family with three kids and a pushchair, staying on the upper floors, went down like regurgitated vomit. The flights from Glasgow were the most frightening, these holiday makers were straight from the school of hard knocks, who may have paid a pittance for this holiday dream but still considered the price to be a fortune. Many had never been abroad before and their expectations of a sunny Spanish Shangri La, were nothing like the reality that they had arrived at.

The best plan was to get them tipsy with welcoming jugs of sangria that had been lined up at a bar adjacent to the apartment and paid for by the company, whilst I worked out which families or groups would be the best for each vacant flat on my list, moving them quickly into the rooms while they were off guard, dealing with any fall-out later. One group of ladies were so much on a budget that they had packed a week's worth of meat in their luggage. In those days, this was as permissible as smoking at the airport. Of course, they ended up with a kitchenette without a working fridge and daily I ran up several flights of stairs to take them what they had requested the previous evening, as everything was safely chilling in a fridge in the staff office.

'Meals on legs!' I chirruped for two weeks.

That was how the summer season of 1988 went on, working, drinking like a fish and partying again like there was no tomorrow, whenever possible. The resort was lively with an amazing swathe of beach front and dozens of bars and cafes. Tables and chairs were grouped together under awnings and large umbrellas shaded them from the ever- increasing power of the Sun, as it rose higher daily as the weeks went on. I shared a large flat with six other employees, rent free, which was part of the generous package I had been given. It was in the old part of the town, a short stroll to the center of the action and had an enormous balcony where I spent many an hour tanning myself, comfortably topless.

My roommate was a Northerner with the biggest breasts that I had ever seen. This girl had also taken the job to escape unrequited love back in the UK, but then started a fling with a Spanish coach driver. When the love of her life turned up from England to confess his regret in letting her go, she poo-pooed him, choosing to concentrate on the shagging gears of Pedro. Apparently 'Knockers' had a terrible motorbike accident a few seasons later and lost an eyebrow. I hoped the thrill of being wrapped around the sexy senor's throbbing Lambretta had been worth it.

The other occupants of the flat were easy to bond with. The girl who had lied about her age to get the job, in fact had taken ten years off it, was a tall, sulky blonde with a good command of the lingo. Together, we would gussy up and prowl into the night receptive to the offers we would receive from the hot-blooded Spaniards out on the town. As time went by, I was able to lick my emotional wounds. I was twenty-eight, my inner soul was learning again, how to protect itself and like a tree, I was developing layers around it. Perhaps I was a weeping willow, bending but not breaking. Or maybe I was a gnarled, old oak, tough and hostile, its shape changing against the seasons to protect its core. No matter what, there would be no fast drugs during the coming summer and the grunting monsters of my nightmares were again, nowhere to be seen. I was my true self once more, how many times would this have to happen to me before I had an inkling of why I did not need the false confidence booster. Before I was able to believe in me?

My body turned its usual deep brown colour, I learnt a smattering of Spanish, settling easily into this new way of life. The wages were generous; and living was cheap, as duty-free prices prevailed and bar and restaurant owners happily gave us reps., courtesy drinks and meals for recommending their venues. Some guests were very appreciative of my efforts to help them and I received many small gifts of gratitude when I waved them off on their homeward-bound journeys. One gentleman however, made a special visit to see me in my makeshift office in a car rental place.

'Gotta present for you.' I looked up with a suitably grateful smile to thank him for the gesture, only to witness a jar of dead cockroaches being slammed onto the desk.

There were constant incidences throughout the months which followed and several of these first-year reps. wouldn't make it. The failure to go AWOL for airport duties would have them sacked on the third strike and be sent home, in disgrace. There was an awful night when a client had had a heart attack and died in his apartment. This terrible scene was witnessed by his distraught family, who had tried and failed, to make contact with the 24-hour emergency pager that should have been carried by a designated rep. Unfortunately, the individual responsible that night had forgotten to take the device with him as he headed out to party. The family were forced to keep vigil over the body until the office opened in the morning and that errant rep. too, was sent packing.

Then, the inevitable happened. The young Mr. R., he of the hardened heart, couldn't help but make the occasional contact and me of the damaged soul, wasn't strong enough to realize the best thing to do was ignore this, grow some more rings around my own heart, keep my distance and draw a permanent line under his existence in my life. He asked if he could fly out to meet me for a week. Silly, stupid girl, I agreed immediately. I rented a cheap studio apartment, put champagne in the fridge and nervously looked forward to his arrival. Mid-morning on the day his flight was due in, I was ready to hop onto a transfer coach to surprise him at the airport, when the office called me in. Gatwick had faxed over details of a passenger who had missed the flight, young Mr. R.

'Is this your idea of a joke?' My voice was unusually cold on the phone when I rang him, demanding an explanation.

'I over-slept.' He was surprisingly contrite.

'You're pathetic!'

'Sorry, I'm booked on another flight tomorrow.' That night I hardened my own heart and went out to join in with a fiesta, one of those crazy Spanish nights where no holds were barred and the whole town went bonkers in a bid to outdo each other in the party spirits. Every bar was crowded and the music playing loudly from each one, vied with each other. The whole town was a symphony of pounding musical rhythms and night beats that the revelers couldn't resist moving their bodies to. I bumped into a luscious guy who worked for another holiday company, our eyes locked with a sudden sexual thrill and we stayed together until dawn, when we drank the champagne I had bought as we watched the Sun rise. He was a seriously good lover, and I made a connection with him on many levels, before sleeping off the antics of the night before. Dreaming not of the man at home, but the guy I had fucked and laughed with and talked deeply to, as the Sun had come up.

'He can make his own way here.' I decided, once I had confirmation that the young Mr. R. had finally boarded at Gatwick. At the last minute I hailed a coach and took the short ride to the airport. There he was, with a battered, old suitcase in his hand, walking out of the airport building, waddling like Charlie Chaplin, shielding his eyes from the fierce glare of the July mid-day Spanish Sun and I was lost.

The week we spent together was fun filled and full on. I introduced him to secret drinking venues away from the gaggle and blare of the tourist crowds. He found the local gay bar the most appealing, funny that. We reps. often went there, just to chill and be left alone. The advent of this male friend of mine had the bartender in spasms of hysterical laughter and lust.

'Guapo! Guapo!' he had squealed, gazing dreamily at the young Mr. R. who's own facial expression was unreadable at the time. It wouldn't be for many years later, when I thought about that evening, that I realised his face had been hiding embarrassed delight. I watched him as the week went on and for the first time ever, I had control. He was on my territory now and it felt damn good. Clubbing the nights away and ordering meals in my limited Spanish, impressing him with my confident style, even though I secretly knew that what was served wasn't quite what I had intended to ask for. I was having a ball, but we had no real sex though. There was no intimacy, wrapped in each other's arms waiting for the splendour of the sunrise, funny that too. At the end of the week when he confessed that he didn't like me being there, my retort was simple, I would only go back if we got married. End of. Silly, silly, stupid, stupid girl.

I watched him disappear back into the busy airport building and stayed to watch his plane take off. Raising my head, I followed the aircraft as it banked around and became a dot in the sky, to vanish as if by magic, into infinity. He was gone. I took another coach back into the resort. Bumming free rides was the norm for us lucky members of the airport duties club and all the coach drivers knew me.

'Hola Guapa!' They would wolf whistle their appreciation, before gesturing me to climb aboard.

The return of the young Mr. R., to England, didn't hurt quite as much as I had feared, so I simply got on with the serious matter of living my dream. 'Wonderful Life.' could be heard playing on the radio one afternoon, as I sat in a prime position at the front of a coach full of tourists, talking to them over the microphone, delivering my welcoming speech with practiced aplomb as we sped towards the resort. The windscreen was so wide, with its panoramic views of the surrounding majestic mountains, that panned to the blues of the sea and the sky. My side window was open and the cool air blowing through it felt so good. The words of the song resonated through my head, as the sunlit lasers of light bounced their beams off the parched motorway. The combination was up-lifting; and I was happy, so very happy to be myself, living that moment.

I had kept in contact with my parents this time during my months away. They had the telephone number of the payphone in my makeshift office, and they were eager to hear my voice, sounding cheerful and hopefully drug-free. They must have crossed their fingers for me and my new, brighter future, back in their English retirement haven where they too were living their dreams carrying out projects, like designing the perfect flower bed. A week or so after I had thoughtfully watched one particular plane dip out of sight, they rang me with panic in their voices. The young Mr. R. had rung them to invite them to a wedding, my wedding! my wedding to him! My face must have been a picture of stunned astonishment as I took in the momentous conversation I was having. This had changed everything in the blink of an eye; this one thing that for years I had yearned could happen and suddenly the new life that I had been creating for myself became irrelevant. Silly, silly, stupid, oh so stupid girl.

I wrapped things up in Spain, early in August 1988. I said my goodbyes, vowing to stay in touch and flew home with a suntan to die for, and a healthy amount of money in my handbag. I had been unable to spend the wages that I had been paid, thanks to all the freebies I had enjoyed, there had to be some compensation for that jar of dead cockroaches. The company was used to this type of staff-leaving-early scenario. Many girls did exactly what I had done, taking a plunge into the world of a holiday rep., due to the unrequited love of boys at home. Many would also jack it in early, to go home triumphantly to bag their prize when those English boys realized what they had potentially lost. Others would stay in the game for years, allocated to several resorts over the seasons and maybe climb the ranks, or even fall for a local and produce beautiful, sun-kissed, squeezable children. Others would meet tragedy, such as fatal accidents, often on a motorbike, but some, like Knockers; would merely lose eyebrows.

Chapter Eight

Some Really BIG Mistakes

Tomorrow was Wednesday 24ᵗʰ December 2014, Christmas was nearly here and today I planned to venture out in my car, wary of my bandaged leg, but determined to get the final bits and pieces needed for the perfect celebration. Cuckoo's father had come to get her and the Beloved Pooch the night before and Mr. R. and I were laughing as we debated who would play whom in a movie, when the Big Man walked in, picking up on the silly conversation.

"The Godfather' would suit you' The beautifully filthy Big Man directed his comment at Mr. R.

'I see you in 'The Hulk'!' Mr. R. had replied.

'Touche mate!' There was an easy banter between them, that wasn't malicious.

'Nope, he belongs in a Bond!' I protested, pointing at the Big Man before hugging him tightly, loving the familiar smells of dirt, sweat and the always underlying, tangible scent of promised sex. The two men got on fine, though there were no reasons why civilized people should not, under the circumstances. The book had been closed on my relationship with Mr. R. long before our encounter on fireworks night, so there were no grudges and of course since his sad confessions of appreciating men in every sense, the three of us were able to play our parental parts in Cuckoo's life, with no messy complications inherited from the time when I had been married to her father.

This was to be a night without Cuckoo or the Beloved Pooch, a blissfully simple evening, with no one to please, but ourselves. Christmas music spanning the decades was playing and we acknowledged with smiles, as we did every year, that those amazing anthems were so vintage. Slade belting out 'Merry Xmas Everybody.' Lennon huskily singing 'Happy Xmas' and The Pogues, with the ghastly lyrics of 'Fairytale of New York.' The happy theme and the promise that war was over, were however, a million miles from the truth this Christmas. War was very much alive, its shape, shifting into different guises. Glimpses of the many changing faces of the cunty, grunty monsters, in every image of military action and worldwide conflict. There had been beheadings posted on the Internet, the most recent manifestation of the way the enemy could adapt, to ensure that the evil lived and breathed. I couldn't comprehend how such monstrosities could be allowed, let alone be available for anyone to look at, if they had the stomach.

I was also aware of more pressing, personal problems, my injured leg was hampering my ability to exercise or bathe properly, I was getting porky, and my legs were turning into hairy forests.

'I'm starting to look like 'The Fly.'' I wailed, referring to Jeff Goldblum's morph into an insect, in a certain film of the same name.

'And I can't fuck you properly, baby!!'

'Oh babe!' He smiled in sympathy at my outburst. I really needed to get a grip, as there was much to do in the planning of the military operation for our Christmas feast, including the serious matter of stuffing the turkey.

'How's the writing coming along, I hear you rambling in your sleep.'

'I want him to hear me!!'

'I know babe, why don't you go and see a medium, that might help.'

'I did once, years ago, before he died, funnily enough with a work friend, it was quite an experience!' I frowned, remembering the cold village hall where about fifty sorrowful people had gathered, in the hope of contacting their loved ones who had passed over.

'It was a bit scary to be honest., but someone once told me he's watching over me from the spirit world, full head of hair apparently. Maybe one day he'll hear me, this way.'

The subject matter was getting too maudlin and trying to cheer myself up, I thought about how our sex life had been prior to my accident, when we were been extremely energetic in the sack. In bed, on the settee, in the woods and wherever else we came together, his magical witchcraft had always encompassed me totally and I remembered lying wide-legged, wild and uninhibited.

'I'm yours!' I would scream, as primevally the Big Man covered my body, ramming his cock deep into me. I had vowed never to lie to this man and one night early in our relationship I had sobbed a confession to him.

'I need to tell you something, baby.'

'You've slept with your ex?'

'No!! Never!' It had only been some stupid personal fact that I needed him to know. It was so important to me that I had laid every facet of my body and soul bare to him.

He would spread my legs even wider, gripping my arms as I wrapped them around his back, pumping furiously, feeling my body respond with orgasm after orgasm.

'Greedy girl!' He laughed the words countless times, dripping with sweat from the delightful exertion of fucking his woman senseless. Flipping me over like a ragdoll, my face pressed against a pillow, he would fuck me from behind, my bottom rising automatically to ensure that I could take as much as possible. Sometimes this would lead to the taboo pleasure of anal sex. Slowly and carefully, he would slide his cock into the tight hole, until I relaxed against the pain and was able to move with him. His favorite position was to have me straddle him, with my hair draped over his face. He would suckle my nipples to hot, erect peaks and sigh deeply, as he heard the familiar noises that I made as I came again. I would raise my head at the crucial moment, locking my eyes with his, needing to watch his eyes change color, his pupils exploding like black fireworks into the vivid blue surrounding them. We were clamped together totally, our breathing harsh and deep, both caring about nothing but that moment. It was raw, basic copulation and we would stay con-joined when it had ended, united for a few more minutes until our racing heart beats slowed down and we laughed, in awe of what had just taken place.

He once falteringly asked me if I had had enough.

'Are you bored babe?'

'Seriously baby! You must be kidding!' I teased him back and scolded him never to ask me that again. I would shit on the women who had planted that doubt in his mind and driven him away, but I gave praise for their mistakes. The magician was mine now and his carnal alchemy belonged to me alone.

The spell had been adapted of course. Since the accident, my leg had had to be protected from any wanton body contorting, so I would slide into bed quietly to lie beside him, cupping his sleeping balls with one hand, feeling them twitch against my fingers. Taking his cock in my mouth, using my tongue to bring it to life, feeling the muscle twitch in response, hardening as the foreskin drew back to reveal a purple, glistening end that was already oozing. Groaning in response, he would play with my clitoris, teasing and stroking, before moving his hand to my breasts. The foreplay continued until my gasps became guttural and he was ready to ram into me. I begged him to fuck me, playing with myself in anticipation, nuzzling into his neck. He wanted to be bitten there, hard; and dark bruises marked the skin for days afterwards. Sometimes he used his hand to jerk himself off, whilst I madly finger fucked my throbbing, dripping vagina, flicking my clit in unison with his hand movements. Silently, apart from our ragged breathing, we brought ourselves to a joint climax. It didn't matter how we came together; the result was always the same. It was a total turn on, a unique, urgent coupling, the like of which I had never felt despite all my previous experiences.

The Big Man had given me complete physical and mental fulfilment and there would never be anyone to better or replace him. His fingers and thumbs were thick, just like his cock. Even the action of brushing them against me created a spark of electricity in my body and I never tired of looking at him, studying his face surreptitiously, reveling in stroking his skin. We would bemoan together about our battles against weight, neither of us being naturally skinny, although his stomach delighted me even though he complained about its size. Its imperfection just made him more perfect in my eyes and it was indeed a splendid belly. He always accentuated his assets, barrel-chested and with tree-trunk like arms, his upper body was honed from the physical exertions of his work. He wore his trademark, black, sleeveless vest tops, come summer or winter and his face and top half of his body were permanently tanned, whilst his legs, invariably covered in shorts or jogging bottoms, were always paler than the rest of him.

'You look like a choc ice!' I once poked the good-humored fun at him as he sprawled naked on the bed.

'Eat me then babe!'

As for his tattoos, those ferocious dragons and mythical creatures that were inked on his arms, were always on show, oiled and supreme. They must have taken hours of work and pain. Tattoos were the norm these days sleeves, black symbols and tributes, to whatever or whoever, were easy to spot. Girls too sported the inking's proudly, but these works of art were vintage, with colours that were still so strong and proud. Again, he had set a precedent back in the day. And again, for the millionth time I would look at him with wonder, to worship at his altar.

'It's time for bed, babe.' His quiet voice interrupted my fantasy, reading my mind apparently. Seeing the invitation in his eyes I followed him upstairs, where despite the constraints of my bandaged leg, we played out as much as we could of what I had been recalling earlier, after which we both fell fast asleep, as my dreams once more took me back in time.

A lifetime earlier oblivious to these wonders that were waiting for me far into my future, I flew back from my Spanish world, excited for what was to come. Hardly able to believe that I would soon be the Mrs. R. who I had always dreamed of becoming. Suntanned and svelte, I was bright-eyed and healthy, a hugely different sight from the sniffling wreck who had taken the outward-bound flight to Reus airport, less than four months previously. The next few weeks flew by in a whirlwind of activity and planning as our mid-September wedding loomed in 1988. I went backwards and forwards to my parents again, the two-hour train journey was nothing to a well-seasoned traveler who still didn't own a car, despite having passed the driving test.

Reception venues were visited and discarded. After their initial shock and probably a hint of horror, that Daughter Number One was actually going to marry this chap after all the trauma and bad history, my parents had resigned themselves to the fact and offered to host the event in their sleepy Devonian hometown. Clothes shopping with my mother was next on the list and I eventually found my dream outfit. This was going to be a low-key registry office affair, followed by a sumptuous wedding breakfast in the most grand and prestigious hotel in the county, so a full-blown, white, traditional dress with veil and trail, would not have done at all. I was also still wincing, from the memory of the peach taffeta bridesmaid dress. I chose a cream suit instead, the jacket had built-up shoulders, so current for its time and the shoulder pads would eventually date the look as being textbook 1980's in fashion history, but in 1988 it was just perfect.

When I had finally landed back at Gatwick, the young Mr. R. had seemed awkward, bashful even. No real conversations took place between us, no final meeting of our minds and there were no apologies or explanations from either of us about our past demeanors. We just slid back into a life together, a life that we seemed to have learnt nothing from, a life of boxing around each other where the old frustrations still sat in the wings and nothing felt any better. Funny that. Did he regret his spontaneous proposal to my parents? In the cold light of day, was this going to be the biggest mistake he could make? It was also strange that I hadn't realized, that at any point he had never actually proposed to me. However, the day of the wedding was approaching fast; and this was enough to quell my scared, secret inner niggles, that things were not going to be okay.

A splendid wedding it turned out to be as well, as everything went according to its carefully laid plans. My father decorated his green Jaguar, his ultimate pride and joy and a symbol of his success. A tasteful white ribbon adorned the bonnet, advertising that precious 'bridely' cargo was being carried that morning, as he proudly drove me to the registry office. The car passed the bridegroom, walking with his besties, en route for the ceremony, all suited and booted. Strangely the young Mr. R. looked fierce and withdrawn, was he hung over maybe from the night before, or was it just cold feet?

The reception was grand, my father in his proud role of Father of the bride, delivered an eloquent speech to the varied group of guests, many of whom would be attending their own and each other's funerals in the next decade or so, my own father included. The groom's family and friends laughed merrily, as the speech concluded that a Panda was not only for Christmas, but for life, whilst my side just looked politely baffled at this strange reference to a black and white bear. They all sat at tables laden with shiny glasses and cutlery, merrily drinking free champagne. Wearing new dresses and suits, their faces were flushed, heated by the alcohol, as with beaming smiles they paid court to me, the tanned bride at the top table. The younger element, friends from home, were secretly appalled that the young Mr. R. had decided to marry me. I was well known as a loose cannon; a habitual drug user and the legacy of my past antics had badly colored their opinions. Hypocritically, they kept their thoughts to themselves as they freeloaded on the plentiful booze and food supplied. Queen for the day, I took the accolades and with my eyes shining I drank the day in, but I ashamed to admit that later that evening I was fumbling in my cream satin clutch bag for the wrap of speed that I had hidden in it.

Back to day-to-day life, we newly marrieds tried to create a future. I found work easily, my father had bought me a car, a suitably reliable banger and I tried desperately hard to be the wife who I thought would make us both happy. The dream for me was a home-cooked meal, a bottle of wine or two and a cuddle in front of the television. Was that honestly too much to expect and ask for? Frankly, yes. The look of withdrawal I had seen on my husband's-to-be face on the morning of our wedding, had not lied, because those cold feet of his were never going to be warmed by my attentions. Slowly, nails were hammered into my marital coffin and my silly dream of cozy nights for two, remained just that, a silly, little dream, never destined to be a reality. The sexless, pointless and totally futile relationship was morphing into a marriage of the same sorry quality and my dreams of a warm and peaceful future as a happily married woman, faded, until even the memory of them was invisible. The party Panda creature roared and the dependence on the availability of speed to sustain that persona, grew again.

Christmas 1988; was our first as a married couple. The young Mr. R. wasn't into the whole Christmas thing at all, seeing it as a commercial exercise and unable to embrace the magic, even for his daughter when she was born and old enough to believe. He really was a damaged soul too, but I was never going to be the one to heal him; if such an elixir existed, I would never find it and by staying with him, I simply became more damaged myself. The opportunities to distance myself forever had been offered several times, but my stubborn, foolish self was never wise enough or brave enough, to understand that these had been the only paths to have saved my sanity. One day I would look back and smile at my folly, but not this day, this Christmas Day in 1988.

As a boy, the young Mr. R. had owned a guinea pig, a smooth-haired, ginger piggy. In a moment of genius, I decided to buy him an identical piglet and hid it in a spanking new hutch in our garage, as a Christmas present. What else would you buy a tin man other than the chance to have a heart?

'Surprise!' I led him into the darkened garage and flicked on the light. What he really thought was unclear, but the gesture seemed to touch him; and I cosseted the guinea pig with love and attention, treating her like a surrogate baby. What a stupid, love-deprived creature I had become. Owning little mammals was a rite of passage for children who dreamed of such pets, but what on earth was the excuse for a twenty-eight-year-old woman who cared so deeply for a fur baby. I was such a different person from the free spirit of the torrid climes that I had experienced over the recent summers. It was a far, heart-rending cry away indeed. The memory of how to be happy, really happy, had vanished again and been replaced with a love of a little animal and a need for Billy the Whizz.

I lost my job of course, running in the fast lane at the weekend took its toll and my ability to be able to function on Monday mornings barely allowed me to raise my head from the pillow, to croakily make a sick call to work. There were plenty of other employment choices and in my trusty banger, I drove to a succession of temporary assignments. Cold calling, computer inputting, credit control, tele-sales and filing, all proved to be so suffocatingly boring that I was prone to falling asleep at my desk in the afternoons. After a week or so in each office the manager would call my agency and regretfully advise that I was no longer required, I would simply shrug my shoulders and wait for the next appointment, using the few days of free time that I had been given, to visit my local dealer.

I came home one day to find the stiff dead body of my beloved pet, I was beyond grief, desperately trying to revive her, rocking with despair. There was a somber funeral, as a small boy from next door watched with great interest.

'Is it dead?' he had asked me inquisitively.

Gravely aware that the little chap could be a sensitive soul, I gently tried to explain.

'Dig it up!' Came his answer. A comment that just about summed up my life. Ridiculous. If only I had known that somewhere else in the world at that very moment, a soldier was fiercely guarding the Berlin wall. A seriously sexy soldier, who was to be my future soul mate.

The marriage limped on. I could frequently taste the ashes of disappointment and regret, mixing badly with frustration. This gritty concoction was washed down with alcohol and banished to a corner of my mind, where these saddening feelings didn't bother me as much as I firmly locked them away with the key of my now, very leaden heart. The house wasn't a home, merely bricks and mortar, where two people were starting to withdraw from each other at any opportunity. I was starting to rely on my own escapes and was drawn back into the netherworld of drug users. That parallel life was still there in the shadows and I was welcomed by the grey-skinned figures, who probably hadn't even noticed my absence. If the monsters who prowled my sub conscious couldn't quite seize my soul, they damn well were willing to settle for stealing any other part of me that they could and my peace of mind along with my sanity, were victims to the theft.

1990, the year I turned thirty, limped brokenly into 1991 and the young Mr. R. and I were by then leading separate lives and separate sleeping arrangements, when I did sleep. I found another job that appealed much more than the others and I began to run a video shop. The long twelve-hour shifts every other day were isolating me even more and accelerating my descent back into regular drug use; and into a much deeper and deadlier dive than I had ever taken before. One day the Barbarian walked in, I had looked up as the door of the shop opened. Much of the time there were few customers, and it was a lonely job, but I was perfectly happy with this, busying myself with vodka and coke poured into a mug for appearances sake, with regular snorts and oral fixes of the white stuff. We burst into laughter when we saw each other. Still as tall and imposing, he towered above me as we talked.

'Where have you been Catrin.'

'Where haven't I been!!'

'You're wearing a wedding ring!'

'Ha.'

'Everything ok?'

'Not really, it's all just one big mess to be honest.' I didn't have the courage to tell him the truth about my sham marriage, that was now well and truly, broken. Having once made the vow to my new husband that I would love him for better or for worse, I was now dancing to a death knoll of a tune that was lamenting a turn of events for the worse, for the so much worse than I could ever have imagined, when the dream of this marriage had promised something so much better. I turned to my father for help. He had seen how Mr. R. and I were together, distanced and awkward in each other's company whenever my parents had visited us and he loved a financial opportunity, especially one that could prise me away from my current situation. He must have tried to ignore the signs of my unstable frame of mind, probably not wanting to see any signs in me of having relapsed into the drug user who he had once glimpsed and feared.

I woke up with a start on Christmas Eve 2014, wondering what the time was. Checking my alarm, it was three a.m. and I looked up into a crystal-clear winter night sky through the open bedroom curtains, seeing a multitude of dazzling stars, hanging suspended against the black background, looking for my special star. I watched its stellar, silver beauty as it dominated the dark, pulsing with a strange inner glow. It looked very much like the one that I had been fascinated with during those magical nights on holiday in October and as I drifted off to sleep, I spoke to my father again.

'You were right again Dad; I had fallen backwards again.'

'I know, Catrin.'

Had I imagined the answer, having desperately wanted him to hear me for so long.

'Are you there, Dad? Daddy!' I lay there for a long time, wide awake, listening intently, but the only sound I could hear was that of silence.

It was easier for him to blame my husband and he bought the house from the young Mr. R., lock, stock and barrel, leaving me sitting pretty with a plan hatched to install paying lodgers, whilst I was to be the live-in landlady, another very bad plan. It was now the spring of 1992 and I was feeling rather smug with the way things had worked out, staying at home much more where I could let my lifestyle have free rein. I could smoke and drink and do whatever else I wanted, whilst pleasuring myself in the king-size bedroom I commanded, to enjoy the fucking skills of a foreign lover who I had recently taken. These were considerable, as was his wildly controlling nature, yet I loved the emotional grip in which he held me, having felt invisible, I now felt wanted and as my new macho squeeze worked evenings, I could combine my illicit drug use with my new-found sex life and still be home by midnight. I was a proverbial Cinderella, with no one any the wiser but the ghost of a little guinea pig and probably a few mice.

It had been four years since my drug-free, happy and confident stride through Waterloo station, with my new uniform and name badge proclaiming my giddy, enviable place in society. I was looking now forward with the false confidence that only amphetamines could provide, to the next episode in my chaotic life. Silly, stupid girl. I had no idea of the Armageddon that I was going to have to face and the level that I was going to fall to. The monsters in the abyss were slowly awaking up, their eyes on the prize that they had lusted after eight years ago, since they had first seen me in the light of a campfire in 1984. My soul.

Chapter Nine

From Despair to Devotion

Finally, it was here, Christmas Day 2014! Our ninth Christmas together, for the Big Man and I, and along with Cuckoo, we all filled it with present-giving, excellent food and far too much alcohol. My vow to hold it all together enabled me to enjoy the day and most of the evening with my little family, including the Beloved Pooch, until about ten p.m. when I suddenly hit amnesia. After slowly marinating my body with red wine, vodka and port and having started the day with a glass of chilled bubbly, despite my every wish not to, I passed out.

'Ma!! You really should control your drinking!' These were Cuckoo's cross words, the next morning as she flew off to join her friends for an annual Boxing Day charity pram race, a fancy-dress pub crawl. She Facebooked me later, with a photo of them all dressed in pink, piggy onesies, with joke shop snouts attached to their noses. I was obviously forgiven then but that knowledge was tempered soberly by a very sobering thought.

'Oh my God, beware the wolf, little piggy's. Silly piggy's, you have no clue as to the powers of the jaw-gnashing, salivating, flesh eating, wolverine monsters.'

Cuckoo was forward bound that evening to join her father for a Boxing Day dinner gathering. The party included a friend who was a girl, who secretly yearned to turn him. Another lady would be joining them; she had battled cancer once and their bond had survived since 1980. It would be an interesting situation and I could have been forgiven for fleetingly wishing to be a fly on their wall that night, watching as these two women fawned over this good-looking, divorced man with his amusing ways. Mr. R.'s vicious tongue was sheathed these days it seemed, maybe he had finally stopped using it as a weapon, or maybe he had worn it out on me over the years.

The presents that we had exchanged on Christmas Day had gone down extremely well, a Santa sack made of red felt embroidered with her initials, that had been Cuckoo's since she was a baby, had bulged with gifts appropriate for a twenty-year-old young lady. The special gift, la piece de resistance, the be-jeweled, rose-gold watch had raised a gasp of pleasure and as she unwrapped and admired it, our first Christmas with the Big Man came to mind. On Christmas Eve 2006 a stony-faced, twelve-year-old Cuckoo had been sitting petulantly at the dinner table, wearing a paper hat and clearly hating every moment. He had stayed over that night, but even the promise of the heap of gifts waiting for her downstairs couldn't persuade her to leave her room on Christmas Day morning. The Big Man had sadly taken the cue and reluctantly had to walk back to his rented flat, in the cold, early light. It was far too early to hope for acceptance, the fact that I had found love so quickly had upset the confused teenager, but approval of him would eventually come and was now very evident.

'Hiya! Love you!' Were some of the fond words that she directed at her stepfather, as she careered through her days. This first Christmas together however, I was glad to see the back of my daughter, understanding now, my own lovely mother's utterings of those same words. Once Cuckoo had been collected by her father, I called the Big Man and he hastily returned.

'I'm sorry about that baby.'

'It's ok babe, I get it.'

'Do you wanna open a present?' I had bought some sexy lingerie and now quickly disappeared to change into it, donning a black mac and knee length boots at the same time, tying a label around my neck with some Christmas ribbon. The desired effect was immediate. He stripped me naked and fucked me long and hard, panting furiously and laughing as he pounded into me. Taking it all, I laughed back into his eyes. We had finally met our perfect matches, soul mates too lucky for words that we had found each other that fateful night and more poetry would be written, exclusively for him.

'You take me to a place I've never been.

I've seen it many times before, ccasionally I've dreamed.

And you will smile, that now I know,

I have the chance, to see the stars, to watch the world; and make it dance, and feel, so very special.'

We spent Boxing Day 2014 quietly together, nursing hangovers and tucking into left-over turkey.

'How's the book coming along babe?' He asked me again later when we were snuggled up together in bed.

'Yeah, it's ok.'

'As long as it's not upsetting you, all those memories.'

'Yeah, there's a lot of them baby.'

I decided to change the subject, reliving my past as I slept was upsetting me; and I didn't want to dwell on it.

'Do you remember Christmas 2006 and my special present?'

'Yes babe!'

I took my own cue from him at that moment, led by the expression in his eyes, the pupils enlarging with desire and we reenacted the effect of that special present, minus the fancy-dress outfit that I had worn eight years ago. Falling asleep in each-other's arms, as my dreams re-visited 1992.

NO EXAGGERATION

I did not feel particularly special then, as the relentless cycle of ups and comedowns took its toll on me. Not turning up for work became another nasty habit that I had developed, along with syphoning off the rent money that I was supposed to send to my trusting but conveniently absent father. My next job was so much more suited to the new lifestyle that I had embraced, working behind the bar of a hardcore rave club. It was smoky and loud, a veritable den of iniquity that was also guaranteed to source any illegal substance required. Drug-infused, I necked my bombs of speed and helped myself to vodka from the optics, driving erratically home at five in the morning with a wad of cash, my nightly earnings, stuffed into the pockets of my jeans. Safe behind the bar I juggled drinks for the punters laughing at their slurry chat-up lines, not in the mood for romance at any level these days. My foreign lover had left the country, leaving me behind, a little bit heart-broken and a lot more relieved, as once the novelty of his need to try and control me had worn off, I had seen it for what it really was and hadn't liked it.

Too high, with glittering eyes, I would watch as the club goers gyrated with wide open 'gurning' mouths and brightly lit eyes, with enlarged pupils that matched my own. Occasionally I would see 'straight' people who had ventured with daring intent, into the late-night venue. They never stayed long, their bravado was extinguished as soon as they entered the club that was illuminated by a thousand lasers, all throbbing in unison to an ear-splitting level of repetitive sound waves. Horrified by the regular clientele who moved like a swarm of bees to the hard-core beats, they would leave as quickly as they had arrived, this netherworld was too dark and dangerous for their tastes. Oblivious to the fact that they had been viewed with such horror, the night creatures would continue their demonic, tribal dancing until daylight forced them back into the murky holes from which they had crawled out. I was promoted to the giddy heights of a being a female bouncer, wearing a black puffer jacket showing 'Security' emblazoned on the front of it, I manned the door with equally blazing eyes reveling in the stupid power, standing next to giants swollen by steroids, whilst I too was equally pumped with my usual poison.

The early years of the 1990s had seen subtle changes in music, fashion and technology and the latter part of 1992 saw changes in the lodgers whose hard-earned rent money was also feeding my lifestyle. One by one the decent ones left, forced out by my erratic behavior and wild-eyed, nocturnal habits, whilst the addition of a regular presence of some of the Machiavellian characters I was mixing with, was upsetting and threatening them even more. Gradually they took up residence in the house, bragging about criminal records and openly sharing out the proceeds of theft and large-scale drug dealing, with snapping-jawed dogs at their feet. I had finally opened a true Pandora's box and out flew the demons as the mouth of the abyss opened wide; and in I tumbled.

I was trapped in an underworld den, where bonfires would be lit willy-nilly, tyres and other rubbish burnt freely, as the fire starters danced manically around their white-hot tributes to evil, it had been bad enough when I went a-visiting but now they lived with me. The neighbors were outraged and mob-handed in their desire to stop the insanity that was brewing like the worse thunderstorm. Its dark clouds were gathering strength and momentum, mingling with the acrid smoke from the weekly bonfires, the fierce flames acting as gates to this new and deadly Hell. Old friends, who had come to see me once never came back, even the Barbarian, accustomed to mixing with such people, was disturbed by the scenes in the house and he too failed to return. My ability to be able to work was now at zero tolerance and I sold my trusty banger for an ounce of speed. Trapped in the vicious circle of depravity I spiraled further downhill, becoming a physical and mental wreck.

I forwarded minimal sums of rent to my father and made as little contact with him as possible, which started worrying and puzzling him. My parents visited once in the autumn of 1992, staying at a hotel. My frantic need to keep them away from the property somehow got me through an evening with them, my sole mission now was to desperately keep them at bay and the taste of rancid fear was omnipresent in my mouth. Acid tabs were offered and always taken, to numb the terror that I was feeling about the monstrous situation that I had created. The house had become one of virtual horrors, inhabited by a nest of human vermin. The events of the Eighties might have been peppered with colorful highs and lows, salted with many tears and regular dustings of white powder, but ten years on things were worse than they had ever been. I never really understood how I dragged myself through those warped months, with my sanity on the edge and my body and mind obliterated, almost to a point of no return. No matter how many rings I had developed around my soul, they weren't going to protect it now and it wasn't until many years later that I would realize I had temporarily sold it.

My parents had to finally face their own fears, that not only had I derailed but that I had crashed the gravy train that they had unwittingly supplied; and by the New Year of 1993 my time of living nightmares was nearly over. One icy, cold February my father arrived unannounced on a Sunday morning. Assessing the scene that he was looking at, wearing a grim and deeply worried expression, he could see that his fears had become the worst imagined reality. The property he had purchased for me was now nothing more than a squat and the suntanned, laughing, healthy bride who he had proudly escorted to her wedding over four years previously, was nothing more than a shell of her former self. My few possessions were stuffed into black bin sacks and piled into his car. No white ribbon was present for this occasion; black armbands would have been more appropriate as I was carefully helped into the car. With neither of us looking back, he drove me back to the West Country.

Within days he had summoned a group of burley men, rugby-playing local builders and tradesmen. He had told them little of his reasons for asking for their help, but they knew enough and could see by his face that the mission could be challenging. They drove East single-mindedly, two or three vehicles following his lead. Back at the house the rats had already deserted the ship having stripped it of anything worth taking, after they had silently watched from closed curtained windows as I had been led away with my pathetic rubbish sacks, containing everything that I owned Apparently, they had left unpleasant reminders of their siege. Dog-piss-soaked carpets, filthy piles of rags and the blatant debris of drug taking were all evident, with makeshift bongs and used needles scattered in every room. That the electricity supply had been tampered with became clearly obvious to the somber eyes of the crew that my father had hired. No questions were asked about how, who, or why, the property had come to be in such an unbelievably dire state; but they willingly helped him to reclaim it.

One little rat had remained, a skinny runt who had locked himself into an upstairs bedroom and refused to leave. A fifty-pound note persuaded him to scamper off into the night and the windows and doors were all boarded up, before the men set out for the three-hour trip home and my father could work out his next plan of action for me. The disposal of the house was a minor detail in his eyes; and it was sold for a pittance. He instructed an agency to deal with any aspects of the sale. He had no interest in this, apart from recouping some of his original investment, making out that it had been an empty property that he had owned and that squatters had managed to break in. He was finding it hard to come to terms that his Daughter Number One had been mixed up in the carnage, let alone admit this to a smug, slick estate agent.

I suddenly awoke in the dark, early hours of December 27th. 2014, with the sweaty lurch that swings the mind out of a nightmare back into consciousness. The Big Man was fast asleep; and I lay there trembling, sickened by the specific memories that had risen from my past to confront me.

'Oh, this is unbearable Dad! I don't want to remember!' And in a flash, I was sure I heard him answer me.

'You have to Catrin, you have to see this again!'

Exhausted and confused, I fell back to sleep, unable to prevent these ghostly facts from reinvading my head.

My exodus became common knowledge on the local grape vine. My immediate neighbors breathed long and painful sighs of relief, cursing me for a long time afterwards. The young Mr. R. also heard of my departure and he too breathed a deep sigh, whether it was in thanks for my safety or a similar curse, was debatable. I was finally safe and once I had been dried out, sleeping for days and sloughing off the ravages of six solid months of self-abuse, my father began his version of my rehab process. As always despite the trouble that I had caused him, these emotional and financial burdens which again I had piled on his shoulders, there was and always would be my father's well documented opinion. He would not sever that umbilical cord, even with this new, mighty blade that I had wielded on him.

He warned me however, just once, that should I bring any shame on my mother in the future he would have no choice than to disown me. He believed that this would not have to be the case and hoped by my sad and solemn nod of agreement, that this awful episode would never be repeated. He was praying that maybe, finally, his eldest daughter's demons which had haunted both her and her parents, had been banished. Sadly, his fervent wishes would eventually prove futile, but for now, having spent their energies in temporarily capturing my soul, only to have it escape their clutches, the monsters withdrew into the shadows to sleep and dream of the taste of its purity.

My main feeling, once normal thoughts recommenced in my head as the mental cobwebs cleared and I was able to see the world through calmer eyes, was one of relief, coupled with a few other emotions. Self-shame, failure and regret to name a few, plus the awful knowledge of the pain that all this must have caused my father, but time passed, and time healed again, as days turned into week and normality took its place back in my life. I looked for work and did my best to mend the damaged relationship with my mother, who despite loving her Daughter Number One, frankly hated me for my recent actions, another sentiment that I was to remember all too well in the future. The three of us muddled along quite happily together as spring blossomed into an early summer in 1993. Large gin and tonics on a Friday night were part of his amateur rehab scheme and as the evenings lengthened slowly, my father and I would sit comfortably together on the raised terrace, drinking and smoking. Lobbing cigar butts and cigarette ends into the flower bed below, we talked quietly, reminiscing of star gazing and past happier times.

I found a job after several attempts, having followed-up a vacancy for a receptionist at a local hotel just a ten-minute walk away. It was a cross between a rest home and the iconic location of the sitcom 'Fawlty Towers', where Basil and Sybil berated themselves for the pleasure of their television viewers. The owner-cum-chef was as equally barmy as his television counterpart, temperamental in the kitchen and roaring at his staff over the slightest error.

'How do you expect me to serve your guests after that!' I told him crossly after each loud tirade, at which his big, bearded teddy-bear face would split into a grin. Trays of tea were served on the patio on arrival of each party. The ladies were usually seventy plus, having spent a pleasant drive being chauffeured by their husbands whilst happily hen pecking them and criticising their driving. The first stop for these long- suffering men was at the bar of the hotel for a swift snifter and a sideward glance at me, the nubile, new member of staff, whilst their wives who were always well coiffured and elegantly dressed, continued to nag their down-trodden spouses.

One afternoon, the biggest seagull poop in the world splattered down the back of the latest female arrival. Her reaction was immediate and totally understandable. Shrieking with anger she leapt from her chair, flapping her arms like the wily gull that had just dive-bombed her. Silently trying to control my laughter, I hastily retreated to the kitchen with the tray of tea that I had been about to place sedately on the wrought iron table. Seagulls were rife in this seaside town, aerial predators with no fear that would swoop at ice creams, terrifying children and dogs alike. I was doodling around the local shops a few days later, as happy as I could be in my new-found haven, when my foot met a similar fate.

'Nooooooo!!', I didn't give a toss who had heard my outburst, as I viewed the dribbly deposit. There it was, a smelly, foul puddle of regurgitated fish and doubtless ice cream, plus anything else that the squawking beak of the beady-eyed creature had gobbled up.

'No way!!', I shouted out-loud again in dismay, as I surveyed the putrid mess that was covering my shoe.

'That be lucky, that be.' Commented an old, salty sea sailor who was passing me in the street and tipping his cap, he winked at me.

'Lucky?!' I laughed back. But maybe there had been something in the old wife's tale after all, as slowly but surely my luck started to change.

There were still many moments of loneliness to come and certain songs would remind me painfully of lost opportunities and cause me to anguish over what might have been. Sudden tears would fall as I walked alone along the seafront and bitter regret for the failure of my marriage would still rise like bile in my throat, even then. Despite all the turmoil I was failing to recognize that the fault of that, had not been mine alone. I made an appointment at a drugs clinic.

'You still using?' A kindly-meant professional asked me, whilst signs in the toilets instructed that used needles should be disposed of safely. We talked of blame and feelings, as he suggested that I should vent my anger at my childhood.

'Cods Wallop.' I thought it, didn't speak it; and never returned to the clinic, understanding one thing at least. The blame for my disasters should never be laid at my parents' feet.

'Drugs would have found you young lady.' I remembered his words as clear as day and accepted fully that this would probably have been the case, with or without the deadly addition of a certain white powder to my drink one night, by a younger Mr. R.

'Yes Dad, I know that, now.' I confessed to him, many years later.

'Good, Catrin, you're finally learning.'

I made a few friends amongst the staff at the hotel; but refused all invitations to go out socially and then another letter arrived.

'Why in God's name can't he leave you alone!' My parents ranted, but against their wishes and despite their fears, I arranged to meet up with my estranged husband and booked a night in a hotel in a nearby town, looking forward to keeping the longed-for liaison. My detox regime of working, sleeping and eating well was paying off. Our time was spent drinking, but once again there was no real conversation, no meeting of minds. At the end of the weekend, we went our separate ways, and he became the only focus of my life, again. My blinkers were firmly back on, as the idea of another reconciliation became my only goal, again. I had chosen not to remember the several times over the last twelve years that I had been in this position and how often I had followed my deluded dreams back to a situation that was always going to end in heartache.

Our next rendezvous was in Brighton, funny that, but I did not even question his choice of venue. We trawled the bars and clubs, exploring dark places crammed with strange people and at the end of this second weekend together he diffidently suggested that we give our marriage another go. Try again perhaps. The young Mr. R. had also learnt nothing about our doomed relationship. He too had chosen not to remember how our reunions had always ended badly. In October 1993 I packed my stuff, again and left my parents' house on a one-way ticket 'home'. They had gone abroad on holiday, indicative of the trust that they had managed to establish in me, and I left a carefully written, loving letter, with small gifts for them, as another attempt at a fresh start was to begin.

I found work and kept my nose clean, literally, there was no desire for a drug hunt now. I was content and happy; and the young Mr. R. seemed to be the same, but our sex life was still practically non-existent. Even so, a month or two later a missed period caused me to visit the doctors. A urine sample was supplied as requested and the unexpected result a few days later showed that I was pregnant. The enforced clean living and looking after myself had restored my thirty-three-year-old body to a state of readiness to welcome the embryo and the baby was to grow beautifully, this time. My parents were astounded by the news at first. but resigned themselves to the fact and visited several times, delighted to be witnessing the sight of Daughter Number One as I blossomed, my stomach slowly swelling. I attended a few pre-natal classes, sitting quietly, watching as other women discussed the merits of different baby seats.

'We haven't got a car'. Was my only sad, silent reaction, as I listened to the debate. The young Mr. R., now a proud father-to-be, owned an old pick-up truck that was perfect for lawnmowers, but was hardly a suitable chariot for transporting a newborn.

'Any questions?' Trilled the lady holding the class.

'What do I do with the baby?' Shyly I asked the one question that was burning for me, as heads turned to look at me with ridicule.

'Sod you and your baby seats.' I glared back at them, wishing I could be brave enough to say the comment out loud. I didn't go to any more classes after that, but I pored over a book that I had been given, following the development of my baby during each trimester. Worrying secretly whether my previous lifestyle would take its revenge on my precious cargo, as my bump kept growing and growing, whilst my father bought me another reliable banger and the young Mr. R; and I prepared a nursery, acquiring the wretched baby car seat which had given me so much angst.

'I'm not ready!' I sobbed down the phone to the expectant grandmother, not meaning the nursery, the damn car seat, or the hold-all packed with maternity bras and other stuff in readiness for the big day. I meant the responsibility, the ultimate responsibility of looking after a newborn.

'I don't know what to do with it!'

'Bit late for that!' She had laughed from the other end of the line.

The young Mr. R and my-self still enjoyed a drink or two. I wasn't against a few pints of lager or a couple of glasses of red wine. Broccoli though, become a staple part of my diet. I ate and ate, stuffing my face with good food, far too much of it but eating for two was blissfully the best excuse I could have, for that third portion of lasagna or roast dinner, always accompanied with heaps of broccoli. I had read in my book that the stalky-green vegetable was excellent for the body, full of iron and folic acid. The book had become my bible during the spring; and early summer months of 1994, as my only focus was to ensure that this latest adventure would have the most perfect of outcomes.

In the final weeks of July 1994, the end of my pregnancy approached; and arms and legs would visibly punch me from inside. Two weeks after my due date, on 9th August I was admitted to hospital to be induced, as baby seemed to have no desire to leave its comfortable, warm, watery world. Twenty-four hours later, after all sorts of nonsense; my daughter was delivered successfully; and I finally met my beautifully ugly ten pounds and nine ounces of bouncing baby girl. She certainly was the cuckoo in the maternity ward nest, with her shock of black hair and chubby arms and legs. I held my Cuckoo so tightly and shortly afterwards made another sobbing telephone call to my parents. Now, as dawn broke on December 27th in 2014, I cried again in my sleep.

'Oh Dad! What did I do to you!'

'You sent us to Hell, Catrin.'

Had I imagined hearing his voice again? I wasn't sure of anything anymore.

A parent now myself, I was starting to understand what I had put them through during all those dark years and I was able to offer up their latest grandchild, as the only peace offering that I had to give them, something worthy, to prove that my apology was heart felt. For the next two years I continued to do so, travelling up and down the country in my new, reliable, old banger, with baby strapped safely in her car seat in the back of the car. Those few short years were good indeed, until one day in August 1996 I received the awful, awful news that my father had terminal cancer. The stars had aligned again, not with benevolence this time and that sloppy, shitty seagull luck was about to run out.

Chapter Ten

Sailing Towards the Light

Christmas was nearly over; and it was New Year's Eve, the last day of the old in 2014. The Big Man and I were both feeling the lethargy caused by a lack of exercise and too much food, but blissfully enjoying the indulgence, aware that come mid-January we would be firmly back to our individual working grindstones. It was time to mark up a new calendar with important dates for 2015. I was going to be fifty-five in the May, where on earth had all those years gone? On our most recent visit to the hospital clinic my wounded leg had been presented again for inspection and it still wasn't healing properly. It had only been a few weeks since my accident, but it felt like forever. A series of dressings was next prescribed, followed by a wrap of thick wadding and crepe bandage, mummifying my leg from heel to knee. The dressing procedure was to be carried out every three days and the medics were perfectly happy for the Big Man to continue this good work for a few weeks, until they would see me again. Considering my excesses of previous decades, I concluded not for the first time or the last, that I wasn't really in a bad physical shape but there were many photographs of the Big Man and I from several foreign holidays, that proved I had looked better. We stared out from the frames, laughing and brown, arms wrapped around each other. Maybe there was a hidden portrait of me somewhere, deteriorating ala Dorian Grey. Laughing at this bizarre idea, I promised myself that the sultry bitch in the photos with him, would be back.

NO EXAGGERATION

The Beloved Pooch had gone to Daddy Two's again. He was probably also being accompanied by his faithful girlfriend, the friend who was a girl, who even though there would be no barking up his tree for her, had stayed loyal to Mr. R. She owned a female Jack Russell, an adorable, pudgy, black and tan bitch, who our own little doggy stallion had claimed as his own and despite the neutering operation he had undergone when quite ready, he happily humped away during these double dates.

'Now that's wrong!' I had laughed when I witnessed them in action. I quite liked the girl who was a friend. They would probably have a quiet evening in getting 'trolleyed', mindful of the fireworks that terrified most animals. Doubtless too, Daddy Two would at some point look up to the stars and think poignantly of his lost love. At home alone, blissfully alone, we drank copious amounts of alcohol, chomped on a well-planned dinner and at midnight, he steadied me around the block, watching those fireworks explode around the same stars. Waking up on New Year's Day we were intent on welcoming the New Year in another fashion.

'I like that, babe.' I heard his familiar, whispered words, with squirming pleasure.

'Babe, I'm coming.' It had started gently, building to its usual crescendo as the magic erupted again. I had read somewhere that the average couple had sex eighty-nine times a year, which was less than twice a week. In fact, it was 1.711 times a week (and a bit), to be accurate. At the beginning we had fucked every night, pulling out the stops at the weekends, eight years on the urgency was still overwhelming and it was seriously in excess of 1.711 times a week (and a bit!). Our activity that morning must have counted for at least three weeks' worth of the sexual equation. When we had finished our personal contribution to that bizarre, erotic calculation, we lay on our backs in silence for a moment.

'I've been talking to him, baby, in my sleep.'

'Your father?' The Big Man raised one eyebrow quizzically, rolling over onto his side to look at me.

'Wow! Has he finally answered you?'

'Yes.' I too rolled over, away from him, I really wasn't sure how I felt about my dream talking and I wasn't ready to talk about it in any depth, even to my husband.

'Tell me when you're ready, babe, there's no rush.' As if he had read my mind.

'I love you so much baby, Happy New Year!'

The first television news broadcast of the year had revealed pure tragedy. Apparently three youngsters had died in London as a result of taking dodgy ecstasy pills; and two had been axed to death in a pub fight, the result of boozy rage. In years gone by there had always been some disaster to mark the introduction of the New Year. There had been a tragedy in Hong Kong at the start of 1993, when revelers were crushed to death in the street in a stampede of people; and a Tsunami in Thailand in 2004, to name but two. All was quiet though, on New Year's Day in my life as 2015 opened its doors to the world and as I dozed in the aftermath of our delicious act of copulation, the past continued to own my dreams.

All had indeed been quiet on that cold April morning in 1997, eight months after the appalling diagnosis of the terminal disease; and a week after my father had closed his eyes for the last time, seeing an iridescent light as he passed away. All was very quiet, as we as a family prepared for his funeral. I had last seen him ten days before he died. The logistics of life at home forced me to return to it, with the sad, certain knowledge that I would never see him again, in this world.

'I Believe I Can Fly' by R. Kelly played on the car radio as the young Mr. R. and I sped back to the base that my father had gifted to us, the greatest gift yet. My parents had disliked the locality that I lived in with their precious, new granddaughter and before the drugs and chemotherapy being used in a futile attempt to prevent the cancer doing its worse, whilst he still had his facilities my father had set about putting his affairs in order and making some final arrangements for his family, for their future without him. He had bought us a four-bedroomed, sprawling, detached split-level property. The first time I had viewed it I found the experience sickening, accepting the gift whilst my father clung onto life and feeling nothing but pure adulation for the man who had never stopped believing that I too could fly. It was a bitterly sweet moment.

As I explored the property, the Sun was setting over a panoramic view of the surrounding area from the back of the house. Like the Titanic it loomed majestically, an ocean liner of a place, its huge glass windows reflecting the beauty of the sunset. Ironically however like the Titanic, the house was going to be part of another sequence of events that would take me down in another spectacular fall. I spotted a lamp post in the back garden, that was duly switched on by the eager seller.

'Narnia.' I had murmured. Unaware that the monsters in the abyss that I had managed to escape from, were lurking in the dappled evening shadows. They hadn't finished with me yet. They had nearly had my soul once and their hunger for their pound of my flesh wasn't satisfied.

For the first few months after my father's death, I continued to travel back and forth, to stay with and support my lovely mother. My promise to him during that quiet afternoon when he had become bed-bound was fresh in my mind; and it was time to keep the vow. My first visit was for two weeks to help the grieving widow deal with the initial shock. Cuckoo was not even three, so no schooling was being compromised and she always accompanied me, strapped into the little car seat, safe in the back of my trusty, old banger. These visits gave me and lovely mother plenty of time to talk, conversations that led to more confidences now that the immediate stress of thinking only of her dying husband was alleviated a little and she spoke many times about events in her own younger life, which had never been voiced to me, until now.

I already knew that my maternal grandmother had died when my mother was a child aged ten, but the facts of that sad story were finally revealed; and a terrible childhood secret was out in the open. My grandmother had jumped off a high quay in a port, heavily pregnant. Some brave soul had jumped into the murky water after her, but neither she nor the unborn child had survived. My lovely mother had been raised by relatives, as a frightened, young girl. This was a most tragic story.

'Why didn't you tell me before?' I asked as I stroked her face.

'I could have helped you carry this burden Mum.'

'You mustn't tell your sister.' Her request was telling indeed, and I solemnly promised to keep the secret as she told me more stories, which would also never be repeated. We spoke of family history, heartbreak and happiness, during confidential chats that contained smiles and tears, history and hope, all randomly stirred with the spoon of circumstance. These verbal ingredients were reminiscent of the making of cakes that we had done together when I myself was young, our heads bent over the mix.

'Don't lick the bowl!' Mother would scold, half-teasing, offering me the spoon instead although my sneaky, surreptitious fingers would always take a naughty swipe when she wasn't looking. I realized many years later, that my life could be compared to slices of a cake, some parts inedible, the taste of ashes and shite, sticking like salt to a slug. Some portions bitter-sweet, doused with regret and eventually the final piece, the best bit, being saved for last. Melted, dark chocolate, sour cream, Morello cherries and succulent strawberries, topped with a drop of liqueur and a scoop of cold ice cream. A perfect recipe that I would create in the future, when I was to learn that I deserved the irresistible combination, but in April 1997 I simply learned to listen. The only thing I could do for my heart-broken, lovely mother; just listen, as the stories were repeated.

'Have I told you about the time...' And I would patiently listen again.

Relations were reasonably cordial with Cuckoo's father, but the many-times-shattered mosaic of our life together could only be stuck back so many times, until no matter how much cement was applied, the cracks in it could not be fixed without permanent damage. As always, our sex life was intermittent and as always, there was absolutely no meeting of our minds. There was just a mutual adoration for our girl, that was temporarily keeping us on the right tracks. The end of the Nineties limped on for us, as had the start of the decade. The only difference now was that we had our daughter, for whom our devotion was absolute. There were annual foreign holidays, courtesy of my mother, who simply wanted to try and keep her own daughters and their families united and as close to her as possible. Geographically we were all miles apart. Daughter Number Two up in the North, me in the South and lovely mother in the West, but this didn't stop her wishing that her daughters could develop a closer bond.

'I would love to have had a sister.' She had admitted sadly to me several times.

'How do you know you would have liked her?' My gentle answer was always the same.

That was the crux of the problem and why my mother's wish was never going to be granted. Daughter Number Two felt that she that had always lost out and began to resent me for that belief, which was so far removed from the truth. We had both treated with equal amounts of love and affection. Her issues continued to fester, she knew little about my tribulations, our parents had divulged hardly anything to her, but she had gleaned enough to decide that my actions had been unforgiveable.

She had never been able to walk in anybody else's shoes and apparently had stated categorically to our mother that she would have quite happily cut that well documented, hypothetical cord, should her own children have been so naughty. Luckily for them they were quite well behaved, there had been no dubious crossroads in life to tempt them down murky paths and certainly no ferry man to pay and they certainly wouldn't have dared to challenge her to a game of Monopoly. Even so, during those expensive Spanish holidays, truces were called, and the cousins played in the sun, where sandcastles and siestas were the order of many blissful days, whilst we adults maintained a degree of civility, lazing on sun loungers with a few beers.

I repeated the journey to see lovely mother many times, with Cuckoo strapped safely into her car seat and she sleepily watched out of the window, as I carefully drove us. Sometimes it was raining and maybe she too was counting the trickling drops that were running down the window, as I had as a child in the back of my father's car, until the lull of the road forced her own eyes to close, to fall into the arms of a sweet slumber wrapped in an accompanying blanket of a sense of safety. She would never have remembered those pilgrimages to see her grandmother nor the time we had driven further on, to scatter her grandfather's ashes in the Welsh countryside.

Sleeping soundly on during New Year's Day 2015, I had another dreamscape conversation.

'I wish my road had always been that easy, Daddy.'

'I know Catrin, but you made it, safely, in the end.'

Back at home during the 1990's, Cuckoo and I cared for several little animals together over the years. One Christmas morning a treasure hunt led her to a pet hamster in a cage.

'What are you going to call it?!' I asked her gleefully, watching the amazement in her wide, shining eyes as she stared at her first longed-for pet.

'Smudgy!' She had declared firmly. A short hamster life was to be had and a tiny grave was to be dug. The demise of Smudgy was followed by the introduction of several more furballs, a large, black lop-eared rabbit, which she named Barney and a rescue guinea pig called Ralphy, who was black and tan and squeaky. They lived happily if not messily together, until a rogue fox snatched them both with its jaws and Cuckoo and I shed tears over two more shallow graves.

I adored being her mother, having carried my baby, worrying and fretting for the unborn child, I now embraced my role. Any doubts or reservations pre-birth, had been wiped away by that first sight of my Cuckoo and I knew exactly what to do. It was my turn to make cakes with my daughter and tease her about bowl licking. When fancy dress costumes were required, I pulled out all the stops to make them perfect for her. Easters, Birthdays, Halloweens and Christmases, all marked the passing of the years of her life as she grew up, when I always ensured that her excitement was rewarded. It was at Christmas when the magic was especially potent and a heap of presents was successfully hidden away, until she finally fell asleep on Christmas Eve.

'He's been!' I could still hear her squeal of joy at five a.m; and remember watching indulgently as she scrabbled through the pile of wrapped packages and boxes, gifts that had been copied to a T from her carefully written letter to Santa. We pored over homework together and argued about her choice of fashion. We made packed lunches and tossed pancakes; and I regularly ferried her to her friend's houses for parties and Brownie meetings, tucking her into bed every night with a bedtime story or two, and a loving kiss.

My innate desire to drink and take a few drugs was now tempered by my responsibility for my daughter. I had been able to replace the temptation during my pregnancy, with broccoli and an absolute determination that I would put nothing into my bloodstream that might harm my baby, but despite the total fulfillment that my daughter gave me, the other areas of my personal life were as lacking as ever and the crutch provided by illegal highs was as necessary as it had ever been, as a substitute.

Whilst all the while the monsters were sleeping nearby, until the day that they were going to wake up, refreshed and ready to play a new game, curved ball.

This was the basis of the end of the 1990's, raising and nurturing our daughter, whilst indulging in our favourite vices at secret opportunities. Mr. R. and I had occasional weekends away in Brighton, (funny that), when Cuckoo was looked after by caring relatives. During these jaunts where we frequented gay night-clubs, it was strange that they were the only times when we seemed to be able to get along in harmony, laughing and joking with each other as if being able to allow his homosexuality to flourish, enabled him to be magnanimous towards me, but I was still so very lonely during those years. Watching other couples meandering around hand in hand, exchanging kisses, made me so jealous that it turned knives in my heart.

Inevitably I found physical comfort elsewhere, sexual frustration and that heart-breaking loneliness led to fleeting glances from others to turn into sordid sexual encounters. Male or female, I wasn't choosy where the welcoming caresses came from, but every time I was left emptier than before as my heart-broken soul cried out for help, it's sad lament only being heard by the monsters who were slowly waking up. Mr. R. inevitably got wind of my infidelities, which was just another nail in the coffin that was getting ready to act as the final resting place of our marriage.

New Year's Eve 2000 saw the millennium exploding in a sky that was lit up for hours at different times throughout the world. A torrent of psychedelic-colored ribbons of fire exploded into glistening handfuls of stellar confetti, as a new century was welcomed. A fresh nightmare was to swiftly follow my drunken appreciation of that night, when in January 2000 Cuckoo's Father was diagnosed with lung cancer, although apparently this was the right sort of lung cancer, if there could be such a thing. Not the splattered tumors of a cancer caused by smoking but a solid lump growing at the bottom of his left lung, that surgery should be able to remove completely. Keeping this from our daughter was impossibly difficult but a six-year-old child can be deceived; and the five-hour operation was successfully performed.

Mr. R. made a full recovery after my vigil at his bedside, when I had rejected the idea of God and discovered the Something instead; and the scar he was left with from shoulder to waist, was the only physical reminder of this episode. The scars to his mind however, although less visible were lethally damaging for our already broken relationship, as he started to follow his secret desires more freely. Having faced his own mortality he had finally found the courage to admit to himself the path that he really wanted to travel on. Not to me though, not yet, I had turned forty that year and we were starting to hate each other for our own reasons, still limping on, financially bound to each other, emotionally, poles apart.

This pathetic pattern continued for several more years, until one final incident, one last betrayal acted as the catalyst that I needed to come to one of the most important decisions of my life. During one of those weekends in Brighton in February 2006, when I was still happy to accompany him, jabbering away drunkenly to new-found gay friends whilst he played the flirting game in earnest. Suddenly he disappeared from the bar that we were drinking in, terrified that the always potential homophobic male had caught his eye, I spent all night searching for him. Bone-tired at seven in the morning I let myself into the pokey bedroom in the hotel that we had checked into the day before, to find him lying in the double bed with a guy I who vaguely recognized from the previous night. The unwelcome visitor was casually also smoking a cigarette. I ran, emotionally drained and completely exhausted, stumbling on, walking in a vacuum, surrounded by happy tourists in search of breakfast, when a BMW shrieked to a halt in front of me. It was the owner of the hotel, brandishing the checking in form that I had signed when we had arrived at the hotel.

'Can't you read!' He shouted at me.

'Fine for smoking in the bedrooms £200!' He read the wording aloud, angry saliva spitting out from his mouth. Marching me to a cashpoint he ordered me to withdraw the money and with shaking fingers I did so.

'It wasn't me though, I wasn't even there.'

'I don't give a shit.' He snatched the cash out of my hand.

I would never visit the place again and the memories of the nightmarish events took a long time to fade into an acceptable form. I knew the city well; at its best it was a draw for many visitors on many levels. Innocents who took trips to the famous pier with its bars and funfair, also strolled through the winding, pedestrianized streets of 'The Lanes', window shopping the shiny jewelry on display. They ate hot dogs and donuts that left salty and sugary crumbs on hungry lips, as they explored, peering with jaw dropped faces, into strange shopfronts where blatant transsexuals wearing high heeled shoes, tried to lure them in. Most of these tourists would turn in before midnight, to sleep log-like after their extraordinary experiences during their day, whilst the town stayed awake all night for those who wanted nocturnal fun, its bars and night clubs blasting out music until the morning.

I had however seen many times, the flipside of this. Visiting shady dives, where fucked clientele stumbled around incoherently. Using toilets, where I saw self-harmers blatantly gouging fresh wounds into their arms and watching children selling perfume, wearily wandering from pub to pub on cold nights, their heads wrapped in scarves to hide the wispy patches of hair caused by alopecia. They were homeless creatures of no fixed abode, girls my daughter's age who should be warm and safe somewhere else, not dossed down under a railway arch, prey to anyone passing. No, I would never go there again and that morning I swear I felt my heart break. The monsters had finally woken up, their first curved ball had met its target with as much demonic force as they could muster; and I had taken a direct hit.

'Is it over?' I had asked Mr. R. a few weeks later.

'I don't know, is that what you want?'

'I don't want this!'

'Stop being a cunt. then, a fat, lazy, useless cunt.'

'You bastard, if my father was alive, he would kill you for calling me those names, no more, it's over.'

As I slowly awoke in the late afternoon of New Year's Day 2015, I sleepily recalled my latest exchange with my father.

'He called me names Daddy, so many bad names.'

'You were never a bad person Catrin, just foolish.'

'Who called you names babe!!' The Big Man was leaning over me as I opened my eyes.

'It's nothing baby, just dreaming again.'

We spent the evening in peaceful silence, turning in at midnight, when more memories flooded my head.

A few weeks later, in March 2006, I put our house on the market, but selling it was going to prove to be a long-winded process, there was so much essential work needed and potential buyers were wary of the white elephant that they were viewing. I was at rock bottom and only the need to try and look after my bewildered twelve-year old Cuckoo, saw me through this period. I was forty-six, worn out, worn down and feeling as fat, ugly and useless as he had told me I was. I found a little house for sale and I could see it from the back windows of the one that I was desperate to leave. Nightly I would stare down at its roof, illuminated by a streetlight; and the view became my only bit of hope for a better future. My lovely mother was aware of this state of affairs; and kept her distance, whilst worrying constantly. A strange birthday card had arrived for me on 2nd May 2006, a picture of a boat at sea, sailing towards the Sun.

'Sail towards the light, the Sun will always be there,' was inked in her familiar handwriting. On my next birthday in May 2007, long after the dust had settled and I had found my oasis and the Big Man, a similar card had arrived at the new house. This time it showed a boat moored in a harbor, safe after its long journey, but for now I was paddling furiously towards the light as if my life depended on it.

The time leading up to the day of the move, once the Titanic had finally sold for a fair asking price, were relatively calm. Our accumulated possessions were divided amicably, all the fight had gone out of myself and Mr. R. and we were resigned to this final separation, but there were still small, heartbreaking moments that marked the final weeks. I watched my Cuckoo solemnly decide which of her collection of many cuddly toys had to be sacrificed, as there simply wasn't the room to pack them all and was that regret that I glimpsed on Mr. R.'s face as he too studied her. After all this and all that complete shite, did he have the gall to feel regret!

The morning of the move dawned, one last tear, one big breath and it was done. The lorry was loaded with my half of the contents and two minutes later it was being unloaded in the house down the hill, that for so many lonely nights I had stared at longingly. An estate agent was waiting for me with a cheery smile and a set of keys. It was done. The rather good-looking lead removal man eyed me up.

'You look different.' He remarked.

'It's called relief!' I replied. His equally ugly, skinny mate carried a small sofa into my new living room.

'There's your new shagging sofa, missus.' He cackled.

'You can't say that to a client!!' His partner looked apologetic.

'Yes, he can! and no it isn't! That's my new shagging sofa.' I had laughed in retort, pointing to the three-seater being gingerly lifted into place.

Those terrible months in 2006 had seen the weight drop off me. Stress had at least one silver-lining. I had my teeth fixed, replacing the front caps that I had fractured in a drunken tumble that I had taken during the long waiting game. I also had a new hair style, new clothes and after the final financial settlement from the sale of the house, I had a fair bit of money in the bank. I became a regular visitor to the local pubs, albeit briefly, thanks to that stellar intervention on Bonfire Night a few weeks later. Cuckoo's time had also been divided between her parents, allowing me some free time and I would prop up the bars, happy that she was with her father, confidently newly single and aware of the appreciative stares from male drinkers. Having been ground into the dirt with verbal abuse for far too long, I lapped it up, with no intention of ever taking up their unspoken offers until the night I met the Big Man. Mr. R. was apparently outraged by the fact his wanton and unwanted ex-wife had met someone else so quickly. Despite the fact that patently he had done everything to prize me out of his life, the process causing me more pain than having teeth extracted without anesthetic, he was beside himself with anger. A final volley of verbal abuse was launched at me down the phone.

'Cunt! Whore!'

'Ever call me that again and I will start telling the truth about you.' My answer was calm; and he never did repeat the insults, as gradually our relationship became amicable.

'Another of life's ironies, there's no such thing as never.'

Of course, it was generally assumed that I was the big bad wolf. My outrageous, drunken behaviour had ruined many social get-togethers and worse of all, I was a bitch who had cheated on her husband, but I kept my council and kept away from all aspects of my former life. The Big Man was all I needed and eventually, as my change of lifestyle proved to be permanent, the gossipmongers began to think that they could have been wrong.

He took me for lunch shortly after we had met; it was his choice of venue, a local pub. Nervously I tried to explain that locals might approach us. He laughed, not fazed at all by the possibility.

'How's Panda?' A half-cut regular asked as we walked in together.

'I don't know, haven't seen her for a while.' I retorted and locked eyes with my savior who winked straight back at me. That was the moment, the pivotal moment that the train crash my disaster of a life had been heading for, was finally prevented and the unravelling of the pandemonium had begun. I had finally beaten my monsters, whether it was my many desperate prayers to the Something over the years, or simply that they could sense the guardianship of my Big Man, this new keeper of my soul. Whatever the reason, they seemed to have finally accept defeated as I worshipped at his altar and could feel for the first time since the trickling raindrops that had lulled me to sleep in the back of my father's car, the most delicious sense of safety and belonging.

Chapter Eleven

Dreams and Nightmares

The first newspapers of 2015 were full of the stories of fireworks around the globe; and there were more accounts of other unfortunate events that had happened during the massive world-wide celebrations. Five young men had now died, taking pills laced with something called PMA. It stood for para-Methoxyamphetamine, a design drug with serotonergic effects, whatever that meant, who knew or cared, the active ingredient was still able to kill the person who opted to swallow the damned stuff. A picture of the deadly tablets stamped with a 'Superman' logo was published, as apparently thousands had been produced and were in active circulation.

'Have you seen the news?' I asked Cuckoo when I finally managed to contact her.

'About those Superman pills? It's ok Ma, we only took MDNA.' There really wasn't an answer to the matter-of-fact comment, not one that I could easily find.

After a few days at home, where Cuckoo recovered from her latest druggy, piggy binge celebrating the New Year; and with her physical and mental mojos restored, she went back to London, where the last term of her university course would start the following week.

'Stay safe x.' I texted her.

'Always do Ma x.'

'Really, little girl?' I spoke that thought in my head only, before I sent a reply, the new term of endearment for my messy daughter suddenly feeling very appropriate.

'Love you little piggy x'

'Love you too Ma x'

Another visit to the hospital was due and I was feeling really miffed with my own physical and mental mojos, they too needed some serious restorations as well. The weight that was thickening my middle had continued to spread and my hair was lank; and sprouting grey fiercely from the crown of my head. Where was that sexy, sultry bitch now? On examination, the weeks of dressing and redressing had still not been effective enough and the gash in my leg seemed to smile at us from the consulting room bed.

'Looks like a.........!' The Big Man had chortled as I stopped him in his tracks, knowing what he was going to say.

'You're not funny!' I scowled, secretly agreeing with the unspoken analogy that he was about to make, as indeed it did look like a scabby fanny. I had been quite proud of my legs, not so much the rest of my body as I had grown older; and our trips to my lovely mother's always began with the same question from her.

'I hope you don't mind me saying...' Was always the cue for my dutiful Daughter Number One's eyes to roll for the umpteenth time.

'Go on.' Gritting my teeth, I would wait for her latest observation.

'You're getting stout.'

Middle-age-spread syndrome was commonly attributed to over fifty-year-old women, who either remained impossibly skinny or got stout. I was firmly in the latter category and sideways glances into mirrors would reconfirm this sad case of stoutness. I was stouter than ever now, with my ever-expanding, self-amassed wine belt of middle age. New Year's blues had set in for me big time;

and more depressing thoughts crossed my mind. The presence of cancer in my life for example, which probably didn't stack up the odds for my long-term future too well, as it had waved its nasty wand at all my immediate family. Even the sister, Daughter Number Two, had taken a bullet from it. Bloody marvelous and now one of my legs was going to have a beauty of a scar when it finally healed, I was really feeling sorry for myself now.

Scars were something I should be used to, my gall bladder and appendix had both been removed along the way. Having Cuckoo had left me the caesarean scar and I had a war wound from a broken nose caused by a drunken fall, and evidence of other sundry mishaps. These marks luckily only revealed themselves when I was tanned, as scar tissue has no melanin, still, the list went on and now I had a five-inch slash in my left leg, bloody marvelous indeed! I was however also very aware, that had I fallen face first the night of that freakish accident, it would have been my cheek and possibly an eye that could have been ripped off, so everything considered, a maimed left leg was a lucky escape. That evening the Big Man carefully redressed the injury with the three types of medicated dressings, a roll of special wool and crepe bandage, finishing off his handiwork with plasters and safety pins. I watched him as he concentrated on his task, thinking about another procedure that he enjoyed indulging in.

He regularly shaved me intimately and the experience was a complete turn on. I would lie back as instructed, my legs wide open, watching him again, glasses perched on his face as he razored away with the electric shaver that he had purchased for this very purpose. His thumb, lingering on my clitoris would make me squirm with desire, knowing what would happen once he had removed all my pubic hair, leaving me bristle-free, smooth and fuckable from any angle. It was the most personal and sensual experience that I had ever known. Dripping wet, I would wait in anticipation for him to bury his face between my legs, lap up the juices and drive me to countless orgasms, laughing as I writhed under him. His cum-covered tongue was then dipped into my open mouth and, playing with my own nipples that were hot and erect, I orgasmed again. He replaced his tongue with his cock, ramming it in and out of my soaking wet core, watching as it was swallowed up. This mindless fucking would go on and on, but we would be aware of nothing but the intense pleasure of the moment. Heart's racing, until one last magnificent orgasm engulfed us both and we eventually pulled ourselves apart, laughing and in awe of the power of our coupling.

We still had plenty of time together at home during the first week of January 2015. The yard that the Big Man worked out of was locked down for a few more days, snarling guard dogs prowled around it day and night, so God help any scallywags who were tempted to break in, attracted by the expensive armory of trucks and machinery. The weather outside was cold and bleak, but it was warm and cozy inside, as we cotched up together in the evenings for nightly movie fests. 'Night at the Museum' was showing, where all the exhibits had come alive, we had once visited the real Natural History Museum during a rare trip to London, when visiting Cuckoo. The stuffed and sightless relics made me wonder if they did really come alive at night once the doors were locked. It was a fascinating place, with dinosaurs moving and roaring realistically. Many types of insect and snakes were on display and then there was a hall of dazzling gemstones, hewn from the earth. It was a place to which we vowed to return. We later watched 'War Horse' the film. We had seen the London theatre version and the story had reduced me to tears, as I fell in love with the puppet horses. 'Joey' and 'Topthorn' were made magically real by the skilled performance of the puppeteers. The evening was relaxed, as was I when we climbed the stairs to bed; and memories of my relationship with the Big Man crept quietly into my dreams.

It hadn't been a complete bed of roses at the beginning. In between the euphoria of the first flushes of our new-found passion, doubt and suspicion had crept into my head. Unable to believe this amazing man was as genuine as he seemed, I was terrified at the way I was falling for him.

'You're not welcome here!' I had screamed at him during a drunken night shortly after meeting him and then apparently, I had punched him in the face. The next morning with no recall of any of this, I looked at his bruised, swollen mouth with disbelief.

'Oh, baby I'm so sorry!' I hadn't been attacking him; it was the ghosts of the past which were still haunting me. The monsters might be impotent against his powers, but they had still left hideous scars on my mind, marks that would take a long time to be erased. Somehow, he understood and forgave me, nodding his head sadly. During another evening when I was home with my Cuckoo, who was far too young to leave on her own, he had rung me from the local pub. There was laughter and noise in the background; clearly, he was having a good time without me and I had slammed the phone down in temper. An hour later there was a frantic tapping at the front door, he had staggered back to be with me, muddied jeans and a cut to his face proving that he had taken a couple of tumbles along the way.

'Can I come in babe?' He stood there head down and bashful, as I gave 'vampire permission' and I started to learn to trust him with all my heart and soul. A few months after that first chance meeting at the firework party, he gave up the room he was renting and moved in.

'What if I'm making another mistake, babe?'

'What do you have to lose baby?' I replied, knowing that there was so very much to be mutually gained. He had nothing, no passport, no old photos, only his much loved and prized medals and an old banger of a car. Nothing but pride and sensitivity and so much love to give me. I had it all on the face of it, my house and possessions, but I had no one to hold and to be held by. I had never had anyone to make me feel this adored and safe. I hadn't felt safety like this for a long time. This was a kind stir by that spoon of circumstance, the mix so overdue for both of us was simply perfect, having both come out of destructive relationships the previous summer, leaving our old lives firmly behind.

'Why did you stay?' I once asked him, but I already knew the answer, having lived it myself.

For such a highly sexed man I was impressed and touched that he had been celibate during the months that he had been on his own. Any woman he had encountered would have fallen for his charms, not that it mattered if he had dallied before we'd met. We were together now, that was all that counted. He had had offers of course.

'How come you didn't want them?' I asked him curiously.

'Guess I'm just choosy babe.' He answered my question with a small smile playing around his mouth.

'Wow, I'll take that as a compliment then!'

Time passed and the trust continued to grow; and after hearing his own stories of the horrific highlights during the turbulent nine years that he had spent in that previous relationship; I completely understood his fears of getting it wrong this time.

In mid-January 2015 I found my-self staring again out of the kitchen window. It was so cold, so bitterly cold and I tried not to think about the occupant of the small grave at the bottom of the garden. As I continued to gaze thoughtfully, a robin was looking back at me from a bird table. The back garden was an oasis for wildlife, my Big Man the gatherer had planted trees and bushes, and positioned strange objects randomly, metal orbs, pottery urns and an oversized wooden mushroom. His pride and joy; was a gigantic tropical plant that he had planted from a cutting, a 'Gunnera', native to the Amazon, that he had named 'Gruber'. It was hibernating now; the roots had been lovingly covered with hay and tucked in for the winter. Come the spring, it would wake up and produce tentacles of growth that would morph into huge leaves. At its peak it would be fifteen feet across and ten high, taking over the whole of the garden, thriving on the water that he pumped religiously into the roots. The scene was in total contrast to the other patches of garden on the housing estate, not a neat lawn and patio, instead it was a sensory riot.

I smiled to myself remembering years past, when as 'twitchers' in our own hide, watching from the kitchen window during springs and summers, the Big Man and I had regularly seen blackbirds, magpies and robins. Then there were the jays, finches and pigeons, squirrels and tiny mice, who together with the odd, long-tailed, pointy-nosed rat, all played out their parts in the obvious pecking order in this unique organic micro world. The pigeons after landing, were awkwardly cumbersome on the ground, their necks portraying the 'Egyptian Walk'. Magpies, the predators, were busily snapping their beaks, intent on stealing eggs from other bird's nests, sailing down arrogantly to do so. Blackbird versus robin, the constant cat and mouse chase was hilarious to see as the fat robin red breast, its chest puffed up against the cold in the winter, winged down to pick up a tasty morsel from the laden bird tables, the blackbird would be waiting beady eyed, to scold it away. But soon the cuckoo would invade, to lay its eggs in blackbird's nest, giving it more to worry about than chasing little robins.

I suddenly thought about the theory that a robin might represent a reincarnated person, or an animal and I wondered if it could possibly be that the tiny bird staring at me unblinkingly, had once been a rabbit, or even my father. Contemplating the still freshly dug grave, marked with a plastic daisy and a pottery bunny, I remembered the awful night when a fox had murdered our big, black, lop-eared Barney bunny; and his squeaky, poo scattering guinea piggy companion. Were they too now part of the merry robin population who graced our crazy back garden? I had woken up with a jolt in the early hours after the night that they had been taken. I had been dreaming that Barney bunny had appeared from water, his fur slicked back, like a seal. I analyzed the dream later, to find out that it meant that the subject was in trouble. Decapitation by a fox surely was in the trouble category. I dreamt a lot even then, and a recurrent dream of mine had literally been of poo, proper poo. Shit, shit everywhere, overflowing from toilets and drains. I had read that this meant that that the dreamers mind was trying to expel mental baggage. Whether that applied in my case or whether it was a flash back to the Greek island of 1986, that dream had stopped when I met the Big Man, and this fact was not at all lost on me.

My mind wandered on as I gazed into our garden and I cast my thoughts back to the terrible August Bank holiday telephone call from lovely mother, three years previously.

'We have a problem.' She had told me, confessing the diagnosis of her breast cancer.

'Why haven't you told me you were having tests!' Not for the first time I scolded her, yet once again I knew the answer to my own question. I too would have protected my own daughter from such a vile truth, until totally necessary.

Shortly after that bombshell, I'd had another dream, I was talking to my father at my old house, the house he had never visited. The railings of the massive, raised decking were festooned with garlands of flowers.

'Money doesn't matter Catrin.' He'd said, as clear as day.

'It's your health that counts.' He had continued. My father's dreamscape words were never forgotten either and the sight of a cheeky robin would always evoke in me a sense of reincarnation and even more sorrow.

'I think money does matter a little bit Daddy.' I muttered, still staring out of the window, my mind firmly back in the cold January present.

'It doesn't necessarily bring happiness with it, Catrin.'

I suddenly realised that I was talking with my father again, but this time I wasn't asleep.

'Are you really here, I'm not dreaming?!'

'Yes Catrin, I am.'

The front door banged closed as the Big Man walked in after finishing work early and the sweet dialogue between me and the man who I had been desperate to communicate with, abruptly stopped.

'You ok babe?!'

'What time is it baby, you're early!!'

'Not much work today, too cold, how long have you been standing there, you look like you've seen a ghost, sure you're ok!!'

'I don't know, he was here though, I was talking to him for a split second, not in a dream!! Really talking to him!'

I didn't know how long I'd been staring out of the window, It must have been for been a few hours, my waking mind dipping and diving between the flashbacks of my dreams. As I slept that night these were accompanied by memories of Cuckoo's behaviour, that swirled around my head as the story that I had longed to write continued to form in my mind.

She was deeply unhappy, back in the day.

'Do you think it's because you and her father have split up?' My lovely mother asked the question during one of our regular telephone conversations.

'Well of course that's a lot to do with it, but she won't understand why I had leave him, not for a long time, one day she will.'

'Maybe it's because you met someone else so quickly?'

'That couldn't be helped Mother.' My tone of voice turned unusually cold towards her as I answered the question.

My daughter had started playing truant from school, drinking, smoking and mixing with the wrong characters and what should have been a blissful, few years were anything but. As I tried to control the little beast, things became more and more impossible to deal with. I was starting to dread the sympathetic grimaces I received from the other parents of sensible pupils, as they picked up their offspring on the daily school run and I was waiting for yet another appointment with the headmaster, to discuss Cuckoos unruly attitude. The Big Man stood by my side unfalteringly during these months of turbulence, solidly supporting me as I tried and failed, to rein her in.

On New Year's Eve 2008 we had decided to go to a gala dinner at a local hotel, planning to stay the night there. We had locked the house down with precision, knowing how Cuckoo's mind worked and terrified of giving her an opportunity for access to a free house. Dropping her at a friend's house for a sleepover, we headed off for our much-needed night away. The next morning Armageddon was waiting for us at home. Despite all our precautions Cuckoo had managed to get back into the house, having slyly undone a top window in the living room so a skinny friend could wriggle through it. God knows how many New Year's Eve rug rats had descended on the place and we gazed at the devastation, appalled and sickened by what we were seeing. Dead tropical fish were floating in the Big Man's much-loved tank, there were broken glasses everywhere and ketchup and fizzy drinks had been sprayed wildly over the ceilings. The list went on, as we investigated further.

We turned slowly to look at the four remaining and very unwelcome house guests sitting around the kitchen table. Cuckoo was slowly rocking, the physical effects of whatever drugs she had taken the night before were blatantly visible in her pinched, grey face; and for a horrifying split second, I swore that I saw an embryo monster grinning at me from within her eyes. I could taste fear in my mouth as the thought that the grunts had somehow managed to shapeshift into the mind of my precious daughter, passed violently through my own. The rest of the day passed in a haze, after I chased the unwanted guests from the house.

'Get here NOW!!' I rang Cuckoo's father with the order. Of course, it could have been a lot worse, I had heard of such events where windows got smashed and furniture ended up in the garden, even so this was too much to stomach and the used condoms that I found in our bed made me feel physically sick.

'It wasn't supposed to be like that!' She had sobbed as I held her later; but finding a childishly handwritten check list turned the knife in me with physical pain as I read it.

'Get booze and fags. Hide Mum's jewelry. Cover anything that might get broken.'

Several times after the episode was put behind us, I would tell my Cuckoo that I loved her but hated her for what she had done, repeating the sentiment once spoken by my own mother, history sadly repeating itself. We tried to carry on as calmly as possible, praying the girl would turn a corner. I was increasingly starting to understand my own parents' past anguish; and the sage comment about never cutting the umbilical cord was always in the back of my mind. One way or another we managed to help Cuckoo acquire enough grades to get into a local college to study fashion and design. But understanding that she hadn't done nearly enough, she broke down and cried in my arms again.

'I didn't do well enough.'

'You can fly economy, or you can fly first class, but you're still going to get there darling.' Her face told me she understood what I was saying, and it was one of the first times that Cuckoo would appreciate that her mother could actually talk sense, whilst I tried to forget about the thousand pounds that we had spent on private tuition. This was becoming a miserable and depressing time, had my own monsters not quite given up in their desire to inflict more pain, on the woman who the girl who had dared peek into the darkness had become?

It would soon seem that my innermost fears were true, as she attempted an overdose a few months later in the late spring of 2009. We had had a physical fight as I had desperately tried to get her into my car for school. I dashed her to A & E; and we were sent straight into the children's department where I was subjected to countless questions by a po-faced, snotty, young social worker. She pointed to the notes she had made about a bruise on Cuckoo's arm where I had slapped her, suggesting that I might have violent tendencies towards my daughter. This newly trained professional explained that it was her job to make sure that it was safe for the child to go home. Barely controlling my fury, I managed to stay silent, knowing that this was dangerous territory. I rang Cuckoo's father, who came straight away.

'Nice tattoo, what does it mean?' He had remarked, admiring the new inking on my back.

'It's my guardian angel, love. She's not doing a very good job.' I replied, as we waited to see the doctor before the girl could be discharged and a horribly familiar thought crossed my mind.

'Oh please, beware the wolf in sheep's clothing, my lovely little girl.'

My guardian angel was also going to be powerless against the next event that was going to happen that summer. The most horrific event yet for my Cuckoo took place just as we were starting to see the light; and when maybe, just maybe, we were turning a corner. She was going to be fifteen that August of 2009 and she had been invited to go to an upmarket holiday camp for a week, with some of her father's family members. Glad of the respite I waved her off merrily, looking forward to some peace and quiet. Four days later I took a nine-a.m. call from an unknown male, a surgeon asking for permission to operate on my daughter. There had been an incident and Cuckoo's eye had been injured. Horror pounded through my mind, as I screamed down the phone at the unseen consultant.

'You have to be fucking joking, who is this!! It has to be a mistake!'

It was no mistake; and he allowed me to calm down before he explained further. I rang my Big Man and Mr. R., but they could hardly recognize my voice and within an hour, which seemed more like a lifetime, we were on our way to a hospital that was a good two-hours' drive away. The Big Man drove, he was outwardly solidly calm and determined to get us there as soon as possible. It transpired that Cuckoo had found an unwelcome admirer who had been stalking her relentlessly. When she finally rebuffed him with a few choice words, he had picked up the nearest thing he could find to throw at her in a temper. Naturally, it had to be a piece of flint, shaped like a medieval spearhead and of course he had to have a particularly good aim; and the sharp stone had sliced through her left eye. She had struggled back to the holiday accommodation and was rushed to the nearest hospital, where emergency surgery was prepared for after the necessary call to her next of kin. Me. All this became horribly clear during the hours that followed our mercy dash to her side.

The poor adult in that camping party had stood vigil all night beside her bed. He explained that he had decided it was safer not to ring me until it was light, as he raised tired eyes to mine when I burst into the ward, guilt racking his face.

'It's not your fault!' I cried as I looked around frantically for my daughter and there she was, pale and fragile, with a patch over the injured eye, slowly opening the other one.

'Ma, you came.' Her faint, little words broke my heart as I held her hand.

'We would have walked darling.' The Big Man held mine, kissing her cheek softly whilst Mr. R., watching with anguish, waited for his turn to gently hug his daughter. It was explained that twenty invisible stitches had repaired a split in Cuckoo's cornea and saved her eye. That night, we three exhausted adults found a local hotel, happy to leave the girl in the hands of the medics, having stayed with her until the unpatched eye closed tightly and she fell into the deepest of sleeps. We hardly slept ourselves, all too scared as to what we would find underneath the dressing the next day. Back at the hospital, first thing the next morning, we held our breath as the surgeon re-entered the room to gently remove the dressing and reveal his handiwork. Exhaling in unison and with acute relief, we saw the amazing extent of his ability.

'Thank you.' My heartfelt words seemed shamefully inadequate.

'Can we take her home?' We found a wheelchair and Cuckoo, wearing an oversized hospital dressing gown and huge sunglasses, was taken to the car.

'She looks like 'Amy' coming out of re-hab.!' I nudged the Big Man, pointing at her black-dyed locks tumbling around her shoulders. The return journey was much more sedate, as mindful of every bump in the road we all had time to mull over what had happened. The police were brilliant, the CPS took the case forward to prepare for prosecution, but for us there was only the painful task of starting Cuckoo's recovery program. Completely traumatized, the need for a sequence of various medicinal eye drops, several times a day, made her rage at me.

'I don't like it! It stings!!' She ranted, but shaky-handed I successfully administered them; and the healing process slowly commenced, until the time came to have the stiches removed at an eye clinic.

'Brave girl!' The expert had murmured as he skillfully took them out one by one. We were offered cosmetic surgery to reshape the pupil, which was now shaped like a cat's eye, Cuckoo deliberated this and refused.

'I like my eye as it is.' Pure relief passed through my mind at her decision and as she recovered, because her eyes were naturally dark, the damage wasn't obvious. I knew though and every-time

I looked at her, the knowledge of its existence tore at my heart strings. Surely, we deserved to turn a corner soon and find a straight road ahead. We approached another Christmas together, with trepidation. Only our wedding; planned for the following February 2010, was giving us a tiny light at the end of this hideously black tunnel.

Chapter Twelve

Debating Drugs and Other Nonsense

Yes, January 2015 was particularly cold. The Big Man was working hard again, thundering around the countryside in his truck, with its elevated cab and wheels higher than me, that clung to the early morning, icy roads like a limpet. We had had other cold Januarys, when thick snow on the roads had made it impossible for my car to deal with the adverse weather conditions, slipping and sliding as I struggled to control it in panic. This time however, I didn't have to face those fears, as I was still at home playing the long game, waiting for my leg to heal. He came home one evening to greet me with a few delighted words.

'Babe, I think it's gonna snow tonight!' It didn't snow that night or the next, but the wind whipped the artifacts in the back garden into a destructive frenzy, as everything was flung around or toppled over. Gruber slept on obliviously, hibernating in its bed of hay, but everything else was upside down and the Beloved Pooch whose hearing was as keen as mustard, kept me awake for hours, shivering and frightened by the alien noises, forerunners of a potential storm.

Our last evening with Cuckoo before she went back to London life, was shortly after her New Year's Eve's festivities. She had appeared with mascara smudging her piggy cheeks, reciting proudly the list of drugs that she had managed to score. We held our tongues, there was no point in remonstrating; but I was still deeply concerned. She; and her friends so reminded me of myself at their age, before my descent into the abyss and the memories made me recoil as that horrible thought crossed my mind again.

NO EXAGGERATION

'Oh please, please, little piggy's, please beware of the big bad wolf who will always be   there, forever accompanied by the cunty grunts, snuffling at the outskirts of your lives.'

We packed Cuckoo back off to the London flat she was renting in Greenwich during her final term at uni. The landlord had sent me a stern email over Christmas, complaining about the dirty, shoddy habits of the girls who were ruining his property. There was no sympathy for Cuckoo from myself or the Big Man as we viewed the photographs that had been attached to his message. A curtain could be seen hanging off its rail and there were pictures of overflowing ashtray, which also named and shamed the students, but Cuckoo just poo pooed his attitude.

'You have to take this seriously, it's his flat; you revoltingly messy creature!' Driving her to the station, I let rip with annoyance.

'Calm down Ma!' Was her only retort, before she boarded the train.

'God, you really are a little pig!!' I spoke the words aloud and they drifted off in the dank, dark evening air, as I waved goodbye.

'Home safe! x' Her text came through a few hours later and I felt my usual relief on receiving the message.

'Make sure you sort it out, I love you piglet x' I texted in reply.

I knew that I was drinking too much during my long-haul holiday at home, that January in 2015 and the words of long forgotten songs were often reducing me to hiccupping tears. Any good lyrics set to the right music, had the ability to reduce my mood into one of raw emotion. Many events in my life were marked by songs that still had the power to move me and the collection of bits of poetry that I had scribbled down over the years were a tiny tribute to my understanding of the power of the written word. Smoking the odd joint with my Big Man these days was my only druggy vice, apparent from too much red wine and far too many cigarettes, maybe fifteen a day, a nod to the fact that a proven chemical reaction exists between nicotine and alcohol, making you want to smoke more.

The Big Man could sink vodka like the trooper that he was and roll a few more spliffs for himself as an evening went on, with no obvious detriment to his own behaviour. The first was always enjoyed in the bath, washing away the crap of the day and relaxing his mind. I was a lightweight in comparison and he was well aware of it, knowing exactly when I was about to tip over the edge, though I would always strenuously deny it as I sucked on the roach so hard that it popped out of the end of the joint.

'Sorry.' I would splutter.

'Take it easy babe.' He would gently remonstrate, tolerant of my inability to pace myself, whilst I felt so safe with him even in my muddled mindset, always so safe under his wing. Sometimes if it was blowing a gale, we would venture out of the house into the dark and enjoy a slow amble around the block, walking the Beloved Pooch, sharing a spliff, cupping it in our hands to avoid it blowing away. He had never let me fall; no matter how wrecked I was, he steadied me.

Laugh! Stoned laughter was the best, watching Saturday night television and cracking up over silly things, everything was so ridiculously hilarious at times like that. Yeah, stoned was nice, as eyes slightly glazed over, and everything took on another perspective. Not too different, a little muzzy here and a little sharper there, a potent companion to the effect of the wine. However, after a glass too many or a lug too strong, there was the danger of a sudden 'whiteout', with very messy consequences as nausea took over. Later, there would be the midnight munchies and a frantic wave of an insatiable desire to eat anything that came to hand. Scrabbling through the fridge in the darkened kitchen, I would be on my knees, greedily devouring its contents and feeding the eager Beloved Pooch with my fingers, sharing every morsel. Waking up groggily the next day, I would stare at myself in the mirror as the telltale remnants of the illicit feast that were stuck around my mouth, named and shamed my secret, nocturnal activities, the excess calories sticking to and thickening my waist, stoutening it even further. This certainly wasn't an appetite suppressor.

Sulfate had been so easy to get addicted to, as every mental and physical edge was sharpened and everything and everybody, became acutely fascinating. Watching paint dry would have become interesting, as I waited feverishly for the moment that the drug would hit my bloodstream, impatiently counting the seconds until I felt the desired effect of taking the revolting powder. It was often in the form of a 'bomb', a generous amount of speed wrapped in half a cigarette paper, swallowed with a gulp of liquid that would direct it into my stomach. Sometimes I snorted the dirty drug, shaking my head in disgust as the pain in my nostrils masked its stinging, eye-watering passage, straight into my blood stream. Either way, the result was always the same, a familiar rush as the speed took control and I felt and looked more perfect than ever.

My skin developed an inner glow and my eyes brightened to a duck egg white, the pupils enlarging into pools of melting, dark chocolate. I would feel invincible, extremely attractive and not the least bit hungry. Taking a bite of anything would now feel like chewing a piece of carpet. My gullet, however, would open wide, thirsty for gallons of cold alcohol. The effects of this cocktail could be maintained for hours, no wonder it was called speed, the whole experience while it lasted, speeded up everything. Running at one hundred miles an hour, body and mind galloping together in a human 'Grand National'. You couldn't get drunk, alcohol just blunted the edges of the sharp, serrated state of being.

I had tried to explain this to Cuckoo so many times. The obvious pitfalls of taking drugs cut with even more toxins and the perils of killer pills, were spelt out to my daughter but there was also the other risk. Drugs could give you so much of a better time if in the mood for partying, providing a much better buzz than simply drinking. Trying to socialize without the added fix would leave you craving the additional high, hence the danger. Desiring fast drugs for a guaranteed good night could lead to a slide into reliance, that could quite easily turn into dependency and possibly addiction. Cuckoo continued to make light of my fears and advice, whilst I kept remembering my own youth and continued to worry.

A few days' recovery would restore my body after such dabbling, my appetite still curbed, as sleep finally took over. Hopping onto the scales, elated, I discovered that I had lost a few more pounds. This cycle had started for me at Cuckoo's age, euphoric highs followed by evil comedowns. Smoking weed and getting drunk would leave you 'hanging' admittedly. Headachy, thirsty, bloodshot eyed and groggy, but this could be slept off in a few more hours to make you able to face the world again, fresher-faced and cobweb-free. Coming down from regular speeding was dragged out and sleepless, hitting a flat bottom you would stay there for hours and when the eyes eventually closed, it could take days to resurface to normality. The crystal- clear, wide-eyed look of a speeder was replaced by the dead, dull eyes of a shark. It was always in the eyes, those windows to the soul and I would always know forever after, exactly what someone had partaken of, simply by studying their faces.

I'd never particularly taken to cocaine. Speed was the poor man's alternative, at ten pounds per wrap versus sixty for coke. Speed was harsher whilst cocaine was too subtle for me. The effects of the latter were similar; but they were more diluted and certainly more expensive. Lines of coke would have to be snorted much more often, to achieve the same effect as a speed bomb. Ecstasy was another matter, swallow the pill and prepare for take-off if you were lucky, as duds were common. and it was always a lottery. Even lucky pills could involve severe vomiting, preceding the slow, mind-warping buzz that stretched its flapping wings, transporting you to a mental state of strange, elated ambience. It was not a drug to be taken if wanting to stay at home, as going out became compulsory. It caused toe-tapping body movements; you were as lithe as a panther on the run; limbs moving in pure harmony with each other. You saw smiling faces everywhere, during hours of dancing and gyrating, with no desire for alcohol. It was a complete love drug, total strangers would become best friends, speech was hard, but unnecessary and probably impossible above the thumping musical beats of whatever nightclub you had stumbled into. It was no small coincidence this was called ecstasy. It was a shame about the telltale movements of the mouth, this gurning was as involuntary as the rest of the drug's effects.

Acid had the same mind-bending power, but that similarity ended there for me. Paranoia would swamp my thoughts with a flick of the LSD's whirring, buzzy wings and avoiding people became essential as the inevitably unwelcome hallucinations started. Face distorting, jingly, jangly, jumpy sensations, that took complete control. Unlike its sister drugs, the end of an acid trip came with sobbing relief. I couldn't speak for heroin, despite the deadly offer in the bender camp of the Eighties, but I had watched as it was smoked and injected, seeing some sort of moronic trance-like state overcome the user. I never saw the point of this and was never tempted, but what a despicable thing to be proud of, never having chased the dragon. It was as if I was discussing pizza toppings, smack, coke and Billy, with a side order of acid marinated weed and I was more than happy that red wine with a spliff on the side was without a doubt, my chosen chemical takeaway these days.

I knew little about the menu available to Cuckoo's generation. M-CAT, otherwise known as 'Mandy'; and Ketamine, both having the addition of horse tranquillizers or plant fertilizers as active ingredients. Nor would I ever want to understand why the survivors of my own generation who been involved in the black market of illegal substances, were still craving such satanical highs. One thing I did know was that no matter how Cuckoo would remonstrate that her mother didn't know what she was talking about, this subject had been studied to the highest level by me and I was at a university degree level of education, in the subject of drug taking and its consequences.

Sleep evaded me again, for much of the night of the storm in mid-January 2015, as the Beloved Pooch refused to settle and I was still wide awake at dawn, talking to my father.

'That was a terrible confession, Daddy!'

'Told you drugs would find you, Catrin.'

When I finally managed to drop off, I was taken back to 2009 and the events after Cuckoo's terrible incident with her eye. Autumn had arrived and she was healing well. By some miracle, the horrible experience had slightly curbed her behaviour and the idea of getting her a puppy seemed logical to us. It was something to be responsible for, something to love and be loved by, and something that could soften the heart strings of this teenager. She had caused so much strife by her own actions, which had been caused in turn by her own pain. It was something to take her mind off the trauma of the summer and sadly, the hopping presence of cuddly Daisy bunny just didn't cut it. I had a friend at work who knew of a two-year-old black Patterdale Terrier that needed rehousing. He came with a wicker basket and a complete lack of having been taught the essential socialization skills for a dog to able to integrate happily with humans. The scared animal had been mistreated, although not physically and a shiny coat plus the obligatory wet nose, also accompanied him when he arrived one Saturday morning.

Mentally scarred, it bit the Big Man that evening and by midweek had created havoc with his growling, snarling traits, whilst Cuckoo was firmly on the little devil's hate list and a chance nip out of her outstretched hand was the last straw. Maybe it had been children who had teased it, but regardless he had to be banished to whence he had come, leaving her more devastated than before. There was a happy ending for the dog, as he was given another home by a childless couple and there was also a happy ending for Cuckoo, as her stepfather-to-be got wind of a litter of pedigree Jack Russell Terrier puppies. Much as I would have liked to give another unwanted doggy a new home that December, it was my daughter who personally made her choice from the bundle of six squirming pups. Ten days before Christmas 2009, she wrapped her new companion in a blanket and we brought the fur baby back to the house, to become the latest member of our family.

The court case for the attack on Cuckoo dragged on over that winter. In April 2010 she was instructed to appear to give video evidence in a courthouse in the same town as the hospital in which she had been treated. We waited, as a very brave Cuckoo was examined and cross-examined by a series of lawyers. The boy was found guilty of course and he was sentenced to the crime of GBH, an intent clause having been removed. I was quite happy with the decision, he had thrown something deadly for sure, but I doubted whether he had really intended that the action was to deliberately maim. Three thousand pounds of compensation was awarded, to be paid on her eighteenth Birthday, over two years away and with a lot of support over the next two months, she managed to achieve enough 'EasyJet air miles' to board her flight to the college of her choice to study fashion and textiles. It was a time of great relief, adoring the Beloved Pooch, loving my Cuckoo and worshipping my Big Man, whilst temporarily, peace was reigning in our lives.

The Big Man had told me stories of his past family life and they were poignantly lonely tales in my eyes. No perfect childhood for this little boy and there had certainly been no feelings of safety associated with raindrops. His father had abandoned the family long before the Big Man was old enough to remember him, but tragically he did remember the violence he suffered at the hands of a wicked stepfather and the fact that his mother had turned a blind eye to the abuse. There was an older sister, who had escaped when she was sixteen. Two years later when he reached the same age, he left the place he knew as home, marching straight to an army headquarters and just as I had, didn't look back.

He told me about his first wife who he had met in Germany, explaining that the marriage had eventually disintegrated. I reflected that in all honesty the life of an army wife must be so hard, there would be so much enforced absence and an inability to really understand the tribulations that their men had to face. Only the most rock solid of relationships could have survived, he had been so young and while I was bouncing off the walls to 'Band Aid' in 1984, he was soldiering, whilst trying to maintain a family lifestyle. This was a most complicated story; how could he have been expected to deal with the responsibility for the children that came along, when he had no such grounding himself. I tried to understand why it had been easier to leave them for the arms of a new lover, rather than struggle with such alien emotions, whilst regularly accusing him that he would leave me too.

Despite this tiny misgiving, when we made the vows at our wedding ceremony on 13th. February 2010, I held his hand and gazed into those serious, blue, sexy eyes, which were looking right back into mine, finally trusting him completely.

'I think I could love you.' He had commented soon after we met and I so wanted to dive into this headfirst, dive deep into it without hesitation. Arms outstretched, legs behind me, I so wanted to perform a perfect 'splash-less' dive into his ocean but was terrified to take that leap of faith.

'I think I'm falling for you too, but I don't want to be taken down again.' I had replied, longing to believe him.

Had we met in another time, an earlier era, it would have been a non-starter. He was too keen and controlling and I had been too unstable, too self-absorbed and more interested in the chase. That adage of women not being interested in the nice guys was timeless and my daily fix of a certain reality chat show, proved this still to be true, even among women my own age who really should have learnt that lesson in love. I loved the shrieking onslaughts from the creatures who stormed onto the stage during this television program, where family dirty washing was rinsed in public for the viewers to snigger at and enjoy. These banshees made me feel rather moral, even though my past antics would have made them look like nuns. They always had bad teeth, bad hair, bad attitudes and very bad choices in men.

I was also powerfully aware that among many of my separated and divorced colleagues at work, a lovely bunch of girls, only a few lucky ones had been successful in finding a second Mr. Right. These women were attractive and friendly, jolly good catches one and all, but let down by crappy internet dating and futile nights out in clubs, where the randy single men they encountered were usually half their age and only interested in a clumsy grope with a 'Milf', I had dreaded the prospect when facing singledom, thanking the stars once again for their alignment that Bonfire night, knowing that if I had had to rely on the Internet to find the Big Man, I would have looked in vain, computers being one of his least strong points of interest.

I loved the Internet but for other reasons, such as trawling for holidays, e-mail communication and the ability to be able to use Google for whatever was of interest to me. I would be the first to admit that I would be a bit lost without access to the 'Net', but I tended to stay in the shadows of Facebook, whereas I had friends who updated their profiles daily.

'Just got in from work. (:' Smiley face.

'Feeling fed up.):' Sad face.

What on earth was that all about.

'Having a poo!' Would have been much more interesting and of course a photo could be uploaded and added to the status, in all the lurid technicolor it deserved. I did post the odd nugget from my life, pictures and all, though maybe not the contents of the loo and apart from anything else, it was a very handy medium to allow me to keep track of Cuckoo's own widely publicised antics.

She of course would not be able to imagine her world without the Internet or a mobile phone and I still fondly remembered the advent of that amazing creation, when the handsets were bulky and primitive. A 1980's film was always recognizable by the size of the actor's hair, male and female, and the bricklike appearance of the mobile phones that they proudly waved about. If you had been born post 1990, texting was the norm, closely followed by camera phones, video phones and Internet phones. The trouble was that these 'gismos' had become so indispensable that they were practically a permanent feature in the user's hand. This had irritated me immensely on many occasions when I would snap at my daughter.

'Put that blinking phone down!'

Me and the Big Man had been dragged reluctantly into owning such phones ourselves and we discovered that the ability to send photos instantly was quite awesome. One summer, relaxing in the garden, I started laughing on realizing that we were both intent on these newly acquired items.

'How funny, look at us baby!' We had laughed together then, acknowledging the behavior that we despised in others.

Had we successfully met at a younger age, doubtless we would have had beautiful children, but aged fifty and rising, this was the last thing that I wanted.

'Do you think you might be pregnant babe?' He had asked me one time, with an unfathomable expression on his face, after another missed period, that was only marking the start of my menopause.

'God, I can't think of anything worse baby!' My reply was heartfelt, as the look in his eyes crossed from disappointment into extreme relief in a split second. There was not supposed to be any more babies for me; and my third time lucky child was more than enough for both of us, which considering the amount of time, money and attention that she was managing to extract from us, was probably just as well. No more babies, just Cuckoo, the Beloved Pooch, Daisy bunny and an ever-increasing collection of tropical fish, whilst I continue to wonder how the two previous women in the Big Man's life had allowed themselves to lose him.

Chapter Thirteen

Beloved Pooch and the Bee Tree

January turned into February early in 2015 and the New Year was marching forward determinedly, the old one forgotten. I had not forgotten however, the telephone conversation I had had with my lovely mother a few days after New Year's Eve. She had flown back from the North, having spent Christmas and New Year with Daughter Number Two and her family. The captain had apparently announced that they were flying over the Brecon Beacons in Wales. My mother's voice broke as she sadly told me how she had imagined a little pile of tiny, cold stones, somewhere down there, the ashes of her husband, my father, entombed forever in a bleak wilderness.

'Oh, Mum, I miss him too, love you. Happy New Year.' My own voice wobbled, remembering vividly the day of the scattering so many years ago, as I mentally reached out to him.

'I knew you wouldn't like it there; Daddy.'

'But I'm not there Catrin.'

'Where are you?'

'I'm everywhere Catrin.'

'Are you really here!!'

'I'm always with you, never forget that.'

A few days later I had woken up happily on a Saturday morning and padded to the kitchen, to make a cup of tea for myself and the

Big Man. Happy, until the telephone rang, and I was subjected to the contents of a very unwelcome, second telephone conversation Cuckoo's father hesitantly conveying her results from the previous year's university term. She had received D and E grades, for pity's sake. Up to now a C had been the worst mark, with A's and B's being the norm.

'Why didn't she tell me herself?' I asked him curtly.

'I think she was scared to.'

'She bloody well should be!!'

It appeared that the addition of some other letters of the alphabet had brought the successful progressive harvest of the educational fruits of each hard-earned term to a standstill. M D N A. Not for the last time I cursed the decision to allow my daughter the wherewithal to move into the flat just outside of London, where party central was the stop that all her like-minded friends disembarked at by tube or bus, on too regular a basis. These rubbish results were hardly unexpected, given Cuckoo's behavior during the previous term. Drug binges, drinking, all-nighters raging and wasting the days sleeping off the excesses. Biting my lip, I again decided that more harm than good would be done by chastising the errant student. Cuckoo was the first to admit she bitterly regretted the dive in her grades and absolutely admitted that it was all her own fault. So, no looking back, no regrets, they were a waste of time and a waste of energy.

'Sort it out! x' I texted her later.

I had been looking forward to surfing the Net for prospective holidays for later that year; but now, decided instead to help Cuckoo research the viability of eco-friendly retailing, the basis of the most important, final dissertation in this highly critical, final year.

'Sort it out. I love you x'

'Love you too Ma, thanx for understanding x.'

The Big Man and I had enjoyed another good night the previous evening. I was still medically signed off, and he hadn't been needed at work that weekend, so there had been no holding back with no gauntlet of early morning police patrol cars to run, with the danger of breath limits being a bit excessive. Tongue stuck to the roof of my mouth, bleary eyed and hanging, I crawled back upstairs to the marital bed, two steaming mugs of sweet tea in hand.

'Everything ok babe?' He had heard me on the phone.

'Not really.' I sighed.

'God, you snored like a bison last night, babe!!'

It was normal in our world to sometimes sleep apart, as my snoring was indeed legendary. As I drifted off the guttural noises would begin, the decibels bellowing rhythmically, raising the roof and echoing relentlessly around the walls. For a big man, my husband slept as quietly as a baby, emitting putts of vibration as miniscule in volume as a mouse's footsteps. He was easily disturbed by my monstrous nasal concertos, so much so that successful holidays had to incorporate separate sleeping areas. Bed, however, wasn't only for sleeping and I would join him in the morning in quest of my prize.

'Well, I'm awake now baby!' As I wriggled my hands under the duvet, it appeared that something rather impressive was also well and truly stirring.

A few days later, midweek, he hauled me out of bed early for another return trip to the hospital for a review of my leg. The need to swathe it from knee to toe was deemed over and I practically danced a jig in the treatment room. It would still take a couple of weeks before the healing process would be completed, but the deepest most joyful of grins cracked my face on being told I could have a proper bath. In the evening back at home, with bubbles and a razor at the ready, I slid my whole body into the welcoming hot water, whilst the Big Man hovered, just in case I might need him. Despite my weight gain, a good twelve pounds of blubber now and despite the hairiness of my legs and armpits, he loved me completely and hadn't treated me any differently during the previous long weeks when I had been a semi-invalid. Being married had also made no difference to our relationship, but the knowledge that he loved me enough to put a band of gold around my wedding finger, sporting one himself, a message to the world that he was mine, had put an extra band of loveliness around my heart. How foolish I had been the first time around, believing this could be the case in my doomed relationship with the much younger Mr. R.

I could see many similarities between my former husband and my present one. Interests in the weather, politics and gardening, no desire for social networking or gaming, great senses of humor and masters of the one liner. The two guys understood each other as well, which was nice. It was splendid for Cuckoo and just generally good all around. Bad feelings and resentful grudges had never sat easily in my mind, about anything. I preferred a calmer karma, as I had learnt the hard way that destructive emotion and angst, directed towards other people, probably hurt the bearer of such, more than the recipients. All things considered, even considering all the things I had experienced at the hands of Mr. R., during my former darker years, the existence of the feeling of goodwill between these two remarkable men was so much better than if it hadn't evolved.

Then, of course, there were the differences between them. Physically, Mr. R. was wiry built and would do very well on 'Strictly Come Dancing', with his snake hips and twinkle toes. The Big Ma, on the other hand, was built like a pit bull, thickset and barrel-like. He couldn't dance for toffee, but together we had at times caused quite a stir on foreign dance floors with an attempt at a strenuous Lambada. The sexual bond between us marked another remarkable difference between the relationship I had endured and the one in which I now basked. That afternoon he spent a couple of hours pottering in the garden, making the most of some early sunshine, as I admired his rear view from the window. He was hung like the proverbial bull, his balls straining against his trousers, I enjoyed the same view later, as he climbed in after me, into my much-enjoyed bath water. They hung unfettered between his leg and I couldn't resist cupping them in my hand, feeling his cock spring to instant attention.

The following Monday, I found myself home alone with the Beloved Pooch, venturing out timidly to walk him, still terrified of bumping my leg. The wound was closing at the edges, but the healed skin was raised and darkened by the trauma of the accident, this would be one heck of a scar.

'Oh, fuck it.' I must have spoken the words sharply aloud, as his ears cocked at the sound and he looked up at me, concern written in his face. Bless the faithful Beloved Pooch. I knew that to many the idea of a dog being allowed upstairs, let alone in the bed, was absurd and doggy stairgates were often installed to prevent their animals entering forbidden places. This little man had free run of the house plus access to all areas, including the duvet. The only no-go area for him was when sex was on the cards and he was banished to the upstairs landing.

Oh, lovely, bless-able Beloved Pooch, snipped when quite ready at six months old, he was the most docile and happy of neutered doggies. His pointy face was like a gazelle's, with his dark brown, limpid eyes that were outlined with sooty lines of colour, like eyeliner. He had a black, buttoned nose at the end of his snout, that was super inquisitive to any delicious scent that it encountered, a sense that was heightened even beyond his hearing, both attributes so typical of his species. He was not a skinny dog, with a tummy that was reminiscent of a miniature, pot-bellied piglet and he would follow me constantly around the house, his bandy legs weaving around mine. It would be such a shock to his system when I eventually had to go back to work.

During my enforced absence, when I had travelled to look after my mother after her surgery, he had apparently lain next to the front door, waiting for me to come in. He had stayed there all evening for the first two nights and then had given up, sticking close to his master. On the third night, at bedtime, he had jumped into bed with the Big Man and nestled under the covers with him, both taking solace from each other whilst I was away. I had read somewhere that dogs can accept death but not abandonment. Somewhere else I had also read that cats like to please themselves and dogs want to please others, which was so apt and true. I had also heard that dogs can understand up to five hundred words. 'Good boy', 'walkies',' no',' get down', 'get up', 'love you', 'move!', were a few of those he understood, not quite the number that had been cited, although canine understanding was also about the tone of the voice used to speak to them. He was such a sensitive dog, with a permanently slightly worried expression on his soulful face, and any raised voices would send him scurrying to his bed in the corner of our kitchen. We were his world of course, us humans, a bit like fateful Daisy bunny's world had been at the bottom of the garden, his was a blissfully happy and simple animal universe, his tail constantly fanning from side to side as if to prove his contentment. How cruel was it to deem it okay to dock dog tails, as their main purpose was happy wagging, surely? He had the typical markings of his type, but the perfect brown patch on his smooth-haired, white back, had a dribble of color smudged on one side, as if a brush had carefully painted the perfect circle and carelessly slipped. There could be no breeding plans for this loving creature; and he remained snipped, fat and slightly imperfect, with a permanently happy wag, simply just an adorable lap dog, secure in his place in the family.

Two years ago, in the spring of 2013, he had suddenly gone lame in one of his back legs. Momentarily losing the use of it during a slow stroll around the block, he had looked back in surprise and then up at me. A check-up at the vets revealed a genetic problem with both his back legs, which would lame him permanently eventually. Both legs had to have separate surgery. They were shaven and sawn; and the bones were pinned to rectify the problem. This was as worse as if it had happened to my Cuckoo as a baby; and I was not ashamed to say that I had sobbed uncontrollably, driving him to the clinic on the morning of the first operation. The mighty skip truck was waiting as I pulled up, the Big Man knew that this was a step too far for me, having heard the emotion in my voice earlier and he took control as always. That evening we tenderly carried him home, his right leg bandaged and taped. I fixed a necessary 'Buster Collar' around his neck, the inverted plastic lampshade contraption had been designed to stop stitches being licked, but also turned the canine wearer into a lethal, ankle butting weapon.

'He hates me, I hate myself.' I posted a picture on Facebook, two sad doggy eyes staring at me accusingly. Then, between operations the hopping started, once he had realised that he could go faster on three legs, than try to bear weight on the healing one. This looked totally ridiculous, but he could go at a right old pace with his snout pointed determinedly forward and the poorly leg tucked up and under his tummy as I tried every trick that I could think of to slow him down, to make him use it. This three-legged style continued until well after the second operation, when finally, the Beloved Pooch became my four-legged friend again.

It was 2015, three days until 14th February, Valentine's Day, two days until our fifth wedding anniversary and my last few days at home. I had already had to endure several meetings during my absence from work, welfare meetings set up by my manager and we had long conversations that were written-up and counter signed. It was like a court of law, but that was the nature of the beast when it came to the rigid policies that were enforced by my employer. It was a hard-nosed, ruthless business when it came to the staff being unable to toe the company line if their human frailties didn't allow them to do so. I had made the mistake of starting to laugh, but this turned into an immediate frown when the possibility of an absence sanction being slapped on my record was raised, when I finally returned to my duties. Return reluctantly however I would have to eventually, as my leg had almost healed and only a thick, crescent moon-shaped scar gave away the fact that the strange accident had happened at all during the previous December of 2014.

There were no holds barred in the sack for us now and we adjourned nightly into our darkened bedroom for slow, urgent sex, both of my legs wrapped tightly around the Big Man as we panted and groaned, building towards our climax.

'Wow that was intense.' I gasped as we reluctantly pulled apart.

'Thought you could use the exercise babe.' He smiled as he said it and smiling myself inside and out, I continued to dream and plan, and revel in being with him, wondering what adventures were in store for us during the coming year.

The spring season continued to blossom, every day lengthening a tiny bit. Brisk evening walks with the Beloved Pooch, shivering around the block, now became more leisurely strolls. Daffodils had already started to peek their heads out of the cold ground, now they swung on graceful stalks, as the somber greys of winter were turning into fifty shades of green and the whispering of grass blades, jostling with each other in the early evening breeze, was almost tangible amongst the pure, white chimes of snowdrop bells. The Sun grew higher daily and the bird's morning songs were starting earlier and finishing later, the first brave cheeps were accompanied by more joyous trills, as the feathered orchestra built their music to a crescendo of raucous sound. Trees were stretching out their branches, their gnarled, twiggy hands unfurling, getting ready to hold the berries and blossoms that would be heaped into them. Bees still slumbered underground, not ready yet to emerge from the protection of the earthy crypt of winter, but eventually they would brave their first bumbling flights of the year, to swarm around the glorious blossoms, gathering nectar.

I had nicknamed one such tree the 'Bee Tree'. It was on my doggy walking route and at its blossoming height I couldn't differentiate between bees and blossoms, as the leaves and branches were heavy with both. If I half-closed my eyes it became a living, humming creature, as if only its leggy roots were stopping it from launching into the sky. I liked watching the development of the Bee Tree as the world rotated on its axis, stretching the hours of light out a little bit more every day as it did so. I was properly back at work now, settled into the routine of my working life as kindly colleagues made sympathetic noises about the scar slicing through my leg and I was able to put the turbulence of December and January behind me. Content for the now, looking forward to the future and without a clue that it was going to hold more trouble.

February 2015 turned to March. Blue and purple crocuses were winking competitively at the bright yellow daffodil heads. Cuckoo was back in London, revising like crazy to try and redeem the crappy grades of the last term and I found myself silently screaming at the pathetic politics of who were nothing but more than bumped-up, self-opinionated shop keepers. Their world of sales and stock, that were so terribly important to them, seemed trivial and pointless to me. How I fantasized about sticking their policies up the backsides of the line-up of the chosen individuals who I had selected for this fate.

These private thoughts were hidden by my fixed smile, regularly re-embellished with the lipstick that I had hidden in my bra. It was another of the astoundingly laughable policies, that no lipsticks were to be carried freely in pockets. Obviously, there were certain items that I understood should be taboo. Money of course, as it could have been craftily stolen from the tills, bank cards equally, as they could give many opportunities for fraud, I had seen several staff members fall to such temptation over the years and completely appreciated the need for rules, but a lipstick!!

Cuckoo had kept in regular contact that spring, I tried to 'Skype' her once, but frustratingly there was no picture connection.

'It's not working, Ma!' Her cross voice made me smile and I could easily imagine the look on her face as she tutted in annoyance. She proceeded to natter away about the better achievements that she had made with her coursework.

'This all sounds great!!' I replied, knowing that any form of remonstration or verbal expressions of doubt, would always end with the same reaction from her.

'I'm not a child, Ma!!' I tried to counterargue this with logical replies. Reminders of how I had tried to treat her as a free spirit, condoning trips to festivals and holidays away with her piggy crew. I knew though, deep down inside, that my Cuckoo would always be my child, my special piglet and I laughed as I compared this fact with my own lovely mother's regular nagging traits, understanding that these too, were only caused by love and concern.

'I'm not a child Mother!!' Was also my usual retort to her. This mothering mindset was eternal it would seem and as I reflected on my conundrum about my daughter, that umbilical cord catchphrase of my father came to my mind again, which was now so much more understood.

'You never cut it Catrin, no matter what.'

'I'm learning that lesson, Daddy.'

'Why do you call me that Catrin? you're not a child anymore.'

I fell silent, thinking about his question, realising that I probably still was, at times like this.

'You are learning well though!' He seemed to laugh at his own words, just before I felt his presence disappear.

'Come back, I need you!!' I shouted the words, before hearing a last faint reply.

'I've waited a very long time to hear you say that; Catrin.'

Chapter Fourteen

Talking Shop n Stuff

Sunday 1st March 2015 was another non-working day for both of us; and once again I was gazing out of the kitchen window. My fifty-fifth Birthday was in two months. Another sobering thought, that it was only five years short of sixty. Sixty!! I remembered so well my reactions to turning thirty, forty and then fifty. Turning my mind to the much more palatable thought that age was just a number, I vowed that by my next big age milestone, things were going to change. I had other things to concentrate on in the next five years, before being able to make any life changing lifestyle decisions for us both; but was determined that this would only be put on the back boiler, for now. It could come to the fore one day in the future, all in good time. Cuckoo in London, aged twenty, still needed me despite all her protestations to the contrary. The podgy Beloved Pooch would always need me and then of course there was my lovely mother, as the promise that I had made to my dying father had never been forgotten.

Five years was still long enough and now that this new interesting idea of an eventual life change had raised its head, I enjoyed contemplating it from time to time, knowing that something would need to be pulled out of that bag of tricks which I had relied on so many times in the past. The only difference now was that I was planning for two, me and the Big Man. He fancied relocating to the coast, spending the three months of winter on our most favorite sunny island. I favored the island idea, but more as an all-year-round package. One thing was sure though, we would leave our cozy, mid-terraced house when the time came. There would be nothing to keep us in the area and the prospect of long days filled with sunshine, was sorely tempting. The plan would probably have to include learning more of the Spanish language, maybe I should secretly start focusing on the lingo whilst at work, with five new words a day.

'You are a rubbish manager!' This could be my starting point, as I smilingly lip-synced in Spanish at my chosen target, that sounded like very satisfying fun.

We would easily find jobs on our sunny foreign island, it was such an English-speaking place, with its eternal sunshine and holiday vibes that drew an endless stream of visitors from Britain. Bars and restaurants always needed jolly workers, both front and back of house. The vast array of self-catering accommodation would need cleaners and surely the advent of the Big Man as a newly arrived handyman, would guarantee a regular income?

My daydream was rudely interrupted by the warmth of early spring sunshine being replaced by a gust of rain hitting the window, as my thoughts turned to the ladies who I had worked alongside for more years than I cared to remember. Rock solid women, who carried out their duties professionally whilst juggling their personal lives. Mothers, many now grandmothers as well, they had their own stories of joy and grief, personal losses and gains, those inner tales speaking so much about the successes and tragedies that they had experienced. One by one they had all confided in me, spelling out their pasts with faltering whispers that were almost like confessions from their souls. We had a camaraderie between us of which I was proud to be a part, it didn't make the political working nonsense any easier, but a certain look shared after a particularly taxing situation had occurred, was always just enough to enable us to ease the urge to say out-loud what we were really thinking.

There were the lovely white-haired 'Genies', with plenty of bottle and the even lovelier lady of the immaculate eyebrows, whose husband had undergone heart surgery before a second operation that was needed for a double organ transplant, their situation had moved me massively and persuaded me to register us both on the transplant registry list. Then there was the lovely tiller girl who swelled the ranks at the weekend and how could I forget the others with whom I shared my working week. They all knew who they were, blondes and brunettes, chubby and slender, all dressed in the uniform that marked them as 'worker bees' for the company. Individually they were irrepressible and unique, yet sadly, united they were simply a workforce who meant little to the employer.

Admittedly many of our customers were equally lovely, a nice chat and a giggle with them whilst serving, was always a bonus. Humor was probably the only thing for which there was no policy to be able to ban and banter would resonate up and down the shop floor constantly. Cheeky comments would fly around, with me right in the middle, giving my two pennies worth. Some of the staff had been there all their working lives, which I considered to be a terrible fate. In their late sixties, some even early seventies in age, they continued to merrily work their shifts. What had happened to their dreams of up-sticking to a sunny island? Maybe they had never had the vision, or maybe such hopes had vanished in the cold light of ageing reality. I was even more determined now, to cherish my dream for the future and I kept it safe inside of me, tucked into my heart as carefully and as secretly as the lipstick I tucked into my bra. A tiny bubble of alternative happiness, that I would nurture until the right time.

It was always quiet at work; this time of year, post-Christmas and pre-Easter and the assistants turned their minds to naughty conversations, in the absence of customers. The bestselling novel, 'Fifty Shades of Grey', had been made into a film.

'Have you seen it?!' They asked each other, amazed at their own temerity. The trilogy had been a block-busting success a few years previously, a soft porn love story with flashes of S&M to tantalize the eager readers. I had avidly read all three books, finding the experience to be akin to gobbling up a Chinese meal, once you were finished and sated, you wondered what the attraction had been. Bloody hell these ladies were sheltered; and as further timid confessions followed, they went pinker and pinker, blushing with embarrassment when the subject of where they might have had sex was raised. The inevitable mile-high club came up for discussion and I had to sadly admit that I had never got to experience the kudos of sky shagging, simply because I doubted if the Big Man and I would manage to squeeze into an aero-plane toilet. The conversation was starting to get very interesting, as they continued the naughty dialogue. Pubic hair shaving was discussed next and the merits of razors versus waxing, debated. 'Mrs. 007' giggled, her mouth wide open in total disbelief at the subject matter, I had named her because of her husband, who did something so secretive at the MOD, that the tall, slender blonde knew nothing about his work.

'Bush Topiary!' I spluttered, as 'Mrs. Granny Smith', who was excited for her first grandson, gave me a quizzical look from her twinkling eyes, set within a face where her cheeks did indeed look like firm, little apples. They were such a stalwart bunch, including 'The Seamstress', who was as straight as the rows of stitching she could produce, yet who would surprise me with bizarre, factual statements, like the pet goat called Victor that she had owned as a child, that she would lead around on a lead like a large dog. There was the raven-haired lovely, who admitted to trying dope once, her fate had been sealed when she was travelling in Australia where she met a native and returned with him to England, to raise four beautiful children. And what about 'Mrs. Poopoo'?! That bizarre term of affection had come about in a silly, random moment and had stuck ever since.

'The Gander' was the only male in the gaggle of geese, who had a lot to put up with working with this motley, female crew, but who seemed to enjoy every bit of it. 'Mrs. Bubbles' had been named for her love of all things fizzy and alcoholic; and next there was 'The Exotic Flower Girl', a beautiful, graceful Indonesian lady, who was easily shocked by the rest of us but enjoyed it all the same. 'Mrs. That's Not Right' had also joined in gleefully with the bald fanny debate, as we continued to laugh like drains over the outrageous subject matter; and even our usually strict supervisor smiled in acknowledgement of her staff's sense of humour. I had nicknamed her 'Mrs. Chocolate Eclair', as she was crisp on the outside but with a hidden, soft centre. She too would be looking forward to a sun-kissed grand-daughter in the next few years if she but knew it.

It was amazing how many people I had encountered over the years, working in that shop. The life of a chicken from farm to counter, was once followed by a famous royal, who deigned to grace us with his presence. He was later to be accused of underage sex when revelations from the 1970s and 1980s went viral. Many famous men were named and shamed in this campaign to reveal that sordid truth. Several were found guilty and imprisoned. Any debatable actions by this chap would definitely have been refuted and covered up, but the potential for guilt was painted all over his lecherously dissipated face that day, as he tried to show some enthusiasm whilst his secret service minders popped up like meerkats in the throngs of excited shoppers. As far back as I could remember, sexual innuendo had been the norm in those past decades. I had lost count of the number of married, male bosses, who had cast their eyes over me, now however, such conduct was considered highly immoral and totally illegal.

One Boxing Day, I had spotted a famous comedienne with her trademark-bobbed hair and size-thirty clothing. She was accompanied by her husband, another celebrity, towering above his wife, his dark skin pallid with an obvious hangover. As I approached the couple to say what a huge fan I was of the 'tubby chubber', the expression on her face soured and her response was short and cutting.

'That's just rude, screw you too!' I had decided, thinking once again that it was quite amazing how diverse the people were, who you could find in a shop.

On Mothering Sunday, mid-March 2015, Cuckoo arrived home with a huge grin on her face and flowers in hand. She came with gossip and my face became equally broad as she shared it. What a silly saying it was, that you should keep your friends close but your enemies even closer. As far as I was concerned you should keep your foes as far away as possible. Still, news of recent downfalls of former adversaries could still cause me amusement, long after the pain they had once inflicted had receded into the past. The hard lesson I had been forced to learn about letting go of bad karma caused by the actions of others was embedded in me now, but the reasons that the lesson had once had to be learnt were still able to sting me a tiny bit, if I let them.

Cuckoo was on form this time, there was no evidence of the bedraggled girl from Christmas and New Year as she proudly produced an essay that she was about to hand in, three thousand words of succinct presentation. The Big Man and I had willingly played our parts in her research and on reading the bits that we had contributed, we looked at each other and smiled. The next day she flew off again, after I had served up eggs, bacon and thick slices of white bread liberally spread with salted butter. It was a very naughty cholesterol combination, but an irresistible feast for the three of us and the Beloved Pooch gave us his best begging face, as we happily guzzled our delicious breakfast, hoping for a morsel or two for himself.

After my daughter had gone, I sat down to mull over the facts I had heard and to decide what I really thought of the revelations that she had brought home. The problem was deep-seated, but it had not caused me any issues for several years. It involved an old acquaintance and her cocaine habit. She was the sort of person who everyone has the misfortune to encounter at some point in their lives, always feeling themselves to be the victim, with their annoying, bleating complaints of the unfairness of everything, whilst leeching from others and seeing it as their absolute right to do so. There was no Dorian Gray portrait saving her, as the ravages of a badly chosen lifestyle were causing haggard wrinkles to appear in a face, that in its heyday had once been beautiful.

The cunty grunts must have had so much fun, silently carving these lines with their talons. The souls of such individuals would have had no interest to them, as there was no purity to be lusted after within them, only dark recesses that offered cold comfort and selfish ways. It would have been easy for them to manipulate these human hosts, who willingly accepted the dark forces that they were offered, instead of fighting against the satanical temptations. Perhaps it was for pure entertainment only, that these deep and unsightly scars were forged, as the monsters hid, lizard like, behind unsympathetic eyes that had no compassion in them, as the creators of the tracks in their faces watched the world from within them, with hostile amusement. Just as they had done from within the wretched, drugged up creatures who had sat around a campfire several decades ago, where they had first spied me.

I had no sympathy, this supposed friend had been one of those to fling insults at me, when Mr. R., and I were in the death throes of our marriage and I felt completely within my rights to feel the way I did now. I also knew that those insults had done me a favor eventually, because as the abuse was directed at me many times, in a barrage of foul, verbal assault from mouths that mimicked cunty, grunting voices, I had suddenly started to wonder whos life I was living, and the wounding words became important contributing factors in helping me scramble out of the mire of my past. I had spent years cleansing my heart of my hatred of those responsible for their curses, rationalizing that it was only hurting myself and as

I was gradually strengthened by the new rock in my life, I was able to see things dispassionately and had no intention of ever letting the angst back into my head.

Now, as I mentally debated the nugget of news that Cuckoo had shared with me, I came to the conclusion that the fact that this character was about to lose a house, simply drew another line under the existence of the festering cauldron of past emotion. Any vestiges of my past anger were finally extinguished and a small, satisfying smile played around my mouth, as I realised once again, how far removed I was from the person I had been.

'You've come such a long way Catrin, I'm very proud of you.'

'Thank you Daddy I've been waiting a long time too, to hear you say that.'

Exhausted, I decided to take a nap and more of the past dominated my dreams.

After Cuckoo's awful accident with her eye, we had muddled along together for a few years as a family, the Big Man cementing our unit with his quiet ways and strong support. The addition of the Beloved Pooch into our midst strengthened our bond even more, as did the unforgettable day in February 2010, when we exchanged our wedding vows and Cuckoo had helped me with my hair and make-up, giving the child her own special part to play. A precious hour when she fussed around me with eye shadow and hair straighteners, one moment in time that brought us closer together. The long-awaited GCSE results arrived guaranteeing the girl's passage to the college of her choice, not the first-class ticket we might have hoped for if things had been different, but it would do perfectly. Once again, this was a case of everything had to be considered, considering the everything.

Early summer 2012; found me working my way through a minefield of university applications, with finance and housing all needing to be put into place. Cuckoo would be eighteen that

NO EXAGGERATION

August and she was starting to blossom, morphing away from the flushed, out-of-control teenager whose only ambition in life was to party at the local park after dark. As an early birthday present, we had paid for a week in Zante, that most famous of Greek party islands, where she and her friends would be taking their first holiday without responsible adults.

'God help Zante!' Was my first thought on the subject but I was starting to relax, praying that the desperate nights that we had spent trying to hunt the errant girl down were nearly over. Those countless incidences when the police had brought her home and other hideous memories, such as the morning when a random stranger had called the house phone, kindly letting me know that they had found Cuckoo's mobile and went on to describe a shoe that they had found along-side it. My mouth hit the floor in panic, it was one of the high heeled contraptions that she had hobbled out on into the night, the evening before. All this dangerous nonsense and more, I hoped was over, forgotten forever, as with a gesture of my hands, I prayed once again to the Something.

These prayers sadly fell on barren ground, when one night shortly after Cuckoo flew home from her first foreign holiday with her piggy muckers, paler than when she had left, one awful night when the monsters made another unexpected and startling appearance. For one night only, they came out to play. The Big Man and my-self were fast asleep; it was late, gone midnight, when all the telephones in the house started ringing, the house phone and both of our mobiles. She had been out with her friends and had turned into a grunt incarnate. An hour later she lurched through the front door in a state of drunken rage, aiming it all at me, with intense verbal abuse.

'Cunt, cunt, cunt!' Over and over, she snarled the word into my face, an insult that I had sworn I would never take again, even from my Cuckoo, but where had all that rage and fermenting hatred come from? Was it stored up in her mind, locked away into a blackened corner, waiting to be released? Caused by frustrations that she had never voiced in over six years, resentment for having her world tossed upside down? Was it an echo of a memory of how her father insulted me? Had she been listening secretly back in the day, hiding from the wrath in his words and had they been stored in her mind, like evil, cunty, grunty seeds, that would one day sprout? Perhaps it was a deep fury about the awful incident with her eye and the trauma she had endured? Or was it plain, rotten, teenage angst, against a Mother who had only tried to do her best. Whatever the source of her behavior that night, those supposedly impotent monsters had found an opportunity to remind me that they had only been banished, not destroyed.

'Cunt, cunt, cunt!' Again, and again. Enough was enough for me; and with a leaden heart I banished my daughter to her father's house.

'I've finally had my fill of her, you need to have her.'

Her exile lasted six weeks, with her eighteen Birthday, slap in the middle of it. There were no piles of cards and presents with the traditional cake in the middle of the table, with candles ready to be lit and 'Happy Birthday to you!!', to be sung merrily. There were no sprinkles of birthday confetti scattered randomly and there were no celebratory bottles of champagne chilling in the fridge. We visited her at her fathers on the day of course, but it wasn't a birthday, let alone an eighteenth, although the promised three thousand pounds compensation for her eye injury probably made up for this in her eyes. A fortune of spare cash to anyone, let alone a girl, who was soon to enter a different world of university halls of residency and London life. During those six long weeks I would go into my daughter's empty bedroom, and cry.

'You don't have to do this.' The Big Man told me.

'Not if it's upsetting you this much babe.'

'Yes, I do baby.' But I was desperately missing my daughter. Our estrangement continued during those long six weeks, until one Sunday afternoon, with all the phones ringing and beeping with text messages and the sound of sad sobs from my Cuckoo, as she pleaded to come home. In all truth, the weeping I did during that six weeks saved me from the onslaught of the inevitable torrents of tears that all the other Mothers would experience in the next few months, as university-bound birds left home and bedrooms, once noisy and messy, were suddenly tidy and quiet. I had already done my empty nest grieving and so the eventual process of transporting the girl to her new life of independency wasn't as heartbreaking as it could have been, as once again she was forgiven for her actions of that awful night.

'Are you starting to understand, Catrin?'

'Yes Daddy, you never give up on your child, no matter what.'

'Good girl, another lesson learned.'

We had collected the keys to Cuckoo's new accommodation a week earlier and decided to avoid the day of mainstream arrival, when each one of over five hundred students accompanied by parents, friends and lots and lots of stuff being juggled, would have had to jostle for car park spaces and the lifts up to the rooms. The actual moving of her stuff into her en-suite room in a flat with a shared kitchen and living room, was relatively straightforward, though how the Big Man had managed to negotiate his car through central London to our destination, was completely beyond me, as he withstood aggressive cabbies and seasoned London drivers, all vying for the right of way. We unpacked her bags and suitcases, carefully arranging new bedding and the ghastly purple towels, purchased to match the tiles in her new shower room. Choosing the colour of these towels had been one of the foremost decisions in her mind, very trivial, but very important!

We met two of the other girls who would be sharing the flat with her, for at least this first year of uni. They were shyly kicking their heels as all three introduced themselves. Finally, we took Cuckoo for lunch and spent a bomb in the supermarket adjacent to the halls of residency, giving her a bottle of wine for the introductory party that was going to be held later that evening in the common room, before saying our goodbyes. The Big Man had seen the anxiety in his stepdaughter's face, whilst I heard it in her voice on getting home.

'Ma! I don't know what to do!' It was so funny to hear those words from Miss Independent and so heartbreaking at the same time.

'Right, now young lady, get a grip.' My own voice was breaking slightly as I replied, but I was trying to keep strong, for her sake.

'Take that bottle of wine and go knock on doors, sort it out! I love you.'

Later that night, the newly met flat mates had ventured out together to find a night club. Cuckoo had taken flight and there would be no looking back for her as she soared skywards. Life during this first year at university was going to be a veritable feast for her and she became very popular, but money started to be an issue. There was no student bar with a pint costing a mere pound, instead she frequented the cocktail bars of Mayfair and rubbed shoulders with mini celebs at famous nightclubs. Wearing push-up bras, with tousled hair and the obligatory pout of the selfie, she and her band would be queue-jumped in and given access to VIP tables. It was time for my Cuckoo to live the dream.

There was a boyfriend back at home, they had been together for a while, but the relationship didn't last once she had gone to London, their two young worlds having slowly grown poles apart. His horizons were limited to his hometown whilst hers were already reaching to the stars and beyond. Cuckoo had never been a fickle girl and the separation was painful for them both, thought probably more so for him. I hoped he would eventually meet a nice local girl, as there was no future for him with mine and I recalled my own parent's woes about the boy who had helped rob me of their vision of my own university opportunity.

'I wish I had listened to you, Daddy.'

'You never listened then, Catrin, you had to learn to listen.'

Cuckoo continued to thrive, studied, presumably and partied hearty.

'Get a job.' Was my next command to her; the following February, where the compensation money had gone was a mystery, but as I had access to my daughter's bank account, it was a jaw dropping moment when I realized that the three thousand pounds had been dissipated, along with other regular allowance sums that were deposited. Studying the transactions, all I could see was debit, debit and more debit.

'Get a job, sort it out! I love you.' And amazingly she did just that.

'Got a job Ma! It's sorted!!'

She had indeed found a part-time job, whilst the first year of her university life turned into a second and she was tracking well in her quest for a Bachelor of Arts degree.

In September 2013, Cuckoo decided to move into a dilapidated, shared house, complete with a broken toilet seat and a very unhealthy growth of mold, another rite of passage for a seasoned second-year student. Prior to that in the summer recess, aged nineteen, she had taken her next holiday, to Magaluf this time, another birthday present from us.

'Yuk!' Thought I, watching the odd program on the place and laughing as I remembered my own exploits in foreign climes, back in the day. A determined band of the usual suspects; spent a week wallowing in the trough of mainstream Spanish hard-core, drinking and partying. Apart from a bout of alcohol poisoning, and with less evidence of a suntan than Zante had afforded her, Cuckoo eventually flew home safely, her Facebook pictures showing her wearing the most lurid onesie that I had ever seen.

2013 turned swiftly into 2014. It was unbelievable how quickly time was flying, as Cuckoo persuaded us to fund the final move. Having seen the cupboard my daughter was living in and come face to face with the mold cohabiting with her, there didn't seem to be a choice, but increasingly the girl's social networking habits were giving me much cause for concern. Facebook was now splattered with pictures of hell-raising parties and accounts of hordes descending on the flat for up-all-night sessions, at what had become a party central extraordinaire. Malia was on her bucket list that summer, after which she also graced me and the Big Man with her company, by joining us in the sleepy, sunny Spanish backwater island, where onesies wouldn't dare be seen and holiday makers went to bed at midnight as opposed to getting ready to go out.

The free-spirited student continued to dance through the final terms of her three-year course. Her plans for spending the coming summer working in Ibiza, had not yet been formalized, but unbeknown to anyone, these plans once actioned, would have the devastating effects of a mini nuclear fallout to me and give me more sleepless nights than I had ever imagined that I would have to suffer, again.

Chapter Fifteen

Finding Treasure and Lost Family

Easter 2015; fell over the first weekend in April and my attention turned itself to the looming car boot season, with all the fun that could be had within it. I started to think about the stacks of hoarded skip-trove that had been piled around the house over the winter. The Big Man had been gathering madly, bringing home his 'treasures' with pride and would doubtless complain about selling them on. Looking out of the kitchen window again, I could see the first flies of the year, hatching in the deceptively warm, early spring sunshine, buzzing annoyingly as they did so.

'At least Daisy's bottom will be safe this year.' I thought sadly making another pensive glance towards her grave, recalling the flystrike that she had been afflicted with.

All the shops were full of Easter promise, bright yellow and fluffy, fuzzy artificial chicks and ah, bunnies galore, were decorating aisles and displays. Shiny, foil covered chocolate eggs twinkling temptation, were begging to be added to baskets. Inevitably, they were hollow and over-priced, but it was such an important part of the ritual that even the most mean-hearted would surely weaken and buy a few. I remembered with great fondness, many egg hunts with my Cuckoo; and the bright-eyed, greedy friends who she had invited to join in with the game. Their mouths were smeared with chocolate as they gobbled up their prizes, resulting in probably more than the odd wave of nausea as tummies were overloaded with the sweet delight of madly stuffing down their finds. Roast lamb would always be on the menu and wine glasses were filled to the brim, as toasts were made and not a thought was given to the real reason behind these festivities.

The sleeping Gruber in the back garden was stirring. 'Worsel Gummidgy' straw shapes were starting to rise from the ground and the Big Man had started the serious business of watering the plant daily, running a hosepipe from the garden tap to quench its thirsty roots. At night he covered it up with an old sheet, protecting it from 'Jack Frost's' icy, early morning fingers. The warmer weather also saw people starting to throw things away in earnest. Every evening the Big Man came home with a few more nuggets of treasure, waiting impatiently for me to return too, so that I could admire his latest finds and I gave regular thanks to the Something for the privilege of knowing that he was there. Brushing aside the appalling thought of how impossible it would be if he wasn't.

'Good day babe?' Was always his gentle greeting. I would never be able to open that front door without the joy of knowing he was behind it, should the unthinkable happen. It was a small taste of the despair that my lovely mother had had to deal with, so my plea, to please let us have a long, long time together, was made in another prayer to the Something, as it was silently spoken.

Every night there was another bit of treasure winking at me. A baseball cap studded with tiny airline badges, caught my attention. The collection must have taken years to amass, all carefully attached, yet it had been thrown away with the rubbish by someone who just didn't give a damn about its meaning. The owner of the cap probably now deceased, would have turned in their grave to witness such desecration and contempt of their cherished memento. Each little gold and silver enameled badge were now telling me its own story about the life of the collector. Dried and artificial flower bouquets had been arranged in glass vases that once washed, sparkled in the light with glints of pleasurable thanks for being rescued from the gigantic trommel machine, into which once the contents of a skip were unloaded would reduce all and anything to pulp and debris with its thrashing jaws. Antique binoculars and cameras, ceremonial, carved daggers with intricately painted sheathes, bits and bobs, odds and sods, all were carefully plucked from where they had been thrown and brought home for me to admire.

The Easter weekend was finally here, the shop closed for Easter Sunday, one of the few bank holidays deigned important enough not to open for and Cuckoo was due home again. She had more news to share, horrible news, that one of her piggy friends had lost her father to cancer after his battle with it for many years. It was to be Cuckoo's first experience of such raw grief, first or second hand. She had had lost both of her grandfathers, the first, my father, had died when she was just a small child and the second, when she was burgeoning as a stroppy teenager, therefore those deaths could not have had the same impact as this one as she watched her friend break down in anguish. I understood this completely and when she asked me if she should send a bouquet to the family, I replied that flowers simply wouldn't do it.

'What about buying them a star, you could name it after him.'

Oh my God, Ma, that's brilliant!'

You could quite easily buy such a tribute these days and before I fell asleep that night, reflecting on my alternative to flowers, I thought of the many stars I could have purchased in homage over the years. It would have been a veritable cosmos that I would have dedicated to my own father. I had rung my lovely mother a few days earlier. The date, 2nd April, had rung a chord in my mind, being the anniversary of his death eighteen years previously. Not wanting to remind her in case she had not made the same leap in her own mind, I kept the conversation light. Mother sounded bright and chatty, she was having a visitor for Easter and this news dominated our chinwag. The passing of that date this year, would remain my secret; and I was simply glad that I had recognized it. I would have offered the whole universe as a token of my respect and gratitude to the man, but I decided that just remembering, was enough.

'I didn't forget, Daddy.'

'Good girl Catrin, thank you.'

'Don't go, I've got so much to ask you!!'

'I can't stay for long Catrin, the link between our worlds is still very fragile.'

'How is this even possible!!' Once again, it was silent in the room and all I could do was try and search for my star, the cloudy night sky making this heartbreakingly difficult, until finally my eyes wearily closed, and the disappointment caused me to cry in my sleep.

My dreams were dominated by memories of our first forays into the world of selling second-hand goods. It was at Easter in 2010 that we had taken the first step into this chaotic business, with its early morning starts and crazy banter. Our little house had become crammed to the hilt over the few years that we had been together. The treasure mounted up, with every wall surface covered, every shelf adorned; and every cupboard stuffed. The blank canvas of a house that I had moved into was now richly decorated with colorful and random objects, paintings, objects d'art and just the plain ridiculous. Tables, chairs, glassware and artificial trees, the collection was seriously verging on blissful madness. One day an elaborately etched leather saddle appeared, whether it was for an elephant or a camel was unclear, but it was a beautiful, ornate piece that the Big Man had draped over the back of the settee. It was time to recycle other people's throwaways into hard cash. He was reluctant to let go of his findings, but I managed to persuade him eventually, even though he groaned as each chosen piece was carefully wrapped in tissue paper and packed into boxes.

'Not that one babe!'

'Yes; and these, baby!' When I had finished trawling through the skip trove, it was all loaded into both of our cars in preparation for our adventure early the following morning. Newly purchased wallpaper tables were precariously balanced on top of the boxes and with the obligatory float of cash in a bum bag slung over my shoulder, off we went in convoy, in search of the site of one of the South of England's biggest car boot sites. Cuckoo then fifteen and a friend, were squashed into the back of my car as they had wanted to be part of this jolly escapade, though there was nothing jolly about dragging them out of bed at five o'clock in the morning. Grumbling and half-asleep, they had climbed aboard, squashing the Beloved Pooch in between them. Forty minutes later we were setting up our stall, aware that we were surrounded by real professionals who were all busy erecting canopies and clothes rails, before they pounced on us new arrivals.

'Any jewelry? Any vinyl? Any perfume!!' Next, the public started sauntering in, the early birds with an eye for a find, and finally the masses. Men, women and kids, with dogs and pushchairs in tow, were teeming along the rows of vehicles that had their goods on display in open boots and along the sides. What an experience this was turning out to be and we were loving it, along with the pure hilarity of haggling with the prospective buyers. The Big Man chatted up the women, whilst I bartered with the men. Bit by bit our trove of other people's rubbish was turned into coins and notes. The girls were useless at the game, devouring fizzy drinks and burgers they were literally eating the profits of the morning's work. The Beloved Pooch hid in the back of the car, all the raucous noise was far too much for his sensitive ears, but by midday a good couple of hundred pounds had been earned and the piles of stuff that we had no intention of taking home, were dwindling fast.

I had decided to take the oversized saddle, although with hindsight this had been a silly idea for several reasons. It was potentially worth a fortune, but this was a new game to me and the financial rewards that 'eBay' and the like, could offer, had yet to be discovered. I had lain it across the top of the Big Man's motor, more of a feature than an offer for sale. I did not intend to take any less than fifty pounds for it. It was worth much more of course, but the punters kept their cash close to their pockets and fifty pounds would be lovely to earn on this cold, sunny Sunday morning, adding splendidly to the coffers. Busily plying my trade, I didn't notice the random guy gesturing towards the saddle, or the short conversation that he had with Cuckoo and her friend before he walked off with it, but I quickly realised that it was missing.

'Did you sell it!!'

'Yes Ma.' Cuckoo looked sheepish.

'How much did you get for it?!'

'A pound, Ma.'

'What!!'

'He said there were no elephants in this part of the world, Ma.'

'Bloody hell, cheeky sod!!' I had no choice but to laugh at what had just happened, there might not be any elephants in these parts but there were plenty of Indian restaurants, where his bargain find would eventually be taking its pride of place in one of them, for the right price. This was one hell of a learning curve and I doubted that I would ever get my hands on such an amazing item again, whilst promising myself that I would never invite my rubbishy helpers along for the ride for a second time.

That day was the start of a very lucrative sideline and I started to study on-line valuations as the treasure poured in as quickly as we could sell it, deciding that we should next brave a pitch at an Antiques Fair. On arrival we were given a prime position at the event and a chunky table, that was placed in the middle of our wonky wallpaper tables. I covered all three in black cloth and large shells, which we had collected from African beaches and filled them with wrapped sweets, to ensure that customers loitered around our wares as they selected their favourite bonbon. Finally, after carefully positioning all our treasure we stood back to look at it in amazement, grinning broadly at each other.

'We look like proper traders, baby!' I whispered to the Big Man, who smiled back at me in perfect agreement. Any onlooker would surely not have been able to tell the difference between the pitches of we two amateurs and those of the pros. My steel float tin, versus their chip and pin card machines was possibly the only giveaway. I had received a letter from the organizers of the event, asking if I minded if we were filmed, as a well-known female interior designer was making a program about Antique Fairs and would be attending this one. Mind? It was manna from Heaven, as the hall was soon crammed with profiling dealers from all over the country, anxious for their fifteen minutes of fame. Spotting the sound boom as the crew mooched around the stalls, was the closest we got to being televised, but our goods changed hands for wads of notes. and I had to pinch myself as my internet search for their potential worth was proving to be a dream come true. An old ship's bell, a handcrafted Noah's Ark set, pieces of furniture, pictures, ceramics, glass ware ... The list went on and the contents of the tables dwindled until we called it a day. Driving tiredly home with over fifteen hundred pounds stuffed into the float tin, I couldn't help but wonder how much I would have got for the leather saddle, as I also reflected on how much money there was to be made, in what other people would foolishly consider was only worthy of being throw into a skip.

That evening unbeknown to me, the Big Man had covered our bed in ten, twenty and fifty-pound notes, as I languished in a foaming bath, drinking the champagne that we had chilled in the hope of such a celebration for our day's work. Smelling divine and liberally sprinkled with talcum powder and perfumed body lotion, both putting a scented finishing touch to the sensual pampering that I had enjoyed, I padded into the bedroom. He was waiting there, standing butt naked with a familiar glint in his eyes.

'Lie down babe.'

'Certainly, Sir.' I lay on the notes, their cold crunch sending a shiver up my spine, as the expression on his face caused a sudden spasm of sexual pleasure to vibrate through my body.

'How much for this? He asked as he gently squeezed my left nipple, waving more notes in his hand.

'Or this?' His fingers moved to my right breast, watching my physical reaction.

'Maybe this is for sale?' His hand trailed down my torso, lingering over my pubic area, stroking and smoothing the shaven hairs.

'I'm also interested in owning this.' Two fingers were plunged deeply into me, as I started to writhe below him.

'Baby, fuck me.'

'Not yet babe, I'm gonna make you beg for it tonight.'

'Spread your legs.' He ordered, before kneeling down to inspect my exposed, throbbing vagina, using those same fingers to play with the engorged, fleshy lips, slowly massaging them and smiling as he felt my response.

'Baby, I want you to fuck me!'

'Not yet baby, I'm gonna make you come a few times first, I want you really wet.'

The teasing continued, until finally his cock couldn't wait anymore, and he plunged it into me, his own orgasm filling me with delicious liquid spurts of his own as the bank notes moved around underneath me, their sharp paper edges giving a touch of exquisite pain to the skin on my back, the alien sensation only adding to the pleasure of the moment.

'Wow baby!' I was unable to say anything else until my heartbeat had calmed down.

Next, I remembered how life had meandered erratically through the first couple of years after we were married. Cuckoo had scraped through her college course, with the dream of university spurring her on. Her attendance had been erratic, but her tutor had seen the potential in the student, the same potential that her headmaster had seen whilst she was at secondary school and decided to give her several second chances. I would always be grateful to these teachers for believing that my daughter could fly, seeing beyond the turbulence that was holding her down. Had I known that Cuckoo's flight would eventually be a smooth take off into the blue yonder, it might have been easier to deal with the sympathetic looks from the other adults as they picked up their impeccably behaved 'Flossy's'; and 'Freddy's', whilst I was sitting head down in the foyer of the school, awaiting and dreading the next meeting. Not knowing that there would be sweet, future conversations with these model parents.

'Flossy is doing so well!' They beamed with pride as they listed her successes.

'Freddy is studying to be a lawyer. We're so proud of him.'

'Oh, how is your daughter?' Their faces changed to expressions of false concern.

'Oh, about to study for her B.A. actually.' My reply was always nonchalant, but mentally I was licking my finger and swiping the air with it.

I had always wondered if there was a valuable hidden gem amongst our treasure. I had approached local antique dealerships and television programs by now and was getting very bold in my quest to unearth such a rare finding, hoping that I would discover that we unwittingly possessed that one thing that was worth a fortune. The subject was great shakes these days and we avidly watched a regular Sunday night series, where folk would queue for hours to have their cherished pieces valued. The crowd would watch and listen excitedly, as the experts analyzed the antiques that were proudly presented for their consideration. Hopes for Faberge, Monet, Cartier and long-lost heirlooms of intrinsic value were imagined, as the bearers of their own bits of treasure shuffled forward in the queue, to hear the verdicts on them. Mouths would drop open in incredulous disbelief as the hawk-eyed antique dealers gave their estimations for insurance purposes. The disappointment was tangible on their faces when the sums suggested were nothing, compared to those they had hoped to hear. Having sometimes had to wait for hours, often in the pouring rain, wearing rain macs and carrying umbrellas to shield them and their carefully held pieces from the elements. The Big Man and I loved nothing better than guessing our own valuations, glued to the television program, inevitably getting them completely wrong, but enjoying playing the game that we had invented for pure fun.

One day I found Cuckoo's prom dress, whilst sorting out my chosen items to sell next. It had been squashed into the back of a cupboard for a year. A prom had not been on my school agenda when I was sixteen back in the seventies, but these days this event was another absolute rite of passage for school leavers. Cuckoo had fallen in love with the splendid emerald-green creation. Layers and layers of blue and green taffeta and lace; were be-jeweled with tiny diamantes and the strapless bodice was pulled tight at the back, like a corset. It was ridiculously over-budget at four hundred pounds, a designer dress fit for a princess and certainly not deserved, given Cuckoo's general demeanor and regular nasty exploits, but the look in my daughter's eyes as she gazed at the gown hanging in the exclusive boutique that we had found, and the speechless, pleading look that she gave me, sealed the deal. The eye surgery and the cause of it, were both now thankfully in the past and she had done her best to achieve the grades that she needed for the next stage of education. Well hardly her best, but she had tried and so I had agreed to purchase the sumptuous frock for the imminent event.

I recalled squeezing a chubbier Cuckoo into the dress, the afternoon of her prom in May 2010. My actions were causing sweaty moments and as the prom princess-to-be breathed in, she asked me sharply, if there was a problem, painfully aware of my battle with the laces. I was holding my own breath, dreading that any second her over ample puppy fat would win the battle and that the fastenings would snap in defeat. Thankfully, there was no such disaster and with my mission accomplished, we set off to where the other squealing teenagers were gathering. Compulsory limos had been hired at great expense and as the prom goers boarded the vehicles, we proud parents and stepparents waved off our offspring. The girls all looked like Cinderella at the ball, whilst the boys looked equally resplendent in tuxedos that matched the colour of their chosen partner's dress. Jealous, younger siblings were also watching, longing for their day in the limo limelight.

Cuckoo's gown was returned with its wearer, much later the next day. She was just about in one piece, hungover and grubby, but unfortunately the garment was not in good shape at all. Torn, burnt with cigarette butts and noticeably stained, it was a complete wreck and all I could do was make thanks that we hadn't hired it. The dress hid its shame in a dark cupboard, completely forgotten about until I had unearthed it and decided to try and sell it.

On our next visit to a car boot sale, it was draped across the bonnet of the Big Man's car, majestic and knackered, as a teenager wandered over, her huge eyes fixed on her prize with wonderment at the vision in front of her.

'How much, missus?' I contemplated the girl thoughtfully; forty pounds had been my price and as our eyes met, she hopefully produced a twenty-pound note.

'That's all I've got, missus.' It wasn't quite the debacle of the elephant saddle; and the dress changed hands.

'Just make sure you tell your mother it's got damage to it.' I warned her as she skipped off into the throngs of dawdling visitors, her emerald-green dream clutched in both hands. This heralded the end of the prom dress saga, though the beginning of a splendid, new adventure for its next owner.

My tears must have turned to smiles during the night in early April 2015, dreaming of all those silly shenanigans, but a frown would surely have wiped my amusement away; as my suspended consciousness turned to another matter, an email that I had received in June 2011. My serious new husband had spoken occasionally of his mother and sister, wondering where they were and if his mother was still alive. I always listened carefully to him, as we continued to rub along in harmony together in our haven of happily married life. Until one day, when the Big Man's opportunity to find out the answer to his questions, came in the form of this e-mail.

'Now who can this be.' I wondered as I read the message. I had always believed unreservedly the sad stories he had told me, I didn't need proof of his integrity, despite my mother's own initial reservations about the fact that he was such a loner, with no family of his own. I didn't resent her doubts and I would probably have felt the same if Cuckoo had met such a man, a man with no apparent past, however that evidence was now staring me in the face, needed or not. The black typeset of the neat, computerized writing was proof indeed. A niece had found me on Facebook, his sister's daughter. The message was that his mother was indeed still alive, but gravely ill and could he find it in himself to visit, despite the twenty-odd-year estrangement. The e-mail, and its message was a serious conundrum.

Two days later, after we had taken the Beloved Pooch to stay with Daddy Two and locked Daisy bunny safely in her cage with fresh hay and water, we found ourselves speeding down the motorway, for a reconciliation that he wasn't even sure he wanted. His sister was waiting emotionally; and the meat was finally put onto the bones of the stories that he had told me, fleshed out with photos and letters from the past. A visit to a nursing home followed, his mother was being cared for there, after suffering a massive stroke that had reduced her to a catheterized patient, trapped in a hospital bed. As the door opened, her head turned slowly, she had been told that her youngest son had been found and her mind at least, was able to assimilate the fact, as she acknowledged the return of her prodigal with shining eyes.

'Hello Mother.' I had no idea what he was thinking, as he stared down at the woman who had betrayed him so badly when he was just a little boy.

That night we trooped back to their house, ordered Chinese food and drank a lot of wine. I observed them silently, taking in this extraordinary event, watching my husband even more closely, still not sure what he was making about the situation. Once reunited we made several more visits as the old lady faded slowly, until eventually there was nothing more to hope for than a happy and merciful release. The Big Man took the final call one evening early in the following January of 2012, grimly setting off to say a final goodbye. That night was as stormy as they came, the weather was horrendous, the winds were raging like banshees, accompanied by lashing rain and dark, stormy skies. My heart was in my mouth with acute worry, as I pictured him battling the roads during that desperate drive.

'So proud of you, my soldier boy, so proud x' I sent the text several times that night, cuddled up to Cuckoo, with our Beloved Pooch snuggled in between us, staying awake to keep our own vigil for him as dawn broke; and suddenly we heard a robin singing outside the window.

A funeral followed, the cars following the hearse to a local church, with a top-and-tailed man walking slowly in front of the procession of black, gleaming vehicles, inside which sat the family including me, feeling horribly out of place. The Big Man then helped carry his mother's coffin into the church and with one slight falter, took his place at the front in preparation to deliver a speech. The words had been chosen carefully by both of us, until we had compiled something that we were pleased and proud for him to recite. I held him with my eyes, willing him on as he spoke, his army medals shining in the gloomy interior. At the ensuing wake looming strangers slapped him on the back.

'Well done, boy, well done,' they said, impressed with both his speech and strength of mind, bowing to the force of the black sheep who had recently returned to the family fold, a force to be so reckoned with. I watched proudly from a side table as my Big Man, with his polished medals still on full view, held his own with these admiring mourners, who in turn were paying court to him.

We tried to maintain the contact with his family, joining them for meals at wine-glass-laden tables and paid our respects to the grave again a month later, revisiting the old stomping grounds of his childhood. It was a beautiful part of the country, very rural with miles of handmade stone walling, a perfect place for a little boy to grow up in, unless that child had learnt about fear and hate along with the husbandry of pigs and cows. Of course, we had our own constraints of life at home to think about as well. There was Cuckoo's acceptance to university, then my lovely mother's horrible surgery and my own need for a small operation, nothing serious, but these were all important matters just the same.

All these factors meant that as time went by our visits became fewer, as the months of 2012 came and went. Communication became less frequent and more brittle, until it halted completely. The Big Man didn't seem to care, he was as bothered as I was about the opinions of my own in-laws and I started to see many similarities between the two families. Like sheep, the husbands and offspring followed the matriarchal commands, bowing to the will of their wives and mothers, erasing our existence. Eventually the e-mails stopped; and Facebook friendship accounts were deleted, all of which I found very sadly strange. Having supposedly missed a brother for all those years, searching for him desperately, then having the most amazing chance to be reunited, only to throw it away. How odd indeed, and another sage-old saying came to my mind, that there are none so queer as folk.

Chapter Sixteen

Races

Easter was over in 2015, for another year and mid-April brought another national highlight, Grand National day, an important traditional feature in the sporting calendar. Pick a few horses for this famously brutal horse race and then trot down to the bookies, crossing your fingers for the three forty-five afternoon fixture taking place at Aintree. One year we had screamed the roof off the house, as one of our chosen horses had thundered over the finish line in first place, making us over four hundred pounds richer. Cuckoo had been with us, as with bated breaths and increasing heart rates, the three of us had urged the nag on. We had no such luck this year, but it had been worth the money on the lost bets, for the adrenalin rush. The horses gleamed with sweat, nostrils pumping, ears pricking up, as their own heart beats slowed; and they shook their manes. They were gladiatorial beasts, winning machines, acutely aware of the accolades shouted at them by the crowds.

An annual boat race followed, Oxford v Cambridge, a most historic of events. Steeped in history, the oars of the boats would dip faster and faster, ploughing through the water of the Thames. It always reminded me of the terrible day that my father had been rushed to hospital, after suffering from a stroke caused by the chemotherapy that he had been enduring, to try and halt the march of the terrible cancer with which he had been diagnosed. That had been a terrible time, that killer disease always lurking in the wings.

It was a mother fucker of a time, a black, phantom period of fear, morbid sickness, and a prelude to inevitable death. A matter that often dominated my dreams, as it was about to again during a night of disturbed, troubled sleep, at the end of April 2015.

Cancer was a cunty, grunty, grumbling; and crumbling subject, which had to beg a question, if the sickness was often present because of nicotine, why did so many people smoke? I knew the answer, remembering those futile days at the hospice in Exeter, during my father's last weeks in March 1997. I would have a cigarette in the gardens with the nurses, who daily saw the cancer curse sink its fangs into patients and drag them off to its lair. The truth was that it was an addiction a subject that I knew much about, just another evil habit. It was also a smelly, expensive and life-threatening habit, but if some of these seriously ill victims had never smoked a fag in their lives, we smokers were still happy to play a lottery with our own, choosing to indulge ourselves with this smelly, expensive and oh, so enjoyable habit.

This reminded me of the third bout of nasal surgery that I had endured in January 2013. It was only a day procedure, nothing serious but the years of amphetamine abuse when I had snorted the evil powder straight into my blood system, had damaged my sinus passages in the process. It had left scar tissue, necessitating the repeat of the minor operation every few years. I knew that this could have been a lot worse; cocaine sniffing had left many a folk without a septum. I was waiting to be taken down to theatre, when I realized who was in the adjacent bed. Another lovely friend from work, who had been fighting breast cancer for a while, was in for yet another exploratory procedure. Both of us were dazed, recovering from the effects of general anesthetic, as we raised our hands slowly in acknowledgement of each other. Later, I wondered if I had imagined the occupant of the bed next to me.

'Get me home x.' I texted the Big Man when it was all over. Feeling sick and shaky, I waited for him to arrive. Tenderly, he peeled off my surgical socks and helped me into my clothes.

'Home, James!' I painfully croaked; my humor still brave in the face of this adversity.

The lovely, lovely friend later had to resign herself to a complete breast removal and reconstruction, she who had also never smoked a cigarette in her life. Unbelievably, at the same time her own Beloved Pooch, a stunning gun dog, had to have his balls removed due to a cancerous growth. She raised another, more defiant hand a year later, prior to preparing herself for this ultimate of operations. One that would involve so much surgery and trauma, removal of diseased flesh, realignment of muscle, all just to live. She proudly proclaimed that she intended to have an overall beautification prior to admission.

'Upstairs and downstairs, in the lady's chamber!' she had chuckled as she confided in me at work, the week before her surgery was due.

'Just in case anyone is looking!' She was intending to be blow dried, waxed and creamed before they wheeled her into theatre, wearing the obligatory, but scarcely modest-making surgical gown. Trying to keep the conversation light and understanding the depth of my friend's fears, for herself and her own Beloved Pooch, I steered our conversation to the subject of dogs' tails having to be docked, having always frowned darkly at the idea.

'What's the point of it, it's a horrible idea!' I asked her.

'It's to stop working dogs breaking their tail bones.'

'Oh, I suppose that makes sense!' Reluctantly I had to agree that there was a point there.

'What are you two talking about?' Another colleague had joined in with our hushed conversation.

'Dogs' tails and bollocks!' We answered in unison, changing our moods back to ones of a more light-hearted nature, giggling helplessly as we did so.

As April came to an end in 2015, the late spring weather enabled us to spend more time outside. The Big Man had created an outdoor room off the kitchen, the floor was decked; and roofed with opaque, plastic sheets, with both water and power available. Climbing plants had been trained to create a living ceiling and walls, all intertwined with fairy lights. Dangling from the inside of the roof were souvenirs of holidays and he had hung wind chimes that swung in the breeze, melodically singing out their 'Tubular Bells'. A grapevine that he had presented me with once, sat solidly in one corner. Later in the year, at the height of the summer, we would be able to sit within the tent of trailing greenery, naked if we wished, hidden within this secret place that became a veritable oxygen tent, as the foliage breathed out its O2. I sat out there quietly one day on my own, admiring his other handiwork in the garden.

The view was a crazy sight, to us it was nothing but pure magic, but to others it might be looked at with incredulous disbelief, as being simply, breathtakingly mad. I counted twenty-five pots, three bird baths and two bird tables, created from thick slices of aged oak. Large, shiny metal spheres were balanced randomly, polished until they gleamed in the sunlight that bounced off their curves like a laser. There were those wagon wheels, bleached antlers, solar lights and that oversized wooden mushroom; and trees that had been planted as saplings, or self-seeded and allowed to grow. Looking more carefully, other treasures caught the eye. A magnificent pearly conch shell, plastic meerkats on stick, and artificial pigeons, discarded after their use for when clay pigeon shooting was over. They too had been collected by the gatherer in his travels and that were now positioned in the flourishing trees.

The shrine to Daisy bun was still there of course, but by now the garden had overtaken the area that had been her run, and the best, saved until last in this crazy cornucopia, had to be another view of the Big Man's pride and joy, his Gruber. It was flourishing now, rapidly coming to life again after its winter hibernation and the first thick green knobs of its new growth could be seen, slowly pushing their way upwards towards the sunlight. Surfboards decorated the fenced periphery of the garden with military precision, brightly cartooned, they had been abandoned after their use during family days at the beach was over. Rescued from the trommel, they stood guard over the rest of the garden with a renewed purpose. The Big Mans latest venture was filling a metal dish with chicken carcasses and positioning it on top of a ten-foot-tall piece of metal piping to attract carrion-loving birds, its own purpose, to fulfil his dream of enticing red kites down to feast on the mouldering mess.

The bird song was nothing short of delightful, the garden was literally an oasis for every winged creature to find and breadcrumbs and nuts were scattered daily. One morning he proudly announced proudly that he had seen a pair of coal tits, identified by their pink under sides. They must have chosen our garden as a stop-off point after flying in from Africa, their tired wings finally landing them safely, if not in a land of milk and honey, then a delicious alternative of one of fat balls and monkey nuts. As in everything my husband touched, everything that he had designed within this little piece of paradise was deliberately intended and meticulously tended. It was an insane and mental assault on every aspect of every sense, sight, sound, smell, hearing and even taste. I adored it and loved him even more for having created it.

There was another race happening that month, alongside the horses and rowing boats, all vying for first place. Cuckoo was approaching the final furlong of her exams. I was no stranger to the fact that my daughter wanted to spend the coming summer in Ibiza, and I had still had secret doubts about the idea, but, on reflection, could the worry be any worse than when my girl was buzzing around central London, sometimes late at night by herself?

'Home safe x', was the always welcomed text, without which I would try to stop the crescendo of panic that was so familiar when it came to my Cuckoo, so how much worse could it be to know that she was planning to spend a few months on a Balearic island, thousands of miles away from terrorism and nocturnal, underground-stalking psychopaths? She was back in London for now, working hard on the final major project that we had proudly contributed towards, but her antics were bothering me yet again, as she made more frequent phone calls to me, asking for money that seemed to be gobbled up by her bank account, in a tsunami of financial transfers to her. She hadn't done any sort of paid work for a year and at this stage couldn't be expected to, but her requests for funds were outrageous. As I continued to sit in our outdoor room, contemplating my daughter's escapades, I heard my father's words on the subject.

'You can't live a 'Champagne Charlie' lifestyle, Catrin, if you don't have the money.'

'Yes, I know that Dad!'

My reply was unusually irritable, but it wasn't Champagne Charlie that I was worried about in Cuckoo's case and I was becoming increasingly concerned that her penchant for drugs was becoming even more of an itch that needed scratching, as whichever way I looked at it, the amount of money that she was begging me for, just didn't add up to the needs of a student powering through her last term.

'Bloody hell, Daddy.'

'That's just how I felt, Catrin.'

'How did you cope with me?!'

'With difficulty!'

Cuckoo had made another telephone call to me a few weeks previously, asking for more money to fund a one-way ticket to Ibiza. The Big Man was not impressed to put it mildly and so many negative 'What ifs', tumbled from his mouth.

'What if she fails the course babe, what if she can't find a job over there?... what if?'

'What if she passes baby?!... What if she does find work for the summer...what if?'

'She needs more discipline babe!'

'Bit bloody late for that!!'

What was I doing when I was twenty? certainly not flying as high as my daughter seemed to be and there were certainly no B.A. letters destined for my younger self, therefore despite my niggling, inner doubts, I gave my final blessing for her summer adventure. I really should have listened to him more carefully and considered the unspoken What ifs with more thought.

There were four weeks left of the final university term and six weeks until Cuckoo flew to the party island, a centre of sun, sex and drugs. What if this was another case of the frying pan and the fire?

'It'll be fine baby, let her have this experience!!'

'Huh....' His grunt of disapproval spoke volumes, as I tried not to peek mentally at the fact that my agreement to her plans could create more potential problems and pitfalls. Moving the girl into the idyllic penthouse flat outside London had seemed such a good idea at the time, but now it appeared to be the worst one that we had allowed. Why couldn't the stupid child have not stayed in the relative protection of the halls of residence, where she would have had her freedom but not the ability to invite every Tom, Dick and Harry back there to party. Hindsight again, good old hindsight, it was such a shame that it couldn't ever be used in reverse, looking forward and trying to avoid disaster, not looking back to regret it. I gave myself a firm shake; and the fears were relegated again, but it was a short-lived hiatus of calm, as I tried once more to warn her about her lifestyle.

'Don't nag Ma, I'm not a child!' Her inevitable response almost barked at me.

'Yee Gods!' I thought, staying silent on the other end of the telephone.

'It's not habitual Ma, it's not M-CAT. Don't worry, it's only cocaine!' This was very worrying.

April 2015 had been unseasonably warm; and the Bee Tree had already given up its blossom. Swirling down like confetti, it had danced with the midges as it descended to lay a pastel-scattered blanket and the tree was now shrouded with decaying seed pods. Other flowers had entered center stage and daisies smiled as they begged to be made into chains. Buttercups and dandelions, the color of egg yolk, pansies with their dark, sultry eyes, were all now in abundance. The smell of early evening barbecues lingered temptingly and walking the Beloved Pooch had become a pleasure again, not a wintery chore, as off we went around our block, taking in its sensory gifts. His eager jaws would snap at forbidden, plump blades of grass, as cocking his leg periodically, he would water the chosen places. My gaze fell upon dock leaves in the undergrowth and a wave of nostalgia came over me as I remembered picking them for Daisy, a gastronomic treat for a bunny.

I had transferred the promised money to Cuckoos bank account for the flight on 13th May, and a deposit for a share of an apartment in Ibiza town. She would be rooming with a tiny, pocket Venus, blonde friend who had worked such summers abroad before, and I was happy that our girl had a seasoned travelling companion to show her the ropes. They were planning to spend the coming months working in bars and paying their own passage. I tried to stay logical, hoping that their plan made sense, after all how much worse could it be than the temptations that Cuckoo was clearly finding it hard to resist in London? How much worse indeed! I would find out all in good time and I really should have listened more carefully to those What if's, as The Big Man continued to try to make me understand his concerns and make me see his point of view, but I argued every toss.

'Baby, what's wrong with working in bars for the summer?!'

'That's if she finds a job, babe!'

'If she stays here, she'll only kick her heels and pretend to look for a job!!'

'Huh!... I suppose so.' There was that grunt again, but this argument was one that he couldn't disagree with despite his black and white attitude, still he couldn't resist the last word.

'She needs rules babe, rules are rules!!' His words reflected the army training that was distilled in him, something that was a blessing but could occasionally be a curse.

'Yes, but I did it once upon a time!' I didn't bother voicing my final thought, as I contemplated my foreign adventures on the Greek islands in the summer in 1986, with an inner smile on my face.

'And look how that turned out, Catrin.'

'Ok!! You've got a point too, Dad!'

There were times when I didn't welcome my father's input.

The evenings were lengthening now and sitting outside with a glass of wine became a nightly treat. The year was already a quarter through, and Cuckoo was home again to attend the funeral of her friend's father, for whom, as a tribute, she had reluctantly rejected my star suggestion, opting to release fire lanterns with her gang of mates from home and light candles in the dark. She was upbeat and chatty, there was so much happening in her life, only three weeks until the handing-in of the final dissertation and five weeks until her flight to Ibiza. I enjoyed a few precious hours with her, listening as she chattered on, content that she was so happy as we walked the Beloved Pooch together around the streets of the village called home.

It was a very rural location considering its proximity to more urban towns, with its narrow roads flanked by trees and the variety of houses, with large, detached properties that sat side by side with terraces and higgledy-piggledy bungalows. Looking up, I could see the watchful windows of the old house, knowing that the size of the house had nothing what-so-ever to do with the peace of mind of those who dwelled in them and I was reminded of the card that my mother had once sent me, with its little boat bobbing furiously for dear life, smiling at the memory. Cuckoo would never come back to live with us permanently, it was too much of a sleepy backwater, but she knew we would always be here for her, or whether else we laid our hats. Her horizons were vast and reached way beyond this little vicinity, Cuckoo's boat would be a massive cruise ship, there would be no paddling to save her sanity, she would just fire up the engines and enjoy the ride.

There was soon to be another milestone race in the years calendar, the London Marathon was about to begin. It had started in 1984, when seven thousand runners of varying caliber had taken to the twenty-six- mile long run around the City. Now, in 2015, over forty thousand runners were taking part, back in the1980s, only four % had been women but now that figure was over forty %. The competition was multi-national, with professional runners in skinny Lycra and ordinary folk, running for charity in crazy fancy dress outfits. The best time was just over two hours, the average around four, but some of the participants took days to stagger round and finish the course in exhausted triumph. I smiled ruefully, admiring the televised sight, running had never been a strong point for me and these days I probably couldn't even run for a bus. I remembered fondly past school sports days when Cuckoo had been little. She used to insist that I entered the obligatory parents' race, and it was with dread that I watched as the other Mothers galloped past me, all determined to be the first across the finish line.

'Silly bitches, I thought it was supposed to be the taking part that mattered, not the winning!!' Was always my out of breath, silent opinion as I lumbered forward along the freshly chalk-marked lane that I had been given. School sports days had happier memories, such as home-made picnic lunches on blankets, after finding a prime spot on the grassy verge of the playing field and cheering Cuckoo on in the sack and egg and spoon races, adjourning to the pub later. They had been such innocent pleasures for my younger self and my even younger, competitive Cuckoo, who had reveled in both the taking part and the winning. She had always rushed to find me in the family crowd after each race, to proudly present me with a colored rosette or cheap medal, her coveted prize for being placed. Her large shining eyes, and reddened, sweaty face, were always glowing with health and pride. These were vivid and cherished past images of an innocent child that I had held close to my heart, as now I watched those eyes focus on a much bigger prize for completing her three-year university course, her own exciting foreign adventure.

May was looming, bringing its first bank holiday at the beginning of the month and my next birthday. Cuckoo had only five days left to submit her work and I could hear panic in her voice when she called me, summoning up words of encouragement as I tried to soothe her angst.

'It will be fine, power through, sort it out!' Although as usual she had left things as close to the wire as she dared.

The Big Man and I spent this birthday bank holiday weekend in our usual decadent way, mooching around during the Monday afternoon, after some luscious shagging the night before. At four am we had been fucking frantically, witnessed by a full Moon staring in through opened curtains. My stoned eyes had met the benevolent lunar gaze as the Big Man rammed into me. Completely turned on, I begged for more.

'Again baby, Fuck me again!' I cried out louder and louder, as every inch of my body squirmed with desire. The bedroom windows were also open, so what the neighbors had made of this nocturnal howling was debatable, as inevitably it must have stirred them from their slumbers. Hopefully, they would put it down to baying werewolves, paying their own homage to the perfectly round silver sphere hanging magically in the dark. We lay head to tail the next morning, wrapped around each other, literally totally fucked from the excesses of exquisite sexual fulfilment. Slowly waking up, I ran my fingers through his pubic hair that was still its original light brown colour, unlike the silver fox sheen of the rest of the hair on his body and head. As I blew gently on his twitching cock and drew the foreskin back to reveal the tight, shiny end, it grew large and bulbous before my eyes.

'Fuck me again, baby!'

'Greedy girl!'

'Baby, fuck me again!' I demanded as he took control and climbing on top of me, slid inside easily.

'God you're wet, babe!' he gasped as he watched himself pumping in and out, then knowing the reaction he would get, suckled each of my hot nipples alternately. I played with them madly at the same time, using just enough finger pressure to pinch them to twice their length, just enough pressure to add another exquisite touch of pain to the pleasure. Eyes locked, we lay there, panting and laughing as usual.

'Happy Birthday babe!' Happy days indeed.

I had thirty-seven Facebook birthday greetings and a special Mother's Birthday card from my Cuckoo. I smiled, remembering how many of my past birthdays had been spent fucked in other ways, knowing that this had to be the best sort of fucked. These were very happy days indeed, sadly to be a very short- lived happiness.

My birthday this year had coincided with the birth of a royal princess, would they call her Catrin? Of course not, but she was second named for a national treasure who would have been delighted to be a grandmother to this new-born cherub and enjoyed so many girly things with her. Her own children had been boys, so her household must have been very masculine. How she would have treasured the excuse to indulge in sugar and spice and all things nice, if she hadn't died so young in a French underpass. Hounded by the paparazzi who had blighted her privacy for so many years and in trying to obtain one more exclusive photograph, were primarily responsible for what was by many, judged to be murder.

I rang my own lovely mother to thank her for her card and the equally lovely cheque that it had contained; and our conversation turned to the Big Man, who was busy cleaning windows as we chatted.

'He does remind me of your father, you know.'

'Thank you, that's a real compliment!'

As I listened to her, I knew that this was something that I had already thought many times, just how like my father my amazing Big Man was, unbelievably strong, judgmental, just to the right degree and a rock.

'He smelt like chocolate; he smelt like my father.' The sensory emotions that I had conjured up about him during our first encounter, came vividly back to mind.

The following week there was to be another sort of race, a general election and a frenetic desire by all the politicians involved, to make sure they were on the winning side. They were cranking themselves into a frenzy of high dudgeon, making false promises to the voting public whilst slagging each other off in the name of our supposed public interest. Blues versus reds, versus yellows, all boxing around each other with swaggering pomp. There had been a live televised debate involving seven party leaders, which had been most entertaining at least for its comedy value. We listened and watched as scripted statements were delivered with annoying saccharin smiles and gnashing teeth, whilst they sported coiffured hair and expensive suits. We couldn't believe a word of it as the crap tumbled out of their mouths, their words fighting with each other for supremacy. They didn't appear to be listening to each other, though the practiced, slightly cocked-head stance whilst pretending to do so, gave a very good impression of genuine intent, whilst what they were really waiting for was the opportunity to jump back into the verbal foray, with more words saying more nothings.

The papers had a field day ripping this performance to pieces. One of the individuals being interviewed was likened to a half-Terminator creature, ala Schwarzenegger's part in the well-known series of films. This wanna-be member of the government was reminiscent of a camel in appearance as he stared unblinkingly at the camera, with his dark hair slicked back just so; and a smile that was so far removed from his wet eyes, that it was more of a grimace, whilst he brayed like a donkey at the same time. Election fever had the country divided now, the political hopefuls were in top gear and the country would turn out en masse, walking or driving to their designated polling stations to mark crosses on ballot papers. Would the world be any different the day after, when one of the parties had been successfully put into power? I doubted it, just as I doubted their ability to make any real difference in the future. The Big Man and I would vote of course, we would walk the Beloved Pooch to our local polling station. Emmeline Pankhurst hadn't chained herself to a railing for nothing, so we would walk together and place our votes.

My pet hates included benefit scroungers gobbling up my hard-earned wages, whilst claiming all sorts of nonsensical reasons as to why they couldn't go out to graft with the rest of the population, so not to vote, in the hope that the successful party would come down a bit harder on these leeches, would be silly. Politicians on the other hand, if not on my hate list were firmly found on my to-be despised list. For example, there was once a chap who had been high in political office, who had been found suffocated after an incident involving a satsuma, during kinky sex. Not forgetting the corruption that seemed rife amongst these lardy lumps, where expense fiddling featured scandalously high in their remit. I had rarely ever signed on to the dole although the child benefit payments received for Cuckoo had been welcomed warmly, but in general I had paid my taxable dues, reminding me of yet another old proverb, that death and taxes were the only things impossible to avoid.

The hopeful candidates stood to attention outside the church hall where the ballot boxes were set up inside. The guy in purple and yellow was the friendliest and he offered to look after the Beloved Pooch whilst we entered the building to vote, so it seemed only fair that my scribbled cross was made against his name. A hysterical way to decide who to vote for, but much saner than listening to the spin and it might even have been more logical. The date, seventh May, again seemed familiar, I puzzled it for a few seconds until I realised that it was my father's birthday and that he would have been eighty-five.

'How you would have loved this Daddy!'

'I believe you are quite right, Catrin.'

'Happy Birthday! I love you.'

'I love you too.'

'Why can I only talk to you now and again?'

'I already told you, the link between us is weak, but its growing stronger.'

'How did it happen?!'

'Do you remember asking me if you were vindicated yet?'

'Yes! It was after Mum's operation!'

'You made this happen Catrin, you wanted it so much that it did.'

'Are you in Heaven?'

'Well, we both know that you don't believe in God.'

'I don't understand!'

'Yes... that is ......'

He had gone again, his last sentence unfinished. Yes, he would have loved all this fuss and the televised, live coverage as the computerized 'Swingonometers', got going. How he would have reveled in the madness, frowning and laughing in turn with vigorous nods and shakes of his full head of hair, which had he still been alive, would doubtlessly now be snowy white.

Chapter Seventeen

The What If's raise their Heads

One temperate evening as the Sun was setting, later in May 2015, I was ambling around the oh so familiar block with the Beloved Pooch, noticing that the yellow dandelion flowers had turned to wispy, white balls of fluff, ready to be used as clocks by children. One hour of time for every puff and a wish for every breathe softly blown. We lived in the flight path of Heathrow, which was far enough away for it not to be a nuisance, but close enough to be able to watch the planes as they ascended and descended. I looked up to watch the aerial show that they were presenting, gazing at their trails of smoky fumes that were dancing amongst the cloud strata. The white and grey ribbons were spelling out cryptic messages in the bluey grey sky, scribbles that turned yellow and orangey red, as the Sun simmered and slowly dropped below the horizon.

At night, their front headlights were reminiscent of the spaceships that featured in H.G. Wells classic, 'The War of the Worlds', their beams seeming to move like giant, mechanically sighted eyes. It was an awesome illusion to see, especially when the stars started appearing and they too joined in with the display. One by one these stellar lights from age old constellations would grace the ballet in the night sky, especially when it was clear, midnight blue and velvety. At first, they were mere pinpricks of silvery white, then, as they took their graceful place in the heavens, their lights grew stronger; and they became sparkling diamonds with a glimmering majesty, just crystal drops in a celestial, overhead ocean, hypnotically drawing my eyes as they had always done. There was one that always attracted me more, my special star. It was larger than the rest, surrounded by an unusual circle of other smaller stars, that seemed to be paying homage to a superior body, appearing to dance with twinkle toes, around it, whirling and dipping with magical movements, bowing as they did so.

'That definitely looks like the star I that saw on holiday last October, but it's bigger than it was then; and I don't remember a ring of lights around it either.' I mused to myself during one of these spell-bound salutes to the sky, as my father felt closer than ever; and I could almost feel his breath on my face.

'The future isn't written in the stars, Catrin, you won't find any answers there, only ghosts from the past.'

'What do you mean?'

'That there are lessons to be learnt Catrin, so many lessons, here on Earth.'

Instantly 9/11 crossed my mind, I, like the rest of the world had watched the live broadcast with its horrific breaking news, during that fateful morning of 11th September 2001. Aghast, frozen in the moment, unable to comprehend what I was watching, I was transfixed by the atrocity that was being played out, as not one, but two passenger planes were deliberately crashed into the Twin Towers in New York. Evil had raised its head at that moment, cunty, grunty, grumbling evil incarnate, that had roared with a deathly intent. That day had made a difference to the world and nothing was ever going to be the same again.

The act of violence was repeated in London on 7th July 2005, when bombs on the tube system had caused carnage on a smaller but equally deadly scale. Evil in the air, evil underground, bellowing monsters of evil, playing curved ball with humanity. Countless were dead and many more injured, maimed for life. The Twin Towers had toppled like mighty Goliaths felled by the sword of David and from the debris, clouds of thick, toxic smoke had enveloped the City. The hopelessly trapped New York workers had texted final good-byes to devastated friends and families, and some had even jumped to their death. The commuters in the bowels of London, where Hades had come alive, hadn't stood an earthly chance either. It was shit, it was grimmer than grim; and many tears were shed, enough desolate tears to restore the cracked and parched exposed beds of the world's dried-up lakes and seas.

'Were these some of the lessons, Daddy?'

'Yes, Catrin; and more, but nothing was gained from them.'

'Can't you do anything to help?'

'No, we can only observe and pray for our chosen loved ones.'

'We?!'

'Yes Catrin, there are many of us, we are the 'Watchers.' We all watch over someone on Earth.'

'You feel closer.'

'Yes, I am closer, our link is getting stronger.'

'I still don't understand.'

'Yes, that is the problem.'

He seemed to have been able to finish the sentence that he had tried to do, on the night of his birthday.

'Am I supposed to understand Daddy?'

'I hope so, eventually.'

With that he was gone again; and I was left with even more unanswered questions.

Cuckoo had travelled the underground daily and the omnipresent potential of the evil attacking London again was constantly in my thoughts, every time I pictured her scuttling down the steep escalators that led to the tube tunnels that were buried so deeply under the city. She was only a little girl, a tough-talking, bullshitting, clever, little piglet, but she was still a little girl all the same, no match for the cunty grunts if they chose to target her. What a crappy, twisted world to be growing up in. So how much worse could it be to exchange the smog and grot of an urban city for the smiling shores of a party island? A place where hopefully another evil, Isis, the Islamic militants, who were baying for blood from those who they considered to be infidels, would find it almost impossible to infiltrate, its North African cousins being so much more accessible. An island that wasn't being besieged by refugees trying to escape the tyranny of the powers that ruled the countries where the roots of the evil resided. The Balearics should be protected from any of this nonsense. So how much worse indeed could it be for Cuckoo to swap life in London for the balmy climes of Ibiza?

She was finally home for the last time, her stuff crammed into black rubbish sacks, three years of university life that had been dumped unceremoniously everywhere.

'Oh no! Girl what is all this!' I wailed as I trawled through the first few bags, unearthing debris that belonged in a dustbin, not my house.

'Calm down Ma!'

'Calm down! you little pig, how rude!!'

'Get a grip Ma!!' I turned away from her hostile retorts, with involuntary tears in my eyes.

'Are you crying, Ma?!! Pathetic!!' As her last sarcastic, verbal blow hit its target, I tried to ignore the insults whilst still wading through the dross in a futile attempt to cull it, wondering why we had offered to throw her a party the following weekend. It was a celebration of finishing university, a pre-Ibiza wave-off and an early twenty-first Birthday bash, as she would be away for this coming of age.

The theme was going to be piggy, obviously and I had trawled the Internet for party accessories. A pig shaped Mexican Piñata, filled with chocolate pigs and a piggy pass the parcel awaited the excited guests, along with helium balloons on the same theme. On the night of the planned shindig, Cuckoo's besties had arrived, squealing and oinking, little piglets themselves one and all. With bottles in hand, they were ushered into the kitchen and outdoor room.

'Let's keep the little sods out there for the night.!'

'Good idea babe!!' The Big Man had agreed whole-heartedly with this suggestion. We had decided to invite Mr. R., Cuckoo's father and the friend who was a girl, for some adult company, all four of us retiring to the safety of the living room as the volume outside became ear splitting. We were drinking as heavily as the over excited mob outside were and after one too many spliffs had been rolled, I made the mistake of giving Mr. R. a blowback. Things nearly got extremely nasty, and my gorgeous Big Man took complete offence to what he considered an act of intimacy, whilst the girl who was a friend was equally shocked. I really liked the friend, she was short in stature with mind-blowingly humongous tits, the like I hadn't seen since Knockers in Spain had flashed hers around. The lady had amazing, blonde -highlighted hair, masses of it, loved a gin and a fag, and was clearly totally in love with her bestie. It was unrequited physical love of course, but the adoration was written all over her face, hence the random brushing of faces during that brief act of blow-backing came as an unwelcome surprise to her as well.

'I'm sorry, baby.' The next morning, I realized that my actions had really upset my husband. I couldn't understand see why the blowback had been misconstrued, the sexuality of Mr. R. was so out there; and no real harm had been meant. It hadn't even been lip-contact, even so the Big Man was clearly hurt by it and the last thing I would ever have wanted was to hurt his feelings.

'I'm sorry, baby.' I repeated.

'Get on top.' He demanded and fucked me furiously, marking his territory and sealing the wrong, righting it in the only way he knew how. I held on for dear life, the ride exquisite. Eyes meeting at the final climax, as I watched his pupils burst like black fireworks, into the familiar blue.

'I love you so much, baby, I'm so sorry.' I apologized for the third time, recalling the look on his face, when a French guy had innocently asked me to dance one evening during a foreign holiday.

'I see murder in your husband's eyes.' He had garbled in his broken English and quickly backed away. I had forgotten my husband's alpha male mind-set tendencies, as I had rarely tested them and never deliberately. It was awesome being on the receiving end of his possessive nature, a bit like being on the end of his cock, pure testosterone, distilled it would be worth a fortune.

Before the royal blunder of the blowback, some of the earlier conversation during the party evening; had been hilarious. Mr. R. completely faced, had reminded me of another party that we had thrown during my antics at the sex shop. I had purloined several sex aids as accessories for the occasion. Life-sized, blow-up dolls had hung from the ceiling, their plastic, sightless faces staring weirdly down on the party goers. Bondage costumes were available for all to change into and there was a booby doorbell attached to the front door, with a homemade sign, 'Buzz for entry,' above it. The piece de resistance was a wax candle in the form of a large dick, that some idiot had lit and was bouncing around the room with it hanging out of his flies. Wax was dripping everywhere, hideous stuff to remove at the best of times, but this pseudo cock was squirting liquid wax, like cum and doing some serious damage to the carpet and furniture.

Overall, the piggy party had gone very well, the only damage was a broken toilet seat, and I had a horrible feeling that it was me who had knocked it off its hinges, in a sudden mad dash to be violently sick, in a red wine, white-out 'chunder' at its most volatile. Sunday, the next day, was reserved for nursing hangovers and retrieving the countless empty bottles for the bin. Cuckoo and the Beloved Pooch had gone to her fathers for a family dinner, prior to her flight to Ibiza the following Wednesday morning. Fuzzyheaded and not sure if a glass more of red wine would kill or cure, I and my now placated husband spent a quiet evening eating fish and chips, just glad of the peace and quiet.

'They're a lovely bunch of kids really baby.' My comment was met with silence from a suddenly poker-faced Big Man.

'Mm, the army would sort them out babe, no bloody boundaries, no bloody rules.' was his eventual answer.

I still deemed them to be a fine drove of piggy's, despite their propensity to drink and shout, as fast and as loud as possible. Yep, the party had gone with a bang and the pass the parcel had gone down a huge treat, as music was drunkenly played and the timing of the pauses fixed, to ensure that every excited guest had a turn to unwrap a layer of newspaper to reveal a surprise. Childhood was never that far away at times like that and much later the night after the party, I would sleep long and hard, drifting off to the sound of raindrops as they trickled down the bedroom window. The familiar noise reminding me once again of my own childhood and the safety it had given me, as my star glowed intermittently between the clouds that were dappling the night sky.

'Night, Daddy I love you.'

'I love you too Catrin.' His answer came as a gentle whisper and my mind fell into a glorious, peaceful slumber.

The next few days passed in a whirlwind of activity and preparation, as Operation Ibiza went into full swing. I tried to maintain a degree of composure but eventually lost it, screaming and shouting at my daughter. There was a virtual bombsite caused by the weapons of destruction contained within the black sacks that had made a direct hit a few days before. The mountains of clothing and personal belongings had spread from Cuckoo's bedroom, the flotsam and jetsam of her university days spilling relentlessly across the upstairs landing. The fact that she still seemed oblivious to this chaos brought more tears of frustration to my eyes.

'Live with the little beast? Not if I want to stay sane!' I frowned deeply, making the silent promise to myself. We finally prized her out of the front door, with a mammoth suitcase filled with five hundred pounds of designer clothing, another twenty-first present handpicked by the fussy chick to ensure that her Ibizan look passed muster.

'Unbelievable!' I couldn't help but voice my opinion of the obscenely overpriced garments when she had proudly modelled them for us.

'Do you like them Ma!!' Cuckoo had completely misconstrued my statement, assuming I was commenting on the stylish nature of her chosen outfits.

'I love them!!' I hastily replied, whilst thinking of my own not-so designer flip flops and shorts. We waited with her until her lift came, releasing the last remaining helium piggy party balloon, waving madly, watching the car disappear around the corner, its occupants waving back, laughing and pointing to the soaring balloon.

'Have a great piggy flight!' I shouted and Cuckoo was gone.

This was the start of the sleepless, worry-filled nights for me, I really should have paid more attention to the Big Man's morbid 'What ifs', as now my mind developed so many of my own. The next few months were going to give me as much stress as anything else that I had endured where my daughter was concerned; and my texting started in earnest.

'You at airport? x'

'Yeah x'

'You boarded? x'

'Yeah x'

'You landed? x'

'Ma I'm not a child, yes we've landed.'

She found work straight away. From ten in the evening until five in the morning, she was pulling punters into a club. At five thirty in the morning, I was wide awake.

'You back at the apartment yet? x' There was no immediate reply and a knife twisted in my gut.

'You home safe?'

'Ffs Ma, I'm not a little girl, remember.' her eventual answer brought more tears to my eyes, for that was exactly what she was to me and the imaginary umbilical cord twisted my stomach with more stressful emotion, reminding me painfully of its presence, as the What ifs just got worse and worse. Next came the news that the girls had been invited to a party on a yacht. Visions of enslavement and prostitution haunted me. What if Cuckoo was kidnapped, injected with heroin ... 'TAKEN!' Sleep continued to evade me, sleep that had always come so easily was almost impossible to fall into now; and no attempts of counting sheep would stop me seeing images of shadowy monsters lurking with needles, ready to pounce with a deadly aim. Of course, it was all nonsense and the Facebook photograph of Cuckoo standing at the prow of the boat, head flung back staring into the sunset, allayed my fears a little bit. Yet the fear of the What ifs and what manner of What ifs that they could be, continued to haunt me.

'Ma, I don't think I can do this x' She was referring to the job.

'Quit then x'

'Ok! xxx' The attraction of all-nighters had quickly palled; and I found myself transferring more money, my Cuckoo had to eat.

Unlike the sultry climes of the Spanish island, May 2015 in England was basking in the odd afternoon of early summer warmth and a more regular lashing from horizontal rain, depending on the mood of the jet stream. The garden loved the combination, and the canopy of green was spectacular. Gruber was headlining the show, its tropical leaves continuing to burst and unfurl from the Mother lode. I got home from work one evening to an explosion of excited, verbal glee from the Big Man.

'You've seen a red kite baby!!' After weeks of offering up his smelly sacrifices, chicken carcasses, bacon rind and raw liver, he finally had his prize. He had watched the bird swoop down talons extended, to pick up a meaty morsel. I was delighted for my man, mentally doubting with a huge smile on my face, the sanity behind this designer of our garden, whilst also loving him completely for his madness.

The next highlight at the end of the month would be my lovely mother's annual birthday visit. The previous November 2014; had seen the most splendid and humbling of sights, as thousands of blood red, ceramic poppies had been commissioned and planted in London. Hordes of thousands of visitors; had made the pilgrimage to view the spectacle. Several of my work cronies had run the gauntlet of the crowds, to gaze upon the sea of tributes to the fallen in both big Wars, which had blighted England and the world. We had not been able to make the journey, but I had managed to buy two of these unique flowers online and they duly arrived, after the poppies had been carefully removed from the site. They had been sold individually and shipped worldwide, to be replanted in vases and pots as a forever reminder, lest we all forget. One was earmarked as a special birthday present for my lovely mother, who had survived the war herself as a little girl; and the other was for my soldier boy.

Good old British Rail threw a spanner into the birthday plans, by calling a strike over the second bank holiday weekend of May over the few days that Mother was planning to travel to us. The hiccup was too much for an Octogenarian to handle, so the visit was post-phoned; and the weekend was spent in an alternative joyously decadent fashion. We sat outside on the Friday evening, breathing in the sweet air. Gruber was still rising, easily ten feet tall now; and I Face booked a snap for fun, the tendrils of the beast were standing proudly underneath its leaves as I photographed it.

'Giant rhubarb!' I had titled the picture.

'That's a big 'un!' The retorts bounced back to me.

'Yeah, I'm a lucky girl!' I was loving the innuendo, if only they knew!

The covered, outdoor seating area twinkled its fairy lights, and the night was balmy, as we sat for hours, laughing, talking shit, drinking and smoking. The garden was illuminated by spotlights, all the dancing lights were having a magical affect, letting us conjure up shapes and faces again, loving the familiar game. Tomorrow could wait and the evening lingered on, with delightful appreciation from both our sides.

Tomorrow sleepily arrived eventually and the hilarious Eurovision Song Contest was to be the Saturday night highlight. Hosted by a charming Irish chap with the gift of the gab, who had an uncanny ability to deliver one-liners with the accuracy of a world-class darts player. He too liked a drop of the grape I had read somewhere and had apparently been known to fall asleep in his dog's basket, after a bottle too many. The various countries that had entered an act all vied with each other, each worse than the last, it was a howler of a show. Last year, the most exquisitely beautiful, silky-bearded individual had captured the hearts of the viewers. A full-length ball gown and eye make-up to die for had completed his look, as his voice soared like a phoenix into the auditorium, creating a stampede of a standing ovation as he took the accolades. Oh, Eurovision night, to be loved or loathed, but in our case, it was to be absolutely adored.

Bank holiday Sunday dawned, with our usual amnesia about the outcome of the previous night's entertainment. England, nil points as always. Well, what could you expect? The judging was a farce. All the proud, little countries with their harsh ways of life, were given this one opportunity to bedazzle the viewers and their amateur entries were always presented with such hope for a moment in the spotlight. They would then busily vote for each other, cowing under the domination they were suffering at the hands of a dreadful, Soviet leader, they trilled their scores in a tiny bit of splendid individual rebellion.

'Never watching that again babe!' The words came from our marital bed, as the Big Man watched my tongue lingering over his cock.

'You say that every year baby!' My voice croaked through the mouthful of hardening muscle. A Grand Prix in Monaco that afternoon would guarantee to lighten his mood.

'I've been there.' I remarked, remembering the valiant Ford hooked up to a touring caravan, as two little girls and their determined parents set out for another exciting European adventure and I had to wonder once again, why my younger sister hated me so much? The angry, little girl who had lost so badly at Monopoly, had grown into an adult with a bubbling cauldron of black emotion in her soul. For what reason? Her own life had been mapped out with successes. University graduation and teacher training; were followed by meeting the man who she would marry, a pairing for life. She produced two babies who would grow to live blameless, shadow-free lives themselves. Definitely no ferry man! They wouldn't have dared to try and cross such rivers; they probably wouldn't even want to. That in itself wasn't such a bad thing, but when they became parents themselves in the future, would they too opt to cut the umbilical cords, if pushed to it?

'Yeah, I've been there, baby.' I repeated my comment, remembering the familiar mountain road that dipped into the fabulously wealthy harbor of Monte Carlo, as those two little girls safely strapped into the back of their father's car, glanced back up at me from over the years. I continued to watch them with my mind's eye, until they disappeared out of sigh, on the winding route into the millionaire's playground, where they would no doubt make camp with their parents on a tree-lined site; and eat corn beef and frites, before trying to play Monopoly without a squabble.

'My glands are up Ma x' Cuckoo's latest message tweeted.

'Spanish flu x Try drinking orange juice with the vodka, sort it out! x'

'Ha ha. Ma, you're so funny not x'

That evening I rang my lovely mother, who was clearly upset by the necessary   cancellation of the trip that she had wanted to make, to visit us.

'I was your age when Dad and I moved to Devon, I was fifty-five.'

'Oh really.' I didn't voice my next thought, that it was only going another eleven years before he died and as if he had read my mind, I heard him.

'Make the most of it Catrin, as you know, you never know what's around the corner.'

'I promise Daddy.' More worried about the hairpin bends in his granddaughter's current road, than the ones that I had travelled in the past.

Cuckoo posted some amazing photographs over the next few weeks. She and her friend had had their bodies painted, before gracing yet another club opening night. Her next job was to try and tempt holiday makers to pay seven euros to have the same make-over, earning a euro commission for each one. She herself looked like a surreal mermaid, with her face adorned in blue and gold swirls of glittery colour, whilst the decoration on her lower body had turned her into an exotic animal, with gold and tawny stripes embellishing her limbs. Wearing a tiny bikini top, even weenier shorts and a huge grin, she posed and preened for the camera, as job number two was excitedly ventured into and subsequently given up as a lost cause.

'Ma, I only made three euros last night x'

'Quit then x'

'Ok! Can you send me some money then please!! xxx'

She had rung frequently much to my delight, as I was trying very hard not to hound the girl with texts and calls, so to receive more than I planned to make was a big deal for me. A Spanish phone had been bought and the familiar tone indicating that the call was from abroad, always made me smile. It had only been two weeks since the farewell party, but it seemed like a lifetime, although it all seemed to be going to plan. I had taken out travel insurance on her behalf, remembering the unfortunate girl on the Greek island in 1986. I grimaced at my own stupidity back in those days, no wonder I had become super organized with such matters, you just never knew what was about to fly-strike your life. As if to remind me of just that, the following Monday morning a colleague gave me a phone.

'It's your daughter, she's crying.'

The horror of a What if galloped through my mind as I took the call. Cuckoo was distraught and not making any sense. The worse-case scenarios flashed through my mind, as I struggled to decipher her sobbing sentences. That morning, she and her friend had been wandering around in another half-ditched attempt to find employment. Relaxing their guard and tempted by the view of the beach, they had put their bags down. Bank cards, mobile phones, keys to the flat, everything, had been stolen. Her wailing increased in crescendo, as she told me that that her cherished and very expensive watch had also been taken.

'Passports?' I sharply asked the question.

'No Ma.'

'Was there an address on the keys darling.' Thankfully there hadn't been, to give a clue as to what door could be unlocked for further thieving. It was a hideous lesson to have to learn, but if this was the only What if of the season to become a reality, then it could be interpreted as a lucky escape. My heartbeat eventually returned to something resembling normality, as I hastily cancelled her bank card and mobile phone. The watch would have already been sold on of course and the cheap Spanish pay-as-you-go would have been used, until any credit was gone. I texted the number.

'I know you stole this phone and my daughter's handbag I am the Mother, and I am coming to Ibiza to find you, you bastard.' Pressing send firmly, the action made me feel marginally better and I was able to fall asleep more easily that night, the roller coaster of the day having wiped me out. Telling the story at work the next day raised hoots of laughter. 'You should have written it in Spanish!' Indeed, I should, but as my written Spanish was more limited than my spoken, I settled for the slight satisfaction that hopefully whichever little tea leaf had read that text in Ibiza, they would have been spooked if only briefly, by its threatening content.

June 2015 was in full bloom in England, and it was the time of plenty for wildlife. That didn't stop the amazing sight of squirrels busily feeding from the still-laden bird tables at five o'clock in the morning, as dawn broke. Poppies, dog daisies and nettles flourished in abundance, as every plant, growing tall and leggy, reached higher and higher. The Sun was at its peak and that, coupled with more than the season's fair share of rainfall, made every leaf and stalk shimmer with verdant delight. Gruber raised more gigantic tentacles, that were flourishing in response to the tender loving care it was receiving from its Frankenstein master. My lovely mother finally made her planned journey, and her picture was taken under the heady canopy, dwarfing her completely, as we spotted a real cuckoo baby, a large, clumsy brown chick being fed by the unsuspecting blackbirds.

Ascot loomed, the famous racecourse taking it's bow in the year's calendar of events. Drunken fillies in short skirts and silly hats, and stallions in top hats and tails, were all guzzling over-priced champagne and playing to the eager cameras of the news reporters who were covering the televised races. As the longest day of the year arrived, the Summer Solstice, my thoughts returned to my Cuckoo and further back, to my own crazy Greek island of 1986, where the desire for hedonistic pleasures outweighed any other needs, apart from earning a drachma or two. Her inability to earn her own buck was becoming ever apparent and the deep waters she was paddling in were even more troubling. She told me about friends who felt forced to 'mule' cocaine as a way of making ends meet; and now I felt forced to maintain the supply of funds, to prevent this ultimate What if from raising its head.

I knew very well the dark side of foreign places. Spend a week or two as a holiday maker and it would leave you undisturbed; but become a part of its community and the underworld would show itself, beckoning fingers of temptation into one-way streets. More posted photographs continued, showing a deeply darkly tanned Cuckoo. One was taken the morning after the night before, when a group wearing silly attire on their heads and revealing the jaded, faded, wide awake look of having spent a night on the tiles, getting as high as possible.

'Why have you got a cake tin on your head? x'

'Cos I'm baking Ma! x' I found her texted reply secretly quite funny; but was still frowning inwardly.

'No more money, get another job, a proper one, sort it out!' I typed my order fiercely along the line, I was at the stage where I just wanted the girl to up sticks and come home.

'I washed pots from five in the evening until one in the morning for a fiver ffs get another job, sort it bloody out! x'

June galloped into July, Wimbledon raised its roof to many tightly fought tennis matches; and Cuckoo continued to bother me. My stress level was reaching a boiling point after she had shared another nugget of upsetting news with me, she too had been approached and asked if she wanted to make some serious money by selling drugs. I found myself huddled in a crumpled pile of tension and sobbing tears, desperate to extract my wayward daughter from Ibiza.

'I've had enough baby! ENOUGH!!' I shouted at the Big Man. Enough of the worrying, enough of the constant monetary bailouts, just enough. Absolutely enough. Once again, I had been taken to the wire by the errant girl and once again, my thoughts turned to how many tribulations my father had suffered by own behaviours, how many times had he despairingly uttered the word.

'How many times did you say enough, Daddy?'

'Too many Catrin, far too many.'

We already had booked Cuckoo's return flight home for her graduation and I was more than relieved to get the text that she had boarded it safely. Originally, I had booked a third flight to send her back for the rest of the season; but hastily cancelled it, hoping that she too had had enough and that the adventures of the 'Ibizan one', were over.

Chapter Eighteen

Twists and Turns

My overall opinion about the eight weeks that Cuckoo had spent kicking her heels up during her supposedly working summer, was one of incredulous disbelief that it had been so worrying and upsetting. Once again, the truthful relationship that I had always insisted I would have with my daughter had proven to be a curse. Still, she was homeward bound now and safe.

'No way is she going back there, baby!'

'I told you so babe.' I knew he was thinking it, even before he replied. Admittedly the cost of a lost flight was annoying, but it was nothing, compared to the relief that I was feeling. Afterall, what was the value of a few hundred pounds compared to the peace of mind that I was experiencing; now that the What ifs were over.

I turned my thoughts to a much more pleasant subject; Cuckoo's graduation, that was to be held on Wednesday 15th July 2015, a few days away. She had rung me again at work whilst she was still abroad, to tell me her final university results.

'Your daughters on the phone again!! She sounds happier this time!'

'Ma, I got a 2:2!!!'

'Wow that's amazing darling, just make sure you catch that flight home!!' The longed-for university degree had been achieved, the result of the blood, sweat and tears of the last three years of her life. It could have been better, but it could also have been a lot worse and now Cuckoo had much better letters to speak of, B.A.!

After she had originally left for Ibiza, I had rummaged through the stuff she had left behind, throwing away most of it, carefully selecting the items that were worth keeping. I had never seen so much crap in my life, there were clothes, personal debris, items of no fixed abode and with no recognizable purpose, all of which I now lovingly sorted into two heaps, one destined for the dustbin, the other into storage boxes. I had also organized and paid for the hire of the compulsory ceremonial robe and head gear, whilst booking a budget hotel in central London, two rooms for two nights. The actual ceremony was being held at the Royal Festival Hall, but my lovely mother wouldn't be able to attend, as I only had three tickets.

When I rang her to reluctantly give her this unfortunate news, a glass of wine had loosened the old lady's tongue and she totally understood that the three tickets belonged to Cuckoo's parents, Mother, Father and Stepfather. She chattered away quite merrily, happy to hear my voice and relieved that her granddaughter was nearly safely home. Then a small vocal breakdown took place. How she missed her husband, my father, she sounded so desperate. I never wanted to experience such desperation, how did you deal with that degree of desolation, a 2:2 in grief. My bed beckoned and I slept soundly while Cuckoo took that short flight away from the brink of insanity. All seemed well, but the girl was belligerent when she finally arrived home.

'I'm going back.' She blurted out to us the night before we were all due to travel to London, to commence the graduation celebrations.

'Over my dead body!' Was the explosive response from her stepfather, the Big Man.

'You can't stop me!'

'Yes, I can!' It was my turn to erupt, as the thought of having to suffer through any more mental What ifs forced me to spring into a physical reaction. I leapt from my seat and grabbed her passport that was winking at me from her open handbag in a corner of the room. Running out into the back garden I threw it wildly into the dark depths, where it landed near the bushes that had overrun Daisy bunny's grave.

'Yes, I bloody well can!'

The rest of the evening passed in a blur of veiled hostility and yet, even though we were all hardly speaking the next morning, the three of us travelled to London together. The graduation ceremony was superb. Resplendently gowned in the black robe, with flashes of purple and magenta, signifying the amazing achievement of achieving her degree as a Batchelor of Arts, with the obligatory mortar board cheekily perched on her head, Cuckoo took her seat in the vast auditorium at the famous South Bank Festival Hall. Mr. R. had joined us; and we three proud parents looked on, as she waited in line to mount the steps to the stage and accept her accolade. Her father was looking self-conscious in a smart grey suit, with a new goatee beard of the same colour, shaping his face. He was looking good for a guy aged sixty-three, where had all those years gone? He spent most of the afternoon secretively muttering on his phone, to whom we didn't know and nor did we care.

The Big Man was in jeans of course, wearing a black shirt worn in homage of the occasion, together with a purple kerchief draped from the pocket, which was his tribute to the colors that Cuckoo was flying. I had dressed suitably as the Mother of the protégée, in a fuchsia skirt and a demure black top. I had bought tights to mark the fact that having bare legs was probably not quite the right thing, especially as the thick scar slicing through my left leg still drew attention; and could tell its own nasty story to any onlookers. A hole in these tights appeared however within the hour and they went straight into a bin, so it was bare-legged and as proud as the proudest Punch, that I savored every moment of this milestone in my daughter's life. The afternoon and evening were spent drinking and eating, until we all staggered back to the hotel; and the next morning, equally unsteady, we hailed a black taxi and went our separate ways.

Inevitably Cuckoo flew back to the Balearics a few days later, her passport slightly muddied from its nocturnal experience and my heart tried to harden itself against the imaginary danger of the What ifs, that haunted me on her behalf. We had tried to talk, tried and half-succeeded. She confessed that my habit of worrying got on her nerves, I understood that, having sometimes similar feelings towards my own lovely mother; and I could reconcile much of my daughter's emotions with many of my own, but my antics on the sparkly Greek island of the summer of 1986 were still poignantly in my mind. I could almost taste the ouzo, vividly remembering the bristly moustache of the armed Greek policeman, on that night train with its lonely Russian carriage.

'Bag!' I could still hear him bark the order. It was therefore almost impossible to banish the fears and once again I had to wait for the final return of my daughter to the safety net of England and to be able to finally sleep soundly, without fear raising its grunty head in my dreams.

The second two weeks of July 2015 in England were wet and miserable, our back garden was swollen with torrents of warm summer rain. Gruber soared and towered, the promised vastness of its leaves was now a real sight to behold. Baby cuckoos, not one now, but two clumsy fledglings were copying their mother blackbird's teachings, whilst growing to twice her size. Their feathers were dappled brown, and their beaks were constantly open, chirruping for food. The mini cosmos of the postage stamp-sized back garden was an oasis of calm in a world that was clearly going madder; and more inanely insane than ever. The news was full of doom and gloom, tragedy had hit Tunisia, as a crazed, armed fanatic came from the sea, annihilating a beach full of unsuspecting sun bathers in the name of terrorism. London was on high alert and atrocities, such as beheadings in France, continued to horrify right-minded people. Was nowhere safe? please let a tiny Spanish island be safer than the chaos elsewhere. Please let my Cuckoo have built a Mediterranean nest with enough fortification to ward off the evil; and another small prayer to the Something was in order.

Then, there was some other amazing scientific news, Pluto had been landed on, not by a human, but with enough technology for man to see its surface from Earth. Could looking back at the Mother planet pinpoint the problems it endured and nuke them into infinity? Could the evils be strategically identified and targeted? Zapped and thrown into an outer orbit, forever to spin out into eternity, unable to harm again? Cunty grunty space shifters, whirling away until all the badness was wrung out of them by the cosmic tumble drying? These morbid thoughts continued to invade my head and whilst a warm, wet peace reigned in the hamlet that I called home, I continued to try and not to lose sleep over the absent Spanish adventurer, trying even harder to resist the temptation of texting her too often.

'How are you x'

'Good Ma x'

'Got a job? x'

'Yes Ma, I'm a shot girl! x'

'What's a shot girl?!'

'Ffs Ma!! I pour shots!! X'

Pinch, punch, another first of a month and August arrived in 2015, when Cuckoo would be twenty-one on the tenth. How I would have loved to travel and surprise her, and how well I remembered the events of the day of her birth. Heavily pregnant, two weeks overdue, I had been admitted into hospital to have my baby induced, as she seemed reluctant to leave the safety of her secure and happy, warm 'womby' world. All ten pounds, nine and a half ounces of her. August 1994 had been a particularly hot and torrid month, I was literally a beached whale by the end of the long pregnancy, having stuffed my face relentlessly with as much good food as I could eat, broccoli being probably the least calorically laden to pass my lips. Hugely pregnant and swollen fingered, I was unable to find a comfortable position as my baby punched me from within; and little hands and feet pummeled frantically, in its own efforts to find comfort. My face was badly marked with the butterfly mask of melanin, the hormonal plague of many a pregnant woman and both my wrists were splinted to alleviate the pain of carpal tunnel syndrome which I had also developed. It was worse at night, as was everything and I would lie awake, exhausted, trying to quash the terror of how exactly I was going to have to eject my baby. How well I remembered, even twenty-one years later, every stage of those last few week; and every moment of the subsequent labor and C-section delivery, that had all been worth it when I first saw my Cuckoo.

'Does she have a name?' This kindly question had come from the nurse on duty, and I had mulled over her inquiry, my eyes transfixed by the podgy, over-sized bundle, with its shock of black, wavy hair.

It was a ridiculous idea even to contemplate visiting the hedonistic melting pot that San Antonio would have become, in forty degrees of heat and all the madness that the peak of the season would have to offer in August 2015. The Big Man let me ramble on about my crazy yen, always with the same firm answer.

'No, babe, it's a really silly idea.'

'Yes, baby, I know it is.' I would regretfully have to agree with him, until the next time, when I couldn't help but broach the suggestion again. It would have been such a surprise for her, yet was still a fundamentally terrible notion, but one that simply wouldn't go away. The eve of Cuckoo's birthday dawned; and I posted a sad picture online, of a couple of candles stuck into a cupcake. The birthday celebrations had started a few days previously, according to her Facebook page. Forty-eight hours of wide-eyed partying; were followed by a huge meltdown on the actual day, when Spanish flu was once again blamed for her ills. There would of course have been no point in arranging the much longed-for visit to the island, as Cuckoo had apparently slept through her actual birthday, snoring through the comatose sleep of the over-faced, over-pilled, over-done-it and shit-faced shot girl. We had pre planned a week's holiday around her big day, but instead of feeling melancholy, I just tried to get on with enjoying the time at home with my husband and the Beloved Pooch, who was as equally delighted to have our company too.

'How many of my birthdays did you miss Daddy when I wasn't there?'

'Too many Catrin, far too many.'

'I'm so sorry, Daddy.'

'I know you are Catrin, but it's ok now.'

Our minds were turning to the return to our own Spanish island, in less than two months. My sad state of stoutness had reduced and to date, a total of twelve pounds of blubber had been shifted. Conversation turned to the highlights that we would enjoy in our paradise re -visited.

'Fishing babe?' The Big Man enquired hopefully.

'Not this time, thank you very much!'

'We'll see.' Was his pragmatic answer, both of us instantly remembering the debacle of past ocean fishing trips; he may have loved those experiences but my take on them was slightly less fond, for good reasons of my own.

More breaking news came, in the form of the sudden death of a much-loved Liverpudlian singer and comedienne, together with revelations of possible pedophilic deeds by a once-famous now deceased British Prime Minister. He too had a fine head of hair and a love of classical music, along with a trademark, deep bellied laugh. He had never married and had been usurped eventually by an 'Iron Lady'. There had been some other disgusting cases that had come to light on this theme, such as a famous, cigar-wielding celebrity with a love of blingy tracksuits. So much had been done for charity by this gentleman, that nobody wanted to believe the scandals that were being unearthed, but they were sadly proven to be true, as dozens of witnesses came out of the woodwork with examples of his gross sexual behavior. Surely not this much-loved politician though, although time would doubtless tell.

The world continued to spin determinedly around its axis during the summer of 2015, as surely as that famous Iron Lady would have turned, if she had gotten wind of the allegations made against her predecessor in political power. The pair of cheeky cuckoos had fled the oasis that they had found in our back garden, fled the nest in fact, heading for Spain or Portugal, leaving Mother and Father blackbirds to grub around forlornly, oblivious to the trickery to which they had fallen victim. Subtle changes to the English summer season were also seen, the magnificent Gruber had risen to its loftiest heights and the ends of its leaves were crisping, as it began its morph into the end of its life for the year. All the wildflowers that the Big Man had tended to as if they were valuable orchids, had bloomed and seeded; and the nights were starting to draw in.

We had sat outside during one of these magical evenings during our time at home together, after the heat of the summer day had warmed the air, giving us an excuse to pour large drinks and take in the ambience. Giggling helplessly into the early hours, we proceeded to fuck long and hard, the bedroom windows open as always and I woke up late the next morning with dim recollections of the previous night's escapades, squirming with naughtiness tinged with a hint of embarrassment, that the noises we had made

NO EXAGGERATION

during the midnight hours would have been extremely loud again and probably carried far into the otherwise still of the night.

The next afternoon I settled on a sun lounger, suddenly entering 'The Land of the Giants', as I looked up through Grubers papery, thin leaves. The veins were reminiscent of the spindly arms and legs of a vampire bat and the largest leaves that were shading me with its vast canopy, were now brown and crinkly at the edges, the first sign of the demise of the monster plant. A giant dandelion had been lovingly trained to reach for the sky, it was easily eight feet tall with a stalk as pink and as plumb as any mature stick of rhubarb, another crazy creation by the Big Man. The fierce heat of the mid-August afternoon was coupled with the sweet, tinkling music from the wind chimes and the rhymical, bubbling noises from several water fountains, that was all transporting me into an exotic foreign location. I closed my eyes and drifted off into a delightful half-awake state of mind, my body was knackered from the pounding it had taken; and my mind was as equally exhausted.

'Ping!' A message from my phone jolted me out of this very pleasant reverie.

'Ping!' The distinctive sound of a text came again as I was suddenly wide awake, annoyed that my dream like moment had been disturbed but very relieved when I read the messages. Cuckoo wanted to come home.

'Ping!'

'I need a flight Ma x' I picked up the phone intrigued as to why the plans had changed again. It seemed that once she had gotten her own stubborn way to return to Ibiza, the novelty had worn off very quickly. She had also given up her job as a shot girl, after a group of drunken English lads had made naughty comments about her boobs and one had had the cheek to cop a feel. Outrage squawked down the phone. Of course, his action had been totally out of order, but her skimpy garb of push-up bra and tiny shorts was always going to cause a stir of some sort or another. I laughed, as no real harm had been done and after all, if this grope had been the catalyst to bring the girl back then maybe it hadn't been such a bad thing.

'I want to come home Ma, I've had enough!'

'You've had enough!' I thought as I answered.

'Ok I'll book you a flight asap. Just get home and get a bloody job, sort it out!'

The Big Man and I lay in bed on the final day of our week at home in August 2015, the glum prospect of returning to work was tempered by the delightful knowledge that we would be poolside in a matter of weeks. Cuddling me, he told me stories of how he had guarded notorious men in two famous prisons, the Maze in Ireland and Spandau in Germany.

'You were so young baby.'

'I loved it babe.'

'You didn't really have a chance for any fun though!' He had been about nineteen at the time, such a tender age for such weighty responsibility, which explained an awful lot about this softly spoken, serious man. He who found it impossible to keep still, always busy pottering around, cleaning, gardening, always so busy apart from when lying in the sun, when he would raise his face to its glare and stay motionless for hours, absorbing the heat. I couldn't wait to see him assume that pose again, but our holiday plans had to be put to one side for now whilst I concentrated on the organization of the prodigal's final return.

Cuckoo and I had already decided that she would be based at her father's house in the future. We had both laughingly agreed before the start of the summer, that it was for the best, all-round. I wasn't sure that Mr. R. would see it that way though, once the reality of his daughter's slovenly ways became obvious to him. Having happily booked the last flight for her, I started packing her belongings in readiness for the return of Hurricane Cuckoo.

Her Spanish adventures were nearly over, whilst for me it was almost finally the end to the roller coaster of these recent What ifs and dramas. The descent into reality would be a shock to her system, I laughed inwardly, it would be the equivalent of a funfair ride, plunging to the ground in seconds, leaving your stomach at the top. Along with fishing trips, such rides would be on my hate list, the opposite of a bucket wish list, a list of experiences to be avoided at all costs. Another one for my personal loathe list, was the sleepless, drug-induced dancing, that I had once embraced with gusto. The sort that Cuckoo had posted many a video of, showing manic holiday makers with wild staring eyes and gurning smiles, spellbound by ear-shattering DJ sets and flashing lights.

'I can't believe that I found that nonsense fun!' I chattered to myself, carefully folding her clothes. Whichever way I looked at it, I had a feeling of profound relief that my own wide-eyed behavior was firmly relegated behind past doors, long closed. Then finally, there was the latest string of texts between us.

'You at airport? x' .... 'Yeah x'

'You boarded? x' .... 'Yeah x'

'You landed? x' .... 'Yeah x'

August 2015 was about to welcome September in a week or so and there was a hint of chill, in the early morning air. Wasps were changing their behaviour too, turning nasty, foraging with a carnivorous mindset and the world had turned again, madder than ever. Thousands of refugees were trying to find sanctuary in countries far away from the tyranny of their homelands. They hid in lorries, swarmed onto boats, frantic and desperate, many dying in the process. The front pages of the newspapers featured a photograph of the lifeless, drowned body of a small five-year-old boy being carried onto a beach, encapsulating the enormous tragedy of the situation. What a tiny, pathetic, pointless life that had been. The story went viral, and chords were struck in many a heart, as help and housing were offered to the lucky ones, whilst the unlucky were made unwelcome, as they camped in towns all over Europe. Shitting in the streets, robbing as they tried to survive, each action becoming more desperate than the last.

'Where all they all supposed to go?' I wondered time after time, as I watched the terrible story play out in the news. I was deeply saddened for these poor souls, especially the children, as I looked at large, innocent eyes staring at me from the television and newspapers, young victims of yet another relentless evil. But what I was about to find even more upsetting was the fact that Cuckoo was also about to turn, away from both me and her oh so patiently loyal stepfather. Another curved ball was aimed at its target, a final shot from the girl that wasn't expected or deserved, hitting me, its bullseye, with a poisoned arrow straight into my heart.

At first, she had burst through the front door, grinning and clutching a motley collection of souvenirs to give to us. It was blissful to see her home again, even more so to relish the imminent relocation to her father's house. I had spent a whole day making a large collage of old photos for her, cutting them randomly and overlapping them neatly, as a celebration of the last twenty-one years. Love and affection were mixed in with the glue that I used to stick down the craftily shaped snaps. It was terribly important that she understood that the move to her father's house was for all the right reasons, not a banishment as once before when she was eighteen, but of course, that was exactly how she decided to perceive the move. Once Mr. R. had collected her, bags and all, her texts and private Facebook messages became rude and cutting, a What if that I had never imagined could be possible.

My supply of financial gravy had had to stop, which enraged her even more, what a cupboard lover my daughter had become. I blamed myself totally for the creation of this money-grabbing monster, but I also blamed her for having put me in the impossible position that had forced an obscene amount of cash out of me, to avoid her own drowning in the deep water that she was swimming in. It was time to face up to the ungrateful child and for her to be independent, certainly not a severing of that umbilical cord, but I needed to cut the link between our bank accounts.

'You have to give me more money Ma!'

'I don't have to do anything Madam, you need to get a job and sort it out!' I coldly replied.

'Forget it.' She slammed the phone down. It was a horrible way for things to be between us, albeit no matter how temporary the situation would last. Independence was the lesson I was trying to teach my Cuckoo; now that she was finally home safe after three years in London with the associated What ifs; and four months in Ibiza on the same theme. It was time for me to concentrate on other matters and I turned my attention to the imminent holiday that the Big Man and I had been longing for. Clothes were tried on and new beach wear purchased, as flip flops, snorkels and all the other essential paraphernalia of pool to beach life were unearthed. As the date of departure came closer, I was left with one final much more enjoyable dilemma. What should I wear to the airport? For our return to the sun!

Chapter Nineteen

Holiday Adventures

Oh, the joys of holiday anticipation, the packing and unpacking, then packing again in a more suitable order. Oh, the thrills of all the last-minute preparations! Finding out the train times to get us to the airport, booking taxis to drive us to the station and making sure that our passports, currency, credit cards and essential flight tickets were all safely stored in the Big Man's 'man-bag' Going to bed the night before departure day, with our bulky suitcases ready to be closed in the morning. Checking and double-checking locks on doors and setting timers, so that lights in the house would randomly go on and off while we were away. Then there was that ultimate, carefully considered and joyous problem of deciding my airport look! Planning it down to the last matching accessory and donning the whole ensemble, feeling like a glamorous A-lister as the Big Man wafted me into the airport and we strolled through departures into the duty- free shops, sniffing perfumes and aftershaves with a nonchalant air.

Life didn't get any better than wearing the airport look on an outward-bound journey through an international airport. Trying on designer jewelry with feigned disinterest and strolling to the designated gate to sit patiently, knowing damn well that the other waiting travelers were admiring us. Watching out of the corner of our eyes, as fat, harassed Mothers and irritable Fathers cast their own envious side-ward glances towards us, as they fussed

NO EXAGGERATION

around overly excited children. The return flight was always very different, everything just got shoved into suitcases, the complete opposite to the carefully arranged contents of the cases for the outward-bound leg of the journey. Oh yes, the treat of deciding on the airport look was immense and a compulsory part of the pleasurable anticipation of a holiday.

Even though I said it myself, we did make a seriously, good-looking couple. Me, wearing a carefully chosen outfit, exposing just a hint of cleavage and flaunting my newly coloured and styled darkly brunette hair and freshly applied makeup, Cleopatra-like flicks of kohl, smoky shadow and bright coral lipstick. The Big Man was simply sex on legs, wearing his trademark, black, sleeveless T-shirt, his tattoos shining their stories and his numerous thick silver chains embellishing his neck. I always laughed when we encountered the problems we always had, getting him through security. He never willingly took off the dog collar of chunky metal ropes, but they would have to be removed and yet he would still always cause an electronic beep, as the bemused guards stripped him further of belts and watches, his pierced ear and nipple not helping the situation at all.

The previous year, a sticker had been slapped on his passport when eventually the girl who was patting him down, gave up and waved him through. It read 'I've flown through Gatwick!', next to a smiley 'emojo' and was normally reserved for children, but the officer had seen the humor of the situation and as I smiled, watching the familiar show, the uniformed lady rewarded him with a wink as well.

'Is he a good boy?!' She had enquired of me, with a twinkle in her eyes.

'Oh yes, he's very good indeed!' I had answered, grinning back at her.

Yes, sex on legs summed him up perfectly and I was always aware of the glances of underlying attraction that other women made towards him, loving their interest, along with the knowledge that this trooper was all mine.

In February 2007 we had taken our first foreign holiday together, Valentine's Day would be spent abroad for the next few years. The bunny took her first trip to the local pet-shop and Cuckoo was delivered to Mr. R, his role as Daddy Two would not be needed yet, as the advent of the Beloved Pooch into our lives was in the future. This first week that we had spent away together was blissful, when despite the weather being a tad iffy and an off lobster raising its head along with the contents of his stomach, we had the first of our holiday adventures. This was the start of our love affair with a trio of sunshine islands in the Atlantic, gems of places, just tiny volcanic drops in an ocean; and it was also my first experience of him smuggling in bit of 'personal.'

'Naughty baby! Very naughty!!' I had laughingly gasped when he revealed his stash, as he smiled back at me, glad of my approval.

We ate and drank, giggling uncontrollably at times and talking solemnly for hours. Another first for me was the view of foreign stars through his eyes, as he described those he had gazed at when serving in the Falklands. These were similar skies, midnight blue with stars so bright that they twinkled like faceted diamonds, hanging suspended in the pitch-black arena above. Amazingly we had known each other for only three short months, but it felt like we had done so forever, always accompanied with that magically special ingredient of both of us feeling like kids at Christmas whenever our eyes met.

He couldn't fuck me deeply enough and neither could I open my legs wide enough, until after one long night of the exquisite pleasure, eventually I had to beg him to stop.

'No more baby!'

'Lightweight babe!' He had laughed, easing his still throbbing cock out of me as I lay spread-eagled and exhausted. The brief week passed; and we fell deeper and deeper in love with each other, compatible in every physical and mental, level of intimacy. It was inevitable that a few months later he would move in with me and Cuckoo permanently, his few possessions fitting in as well as he did. Any doubts that he and I might have had about this being a potential mistake had vanished, any burns we had suffered at the hands of others were healed and suddenly the future looked bright and secure, with my daughter's misdemeanors being the only cloud on the horizon. The fragile, bobbing boat that I had been furiously paddling to help me stay afloat and stay sane, had finally reached its harbor. There was a new captain at my helm; and he had brought with him those feelings of safety and belonging that I had been missing since I was a child, but that had always evaded me.

In August 2007 I had another holiday to take, one that I was dreading, as it would take me away from the Big Man for two whole weeks. My lovely mother had booked and paid for a family holiday, so Cuckoo and I would be joining the up-tight Mancunian crew, on another Atlantic sunshine island. There was no getting out of this, as it had been planned long before I had met my soldier. Originally supposed to be a treat for Daughter Number One, following the breakdown of my marriage and the chaos that I had survived, it was now a curse in my eyes, but I had to go.

'Don't go babe.' The Big Man pleaded.

'I've got no choice baby, I've got to.'

'I know you have, it's just that I'll miss you.'

'Not as much as I'll miss you.' The next fourteen nights were spent in a five-star hotel, a fortnight that I was barely able to tolerate, counting the hours until I would be going home to him. We rang, we texted, we sex-texted and we missed each other so badly that there were times I had to disappear for a moment or two, to dry the sudden tears that welled up from nowhere. I bought him a present every day, fourteen gifts to take home to my Big Man to make him smile, whilst squirreling packets of cigarettes away in my suitcase, far too many than the acceptable allowance of one measly carton. Costing the saving, it worked out to be hundreds of pounds but the hoarding of the duty free was followed by a piece de resistance, that was the icing on the rancid holiday cake.

We were stopped at customs when we arrived back at Gatwick after the return flight back to England. Tired, irritable and so temptingly close to home, I had sauntered through the 'Nothing to declare' channel when out stepped the no neck, fat, lesbian bitch of an officer.

'Great, just what I need.' As I thought the words; she pointed towards me.

'Anything to declare, Madam?'

'Just a few cigarettes.'

'You won't mind if I open your luggage then, Madam.' There was no humour in the eyes of this customs official, just a suspicious hint of the fact that she knew I had broken the rules. As she carefully watched me fumble with the padlock and duly open my suitcase, there, for all the other inquisitive travelers to see as they craned their necks to watch this extra bit of excitement to the end of their holidays, there, was the shameful layer upon layer of boxes of the smokes that I had unsuccessfully tried to bring home.

'Just a few Madam?'

'I've been to Spain, there's no limit!'

'You've been to a non E.U. country Madam, the limit is two hundred per person.'

'Oh really!!'

'Yes Madam, really.'

Twenty-one years previously when my bags had been searched once before, there had been no contraband, just a pile of smelly, holey clothes but now I knew I was in a big spot of trouble and now there was nothing to laugh about, as the stream of travelers continued to gawp at my suitcase as it was well and truly rummaged through.

'What are you looking at!!' I snarled, as lovely mother and Cuckoo both tutted in united disapproval at the attempted smuggling and my extremely rude reaction. All but two hundred were confiscated and forms had to be signed, marking me as having committed an illegal act. A few hours later I finally returned home to the arms of the Big Man, vowing that never again would I go so far away, without him right by my side.

In October 2007 I had my third foreign holiday, the second of the year with him, when another Atlantic sunshine island had beckoned, and we followed its call having taken all the usual pre-holiday steps involving a bunny and a Cuckoo. It was a boozy week even by our standards. Starting the day with a full English breakfast, we moved on to large carafes of sangria. A large glass jug was moved from spirit optic to optic, red wine and fruit were added and a token splash of lemonade finished off the cocktails, before they were presented to us for our delight, as we sat in the shade literally drinking in the atmosphere. One of these blissful days that week started at sunrise, when we found ourselves being strapped into the back of a sturdy Land Rover truck that drove wildly up through windy, mountainous roads, intent on the volcanic destination of Mount Teide. Stopping halfway at a café in the still and misty morning, the Sun not raging yet, we ordered brandy coffees and listening to the strains of Dire Straits in the background, we breathed in the cool, fresh air, looking at each other with mutual appreciation of the moment. Reaching the summit of the volcano, we stared up at its Jurassic magnificence as it loomed above us stretching into the sky, with small clouds daring to scud across its mountainous peak. It was a place of breath-taking beauty and another sensation of united wonder was felt as we held hands, looking up at the 200,000-year-old spectacle.

Our next stop was going to be Africa, a place that the Big Man had spoken to me of his longing to visit and I spent hours trawling the Internet researching the continents holiday option, during the dark winter months of 2007, finally deciding on the Gambia for our next adventure. The promise its of white, sandy beaches; and swaying palm trees, helping us to tolerate the bleak English skies, occasional flurries of snow and the storms that Cuckoo was regularly brewing up with her teenage turbulence. Finally, in mid-February 2008 we boarded another flight, this time soaring over our island clutch of volcanic drops in the Atlantic, aiming for the country that the Big Man had always dreamed of discovering. I would never forget that first flight to Africa, watching surreally out of the window of the plane as it soared over miles and miles of sandy desert with towering dunes, arid browns and beiges that were rippled by the wind, to give the impression of ocean waves. Nothing could live there, it was the ultimate sand picture, frozen in time for thousands of years. Then, a tiny squiggle of green or two, spreading with crazy fertile fingers appeared, as the plane approached its descent to the coastline.

We weren't prepared for the notorious landing on a tarmac runway so melted by the African heat that it caused the plane to bounce as the wheels hit, causing a few minutes of manic kangarooing before the airliner slowed and stopped. A few moments of stomach-churning panic were felt by the passengers who had never made the trip before, including us, until the plane doors opened to the hottest temperature that we had ever experienced.

'Welcome to Gambia's International Airport.' The impressive sign, hanging above the airport building belied the shanty town appearance of the place and there were enormous gorilla-like policemen patrolled the perimeters, rifles hoisted, their stern, black faces saying only too well that they meant business. The thought of the Big Man's always packed and hidden little stash of solid did not sit well with the sight of these monster men; but running the ensuing gauntlet of getting through the stiflingly hot airport took priority in my mind over that worrying thought, as hopeful locals desperately tried to grab our bags to carry them to the waiting coaches, in return for a tip. Beggars were waiting outside; with outstretched, scrawny hands and one-legged men in wheelchairs jostled with them, all vying for our attention in the hope of receiving a precious English coin.

It was a crazy beginning to a most magical time and an experience that we would repeat three times over the next few years, always February, always Valentine's Day. The memories of the place would stay with us forever, the size of the molten Sun, shimmering during the days and the frozen face of an equally large Moon, that glistened its white, magnetic power at night. The noise of jungle drums and wind chimes, the ebony black people with bright white teeth in grinning faces and the vivid colors of their clothes, turning cheap cotton garments into attire that every visitor longed to own. Their hair was plaited and braided, swinging with the movement of their bodies as they danced through their days. I would have my own done the same during our first visit to Africa, choosing with delight the different shades of wool to be spliced in with my own locks; and picking out the coloured beads that finished off the look.

There were miles and miles of those exquisite, white sandy beaches that I had seen online, but their reality was totally overwhelming, fringed as they were on one side with swishing tropical palm trees and on the other, by the Atlantic roaring its thunder, giving up marbled shells for us to beach comb as we walked up and down the shore. Fruit ladies could be seen with oversized wicker baskets niftily perched on their heads, laden with pineapples, coconuts and papaya. Horses galloped along the surf line, hooves strumming the sand, locals riding them bare backed, urging them on for the amusement of the sun-bathing tourists, it all contributed to the most magical time indeed.

The poverty was unbelievable and so humbling to witness, the locals would bend over backwards to 'befriend' the rich tourists, as we visitors were perceived. With nothing to do but sunbathe, eat, drink, laugh and fuck, we were in a paradise unimagined during these amazing days and nights under the African Sun. The Gambian way was to groom the pale holiday makers, the rich, white visitors were their passports to solvency, or so they believed. The practice was not malicious, merely survival-borne, as the local people had nothing but the donations of the well-wishing guests and the pittance that they could earn, as they slaved hard in the hotels that gave them access to the new guests who arrived weekly. We had become friendly with two of the staff and after understanding the struggles they had to simply survive, we had happily offered to send them ten pounds each month, nothing to us really but a fortune to them.

The Valentines Gambian experience was repeated in 2009 and finally in 2010 the year I turned fifty, when we flew out for what was going to be our last visit, a very special revisiting, for a honeymoon holiday. If we had been spoilt up to now, we were feted during this trip. Our accommodation was upgraded free of charge to a suite, where luxurious, fluffy, white robes, a kettle and a fridge were waiting for us, as gladly accepted extras. Of course, five-star African style could never compete with the opulence of other worldwide destinations, the water sometimes ran a little muddy from the taps and power cuts were regular and expected, whilst mosquitoes were also a huge problem. Malaria was an ever- present danger and 'Malarone' tablets should be taken religiously as a wise precaution for the prescribed number of days, before, during and after the trip. The nasty, blood sucking insects didn't seem to like me nor the Big Man, perhaps this was due to the scent of sex that pervaded our rooms or the taste of a very high alcohol percentage in our blood, which was probably too off-putting. We had however witnessed the handiwork of a greedy mosquito too many times to dismiss the danger that they could bring to unprotected flesh; and fat, sunburnt arms and legs peppered with infected bites, abounded among others staying at our hotel.

I watched one day as my sexy, tanned Big Man, husband now, was approached by a gloriously tall, swaying Gambian woman.

'Room 100?' I heard her ask him.

'Sadly not!' He replied as he winked at me, prostitution being another way to supplement incomes. We had met old men with wrinkled, mahogany brown skin, who were out there for months on holiday, old codgers doing their bit of business with these girls. One offered us Viagra, which was another bit of business. Laughingly we refused politely, we didn't need that stimulant, as deep, frantic fucking started and ended the lazy days for us two honeymooners, often accompanying a mid-afternoon siesta.

Africans have an absolute fear of snakes and a trip was made to a snake farm, where I bravely allowed a boa constrictor to be draped around my shoulders as the Big Man took pictures for Cuckoo. Another stop-off was a crocodile swamp, where the famous 'Charlie' opened one large, 'lizardy' eye at us, fixing us with its unblinking gaze, before sliding back into the pea green, soupy pool, its prehistoric tail the last thing to disappear into the swamp. Our last day was spent lounging on the beach again, the Sun was high, suspended in a haze of torrid heat and we couldn't resist running into the welcoming waves that were lapping seductively. Neither of us had given a thought to the pull of the tide, as it suddenly turned to draw back out and we were dragged back every time we tried to reach the safety of the beach. Legs bleeding from being scraped over miniscule, razor sharp particles of shell, we eventually managed to haul ourselves onto the sand. Breathing heavily, exhausted from the exertion, we lay there for a few minutes.

'I thought we were going to die then babe!' The Big Man croaked, as I caught my breath, nodding in agreement.

Before travelling reluctantly home we promised our friends that we would return one day, but slowly they started asking for more monetary contributions, until we'd had enough of the begging e-mails that they sent from the hotel.

'This has to stop babe.'

'Yes baby, but if we stop sending them money, we can't go back.'

'Why not?'

'It would be too callous, bumping into them and having to pretend that they meant so little to us.'

Our African experience was consigned to the past, whilst the memories of its magic remained in our hearts and as reality prevailed back in England, we reminisced about the joys whilst dreaming of the next holiday and remembering another little trip that we had taken the previous year.

It had been October 2009, when after the shit that Cuckoo had endured with the incident causing injury to her eye, we had felt that she deserved a holiday with us. It was the first time she had been invited, primarily due to the problems she was regularly causing us. Our precious holidays had always been a way of escaping the tribulations that the girl was so masterful at dishing out, even though I knew her actions were hurting her, as much as they backlashed against myself and the Big Man. A schoolfriend was invited along and the sunshine island that we had so enjoyed in October 2007 was revisited, with two belligerent teenagers along for the ride, the shenanigans of the New Year's Eve debacle at the start of the year having been forgiven. It was a budget week, less than nine hundred pounds for the four of us, all-inclusive and allocation on arrival. A sleepy resort was our allocated destination on landing, for which I was very thankful, as aged fifteen and fourteen the lure of the more commercial party towns would have been too much for them and I hadn't fancied spending my evenings trying to stop the little minxes escaping.

We saw very little of them in the event, as the mischief-seeking girls hooked up with other like-minded teenagers and they had a ball rampaging around, wearing different colored wristbands, which identified them as being under eighteen and able to officially only get soft drinks. Of course, it didn't stop the regular procurement of stronger stuff by them, one way or another. Come sundown, the adult holidaymakers who were intent on their own agendas to make the most of this all-inclusive lifestyle, were already too bladdered to care what their kids were doing. The Big Man and I didn't really do justice to the endless supply of free drinks this time, trying to be more sensible than during our sangria days, we enjoyed a few during the day, saving ourselves for the evenings. However, having these two always hungry and thirsty tikes accompanying us, the limitless food and drinks proved the holiday to be exceptional value for the money, despite the slightly ramshackle condition of the hotel.

We treated the girls to a boat trip, a dolphin safari on a sturdy craft that didn't raise my fears of seafaring, although pulling out of the safety of the harbor walls sent the boat into another gear, as it chugged against the waves of the open sea and my sea legs had to be re balanced. The hunt for the promised dolphins was on. With flicks of blue and silver, they followed the boat, aquatic dancers in perfect timing with each other. Riding the swell from the prow of the boat, they gave a first-class show and watching my daughter's face as she squealed in awe, I was delighted that I had invited her along.

Day three saw the arrival of a Welsh couple in the apartment next door, twelve hours later alcohol-fueled rage had descended on the pair of them, and he was firmly banished from the place by an outraged hotel manager. The Big Man and I decided to take the remaining girl, covered in bruises by now, under our wings, only to regret it instantly, as for the rest of the week she shadowed our every move, tagging along with us like a faithful puppy.

'You are angels!' She would squeak every ten minutes, whilst pouring regular disgustingly sweet, gloopy cocktails down her gullet. I wasn't sure how it happened, but the highlight of the end of that night we had spent with her, was an impromptu lesbian romp between me and my new friend, as the Big Man watched with amused interest. This was the first time I had physically demonstrated this sometime leaning, though I had told him of past antics when I had fallen into the arms of other women, so it came as no shock to him. We licked, finger fucked and groaned in front of him, squeezing nipples, tonguing each other's spread-eagled legs and sucking each other's juices, the madness of the moment causing both of us to succumb to frantic orgasms. This went on until the early hours, when after the friend had collapsed comatose onto a bed settee, he took over and fucked me long and hard, totally turned on by the amateur, erotic performance I had given him.

The next morning another boat trip had been booked and I was about to learn that this sort of excursion was not a good idea, in fact that a fishing trip was an exceptionally bad idea, as 'Tagalong' accompanied us to the seafront.

'I'm not in the habit of that!' I mumbled, too knackered and hungover to care, not knowing that the morning was going to be made of the stuff of nightmares. The boat pulled into the harbor awash with blood and fish guts, the smell of the diesel fumes turning my stomach. Somehow, the Big Man heaved me aboard, when aghast, I realized that there was now nowhere to escape to, apart from an upper deck that could only be reached by a very narrow waist-high rail. Eyeing this up with an ever-increasing feeling of panic, I also realised that to try and lumber up to this upper deck would result in the very high possibility of me falling overboard; and I was forced to stay put on the lower deck. Breathing in the diesel smoke, increasingly more and more green-gilled, I sat with my head in my hands whilst the other two attempted to fish. The Big Man was in his element, with a huge rod strapped around his waist, but there wouldn't be a single fish for him to reel in during the next few hours. Tagalong managed to land a Tuna, and as it slid and flopped onto the deck, its blank eyes watching me accusingly, I apparently turned a whiter shade of green.

'Babe, you ok, you've gone a funny color?' I heard the concerned voice of the Big Man.

'Kill me now, baby.' I answered with a dry whisper. Finally, the boat turned its course, picking up speed back to dry land.

'Never again!' I vowed, staggering back onto the jetty.

'We'll see.' Was his reply.

Indeed, we did see just that, when in October 2013 we revisited another sunshine island, six years on. Bunny to pet shop, check, the Beloved Pooch and Cuckoo to Daddy Two's, check. Airport look, double check! We soon found the beach and practically had it to ourselves, the other residents preferring to bake by the pool, unwilling to pay a couple of euros for a sunbed and a parasol. Snorkeling was discovered for the first time and with our bums in the air we scoured the shallow seabed for glimpses of brightly colored fish; giving an underwater thumbs-up to each other with delight at each new sighting. We took bread rolls from the hotel to feed the shoals and the doughy mess encouraged fish from all around to circle us and nibble at our fingers. They swooshed and dived between our legs, with our faces masked and underwater, the experience was nothing short of amazing. I was a creature in my own aquarium and in bliss, floating in the salty depths. Not so much a few days later.

'Fishing?' he had asked hopefully and against all my better judgement I found myself being lumbered unwillingly once again onto an identical boat to the last, where once again I had to stay put, an identically impossible handrail offering me no choice. I sat quietly on a hard slab whilst the Big Man was sent to the upper deck, rod in hand, meaning that I couldn't even have the dubious pleasure of watching him fish. Six hours later, disembarking, I painfully realized that I had bruised my coccyx.

'Ow baby, it really hurts! No more fishing trips ever, ever again!'

'We'll see!'

One tequila-infused night, after my age-old request for 'Moon River', the interjection by the Frenchman who had asked me to dance, ended up in us adjourning to our room, absent a Tagalong this time. Having 'Seen murder in your husband's eyes,' the guy had backed off quickly and nervously; and the furiously drunk alpha male of my husband proceeded to mark his territory. Once we were in private, he videoed me as I sprawled on the king size bed, playing with myself madly, giving him a full view of my fingers bringing myself to orgasm with my legs wide. He zoomed in on the swollen, wet folds of exposed, pink flesh with one hand and masturbated urgently with the other. With a low moan he flung down the camera and drove his cock into me. The next day we played the film back, marking the mini-DVD as 'personal'. It would be awful if that seriously X-rated hardcore porn show fell into the wrong hands, this was for our eyes only.

The flight home was agony for me, my bruised backside was throbbing, and a bumpy landing caused me to shriek out with the pain, joining in with the squealing chorus of the babies on board, vowing for the last time that there would never, never, ever, ever, be another fishing trip.

Married and short of money for the next two years during 2010 to 2012, we turned our attention to the idea of budget breaks at home. I started to collect the coupons published in a national newspaper, where minibreaks could be had for less than ten pounds per person. We were blissfully happy but seriously broke, so this seemed like an ideal alternative to foreign climes and a different type of adventure was on the cards. Cuckoo, the Beloved Pooch and Daisy were boarded again at their own respective holiday homes and the car was loaded to the hilt with enough food and drink to satisfy a small army. The Big Man and I then set off with glee, looking forward to a four-day break in a caravan for which we had invested the princely sum of nineteen pounds. The facilities were typical of a holiday camp, with terrible entertainment consisting of a bloke dressed up as a giant rabbit gyrating on the dance floor, diverting tiny tots from boredom while their parents sank as many pints as possible in the time allowed, before the knackered children would become grisly and need their beds. We preferred to keep our selves to ourselves, reveling in the isolation despite the freezing, wet weather.

We walked daily on the windswept beach, drenched and exhilarated and took a mini railway to Dungeness, home to the famous power station. It loomed in front of us, a gigantic monstrosity. The surrounding habitat was occupied with shacks and strange houses, which were cobbled together rather than built. Each one had a theme, as collections of driftwood and ocean debris, old flip flops; and bottles, which had all washed up on the beach, had been skillfully placed outside the shanty town dwellings, creating a strange illusion of slight madness. We sat on the deeply shelving shingle overlooking the cliffs of Dover, breathing in the cold, salty air. We pottered around the caravan, watching films, opening bottles of wine, mid-afternoon and snacking on crisps and peanuts. Siestas beckoned me and slow fucking sessions always followed.

We repeated the experience the following year, but the unpredictable English weather let us down for the second time when we arrived at this next location, shivering in inappropriate clothing, waiting to get the keys to our next holiday home. We drove slowly around the perimeter of the park, following the map we had been given to a brand-new chalet far away from the maddeningly noisy crowds, to repeat the successful format that we had used the first time. These two minibreaks had been so different from the heat and sophistication of all the others we had enjoyed, but we had relished them all the same. My coveted airport look was swapped for comfy joggers and sweatshirts, and an au natural look, with a slick of moisturizer against the elements was chosen over the kohl and lipstick that I usually decorated my face with. More than happy to sport wellington boots, rather than sparkly sandals, because I was with my Big Man and that would always be enough for me, no matter where we enjoyed that most precious of luxuries, just to be together.

Chapter Twenty

Full Circle

September 2015 was coming to a sunny end and Gruber had been lovingly cut back by the Big Man, put to bed until next year, about to hibernate in its nest of hay. Spiders' webs shone in the sunlight, they were beautiful creations, the gossamer, silky strands woven and intertwined by their busy makers. Not so lovely though when you inadvertently brushed your face through one, destroying the work of the insects and recoiling from the sticky touch. I imagined that such regular destruction must really piss the spiders off. Evenings were cooling and the days were shortening fast. There was a hint of bonfire smoke replacing that of the smell of barbecues, as autumn was putting its stamp on Mother Nature in England. There was another tangible aroma, the sour, damp scent of rotting vegetation, caused by falling leaves that had been shed by many trees, dropping like tears that seemed to mourn the end of the summer. Crispy, dried debris crackled underfoot elsewhere, as new, rich shades of bright red and gold started to colour the scene, and evening silhouettes lined the view from the doggy walk with crazy, black outlines, as those now naked branches pointed hostile talons to the darkening sky.

We had two more days at work and so much more left to do. Newly purchased essentials were crossed off the holiday list, to be quickly replaced by hastily thought of alternatives. Beach towels, passports, sunglasses and snorkels were piled onto the spare room bed, along with a mountain of other necessities. A reservation for Daisy bun at the pet shop was sadly not required this time. Arrangements had already been made to drop the Beloved Pooch off with Daddy Two. His podgy dog eyes met mine again, he was six now, or forty-two in human years; hopefully, there would be many more doggy years for us to enjoy together. The dreadful but essential surgery that he had endured was long gone and with luck he had forgotten the trauma it had caused him. He was such an important part of our family, yet Cuckoo seemed to have dismissed her pet along with us, the honeymoon period with her father was clearly still in full bloom.

Mr. R. had met someone; it must be the recipient of those muttered phone calls during the post-graduation afternoons drinking spree. He was rarely at home during the weekends, so Cuckoo would be home alone a lot which would have pleased her greatly, a free house is always appealing when you have lots of piggy friends to entertain. I was pleased he had found someone else, no one deserved to be lonely, and I just hoped he was treated well as rumor had it that his new love interest was very controlling. Mr. R. of course was nothing if not a big boy, so good luck to him I decided.

'Get a job.' had been my one of my last messages to my daughter. Her Facebook page was plastered with accounts of social exploits, festivals and parties but the two-way communication that I had enjoyed with the girl over the summer, had dried up along with the financial drip that I had been watering her bank account with. Cuckoo had indeed fled the nest. Had I finally lost her? It was just as well that mummy blackbirds didn't grieve overly for the charlatan chicks who had also abandoned the parents for a better offer, scamming little cheats the lot of them.

The Rugby World Cup was in full swing, England v Wales and I turned a framed photograph of my father as a young man in a naval uniform, towards the television, in order that he could see the match.

'Silly really baby!' The Big Man nodded, intent on the game himself.

'You even listening baby!!' And as he nodded again, I knew he wasn't, and smiled. He was a sports fanatic after all, whilst I wasn't a fan to put it mildly, but was quite impressed by the sight of these ripped, muscular athletes charging at each other; and settled down to watch it with him, my eyes occasionally drawn to the photograph that I had positioned, just so.

Later I lay in bed, wide awake; and with the curtains open I stared into the night sky.

'Don't give up on her, Catrin.'

'Never Daddy, but I think she's given up on me.'

I studied the stars shining through the window, painfully knowing that he must have gazed at the same stars when I was Cuckoo's age, feeling the same anguish about his Daughter Number One as I now felt about mine. Exhausted, I stared at the biggest one, my star, that was dominating the dark as usual, surrounded by satellites of small, silver, twinkling, gem-like orbs. My mind was full of those unanswered questions that I had for my father, as I struggled to find the much-needed arms of the sleep that I was longing would wrap itself around me. Once again, sobbing an apology to him.

'I'm sorry Daddy, but I don't know what to do now.'

'Yes, you do Catrin, you need to sort it out.'

'How!!'

'The way you sorted everything else out, the way you defeated your demons.'

I was so horribly aware that history was repeating itself in so many ways, the drugs, the crazy behavior that my daughter didn't see as anything out of the ordinary, the potential spirals into a life of who knew what; and the What if's that might be lurking in the abyss these days. I knew that Cuckoo's achievements were already so much more than I could have ever claimed, but even those precious letters after her name would not protect her if the cunty grunts fixed their sights on her. Just like Charlie spying a newt in the cool, rancid, green-hued pond in Africa, it would be swallowed up in a blink of his Jurassic eyes and with a gulp would be gone. Then there was Cuckoo's silence, was this my long overdue and well-deserved punishment for the years of contempt I had subjected my father to?

'I love you, Daddy.'

'I love you too, Catrin.' His words floated on the breeze that was blowing through the open bedroom window as I wrote a tribute to him and quietly prayed to the Something.

'Watched the stars slip n slide tonight, in a sky of velvet blue, and I fell asleep, with you in mind, please tell me what to do.

Heard the wind caress the trees tonight, with a whisper of your name, and I fell sleep, in the dim moonlight, knowing nothing is the same.'

My words hadn't fallen on barren ground this time, as the next day when I took the Beloved Pooch over to his Daddy Twos as planned, Cuckoo was waiting for me, her face pinched and worried, as if she had sensed the pain that she had inflicted on me with her own airs of disdain. We cleared the air, after several painfully silent weeks and hugged tightly, both feeling the emotion from the grip of the other. Talking frankly, I tried to explain my point of view, Cuckoo listening, trying to understand. The arrogance of her youth being more than a bit of a barrier to a full comprehension as to what I was saying, but we parted happily. She was now the temporary guardian of her dog and as we said our goodbyes, both of us were grateful and relieved that whatever had caused the animosity and the distance between us, was now suddenly not an issue anymore.

Generations in full circle, Father to Daughter, to Granddaughter, feeling the same pain, the same elations, the same despairs and the same joys. Looking through the years at the same stars, eons old, those cosmic Suns that we had all three raised our heads towards at different moments, their lights shining over decades of human age, that were mere blinks of an eye in time, just drops in a stellar ocean.

'I'm sorry, I love you.' I gave her one final hug.

'Ma, I'm sorry too, love you more.' As I drove home, I made a strange acknowledgement of respect to my survival of a past that had been so chaotic, almost unbelievable. Finally looking back, I could see that battling with my monsters had also been a fight for a longed-for alternative. A better future, with someone like the Big Man, who would keep me safe and cherish me the way I had always wanted to be loved.

'The future isn't written in the stars, Catrin, they are only ghosts from the past.'

Remembering these words spoken by my father not so long ago, I was still so eager to have more answers from him.

'Everything ok, babe?' This from the Big Man, three quiet words that encompassed so much, as I opened our front door on the eve of our return to the sun.

'Everything's fine baby.' My smile answered every aspect of his question and our eyes locked momentarily, in perfect understanding again. That night I fell asleep straight away and the next morning, bright and early, we set off hand in hand, dragging our carefully packed suitcases behind us, looking forward to revisiting the little bit of Heaven on Earth that we had found the previous year.

1st October 2015, our plane was on schedule and there were no dramas at the airport, only the usual and expected delay as the Big Man was patted down by yet another security guard. The four-hour flight was smooth and there were no bruised backsides to put up with, or any squealing babies to try and ignore. Arriving at the apartment, the key slid smoothly into its lock, we were back. With our cases unpacked, duty-free vodkas were poured and again we sat until silly o'clock, breathing in the sweet, warm night air and laughing at the shadow puppetry of the tropical palms, swaying as if for our sole entertainment. Sixteen nights of unadulterated sunny, sticky holiday bliss stretched out in front of us and the long- awaited, pleasurable tick list of choices was all ours to be enjoyed again. I was looking forward to lingering in the supermarket, repeating my selections of strange foods, feeling the same irresistible longings towards the squeezing of warm baby flesh, as I fingered sun-kissed fruit and tomatoes. There would be no fishing trip this time, instead we had planned a day trip into the interior of the island, to see the wonders of the volcanic Fire Mountains from the padded comfort of a luxury, airconditioned coach. We were awed by the mastery of the driver, as he slowly steered the vehicle around impossibly narrow bends in the road, stopping regularly for us to look over the edges of the mountains into deep craggy ravines below. The rest of our days would be spent poolside and beach bound; and of course, poetry would be written.

'We sit on the edge of an island, a jewel of a place, just a drop in the ocean.

Watching the climb of the laden airliners, holiday trade and sometime reminders, that home is beyond the horizon.

With sun on our skin and the wind in our sails, we jump fierce, salty breakers, with smiles on our faces, and laugh, as they lash us with white, foamy tails.

We sit on the sand on the edge of this island, drinking icy cold beer, making magic appear in the clouds, as our laughter grows louder than loud.

We sit very still on the edge of our island, together forever and you hold my hand, knowing home is within the horizon.'

It is mid-October 2015 as I sit once again in the apartment, balcony doors open, a light breeze fanning through the flimsy curtains. Now, always, as then, the Sun glides slowly East, disappearing again beyond the horizon of the ocean and the welcoming, cooler dusk of an early Spanish evening greets the night. Welcome again the Moon, to its eternal celestial center stage, it's light as wonderful to my senses, as the soothing, hypnotic swishes of the sound of the tide. Star light will soon seize the sky and another perfect day in this holiday paradise is ending, beckoning another perfect night with sultry fingers. Gentle background music is playing, candles are lit; and both my body and soul are warmed by the day's fierce heat and the potent red wine I am drinking. Eye's half closed, thinking nothing. Acutely aware of the smoke from an expertly rolled joint wafting past me; and acutely aware of the other presence in the room who smells of suntan oil and sex, and who has literally changed my life in so many ways that it has been a mystical experience.

My name is Catrin Thomas, and I am fifty-five years old. I look up at the Big Man as he passes me the spliff and smile, as he refills my wine glass.

'Thank you, baby.' My book was completed, every 'I', dotted and every 'T', crossed. As every story apparently has a moment of truth in it, so every moment of truth has the makings of a story, it would seem. This certainly has been such a story. Would someone one day ask me as to its genre? If so, how would I reply? It has adventure and romance, crime and horror, fantasy, thrills and even comedy. It speaks about sinners and saviors, winning and losing, climbing mountains and crawling away from the abyss. As promised, just in one single year, that feels like a lifetime later, I have finally written my book and told my story. Could it ever possibly grace the bookshelves at airports, resplendent in a shiny cover, tempting travelers with it's potential as a must-have holiday read, with its defiant title, 'NO EXAGGERATION!' beckoning them to lose themselves within the contents of its pages, as fact outweighs fiction with its capacity to spin a yarn or two.

I wonder further, if it could then hold the readers spellbound, eager to find out what was to happen next and if they might recognize themselves in the tale and if, with that recognition, would come shock, outrage, or maybe, simply nostalgic pleasure. Would they be reminded of monsters that they too had battled, conjured up from the depths of their minds, or released by the of opening dark doors from forbidden places. Would they reflect sadly about relationships that they had agonised over, or remember past prayers that they may have made to a Something that they believed in. I smile inwardly, wandering onto the balcony, staring into the perfect pitch black, to gaze at the stars as they twinkle and dance; and to talk to my father for what was going to be the last time. The brightest and most brilliant was still dominating the view, as it had here last year, as it always did where-ever I watched it from. As I watch, the same circle of smaller stars are moving around it, swirling like a mini constellation, with what seemed like needy fingers of light, waving as if to get the attention of my special star that was pulsing in the middle of them.

'I did it, Daddy, I told our story.'

'It's one hell of a story, Catrin.'

'I'm not sure anyone would think it could be true!!'

'Well, we know the truth.'

'I always hoped you were there, to hear me say how sorry I was.'

'Do you remember what my last word was, Catrin?'

'Iridescent!'

'It wasn't angels I saw, at that moment, Catrin, it was stars.'

'Are you in the stars?! Are you my special star!!'

'Yes; and now you finally understand.'

'Why are the others staying so close to you!'

'They want to learn how to speak to their humans, as we do.'

'Why didn't you contact Mother, she misses you so much.'

'I can only watch one human soul, I looked after her whilst I was alive; and you made me that promise to carry on doing that. She will join me one day.'

'I beat my monsters, Daddy.'

'Within and without, Catrin. You may have been responsible for releasing them, but you kept your soul safe. Anyway, there are many forms of monsters, you weren't the only one to have to battle them nor will you be the last.'

'I don't understand.'

'The monsters aren't real Catrin, even though they have the power to hurt and destroy. They are products of human foibles and failings. Hate and jealousy, weakness, addiction, temptation and frustration, are just a few of these, they are dark forces, internal emotions caused by human desires that can influence external circumstances if allowed to, leading to terrible consequences.'

'Why does she hate me?'

'Your sister?'

'Yes.'

'Because you were the first, number one and that always made her feel second best. She has her own monsters, envy, selfishness and arrogance, but she never fought them, they just became part of her. She could never see that you needed help, not judgement, with your battles. Everyone has their monsters Catrin, yours came from drugs, bad decisions and unfulfilled needs, but you've fought them, many humans don't fight they just allow them to take over their souls. Sometimes they want them to, sometimes they enjoy what their demons can give them. You've seen that in people you have known, you've seen the world turning this year and witnessed many evils at work, they are everywhere looking to pounce. Envy, gluttony, greed, lust, pride, sloth and wrath are the seven deadly sins of Christianity and other religions have their own interpretation of these, whilst committing the greatest sin of all in the name of their Gods. You saw this in New York in 2001, London in 2005 and all those other countries only recently. Mankind can be so beautiful, yet so horribly damaged.'

'Can't you do anything about it?'

'I already told you this, there's nothing I can do.'

'That's such a shame, do we all go to the stars?'

'Not all Catrin, only the good souls.'

'What happens to the bad ones?'

'They are banished into the dark.'

'What about animals?' I was suddenly reminded of my wistful wish for a very grassy, ever sunny place in the stars, for all the fur babies I had loved.

'There are no bad souls in animals, any wicked behaviour is always the fault of the way they are treated, they always come too.'

'How many souls are there, in the stars?'

'Thousands Catrin, the little boy you saw drowned on a beach, he's here with me, as are many more spirits, all watching someone, until the time comes to stop their vigils and they can move on.'

'Where do they go next?'

'Further Catrin, into infinity, so that other stars can take their places to begin their own watches. I've been waiting for years, waiting and watching over you, waiting for you to be finally happy. I've seen you with this big man, I've seen my daughter as I always knew she could be, and now it's time for me to leave.'

'Don't go, I've got so many questions!!'

'I can wait a few more minutes.'

'Why can't the others talk to the ones they are watching, like we do?'

'They would love to; they are trying very hard to understand how.'

'Why can I talk to you then?'

'Because you wanted this so badly, Catrin, you made something very unusual happen; and I'm so glad it did.'

'Is there a God or a Devil?

'It's not that simple, but if you look at the difference in the words, God and good, Devil and evil, it will help you to understand.'

'I never believed in God, just the Something.'

'Ah, yes.'

'Are you my Something?!'

'Yes I am.'

When I go to the stars, will I be watching someone.'

'You already are Catrin, that was the last lesson. You already watch over your daughter, my granddaughter and you always will. You should know by now that you can only watch and worry, hoping that the person you care about eventually makes the right decisions, if their soul is pure enough.'

'I don't want you to go!!'

'It's my time, Daughter Number One.'

'Goodbye then.' My sad farewell drifted into the night air, as the Big Man joined me.

'Everything ok?' He took my hand and we stood silently together, as that one splendidly bright star suddenly shot across the sky and vanished, whilst the rest seemed to dim momentarily, as if mourning its disappearance.

'That was him baby, he said he had to leave, I didn't want him to.'

It's said that that we all come from the stars, babe.'

'He told me that we all go to the stars, at the end.'

'He sounded very wise, babe.'

'I don't think I'll hear from him again. I wish you had known him; he really would have liked you.'

'Yeah, wish I could have met him too.'

'I really didn't want him to go.'

'He'll always be with you, in there.' He softly kissed my forehead.

'I wrote my book because of him; you know he was my inspiration.'

'Time to write a sequel then!'

'Nah, I couldn't follow that story.'

I smile again, looking into his eyes, drowning in the blue of them, maybe it was time to write another book, maybe this wasn't the end at all, maybe it was just the beginning.

Milton Keynes UK
Ingram Content Group UK Ltd.
UKHW040648091023
430221UK00004B/231

9 789391 384227